LEGACY

The editor said
"If you don't
write sex scenes
then you're
through."

I said,
"Okay, then
I'm through."

For over 21 years, author Al Lacy wrote for leading publishers Bantam, Dell and Doubleday, using his gifts as a storyteller to write books that would financially support his greatest passion: traveling around the country as an evangelist, leading people to salvation in Christ.

With 47 best-selling novels written under pseudonyms, Al's success as an author was clear. But when faced with pressure to add sex and profanity to his books, he refused—choosing instead to take a stand for his beliefs.

That decision led one of the country's best Western and historical fiction authors to the Christian bookseller's market, where he has launched the exciting new *Battles of Destiny* Civil War series and *The Journeys of the Stranger* with Multnomah Books.

Here is Al Lacy's incredible story, told in his own inspiring words.

Q: How did you get started as an author?

AL: It all goes back to my call to preach. I pastored for several years before I went into full-time evangelism. The church I pastored had fantastic growth, and I didn't want to leave it. But it's hard to explain how God works. It's like being in love…you can't really explain it, but you know it's there.

I didn't want to be gone for weeks on end like an evangelist has to do. But God made it so plain. I've been doing preaching in churches around the country for 21 years now.

The problem is, there are a lot of expenses in evangelism that I never dreamed of. Some of the small churches can't pay anything, but I go anyway.

> It's hard to explain how God works. It's like being in love… you can't really explain it, but you know it's there.

I feel that I should do that—help the young ones get on their feet and go. But that means I wasn't putting anything away for retirement.

I thought,

"What else can I do and travel at the same time?" Then I was inspired by my wife. She said, "Well, you've read Westerns and historical books all of your life. You've talked about writing. Why don't you try writing one?" So I sat down and I wrote a Western novel called *Dead Man's Noose*.

Q: How did you first get published?

AL: I sent *Dead Man's Noose* to a few publishers. Most didn't even answer me. But one wrote back and said, "You're going about this all wrong. You have to have an agent."

So I prayed about that. I said, "Lord, I need the right agent." Then one day when I was flying, I read in the back of a magazine about an agent who was trying to find new writers. I contacted him, he read *Dead Man's Noose*, and he loved it. We signed a contract, and six weeks later, the book was sold.

I wrote several books for that publisher. Then my first editor left, and the new editor said, "I love your work. Your stories are exciting and captivat-

ing. But I want some sex scenes in here."

I told him that I don't write sex scenes. He said, "If you don't, then you're through. I said, "Okay, then I'm through."

He probably thought I would give in. But I will not give in. I have standards. They are based on the Bible, and I won't break them.

After that, I worked for other publishers. But the problem continued over the years. I would get a new editor, and my book would come out with a few cuss words in it. I would call them and say, "Hey, I didn't put those words in there. I don't want that kind of language in there." Several books would go by, and everything would be fine. And then a new editor would come along, and—ZAP—out would come another.

> **I will not give in. I have standards. They are based on the Bible, and I won't break them.**

It broke my heart that my publishing career seemed to be coming to an end, but I wasn't going to bend. God blessed me in that. Just a year ago, a pastor friend asked me, "Have you ever thought about writing for a Christian publisher?" He introduced me to Questar Publishers and Multnomah Books. And so the story goes…

Q: How do you find the time to write?

AL: The fiction series, traveling, preparing for sermons…it just takes a lot of discipline. And I don't watch a lot of television. Football season is rough on me. I love football. Writing takes a little midnight oil some times. But when you love it like I do, it's easy. I love to create stories, almost as much as I love to preach. I am amazed that I get paid to do the two things I love to do the most: preach and write. What a blessing!

> **Football season is rough on me. I love football.**

Al Lacy *is the author of over fifty titles with over 2.8 million copies in print. He lives in Littleton, Colorado, with his wife JoAnna when he's not on the road "winning souls."*

LEGACY

JOURNEYS OF THE STRANGER • BOOK ONE

LEGACY

Bethel Baptist Church
P.O. BOX 167
AUMSVILLE, OR 97325

AL LACY

MULTNOMAH BOOKS

LEGACY
© 1994 by ALJO PRODUCTIONS, INC.
published by Multnomah Publishers, Inc.

Edited by Rodney L. Morris
Cover design by Bruce DeRoos
Cover illustration by Bill Farnsworth

International Standard Book Number: 0-88070-619-8

Printed in the United States of America.

For information:
Multnomah Publishers, Inc.
Post Office Box 1720
Sisters, Oregon 97759

Library of Congress Cataloging-in-Publication Data

Lacy, Al.
    Legacy / Al Lacy.
        p. cm.—(Journeys of the stranger ; bk. 1)
    ISBN 0-88070-619-8
    I. Title. II. Series: Lacy, Al. Journeys of the stranger ; bk. 1.
    PS3562.A256L44   1994   94-15009
    813'.54—dc20   CIP

99 00 01 02 03 — 10 9 8 7 6 5 4 3

To Dennis Fogle, my best friend.
I love you, Denny, more than you
will ever know.

Proverbs 17:17

CHAPTER

ONE

———◆———

Twilight lay its successive layers of purple satin across the sky as the train rounded a curve, jostling its passengers. The mild lurch of car number three bumped Breanna Baylor's head against the window, awakening her with a start. She straightened herself on the seat and rubbed the back of her neck. She was surprised to see a large, beefy man sitting on the opposite seat, facing her. The seat had been unoccupied from the time the train pulled out of Santa Fe, and had remained so up until the time she had fallen asleep.

The big man had bright magpie eyes glittering out through an enormous mat of beard, and the low hairline on his hatless head seemed to leave him little forehead. Breanna noted that he was well-dressed.

Big white teeth appeared, contrasted with his dark, gray-speckled beard, and he said pleasantly, "You've been sleeping ever since I sat down here almost three hours ago. Had you been traveling before you boarded at Santa Fe?"

Her neck was stiff from sleeping in the unnatural position. She rubbed it again as a smile made its small break along her lips. "No. I've been working in Santa Fe for about a month. Too many nights with too little sleep."

13

The man nodded. "What kind of work have you been doing, may I ask?"

"I'm what is known as a visiting nurse. Do you know what that is?"

"I believe so. You travel about, serving wherever medical help is needed."

"Mm-hmm."

"So you're what is known as a CMN, I presume."

Breanna raised her eyebrows. "Are you in medicine yourself, sir? The average person doesn't know about Certified Medical Nurses."

"Not like you are," he grinned. "I'm in pharmaceuticals. My home base is Denver. I've just been to El Paso for a convention, and now I'm heading home."

"I hope we're coming up with some new innovations in pharmaceuticals."

"Most definitely. Just in these few years since the Civil War, we've come a long way, but our research laboratories back East are promising greater things to come."

"Wonderful," smiled Breanna. "That will make my work easier and help me to better treat my patients."

"By the way," said he, "my name is Orville Waters."

"I'm Breanna Baylor," she responded warmly.

Looking over his shoulder, then back at Breanna, Waters said, "The reason you woke up to find me here is that there was a woman sitting beside me in car number two who has a mouth like a triphammer. I mean, my ears were getting sore. So I took a stroll and conveniently forgot to return to my seat. I'll have to go back and claim my hand luggage when we get to La Junta."

Breanna smiled again and turned her attention out the window. The train was running parallel with the Rocky Mountains. Though the mountains were some seventy miles to the west, she could make them out as a dark, sharp-peaked jumble beneath the horizon's indigo haze. The darkening sky above was coming alive with winking stars, like tiny diamonds against a backdrop of black velvet.

Orville Waters gazed upon the young woman by the lantern light that glowed in the rocking car. He thought her just about the most beautiful woman he had ever seen. The spirit of Breanna Baylor was light and quick, and the shadow of a smile stood at the corners of her mouth even when she was silent and sober.

Breanna was still gazing out the window, watching the sparks that flew by like fireflies, when Waters said, "If I remember correctly, Miss Baylor, to earn your CMN you had to work under an approved physician for two years. Is that correct?"

"Two years and four months to be exact. I actually put that much time together with two doctors. I was just under a year with Dr. Jacob Wellman in St. Louis, and the rest of the time with Dr. Myron Hunter in Wichita."

"Ah, yes...Dr. Hunter. I've met him. I never knew Dr. Wellman, but I had heard of him. He died, didn't he?"

"Yes. Worked himself to death, I think. He was a wonderful man. It was after his death that I moved to Wichita to finish what you might call my internship with Dr. Hunter."

A mother was chasing her small son down the aisle, calling, "Tommy, come back here!"

Waters leaned from the seat, scooped the toddler up in his arms, and handed the child, screaming and kicking, to his mother, who thanked him and headed back to her seat.

Waters shook his head and said, "If that had been me and my mother, she'd have paddled my posterior until I went into the sitting-down-and-shutting-up business. I hope we don't come to the place in this country where we're afraid to use strict discipline with our children."

"Me, too," agreed Breanna. "The Bible says 'Chasten thy son while there is hope, and let not thy soul spare for his crying.' "

Waters arched his bushy eyebrows. "Ah, the little lady knows the Bible!"

"I can't say that, but I know some of it."

"Well, on the subject of disciplining children, you know it also says, 'The blueness of a wound cleanseth away evil: so do stripes the inward parts of the belly.' "

"So you know some too," Breanna chuckled.

"Yes, but especially that one. It's Proverbs chapter twenty and verse thirty. Both of my parents quoted it before every licking they gave me."

Breanna laughed.

Waters laughed with her, then said, "Let's see, now...you were telling me that you finished your two years and four months with Dr. Hunter. How long have you been a visiting nurse, then?"

"Well, I stayed on with Dr. Hunter another three years and four months, so I've been a visiting nurse for seven years."

"Seven years?" he echoed. "You don't look old enough."

"Why, thank you, Mr. Waters. The truth is, I started when I was seventeen." Smiling, she said, "To save you the arithmetic, I'm twenty-nine. Almost thirty."

Waters rubbed his bearded chin thoughtfully. "Well, you hardly look it." He had noticed while she was sleeping that she wore no wedding ring. Meeting her gaze, he said, "I'm probably sticking my big nose in where it doesn't belong...but certainly such a lovely young lady as yourself must have had a hundred or so proposals of marriage. Is there some young man waiting somewhere with an engagement ring in his pocket?"

Waters saw Breanna's countenance fall and knew immediately he had tread on tender ground. "I'm sorry, Miss Baylor," he said apologetically, "I *am* sticking my big nose in where it doesn't belong. I've upset you. Please forgive me."

Tears surfaced in Breanna's eyes. Her purse was on the seat beside her. As she picked it up, she said shakily, "It's all right, Mr. Waters. You meant no harm. It's just that I—"

She was pulling a hanky out when the purse slipped from her trembling fingers and dropped to the floor. Several articles spilled out, including a silver medallion the size of a silver dollar.

Breanna started to bend down and retrieve the scattered articles. Waters jumped from his seat and went to one knee. "Here...I'll get them for you."

Placing the purse in her hand, he picked up her belongings and handed them to her. The last piece he retrieved was the medallion. Eyeing it carefully, he said with cocked head, "This is interesting."

The medallion was centered with a five-point star, and around the circular edge were the words: *THE STRANGER THAT SHALL COME FROM A FAR LAND—Deuteronomy 29:22.*

"The stranger that shall come from a far land," Waters read aloud. "This is part of that verse of Scripture?"

Breanna was biting her lips and dabbing at her eyes. "Yes," she choked.

"What does it mean?"

"You wouldn't understand," she replied, sniffing and extending her open palm. "It was given to me by...by someone very special. It's something quite personal."

"I'm sorry," Waters said. "Here's my big nose poking in where it doesn't belong again." He laid the medallion in her hand.

Breanna clutched the piece of polished silver in her fist and pressed it close to her heart. Fresh tears welled up in her eyes. She quickly blotted them with the hanky, fighting to maintain her composure. Biting hard on her lip, she turned her face toward the window.

Feeling bad about what he had done, Waters returned to his seat and said, "I'm really sorry, ma'am."

Breanna turned back toward him, lips quivering, and spoke in a shaky half-whisper, "Please don't feel bad, Mr. Waters. How could you know such a simple question would affect me this way? You're a very kind man. Please don't punish yourself."

Waters figured a change of subject would be best. "I...ah...I didn't ask you what it was that kept you in Santa Fe for a month.

Was it some kind of epidemic?"

Breanna swallowed hard and said, "Yes. Smallpox. Whites and Indians both. Over fifty died...mostly older people and infants."

"That's tough," Waters nodded. "Dying that way, I mean."

"It's tough on the survivors, too. The scars left on the body—especially the face—are terrible."

"Yes. I've seen a few people with them. Has to be hard."

Breanna was about to comment when the conductor's voice came from behind her, "La Junta...five minutes! Train will arrive in La Junta in five minutes!"

"Where are you going from La Junta?" Waters asked

"To Denver. I suppose we'll be on the same stagecoach?"

"Not if you're taking the one in the morning."

"Oh?"

"I've got to hire a wagon and drive to Fort Lyon. My company supplies pharmaceuticals to all the forts throughout these parts, and the doctor at Fort Lyon is expecting me tomorrow. I'll catch the Denver stage that goes day after tomorrow."

"Well, it's been nice meeting you," said Breanna, once again in control of her emotions.

The train was slowing.

"Well, it might have been if I hadn't upset you," he said dolefully.

"Please, Mr. Waters. It's all right."

"Thank you," he smiled. "It's been a pleasure making your acquaintance. Maybe we'll meet again in Denver. Are you going to be there long?"

"I'm not sure. My home base has been Wichita, but if things go as I hope, Denver may become home base."

"Well, I hope everything works out for you. If it is to be Denver, I'm sure we'll meet again."

The train was down to a snail's pace, and the bell on the engine was clanging. Breanna could see lights burning in the windows of houses just outside of town, and she could make out some street lamps near the edge of La Junta's main street. She thought about the remainder of her trip, dreading the stagecoach ride. The Topeka & Santa Fe Railroad ran from Albuquerque through Santa Fe to La Junta, Colorado. There was no railway as yet from La Junta north to Denver. The stagecoach route would take her some sixty miles west to Pueblo, then straight north for a hundred and ten miles to Denver.

It was mid-March, and in Colorado, spring did not come until mid-April, sometimes later. The stagecoach ride would be dusty and cold.

When the train chugged to a halt in the depot, Orville Waters stood in the aisle and asked, "Is there some luggage I can help you with, Miss Baylor?"

"My medical bag is in the rack above your head, and the small overnight bag next to it is also mine. There's a small trunk in the baggage coach, but I understand there's supposed to be a carriage here from the La Junta Hotel, and the driver will handle that one for me."

Waters took down both bags from the rack. "I'll carry these to the carriage for you."

"This is awfully kind of you," smiled Breanna. "Are you staying at the La Junta Hotel?"

"No, ma'am. I'm at the Colorado Hotel, just up the street. There's supposed to be a carriage here from the Colorado also."

Passengers made their way out of the car onto the platform. Breanna and Orville moved amongst them. The carriage from the La Junta Hotel was indeed waiting, parked beside the Colorado Hotel carriage. Waters placed Breanna's two bags in the carriage as she informed the driver that her trunk was in the baggage coach.

The night wind was brisk. Breanna turned her coat collar up and watched Waters hasten back to the train and enter car number two. She climbed into the carriage and took her seat. Other passengers were approaching the carriages, among them a short, stout woman about to board the Colorado Hotel carriage. She had a loud, coarse voice and was bending the ears of an elderly couple who were to board the same carriage. By the looks on their faces, they were not happy with her constant talk.

The driver returned, carrying Breanna's trunk by its leather handles, and placed it in the rear compartment. A young couple climbed in and sat beside Breanna. Both smiled and greeted her, and she returned the greeting. Two well-dressed businessmen boarded and sat in the seat behind them. While the driver was loading luggage in the rear compartment, Breanna saw Orville draw up to his carriage. His face went rigid. He glanced at Breanna, managed a smile, and furtively pointed to the stout woman, mouthing, *That's the woman with the flappy jaws!*

Breanna snickered and shook her head. Her driver mounted the seat, snapped the reins, and moved the carriage toward the street. Waters had just climbed into his carriage, and the loquacious woman plunked herself down beside him. He had a sick look on his face as he looked back at Breanna and waved.

The wind had a bite in it, and Breanna turtled her head into her collar, holding it tight against her throat. The young woman who sat next to her did the same.

"Nippy, isn't it?" said Breanna.

"Quite," smiled the woman. "My husband and I are from El Paso, and it's already warm there."

"I've been in Santa Fe for a month," said Breanna. "It's been cool there, but not icy like this."

The husband looked past his wife and asked, "Is La Junta your final destination, Miss, or are you going on somewhere else?"

"I'm going to Denver. Taking the stage that leaves at seven in the morning."

"Oh, how nice," the woman said. "Harley and I will be on the same stage. We're going to Castle Rock."

"Oh, yes," nodded Breanna. "I know where that is...about twenty-five miles south of Denver."

"We should introduce ourselves," said the young man. "I'm

Harley Carter, and this is my wife, Louise."

"Happy to meet you. I'm Breanna Baylor." She paused a moment, then asked, "Are you visiting someone in Castle Rock, or is this a business trip?"

"It's a wedding," said Louise. "My little sister is getting married. I'm to be the matron of honor."

"Oh, how nice. I love weddings. They're always so...so tearjerking."

"They are that, all right," agreed Louise. "Is Denver your home, Breanna?"

"Well, it might become that. Wichita has been my home for quite some time. I'm a nurse, and there's been a smallpox epidemic in Santa Fe. I've been there doing what I could for those poor people."

"Yes, we heard about it," said Harley. "Quite a few died, I understand."

"Fifty-four at last count," Breanna replied sadly. "Both Indians and whites."

"So you're on an assignment in Denver?" queried Louise.

"Well, not exactly. I...I'm going there to meet someone." *I hope,* she added within.

"Aha!" said Harley. "Some lucky man, eh? Are there wedding bells in the offing?"

Breanna's features tinted. A sharp pang lanced her heart. She didn't want to pursue the subject any further, so she said, "No. It's not like that. I have some medical connections there, though. The way Denver is growing, and people are moving into outlying areas, they'll be needing a visiting nurse."

The carriage came to a slow stop in front of the La Junta Hotel. Moments later, the passengers were in the lobby. Breanna was allowed to register first. When she had finished, Harley Carter offered to carry her luggage to her room once he and Louise were registered. Breanna thanked him and stood back to wait.

One of the businessmen who had been in the carriage stepped

close to her. "Pardon me, Miss. My name is Albert Cross." Gesturing to his companion, he added, "This is George Simpson."

"Glad to meet you, gentlemen," smiled Breanna.

"We overheard you talking to the young couple, Miss," said Cross. "You're a nurse?"

"That's right."

"Well, ma'am, I've had a thundering headache ever since I got on the train at Santa Fe this morning. It's steadily gotten worse. Would you happen to have some powders I could buy?"

"I have some powders, Mr. Cross, but you can have them for free." As she spoke, she bent down and opened her medical bag. She found a small white envelope and placed it in Cross's hand. "Take these, along with some food, Mr. Cross. Your headache should ease off within about twenty minutes after you take them."

"Thank you, Miss. I'll be glad to pay you, though."

"No need," smiled Breanna.

"Then how about letting me buy your supper? You are going to eat, aren't you? The restaurant here in the hotel is excellent."

"Well, yes, but—"

"I'll even treat your friends, here, too," said Cross. "George and I are going to be riding the stage with you tomorrow. We might as well get acquainted."

Louise heard the conversation and tried to decline the invitation, but Cross insisted. Harley finished registering and was told of Cross's offer. He was glad to accept. Introductions were made, and after everyone had checked into their rooms, they met in the restaurant and enjoyed a meal together. Breanna purposely steered the conversation away from her purpose for going to Denver.

It was after eleven o'clock when Breanna entered her room, locked the door, and prepared for bed. Bone-tired, she picked up her purse off the dresser, fished out the silver medallion, blew out the light, and climbed into bed. Clutching the medallion close to her heart, she stared into the darkness. "Oh, John, you have to still be in Denver. I *must* see you. I was such a fool to send you away. I was so mixed up. So terribly mixed up. It wasn't until you were gone that I realized how very much I love you."

Tears filled her eyes and began streaming down her cheeks. She dabbed at her face with the sheet, then broke into uncontrollable sobs, repeating his name over and over. Finally, she gripped the smooth silver disk in her hand and prayed, "Oh, dear God in heaven, You know where John is. Dr. Halleck told me he had passed through Santa Fe three days before I arrived, saying he was on his way to Denver. If he's still there, please...keep him there until I arrive. I love him, Lord. You know I love him with all my heart. I just have to tell him."

Breanna prayed for nearly a half hour. Then as drowsiness began to take over, she carefully reached out in the darkness and laid the medallion on the bedstand.

As she drifted toward slumber, she could hear John's soft, broken voice on that last day she saw him in Wichita four months ago—"All right, Breanna. If that's the way you want it, I'll move on. I will be out of your life, but you will never be out of my heart. From time to time, I may be looking at you, but you'll not know I'm near. I'll respect your request."

You will never be out of my heart echoed through Breanna's mind, then finally faded as she fell asleep.

CHAPTER

TWO

The Colorado sun was shining bright in an azure sky. It was late morning, and the air was cold and brisk. Breanna Baylor was riding the rocking, swaying Wells-Fargo stagecoach on the dusty road between La Junta and Pueblo.

At an old abandoned shack on the west bank of Chico Creek some fifteen miles east of Pueblo, an outlaw gang was holed up. Turk Dunphy, their leader, sat on the rickety porch of the shack in his greasy sheepskin coat, talking to two of his men and watching a third practice his fast-draw near the dilapidated old barn thirty yards away.

Dunphy sat in a squeaky old rocking chair, while Hec Speer and Harold Eggert lounged on the porch step. Dunphy was a mean-looking, thick-bodied man who had an aversion to bathing or shaving, as did the other men in his gang. Their clothes were grimy, and their long, shaggy hair stuck out, matted and filthy, from under their hats and dangled over their collars.

Dunphy reached inside his coat and took a tinder-dry cigar from a shirt pocket. Placing the cigar between his teeth, he fished for a match, flicked it into flame with his thumbnail, and fired the cigar to life. Dunphy's scowling face seldom lifted in a smile except when he opened a sack of money after a bank robbery.

Dunphy kept his eyes on the man shooting a hole in the side of the old barn as he said to Speer and Eggert. "Ever since he took out that hotshot gunslick down in Walsenburg—what was his name?"

"Curly Bender," said Speer.

"Yeah. Curly Bender. Ever since Mack took him out, he's been thinkin' he's one of the elite gunfighters."

"Well, you gotta admit, Bender was one of the best. Mack shore did make him look like molasses in January. Bender barely cleared leather before he was dead on his feet."

"Well, one thing for sure," Eggert said. "Word gets around fast. Won't be long Mack'll have some of them hotshots lookin' him up for a showdown. You know how them gunslicks are. Ever' one of 'em's gotta be top hog in the trough. Don't dare let it be thought that some other gunnie is faster'n him."

Speer chuckled. "Let's hope Mack gets a whole lot faster before he has to face off with the likes of Bobby Lawton, Clay Austin, Rex Hobbs, or Tate Landry."

"Yeah," chortled Dunphy. "He ain't quite on that level, yet."

Rapid gunfire continued to pierce the morning air as Eggert set his beady eyes on Speer and said, "We know Landry's considered by ever'body to be the kingpin. But amongst them other three, who do you suppose is the fastest?"

"My money'd go on Rex Hobbs," said Dunphy.

"I don't know, boss," said Speer. "Word is that young Clay Austin is faster'n a rattlesnake's tongue. And Lawton ain't far behind him."

Turk laughed. "Well, sooner or later those boys will tangle with each other. Then we'll know."

The firing at the barn had ceased. Mack Pflug had emptied his gunbelt and was punching fresh cartridges into the slots. A magpie appeared above the naked-limbed trees that surrounded the yard, making slow, lazy circles. Dunphy watched the bird settle on a thin limb high in a tree near the barn, then called, "Hey, Mack!"

Pflug turned toward his boss. "Yeah?"

"Is your gun loaded?"

"Yeah. Why?"

"Let's see if you can draw, shoot from the hip, and knock that magpie outta that tree."

"All right," grinned Pflug, laying the cartridge box down. Backing up a few steps, he grinned at the cawing magpie. Splaying his hand over the Colt .44 on his hip, he paused a couple of seconds, then whipped out the gun and fired. The magpie seemed to explode, and while feathers floated earthward, the three men on the porch applauded.

"Good shootin', Mack!" shouted Dunphy. "You're gettin' better all the time."

"That's what I aim to do," replied Pflug, walking toward the shack.

Mack Pflug was twenty-four and full of fire. He was the newest member of the gang. Dunphy had watched him take on two would-be gunfighters at once over in Durango, Colorado. When the two men lay dead in the street, Turk Dunphy decided he needed a fast gun in his gang. He made Pflug an offer, and Pflug took him up on it.

The gang had been hitting banks all over southern Colorado, northern parts of Oklahoma and Texas, and southeastern Kansas. They had hit so many banks of late that Dunphy decided to lay low for a while and let things cool off. He had plans to rob the biggest bank in Pueblo, but he would have to wait a few weeks. Right now, the law was scouring the territory for them. In most of the towns, "wanted" posters displayed Turk's face and the faces of Hec Speer and Harold Eggert. The three dared not appear in Pueblo until they were ready to rob the bank and ride hard.

Two other newer members of the gang, Jade Whetstone and Aaron Smith, were in Pueblo buying food and supplies. Like Mack Pflug, they had not yet become identified by face as members of Dunphy's gang.

Pflug drew up to the porch, punching the last few cartridges in his gunbelt.

"You keep practicin'," Dunphy said, "and one day you'll be as good as Tate Landry."

"Not as good as him, boss," grinned Pflug. "Better. Unless someone beats me to it, one day I'll put Landry in his grave. Then you'll have to call me *mister*, 'cause I'm gonna be top dog."

"Well, when you do it, pal," chuckled Dunphy, "I'll be glad to call you *mister*."

"You can count on it," Pflug said levelly. "In the meantime, when I run into these fancy gunslicks along the way, if they don't challenge me, I'll challenge them."

Dunphy took the cigar from his mouth, blew smoke skyward, and studied the red-hot tip. "Mack, I hope you'll go easy on this challengin' gunfighters. Not that I don't think you're good and gettin' better, but you're a real asset to this bunch. I'd like to keep you. Just be careful who you take on, will you? Brace the wrong guy, and it's curtains. You only get one chance with any of 'em. There ain't no second opportunities. Okay?"

Pflug grinned and rubbed his bristled chin. "I appreciate your concern, boss, but don't lose no sleep over me. I know my limits. I've faced off with enough gunslicks now that I've developed a sixth sense about it."

"What do you mean?"

"Well, it's sorta hard to explain, but when I sees a gunnie, there's a certain...well, it's like a little voice inside me that says, 'You can take him, Mack.' That little voice ain't never failed me. When I sized up the last three guys, the little voice spoke, and I knew I'd be the one standin' when the smoke cleared. I've been right, ain't I?"

"Yeah," nodded Turk. "But just make plenty sure you're hearin' that little voice clearly before you face off, okay?"

"Okay, boss. I'll make sure."

"Mack, you ever size up a gunhawk and have the little voice tell you not to challenge him?" Eggert asked.

"Yep. Twice."

"So who were they?" asked Dunphy.

"Well, the first one was Buck Wellman over at Cortez. I'd heard plenty about him. Plenty fast. I was on the street talkin' to a coupla friends when one of 'em bulges his eyes and says, 'Hey, look who's in town.' It was Wellman. First impulse I had was to walk up to him and call him a yella-bellied so-and-so and make him draw. But that little voice inside me said, 'Don't do it, Mack.' So I didn't. Nobody else challenged him, either."

"He got it up in Black Hawk 'bout a month ago, didn't he?" asked Speer.

"Yep. Clay Austin. Austin had just taken out Bart Feathers 'bout two weeks before that. Wellman's gun hand got to itchin'. He figgered it was time to move himself up a notch in the brotherhood, so he rides into Black Hawk and dares Austin to draw against him. Them that tell it say it was close, but Wellman's six feet under and Austin's still breathin'."

"Think you could take Austin?" asked Eggert.

Pflug thought for a moment, then said, "Well...I'm not sure I'm quite there yet. Just the thought of him stirs the little man inside. Seems I hear him moanin'. I think I need a little more practice and experience before I take him on."

Turk clamped the cigar between his teeth once more and puffed a cloud of smoke. "So who was the second dude your little man warned you to bypass?"

Pflug's face stiffened. "The big dude, himself."

"Landry?"

Pflug nodded. "In person. 'Bout a year ago. Town called Sterling, up in northern Colorado. I was there havin' me a good time in the local saloon and this tall, lean, clean-shaven fella comes in actin' tough and like he ain't scared of nobody. Goes to makin' smart remarks just like he was itchin' for a fight. I seen the low-slung hogleg on his hip and figured he's a greenhorn that needs to learn a lesson. I was just about to invite him out into the street when that little voice comes alive inside me, screamin' loud and clear to leave it alone. Just then another fella snarls an insult at this unknown dude, and out to the street they go. After the challenger lay dead in the street, somebody in the crowd said somethin' to the guy still standin', callin' him Landry. I tell you, when I found out who he was and remembered how close I come to bracin' him, I had to go out back and upchuck my lunch."

The others laughed, then Dunphy said, "Mack, my boy, you just keep listenin' to that little voice."

"I'll do it, boss."

"If you don't," Speer said, "you're liable to miss out on the big money we're gonna come into when we rob that bank in Denver."

"I wouldn't miss that for nothin'," chuckled Pflug. Looking at Dunphy, he asked, "When we gonna clean out the Pueblo bank and head for Denver, boss?"

"No hurry yet. We still need to let things cool down around here a bit more. Besides, like I told you boys before, Frontier Bank and Trust in Denver won't be fat and ready to butcher until the gold mines start pickin' up production. It's been a hard winter, and not much goin' on. With spring on the way, and the snow meltin' up there in them mountains, they'll be diggin' the stuff out by the carloads pretty soon. Should make ourselves a big haul."

Dunphy rose from the rocking chair, flipped the cigar into the yard, and grunted, "Let's take the horses over to the creek for a drink."

Noon came. Hec Speer, on duty as cook for that day, entered the shack, built a fire, and threw some salt pork and beans into a pot. They were devouring the last of their lunch when they heard a horse blow in the yard. Pflug scooted his chair back and hurried to the door. He smiled when he saw the other two gang members riding in with gunny sacks packed full and tied behind their saddles. "Jade and Aaron," he said to the others.

A moment later, Jade Whetstone and Aaron Smith came through the door, carrying the sacks on their shoulders.

Whetstone set his sack down with a whump, looked at the dirty tin plates and cups on the table, and said, "Thanks for waitin' on us for lunch."

"How'd we know you'd be back so soon?" parried Speer. "For all we knew, you two were passed out drunk in one of them saloons by now and wouldn't be back till who-knows-when."

Smith laughed as he set his sack down. "We didn't even go into a saloon. We'd have eaten lunch in town, but we was in a hurry to get back here."

"Yeah," chirped Whetstone. "We've got some news for Mack."

Pflug's ears perked up. "News for me?"

"Yep," nodded Whetstone, grinning at Smith, then looking back at Pflug. "You're gonna like this."

"So let's hear it."

"We saw us a fast-draw shootout in town. We watched some greenhorn smart-aleck challenge Bobby Lawton."

"Bobby Lawton! You're kiddin'. It ain't been more'n a week since l heard he was somewhere in Kansas. Coffeyville, I think it was."

"Well, he's in Pueblo right now," Smith said. "We was on the street, about to go into the saloon, when we seen Bobby and a coupla his pals come ridin' in. They hauled up to the hitchin' post right in front of us. They was plannin' on goin' into the Bullhorn, but by the time they stepped up on the boardwalk, this here wet-eared kid walks up and calls Lawton an overrated, slow-handed, poor excuse for a gunhawk."

"It was sorta funny," put in Whetstone. "Bobby looked at the kid like he couldn't believe such brass. Sneerin' at him, he told the kid to get lost. He had more important things on his mind. He and a gunnie named Lance Pierson were meetin' there to shoot it out."

"Lance Pierson!" Pflug gasped. "He's an up-and-comer. I wonder how come he and Lawton chose Pueblo for one of 'em to die."

"Don't know," said Whetstone. "Nobody said. Anyway, this kid said he'd save Pierson the trouble of takin' out Lawton. *He* was gonna do it."

"So Lawton treats the kid like a pesky fly and tries to shoo him outta the way," Smith said. "Said he and his pals was gonna wait in the saloon till Pierson showed up. When Lawton started for the saloon, the kid jumped in front of him and said Lawton was all hot air and was afraid to face off with him."

"Well, that done it," snickered Whetstone. "Lawton looked real perturbed about then, so he tells the young punk to step into the street. They squared off, and that kid didn't do too bad. He cleared leather and had his gun comin' up when Lawton's slug plowed into his heart. Everybody was talkin' afterward about how the kid came within a half-second of bestin' Lawton."

"Pierson hadn't shown up yet, even after they'd carried the kid away and Marshal Collins made his usual inquiries among the spectators as to whether it was a fair fight or not," said Smith. "So we hightailed it on back here to let you know about it, Mack. We know you been talkin' about movin' up in the ranks by takin' on the likes of Bobby Lawton. If you get goin' right away, you'll probably still find him in town."

Eagerness showed on Pflug's craggy features. "I appreciate this, boys. I'll saddle up right now."

"Wait a minute, Mack," said Dunphy. "What about that little voice inside you? Lawton is pretty high on the ladder."

"Yeah, I'm listenin', boss. And I'm hearin' him say, 'Go get 'im, Mack.' When word gets around that I took out Lawton, I'll start gettin' some respect."

Dunphy frowned. "But what if you get to town and find out that Lawton and Pierson have already had it out, and Lawton's dead?"

"Then I'll challenge Pierson," came the quick reply. Mack thought a moment, then added, "That is, unless the little voice tells me it ain't the right time. But I don't think Pierson can take

Lawton. It'll be Lawton I'm challengin'."

"Yeah," mumbled Dunphy. "That's what's worryin' me. Mack, you'd better forget this 'little voice' thing and stay away from Lawton."

"Hey, boss," chuckled Pflug, "don't be an ol' grandma. I know what I'm doin'. I'll be back in no time. If Lawton's still in town, I'll take him out and you'll have an even bigger name workin' for you."

While Dunphy was shaking his head, Whetstone said, "Mack, Aaron and I'll go with you."

"Suit yourselves," Pflug replied, heading for the door.

As Whetstone and Smith followed, Dunphy said, "He's bull-headed, boys, but do what you can to bring him back alive."

Dunphy swore and said to Speer and Eggert, "These gun-slicks. I have a hard time figurin' 'em out. Looks like they all got a big ego problem."

Both men chuckled and started picking up tin plates and cups.

"I guess that's it, boss," sighed Hec Speer. "And that ego problem puts 'em in their graves long before their time."

"Well, I hope Mack don't play the fool. We need him. He's plenty handy to have along when we do these bank jobs."

Word had spread through Pueblo that Lance Pierson was on his way to face off with Bobby Lawton. Main Street was lined with spectators. Seeing Lawton cut down the greenhorn earlier had only whetted their appetite for more. Most of them were collected near the Bullhorn Saloon where Lawton and his cohorts, Dick Freeman and Hoagy Byers, waited at a table inside. Eager eyes searched both ends of the street, watching for the appearance of Pierson.

At two o'clock, Marshal Jack Collins and his deputy, Willie Yarrow, came out of the marshal's office a block away. Together they moved side-by-side down the middle of the dusty street, which was eighty feet wide from hitching rail to hitching rail.

Collins was in his early fifties and was developing a paunch. He wore a heavy mustache that drooped over the edges of his mouth. It matched his silver hair in color. Yarrow, tall and thin, was in his late twenties.

Collins was aware of eyes watching him as he moved up the street. A murmur rippled through the crowd, voicing the disappointment they would feel if Collins ran Lawton and his cronies out of town.

Collins's features were solemn as he drew up in front of the Bullhorn and said, "Clear the way, folks. Willie and I are going inside."

"You ain't gonna stop it are you, Marshal?" asked a man.

"If I'm able," Collins said. He noted the town's only physician, Dr. Harvey Roberts, among the crowd. Halting, he frowned and asked, "Doc, what're you doing here?"

There was a sober look in Roberts's eyes. "If Pierson shows up and this shootout transpires, a bullet or two could go astray. I don't give a flip if these ignoramus gunslicks blow holes in each other, but with a crowd this size looking on, it'd be easy for a stray bullet to hit somebody. Figured I'd be on hand just in case."

"I appreciate that, Doc," nodded Collins, "but I'm putting a stop to the whole thing. After I'd settled that Lawton and the kid fought it out fair and square, I figured Lawton would have him a drink and ride on. He didn't tell me he'd come here to meet Lance Pierson."

"Better be careful, Jack," said Roberts. "Lawton's a mean one."

"Yeah, I know. But Pueblo's my town, and I'm responsible for it. I left my office with the same thing in mind as you. I don't care if Lawton and Pierson blow each other to kingdom come, but I don't want any of these people getting hurt...or worse."

Suddenly a man's voice cut the air. "Here comes Pierson!"

The marshal pivoted, and his gaze swerved to the south end of the four-block-long business district. Three riders moved slowly between the lines of gawking people.

Marshal Collins had seen Lance Pierson on a couple of other occasions. It was him, all right, flanked by a couple of toughs. Deciding to deal with Pierson instead of Lawton, Collins pushed his way through the crowd and moved into the sunstruck street. Yarrow was on his heels.

Lance Pierson was a straight column in the saddle, his back like a ramrod and his shoulders squared. He and his partners reined in as Collins approached. His features were rock-hard. Smiling in a tight, acid way, he nodded, "Marshal."

"So why'd you two pick my town to shed blood in, Lance?" queried Collins, voice level.

"By the looks of things, I guess he's here, eh?" Pierson's hard gaze was scanning the crowded street.

"You didn't answer my question."

"Well, I'll tell you, Marshal, it's like this. Bobby and I bumped into each other a few days ago in a little burg down south of here. I'd been thinkin' about lookin' him up so's we could square off. We talked about it and agreed that since we're at about the same level on the ladder, we'd best have it out where more people would see it." Looking around at the crowd again, Pierson added, "Looks like you done got us a real good audience. They'll tell it far and wide when I kill Bobby right in front of their eyes."

Collins fixed Pierson with smoldering eyes. "I really don't care which one of you walks away, Lance, but I do care if some of these people get hit with a stray bullet."

"Won't come from me," parried Pierson. "I'll only fire one slug...into Bobby's chest."

Collins was about to speak again when there was a gasp from the crowd. All eyes were focused toward the Bullhorn Saloon. Collins turned to see the spectators quickly making a path for Bobby Lawton as he crossed the boardwalk, sided by Freeman and Byers.

Lawton said something to his friends, and they halted, allowing him to move out into the street alone. At the same time, Pierson left his saddle, telling his partners to take his horse and keep an eye on Lawton's cronies. They dismounted and led Pierson's horse away.

Marshal Collins motioned for his deputy to step aside and placed himself squarely between the two gunfighters, who stood facing each other over a distance of forty feet in the center of the street. Yarrow backed toward the crowd and came to a halt next to Doc Roberts.

With his back to Pierson, Collins set his gaze on Lawton and said, "You didn't tell me this was planned, Bobby."

Lawton was a cold-blooded man with shrewd eyes and hawk-like features. "You didn't ask me," he growled. "Now get outta the way, Marshal."

A cool, stiff breeze whipped along the street, picking up dust and flinging it against the spectators. There was a smell of death in the breeze.

No one noticed the three riders who came in from the east on a side street and dismounted. They filtered into the crowd and threaded their way closer to the scene.

Marshal Collins regarded Lawton with a hard, steady gaze. "Why don't you two go somewhere outside of town and do this?"

Collins heard Pierson chuckle behind him.

A serpentine grin curled Lawton's mouth. "Now, Mr. Lawman, you know why we choose a public place to settle these matters."

Collins knew there was nothing more he could do. Both gunfighters had their toughs with them. Even with Yarrow to back him up, he wouldn't have a chance. Most of the men in the crowd carried guns, but Collins knew they wouldn't side with him if he went up against the four toughs. The gunplay was going to happen.

It was the same old pattern that had been going on in the West since the end of the Civil War. The men who had fought on either side had tasted of violence. The war had changed them forever, though for most it didn't become evident until they returned to their homes and found their old way of life dull and boring. For many, violence had become an integral part of their lives.

So they drifted west in search of excitement and adventure, wearing sidearms. At first the revolvers were worn for protection from wild animals and hostile Indians. But hard liquor and hot tempers soon found them using the guns on each other. The man who cleared leather the fastest and shot the straightest wore a badge of honor among the hard-living wanderers of the West.

Thus was born the gunfight, spawning a new breed of heroes throughout the western states and territories. There was a pride in the gunfighters that ruled them with an iron hand. Just or unjust, it gave them a measure of dignity they would risk their lives to maintain.

Collins held his gaze on Lawton, wishing he could force the gunplay to a less dangerous place. From behind, he heard Pierson say, "It's time for you to move out of the way, Marshal."

Collins sighed. He knew it would do no good to warn the onlookers of the potential danger. He might as well do as Pierson had said. Lifting his hat and running splayed fingers through his thinning hair, he walked toward the Wells-Fargo side of the street and joined the spectators. He glanced at his deputy, who was talking with Dr. Roberts.

Mack Pflug, Jade Whetstone, and Aaron Smith made their way to the front of the Wells-Fargo office, just behind Marshal Collins, and watched the scene in the middle of the street.

Both gunfighters took their stance, their hands hovering over their holstered guns. The crowd looked on, wide-eyed and eager.

Bobby Lawton barked, "Well, Lance, this is what you wanted. Go for it."

"You want it as bad as I do, pal. I've had my share of challengers already...and after I drop you, I'll have plenty more."

"Do it, then talk, Lance."

Pierson's boots twisted ever so slightly just before he reached for his gun. The signal was unintentional, but it gave Lawton the edge. His gun was out and spitting fire just as Pierson's weapon was coming out and up.

The .45 slug plowed through Pierson's chest and came out his back. He coughed and stared at his adversary, a surprised look on his face. For a long, breathless moment, he held himself upright, then fell heavily to the street.

The breeze carried Lawton's gun smoke away while the crowd looked on, almost hypnotized by what they had just witnessed.

Mack Pflug turned to his friends and said, "I can take him."

People standing near looked at Pflug with amazement. Whetstone said in a subdued voice, "Mack, you're crazy! Lawton's a lot more experienced than you."

"He's also slower than me," countered Pflug. "I tell you, I can take him! That dude lyin' dead in the street gave himself away by movin' his feet a split second before he went for his gun. Didn't you see that?"

"I didn't see nothin' of the kind," said Whetstone.

"Me neither," Aaron Smith said. "You better just leave it be, Mack."

Pflug gave them both a disgusted look and said, "The little man inside agrees with me. Lawton's a dead man."

Even as he spoke, Pflug pushed his way through the crowd onto the street.

Bobby Lawton was standing over the lifeless form of Lance Pierson and sliding a fresh cartridge into his revolver as Dr. Roberts knelt down and pronounced Pierson dead.

Marshal Collins was kneeling on Pierson's other side. Rising, Collins stepped around the corpse and said to Lawton, "All right, Bobby. Take your two pals with you and ride. I want you out of my town right now."

Lawton bristled. "I didn't break no law, Marshal. You ain't got no right to—"

"*Lawton!*" bawled a powerful voice. "I'm callin' you right now!"

Lawton's head whipped around. Collins stared in disbelief at the owner of the voice. The crowd quietly looked on.

Mack Pflug stood about ten paces from Lawton, eyes blazing, feet spread slightly, his hand almost touching the butt of his gun.

Lawton eyed him with disdain. "Who are *you?*"

"I'll tell you who I am, mister. Mack Pflug, and I'm the man who's gonna put you in the ground!" Pflug kept his voice loud so everyone on the street would hear his name and remember it.

"Pflug, eh?" snorted Lawton. "Seems I heard your name. You're the dude that took out Curly Bender down in Walsenburg."

"You heard right," Pflug said, figuring such an accomplishment might rattle Lawton some.

It didn't.

"The way I heard it, Curly hurt his gun hand the day before," Lawton taunted. "You knew about it and forced the fight, knowin' you had the edge."

"That's a dirty lie!" boomed Pflug. "You didn't hear it that way, and you know it."

Marshal Collins turned to his deputy and said, "You know this guy?"

"Nope," Yarrow replied, shrugging his shoulders.

"I've seen him around town a time or two, Jack," Dr. Roberts said, "but I don't know anything about him."

Lawton squared himself with his new adversary. "I've never killed three men in one day, Pflug, but I'm fixin' to unless you apologize for your smart mouth and walk away real quick-like."

"I ain't apologizin' for nothin', Lawton. And I ain't walkin' away from the likes of you, neither! So you might as well go for your gun."

The afternoon sun was stabbing Bobby Lawton in the face. He tipped his head downward just enough to allow his hatbrim to cast a shadow over his eyes. His deadly stare locked with Pflug's and remained a fixed, calculating pressure against his challenger. "Loudmouth punks draw first," he said levelly.

Pflug's hand moved like lightning. Lawton's was an invisible streak. Both guns roared, Pflug's firing first by a split second.

Pflug's bullet struck Lawton several inches below his heart, dropping him to the ground. Shock registered on his face as he groped his way to his knees. He couldn't believe this little-known gunfighter had more than matched him for speed.

Pflug took Lawton's slug in the left shoulder, just above the arm pit, and, amazingly, stayed on his feet. He staggered slightly, blinking to clear his vision. When he saw that Lawton was not dead and was struggling to balance himself on his knees to get off another shot, Pflug tried to line his revolver on the famous gunslinger's heart. At the same time, Lawton brought his weapon up for the kill.

Again Pflug's gun roared a split second sooner than Lawton's. The bullet struck Lawton in the right side of the chest, spinning him sideways. His gun spun with him and discharged, hitting Dr. Roberts. Women screamed and men shouted as they saw their beloved physician fall.

CHAPTER
THREE

Breanna Baylor sat on the rear seat of the stagecoach, next to the window on the right side. Louise Carter sat beside her, with Harley to her left at the other window. The women were covered up to their necks with a buffalo-hide blanket. Albert Cross and George Simpson sat opposite, riding backwards.

It was mid-afternoon and conversation in the coach had dwindled. The Carters were holding hands, Cross and Simpson were dozing, and Breanna was looking out the glassless window, noting Pueblo's uneven line of rooftops in the distance. In silent repose, she thought of the man she loved.

Up top, driver Clete Washburn and shotgunner Phil Madsen faced the cold wind with hats pulled low and coat collars up. The sun was reasonably warm, but the forward motion of the stage, along with the natural breeze coming off the nearby snow-capped Rockies, produced a snappy wind.

"Well, there she is," spoke up Madsen. "I like gettin' in before dark. Gives a fella some time for himself."

"Yep," nodded the older man. "And tomorrow is even better. Just forty miles from here to Colorado Springs."

"Don't make me mad," chuckled Madsen.

Twenty minutes brought the Wells-Fargo vehicle to the edge

of town. Washburn guided the team in a right turn onto Main Street and held them to an easy trot as they headed for the business district.

Washburn elbowed his young partner and pointed up the street toward the center of town. "Wonder what's got everybody's interest up there?" he mused.

Madsen had already noticed the large crowd lining the boardwalks. Having better eyesight than the older man, he spotted the two men in the middle of the street. "Looks like a shootout, Clete."

No sooner had the words come from his mouth than there was a double crack of gunfire. Washburn pulled rein, halting the coach. Heads were poking out of the windows below. The passengers had heard the shots.

Everybody on the stage saw one of the gunfighters go down, then grope his way to his knees. The other man was on his feet, but swaying unsteadily. He fired at the man on the ground again. When the bullet hit him, the man spun to his right, and his gun discharged into the crowd. A man went down like a pole-axed steer. There were screams and shouts from the crowd as two men knelt beside the fallen bystander.

Washburn snapped the reins, putting the six-up team in motion. As the stage rolled along the street, people moved out of the way, but kept their attention riveted on the wounded bystander.

Marshal Collins shoved people out of the way to make room for Dick Freeman and Hoagy Byers as they solemnly carried the lifeless form of Bobby Lawton from the scene. Lance Pierson's cohorts had already taken his body away.

Two middle-aged women were attending Dr. Roberts, who now was laid out on the boardwalk. Both were frantic, not knowing what to do. The town's physician had taken the bullet in the stomach and was bleeding profusely.

Mack Pflug sat on the edge of the boardwalk, leaning against a post. Jade Whetstone and Aaron Smith found that the slug had passed through his body, but had torn a gaping hole. In an attempt to stop the bleeding, they were packing the wound with strips of cloth provided by the proprietor of the nearby general store.

Clenching his teeth in pain, Pflug managed a grin and said, "I told you...boys...I could take him."

"Yeah," sighed Whetstone. "You told us. Turk's gonna be plenty mad when he finds out you're gonna be outta commission for quite a while. It could mean delay in doin' that...ah...that job in Denver."

Jade reprimanded himself for almost blabbing about their plans to rob the Frontier Bank and Trust in Denver.

Smith wrapped the wound as best he could and tied it with a thin cloth strip. Shaking his head, he said, "Sure wish that doctor hadn't been hit. I don't know much about patchin' up wounds."

"Probably the best thing to do is get you out to the shack so's you can lay down and get some rest," said Whetstone. "Think you can ride?"

"Won't be a lot of fun, but I can manage."

Both men started to help Pflug to his feet, but dizziness claimed him, and he told them to let him sit a spell, then he'd try it again.

Breanna stood beside the stagecoach with the crew and the other passengers and watched the painstaking way the two women were tending to the wounded bystander. A man and woman walked by a few feet in front of Breanna and the others.

"Pardon me," Breanna said. "Doesn't this town have a doctor who can take care of that poor man?"

The couple stopped and the man said, "That poor man *is* our town doctor, ma'am."

Breanna's eyes widened. "Oh, that's terrible," she gasped. "He's the town's only doctor?"

"Yes, ma'am."

"He doesn't have a nurse?"

"No, ma'am. His wife was his nurse, but she died this past winter. He hasn't been able to find another."

"Well, I'm a nurse," she announced. "Let me get my bag."

"Marshal!" the man called. "There's a lady here who says she's a nurse."

"Well, tell her we need her!" exclaimed Collins.

Whetstone and Smith heard the exchange and grinned at each other.

"You hear that, Mack?" said Whetstone. "There's a nurse here can help you."

Breanna hastened to the boardwalk where Dr. Roberts was stretched out. The two women smiled at her as she knelt down.

"Bless you!" said one, her lips trembling.

Doc's eyes were closed, but he was conscious.

Looking at the women as she opened her bag, Breanna asked, "What's his name?"

"Dr. Harvey Roberts."

Nodding, Breanna touched the physician's shoulder. "Dr. Roberts, can you hear me?"

Roberts opened his eyes and tried to focus on her face. "Yes, ma'am."

"My name is Breanna Baylor, sir. I'm a CMN from Wichita. May I see what I can do for you?"

Doc ran a dry tongue over equally dry lips. "Yes," he said weakly. "Please do."

The people pressed close as Breanna removed the bloody cloths, unbuttoned Roberts's shirt, and examined the wound. Marshal Collins spread his arms and said, "Please, folks. Give the lady some room to work." Reluctantly the people obeyed.

Breanna's face paled as she saw the damage to the doctor's intestines. The bullet had plowed through his brass belt buckle, carrying metal slivers with it. Speaking in a soft voice, she explained the seriousness of the wound to Roberts, then asked, "How close is the nearest doctor?"

"Colorado...Springs."

Breanna knew it would take too long to send for a doctor.

"Dr. Roberts, that bullet and those metal fragments have to come out or you'll die. I've assisted in this kind of surgery before, but I'm not a surgeon. Do you want me to try?"

"By all...means," Roberts nodded, knowing she was right. "You'll need help. Mrs. Nelson...and Mrs. Dodd will help you."

Breanna suspected they were the two women who had done their best to make him comfortable and stay the flow of blood. Turning, she looked at them and they both nodded. Swinging her gaze to Collins, she said, "Marshal, I'll need four men to carry the doctor to his office. I'll do the surgery there. He must not be jostled any more than is absolutely necessary."

"Yes, ma'am," replied Collins, and quickly selected two men from the crowd to assist him and Deputy Yarrow in carrying Roberts to his office.

Breanna closed her black bag, rose to her feet, and turned toward the stagecoach. Passengers and crew were looking on. "I may have to stay here a day or two to see him out of danger. I'll let you know."

Clete Washburn nodded and smiled.

The four men were about to lift the wounded man. "Careful, now, gentlemen," Breanna said. "Be sure to support his torso and legs when you pick him up. All right. Let's move slow but steady."

Maudie Nelson and Sarah Dodd flanked Breanna as she followed the men down the street. As they walked, Jade Whetstone drew up behind the women and said, "Please, ma'am, can I talk to you?"

Without breaking stride, Breanna looked over her shoulder and replied, "If you can talk while we walk. This is an emergency."

"Yes, ma'am," he said, and moved in front of her, walking backwards. "My friend back there was in the gunfight, ma'am."

"Yes, I saw you and another man tending to him. Is he hurt bad?"

"Not as bad as the doctor, but he's bleedin' quite a bit."

"Where's the wound?"

"It's in his left shoulder, near the top of his armpit."

"All right. Bring him to the office and I'll see what I can do. But mind you...Dr. Roberts will have my undivided attention until I've finished the surgery."

"Yes, ma'am. I appreciate it, ma'am. We'll bring him right away."

As the four men who bore the doctor neared his office, Maudie lifted her skirt and ran before them, opening the door. The marshal and his assistants carefully squeezed through the doorway.

As Breanna waited on the boardwalk, her attention was drawn to three "wanted" posters tacked on the clapboard wall next to the door. The posters included sketches of the wanted men, and bold letters identified them as Turk Dunphy, Hector Speer, and Harold Eggert. They were wanted for bank robbery and murder and were reported to be in the area. There was a $1,000 reward offered for the capture of each man, dead or alive.

Breanna asked Sarah, "Why does Dr. Roberts have these posters by his door?"

"Oh, he didn't put them here, Miss Baylor. Marshal Collins has them tacked up all over town. From what the marshal says, those men will kill a human being as quickly as they'd step on a bug or shoot a rattlesnake. They've gunned down bank employees and customers who even looked at them wrong. He wants their faces known so if they ride into town, someone will recognize them and report it to him immediately."

Maudie hurried through the waiting room into the clinic and stood beside the examining and operating table. She made sure the men were careful as they laid Dr. Roberts on the table.

Breanna did a quick survey of the room, noting the single bed in one corner, the glassed-in medicine cabinet, spotless white cupboard, counter with water pump and wash basin, and small table on wheels that held Dr. Roberts's surgical instruments.

Taking a bottle of laudanum from the medicine cabinet, she set it on the counter and smiled at the four men, saying, "Thank you, gentlemen. If any of you care to stay close by, you can remain in the waiting room. A couple of that wounded gunfighter's friends are going to bring him here for me to tend to. No matter how bad off he is, they'll have to keep him in the waiting room until I'm finished here."

"My deputy will stay, ma'am," said Collins. "He'll make sure they keep the man in the waiting room till you're ready for him. I'll be back to check on Doc a little later."

When the men were gone and the door was closed, Breanna gave instructions to the two women as to how they could assist her with the surgery. While Maudie and Sarah were washing their hands in lye soap, Breanna took a pair of scissors and cut away the front of the doctor's shirt. Laying the scissors aside, she loosened the bullet-drilled belt buckle and lowered his trousers just enough to expose the ugly wound. The free flow of blood worried her. Dr. Roberts was in serious trouble, and she could tell by the look in his eyes that he knew it.

"Before I give you this laudanum, doctor, I want to tell you that I'll do my very best," she said. "Like I said, I've only assisted this type of surgery. I've not performed it."

In a haze of pain, Dr. Roberts was thinking of the irony of this whole thing. He had gone to the street in case someone picked up a stray bullet, never dreaming he would be the one shot.

"I understand, Nurse Baylor," he said with effort. "If...well, if I don't make it...please don't blame yourself."

Breanna swallowed hard, nodding. She administered the opium-based tincture, then quickly scrubbed her hands and made the other necessary preparations. Once Roberts was under the influence of the laudanum, she proceeded with the surgery.

After nearly two hours, the bullet and metal fragments had been removed, and the good doctor had been sutured up. He was still under the influence of the laudanum, resting quietly.

While Breanna washed the blood from her hands, Maudie asked, "Miss Baylor, what do you think? Is he going to make it?"

"I can't say right now. That bullet tore him up pretty bad in there. I hope I've done my job correctly, but even if I have, he could still hemorrhage to death. If he makes it till morning, there's a good chance he'll live."

"We'll just have to pray," Sarah said.

"I've been doing a lot of that for the past two hours," sighed Breanna.

Breanna dried her hands on a towel. Looking toward the door, she said, "Well, guess I'd better see what I can do for the gunfighter."

With disgust, Sarah blurted, "Serves him right, however bad he's hurt. Grown men acting like little boys. Somebody's always got to be known as the best bullet-slinger around. Downright stupid if you ask me."

"I agree," nodded Maudie.

"Well, I do too, ladies," said Breanna, "but in my line, I have to work on wise men and fools alike." As she headed for the door, she spoke over her shoulder. "If you ladies want to go home, I'm sure I can handle this patient myself."

"That's all right," Maudie said. "We'll stay. You may need our help."

Breanna opened the door and found Mack Pflug sitting on a chair, eyes closed, leaning against Aaron Smith. Jade Whetstone was lighting a lantern. Breanna had been so preoccupied, she hadn't noticed it was growing dark outside.

"Where's the deputy?" Breanna asked.

"He's out on the street talkin' to someone, ma'am," replied Whetstone.

Breanna nodded. "I can see your friend, now. How's he doing?"

"Still bleedin' quite a bit, but I'm sure you can fix him so's he'll be all right."

"I'll need you two—" she started to use the word *gentlemen* but thought better of it—"I'll need you two men to help me get the doctor onto a bed in here, then we can put your friend on the examining table."

Maudie and Sarah stayed with the wounded man, and Breanna directed the careful removal of Dr. Roberts from the table to the bed. She then examined the patch-up job Whetstone and Smith had done on Mack Pflug.

Pflug looked at her with glassy eyes and said, "How's it look, ma'am?"

"Can't tell yet," she replied, peeling away layers of blood-soaked cloth. "What's your name, mister gunfighter?"

"Mack Pflug, ma'am," he said proudly. "You'll hear my name a whole lot in the days to come. I took out Bobby Lawton today."

Breanna looked into his face for a brief moment. "Well, not by much, you didn't."

"Fool!" Maudie muttered to herself. Then to Breanna, "Do you need us any more, Miss Baylor?"

"I don't think so. You and Sarah can go. Thank you for your good help."

"You don't have to thank us for helping with Doc. We'd do anything for him. But when it comes to fool gunfighters, that's another story."

Pflug glared at Maudie but said nothing.

"Are you staying at the hotel tonight?" Sarah asked as the two women headed for the door.

"I doubt it. I'll probably stay here and watch over Dr. Roberts."

"All night?" Sarah asked.

"Yes. I don't want to leave him. He's not out of danger by any means."

"Do you want us to bring you something to eat?"

"I wouldn't want to be a bother to you."

"Honey, you've got to eat," said Maudie. "We'll be back in an hour or so with some nice hot food."

Breanna's brow furrowed. "You're sure it's not too much trouble?"

"Of course not. We'll see you in a bit."

The two women passed into the waiting room and were greeted by Deputy Yarrow. Yarrow went on into the clinic and asked, "How's Doc, Miss?"

"He's resting easy at the moment. Can't tell you any more than that."

"He's gonna make it all right, isn't he?"

"There's no way I can say, Deputy," she said, removing the last cloth layer and eyeing Pflug's bloody wound. "I'm going to stay here with him all night. If he makes it to morning, his chances will be a lot better than they are right now. It's internal hemorrhaging I fear the most."

"Well, ma'am, if you're going to spend the night here, can I go over to the café and get you something to eat?"

"No, thank you. Maudie and Sarah are going to bring me some supper."

"All right, then. I'll go and tell Marshal Collins how it is with Doc. We'll be back first thing in the morning to see how he's doing."

"That's fine," said Breanna, without looking up. She heard Yarrow leave, then said to Pflug, "I've got to clean the wound and sew it up. I'll give you some laudanum."

"That won't be necessary, ma'am," Pflug said, eager to prove he was tough enough to stand the pain.

"It's going to hurt, Mr. Pflug. Are you sure you don't want some laudanum?"

"I'm sure. Let's just get it over with."

Breanna made Whetstone and Smith return to the waiting room while she worked. Within three-quarters of an hour, the job was done, and the men were called back into the clinic. As they came close to the table where Pflug was sitting up, Breanna said, "Mack tells me the three of you are planning to go back to the farm where you work yet tonight."

"That's right," nodded Whetstone. "We really need to get back. Our boss, Mr. Jones, will be worryin' about us."

Smith and Whetstone exchanged furtive glances.

"I told my patient that he shouldn't be riding that far. It is five miles, isn't it?"

Realizing Mack had also lied to the nurse, Jade grinned and said, "Yes, ma'am. Five miles. Mack's tough. He can make it."

Whetstone and Smith feared Turk Dunphy. Figuring he would be plenty upset by now, they didn't want to keep him waiting longer than necessary. He had been on pins and needles about Mack's shootout with Bobby Lawton. Since Turk, Speer, and Eggert couldn't show their faces in town, Turk would have to wait for any news until the three of them returned to the hideout. Whetstone and Smith had talked this over with Pflug while sitting in the waiting room. Pflug had insisted he would be able to ride back with them.

"Well," said Breanna, "I strongly recommend that he not ride at all tonight. The best thing for him would be to take a room at the hotel and rest."

"I'll be all right, ma'am," spoke up Pflug. Then to his friends, he said, "Let's go, boys. The boss is waitin'."

Breanna shook her head as she watched Whetstone and Smith half-carry Pflug through the door. His knees were so weak, he could hardly stand. She wondered how far he would make it in the saddle.

Closing the door, she went to Dr. Roberts and sat down on a straight-backed wooden chair next to the bed. His color was bad. He looked like a dead man. She was afraid he was bleeding internally.

For Pflug's sake, Whetstone and Smith kept their horses at a walk as the trio moved eastward across the rolling plains by the pale light of a half-moon. Whetstone and Smith rode abreast and the wounded man followed. Pflug rode quietly, hunched over in the saddle. From time to time, one of the other two would look back and ask the wounded gunfighter if he was all right. Pflug would raise his head and assure them he was fine.

It was after eleven o'clock when they topped a gentle rise and the hideout came into view, resting quietly on the west bank of Chico Creek. The dilapidated barn, privy, and tool shed stood in somber shadows beneath the naked-limbed trees. Lantern light glowed through the windows of the shack.

"Looks like Turk and the boys are still up," Smith said.

"I'd say so," agreed Whetstone.

The path they were following ran alongside a ravine for about fifty yards. The ravine was some twenty feet deep and fifty feet wide. Its banks were rock-ribbed and steep.

The ride had taken its toll on the wounded man. He had been feeling light-headed and nauseated for several minutes. A sudden wave of dizziness swept over him, and before he could call out for help, he fell from the saddle, struck the lip of the ravine, and tumbled down the steep bank, arms and legs flailing. Whetstone and Smith whipped around in their saddles and watched helplessly as Pflug disappeared into the deep shadows of the ravine.

Whetstone swore and slid to the ground. Smith did the same. Together they picked their way down the embankment in the dim moonlight and found Pflug unconscious at the bottom. Even in the gloom, they could tell that his bandage had come off and the stitches had ripped loose. The wound was bleeding profusely.

"We gotta get him to the shack," Smith said. "This is bad."

Twenty minutes later Turk Dunphy, Hec Speer, and Harold Eggert came out the front door of the shack at the sound of hoofbeats and horses blowing in the yard.

Dunphy saw the limp form of Mack Pflug cradled in Whetstone's arms atop his horse and hurried to him. "What happened? Did Lawton do this to him? Why've you taken so long to get back here?"

"Let's get him inside, boss," said Jade. "We'll tell you the whole story."

Mack Pflug lay unconscious on his bed. Dunphy held a towel against the bleeding wound while Whetstone and Smith told about the shootout. They explained about Dr. Roberts being hit and of the nurse arriving on the stage just in time. When they finished, Turk looked at Whetstone and Smith and said, "I want you two to take fresh horses and ride hard. Bring that nurse back here as fast as you can. Mack's gonna bleed to death if she doesn't sew him back up quick. Now go!"

FOUR

Breanna Baylor rubbed her tired eyes as she sat on the chair next to Dr. Harvey Roberts, then glanced at the old clock on the wall. Almost one o'clock. *He looks bad, but maybe he'll make it,* she thought. *If only he's not hemorrhaging. If only—*

Suddenly Roberts jerked awake and moaned. Fluttering his eyelids, he focused glazed eyes on Breanna, ran both hands to his midsection, and gasped, "Pain. Awful pain. Help me."

Breanna drew back the blanket that covered him and saw that his abdomen was swelling. Blood! He was hemorrhaging, and the blood was collecting around his stomach!

"Dr. Roberts," she said, struggling to keep her voice steady, "you're hemorrhaging. I'm sure of it."

Roberts licked his lips, nodding. "You'll have to...open me up again. Find the...aperture. Sew it up."

Breanna's heart was pounding. She wasn't sure she knew enough to do it right. But there was no choice. He would die if she did nothing. She left the chair and carried two lanterns to the small table beside the bed. There was no way to get him on the operating table. She would have to do her work where he lay, and she would need plenty of light.

While she rolled the instrument table across the room, she

thought of Maudie Nelson and Sarah Dodd. When they brought her supper, they had offered to stay the night. Knowing they needed their rest, she had thanked them and sent them home. Now she was kicking herself. This operation would be difficult if she had help, but doing it alone was going to be next to impossible. There was no time to run for help. It had to be done in the next few minutes or it wouldn't matter. Dr. Roberts would die.

Roberts was gritting his teeth and rolling his head back and forth on the pillow as Breanna rushed toward the counter to scrub her hands. As she reached for the lye soap, she heard footsteps in the waiting room. *Oh, wonderful!* she thought. *Just in time! Whoever it is can help me.*

The door swung open and there stood Jade Whetstone and Aaron Smith. Her heart sank. She wouldn't dare let one of them get near her patient while she was operating. "I don't know why you're here," she clipped, "but it'll have to wait. I've got to do more surgery on Dr. Roberts. Now!"

"Sorry, lady," said Whetstone, crossing the room with Smith on his heels, "but you have to come with us...*now*. Mack took a fall and tore his wound open. He's bleedin' bad."

"I'm sorry, but I can't be in two places at once. My first duty is to this man on the bed. Your gunfighter friend will have to wait."

Jade reached for her and growled, "You're comin' with us!"

Breanna cried out and jumped to the side. Jade swore and lunged for her again. Dodging him, she dashed to the instrument table and picked up a scalpel. Wielding it in a manner that told him she meant business, she snapped, "Get out of here! This man is dying, and I must operate on him!"

Smith came at Breanna from another angle. Swinging the blade in his direction, eyes blazing, she half-screamed, "Leave me alone! Get out of here, both of you, or I'll call the marshal!"

Both men charged her at the same time. Breanna thrust the scalpel at Jade, but he seized her wrist. A quick, powerful twist sent the scalpel clattering to the floor.

Jade wrapped her in his powerful arms. "You're comin' with us, lady. Our pal is dyin', too. If I have to cold cock you to get you there, I'll do it. Choice is yours. You can come peaceful-like, or the hard way."

Breanna knew if she screamed for help, there wouldn't be anyone on the street to hear her at that time of night. She was helpless. Casting a sorrowful glance at her dying patient, she said, "All right. What you're doing is wicked. You're committing murder by keeping me from operating on him. You know that, don't you?"

"I don't look at it that way," replied Whetstone. "I figure it's just a matter of choosin' which man to save. Now let's go."

Jade released her, and Breanna's hands trembled as she put her coat on, then took laudanum, suture needles, and thread and put them in her bag.

Dr. Roberts's weak voice carried across the room. "Nurse Baylor...it's all right. Don't blame yourself." Dr. Roberts had heard the whole thing. He was going to die, and he knew it.

Breanna felt like a dull, jagged blade was cutting at her heart. The tears began to spill down her cheeks. "I'm sorry," she choked.

"C'mon, lady!" boomed Whetstone.

Breanna glared up at him and thought of the man she loved. *If John were only here, he would handle these animals.*

Steely fingers gripped Breanna's arm, dragging her toward the door. Suddenly Jade stopped and said, "Maybe we'd better gag this little spitfire. She's liable to start screamin' out there on the street. We don't need that."

Smith produced a washcloth from the cupboard, along with a towel. In his haste, he knocked other towels and washcloths to the floor. When he approached Breanna, he said, "Now, lady, I'm gonna stuff this washrag in your mouth. If you try to bite me or give me one bit of trouble, I'll smack you. Understand? One way or the other, you're gonna be gagged."

Breanna would not resist the gag. Smith meant what he said. What could she do against two men? It took Smith only seconds to stuff the cloth between her teeth and tie the towel over her mouth.

Quickly they were out the door and on the dark street. A lone street lamp burned on the corner a half-block away. Jade hoisted the weeping Breanna into his saddle, then swung up behind her. Smith mounted his horse, carrying Breanna's black bag, and they galloped down the street. Breanna managed a glimpse of the doctor's office as they turned onto a side street and headed east. *Dear God*, she prayed, *please don't let him suffer long.*

When they were a mile from town, Whetstone called to Smith above the rumble of galloping hooves, "Haul up a minute!"

Both men reined in and skidded their mounts to a halt. Jade untied the towel and removed the washcloth from Breanna's mouth. "Now, lady," he said gruffly, "you can scream all you want. Ain't nobody out here to hear you."

They resumed their gallop through the night, but Breanna's thoughts stayed in Pueblo with Dr. Roberts. Again she prayed that he would not die a lingering death. Her thoughts then went to the man she loved, and the treasured silver medallion came to mind. She had left her purse on the stage with her overnight bag and trunk. She was sure Clete Washburn would leave her belongings at the Wells-Fargo office when she didn't show up for the trip to Denver. Losing the luggage and its contents she could stand, but not the medallion. It meant more to her than anything she owned.

Dawn had not yet begun to break when they thundered into the yard at the hideout and dismounted. Lantern light still glowed from the windows. Whetstone ushered Breanna into the shack, with Smith following. She glanced at the two men who rose from their chairs, but her attention was on the man on a bed in a far corner. A third man sat beside him, holding a bloody cloth to the wound.

The shack was a large one-room affair, with six single beds shoved in the corners and against the walls.

"So this is the lady, eh?" Turk Dunphy grunted. "Never saw a nurse as purty as her. What's your name, honey?"

Breanna took her eyes off Mack Pflug and looked at the big, thick-bodied man who had spoken. Shock went through her like a bolt of lightning. It was the face of the outlaw leader from the wanted poster. She looked at the second man, then to the third, and recognized them from the posters also. *Whetstone, Smith, and Pflug were part of the gang of outlaw killers!*

Not until that moment had she feared for her life.

"What is it, lady?" growled Dunphy. "You act like you've seen us before."

"No," she gasped. "I—"

"It's prob'ly those posters we told you about, boss," cut in Aaron Smith. "They're all over town."

"So you know who we are, huh?" Dunphy growled.

Evading the question, Breanna looked back toward the bed, and said, "I thought I was brought out here to tend to Mack."

"You were," said Turk. "Get to it."

Breanna took her bag from Smith's hand and headed for the wounded man. Hec Speer looked up at her from his chair and said, "He's not bleedin' as bad as he was, ma'am. Should I let go or keep pressin' against the wound?"

"Keep pressing for now," she said. Turning to look at the others, she said, "I'll need hot water and more light over here. If you can find a way to hang a lantern directly above his head, it will be a real help. I'll also need one on the wall to his side, and another on a small table, if you have one."

When nobody moved, Turk blurted, "Well, what're you guys waitin' for? Get the lady what she needs!"

A fire was burning low in the cookstove. Harold Eggert stoked it while the others hurried about to get the lanterns in place. He poured water from a bucket into a large pan and set it on the stove.

Breanna bent over Mack Pflug, whose eyes were closed. "Mack, it's Nurse Baylor. Can you hear me?"

Pflug's head rolled slowly from side to side. Without opening his eyes, he replied weakly, "Yes, ma'am."

Breanna wondered how much blood Pflug had lost. She must get water into him to keep him from dehydrating. Hastening across the room, she dipped a tin cup into the water bucket and returned to Pflug. He was totally out, now, and could not drink. Sighing, she looked at Speer, who faithfully pressed the cloth to his friend's wound. "He's in real trouble," she said. "Without water, he can't produce new blood."

Speer only stared at her as she took the cup back to the cupboard. The lanterns were now in place, along with a pan of steaming water on a chair close by with a stack of dirty towels beside it. Breanna told Speer to hand her the blood-soaked cloth and move out of her way. Once she was seated and pressing the cloth into the wound, she reached into her black bag and pulled out needles and thread. Looking over her shoulder, she found all five outlaws standing behind her in a half-circle.

"I'm going to ask something of you, sirs," she said levelly. "I need privacy while I work. If you want your friend to live, please go away and let me do my work. Outside would be the best place."

"Let's do what nursie says," grunted Turk. "Outside."

Breanna heard them settle on the front porch and smelled their tobacco smoke as they talked in low tones. Breanna looked at the bloody blanket Mack was lying on. Blood was actually dripping from the blanket and forming a large puddle on the floor. Shaking her head, she studied the gunfighter's pale features. Mack Pflug was not going to make it. He was all but dead. All she could do was suture up the wound and let nature take its course.

Mack's eyes were still closed, and he was barely breathing. There was no way she could administer laudanum. If he came to while she was stitching him up, she would give it to him then. Using the cleanest of the dirty towels, she washed the ragged area around the wound. The fall Mack had taken into the ravine had opened a gaping hole.

It took her a half-hour to close up the wound. When she was finished and had bandaged it, she left the dying man and went to the water bucket at the cupboard for a drink. The cupboard was near the front door, which had been left open. The low, indistinguishable voices she had heard while she was working on Mack were now clear. Her ears perked up when she heard Turk Dunphy say, "The way I see it, we don't have any choice. If we let her go back to town, she'll have the law on us quicker'n you can bat an eye. Once she's got Mack on the road to recovery, we'll have a little fun with her, then kill her."

Turk's words hit Breanna like a sledgehammer. She froze. A coldness swept through her. *These vile men would use her to save Mack Pflug's life, then abuse her and kill her in cold blood!* Panic clawed at her insides like a wild beast.

Breanna backed away from the cupboard toward the corner where Pflug lay dying. As she looked at him, the thought struck her: *If Mack died, they would no longer need her, either!*

Her mind was racing. What could she do? She would have to figure out a way to escape, but it would take time. She must keep Pflug alive as long as possible. As long as he was alive but not recovered, she was safe.

Breanna knew the recovery would never come. He would not live more than a couple of days at the very most. It all depended on how much blood he had lost. He was still bleeding some, even after she had closed up the wound. She wished she could put blood in his veins. She would give him some of her own if it were possible. Sitting down beside Pflug, she laid a hand on his brow. His temperature was rising. This would only complicate things. If he ran a high fever for very long, that by itself could kill him. He was already so weak.

Breanna dashed to the cupboard and picked up the water bucket, which was about three-quarters full. At the same moment, the outlaws began to file through the door, led by Dunphy. As he approached her, he said, "Well, did you get our boy all sewed up?"

"Yes," she said, her throat slightly constricted.

"So where you goin' with the water?"

"He's running a fever. I've got to see what I can do to bring it down."

"He's going to be all right, ain't he?"

Breanna hated to lie, but she dare not tell Dunphy that his prize gang member had little chance to live. "Of course he's going to be all right," she said. "But I want to make him as comfortable as possible."

Turk nodded, grinned, and swung his hand in Mack's direction. "Well, go to it. Don't let me stand in your way."

Breanna hurried to Pflug and used a towel dipped in the cool water to bathe his face. His breathing was shallow, and he looked whiter than ever. While the outlaws sat at the table in the center of the shack and discussed Mack's condition, Breanna thought again of her impending death. *Oh, John! Where are you? I need you! Dear Lord in heaven, You know what these evil men are planning! Please help me!*

John's parting words echoed through her mind. "From time to time, I may be looking at you, but you'll not know I'm near. I'll respect your request."

A shudder ran through Breanna Baylor. What a fool she had been to send John away. Not only did she need rescuing, but she also wanted to tell John how sorry she was for what she had done...and how very much she loved him.

After an hour of bathing Mack's face and wrists with the cool water, his fever subsided a bit. The windows on the east side of the cabin were showing the hint of dawn. Breanna was dead tired. She looked toward the table to find that the outlaws had deserted it and gone to their beds. She had been so preoccupied with her thoughts she hadn't been aware of their movements.

Her heart quickened pace. They were all asleep. She could make a run for it. If she could get out of the house without awakening any of them, she could dash to the barn, bridle a horse, and ride hard for town. She had ridden bareback many times.

Then she looked at her patient. If he had any chance at all to live, *she* was that chance. Though she had no respect for outlaws and gunslingers, God gave human life, and it was sacred. She must stay and do what she could to keep the gunslinger alive.

Pflug was resting peacefully at the moment. His breathing was still shallow, but as long as he was breathing she was safe. Taking a folded blanket from the foot of the bed to use as a pillow, she stretched out on the floor, covering herself with her coat. In less than a minute, she was asleep.

At sunrise Marshal Collins and Deputy Yarrow left the marshal's office and walked down the street toward the doctor's office. They could hear the bawling of cattle coming from the outskirts of town on both the east and west sides. Just south of Pueblo a few miles was the Bar W ranch. It was a huge one, and periodically they drove three or four hundred head of cattle to market at Denver. For some reason unknown to the lawmen, the drovers always split the herd at Pueblo, driving them on both sides of town. Once they were on the north side, they would join the herd together and keep moving toward Denver. They wondered if the drovers did the same thing at Colorado Springs.

When the lawmen reached Dr. Roberts's office, they noticed that the door was ajar. Entering, they passed through the waiting room and into the clinic. The lanterns were still burning, but Breanna was nowhere to be seen. Moving quickly to the bed in the corner, Collins bent over the patient. His eyes told him that Dr. Roberts was dead. He placed his fingertips to the physician's neck. Roberts was cold, and there was no pulse.

Willie drew up beside him and knew by the look on the marshal's face that Doc was dead. "He's dead, isn't he."

Collins nodded. "At least it appears he went peacefully. Maybe not too much pain." Reaching down, he lifted the blanket, placed Roberts's hands underneath, then covered his face.

Looking around, the deputy said, "I wonder where Miss Baylor is?"

"I don't know, Willie, but this is strange."

"What do you mean?"

"Miss Baylor isn't here, but the lanterns are all burning and the front door was ajar."

"Is odd, isn't it? Maybe...maybe she was so tired, she thought Doc was doing okay, so she decided to go get some rest at the hotel. Maybe she just forgot to put out the lanterns and close the door."

Shaking his head, Collins said, "Nurses are very efficient, Willie. I can't believe—"

The marshal's eyes fell on the scalpel that lay on the floor. Picking it up, he said, "Something's awry, Willie. No nurse is going to drop a scalpel on the floor and leave it there."

"Hey, look over here!" exclaimed the deputy, moving to the cupboard. "These towels and washcloths on the floor..."

"She wouldn't walk out of here leaving the place like this. Not if she was leaving on her own accord."

Yarrow's brow furrowed. "But...why would someone come in here and force her to leave?"

"Good question. Why would they? But the evidence is here. I'm afraid Miss Baylor was taken from here against her will. Let's check at the hotel, just to be sure. If they haven't seen her, we'll check with the Wells-Fargo people. If they've heard nothing, our suspicions will be confirmed."

Rubbing his chin, Willie said, "We might check with Maudie and Sarah too, Marshal. They were going to bring supper for her last night. They might know something."

"We'll do it," said Collins. "Let's go."

Leaving the doctor's office, the lawmen hurried up the street to advise the town's undertaker of Doc Roberts's death. They hastened to Maudie's and Sarah's homes next. The two women had not seen Breanna after they had taken supper to her. The lawmen went to the hotel, but the desk clerk had no information about Breanna

Baylor. At the Wells-Fargo office they found the Denver-bound stagecoach being loaded with baggage. Passengers were collected on the boardwalk, waiting to board.

"Howdy, Marshal...Deputy," grinned Clete Washburn as the two lawmen drew up.

"You seen anything of the nurse...Miss Baylor?" Collins asked.

"No, sir," replied the driver. "She said she'd let us know if she was gonna stay here to take care of the doctor."

The Wells-Fargo agent emerged from the office and approached Washburn. After greeting the two lawmen, he said, "Clete, what about the nurse? Do you know if she's going with you on this run?"

"Marshal and I were just talkin' about her, Barry. He was askin' if I'd seen anythin' of her."

"Have you?"

"Nope."

"Wasn't she to let you know by now?"

"Yep. She knew Phil and I were stayin' at the hotel. She coulda got a message to us anytime she wanted."

"Fellas," said Collins, "I'm afraid Miss Baylor may have been kidnapped."

"Kidnapped!" blurted Washburn. "What do you mean?"

When the passengers heard the word *kidnapped*, they immediately crowded around. Louise Carter looked at Collins and said, "Marshal, I hope you're not talking about Nurse Baylor."

"I'm afraid we are, ma'am."

"What has happened, Marshal?" queried Albert Cross. "Are we understanding correctly that she has been kidnapped?"

"Looks like it," nodded Collins. "Just about has to be the case."

Marshal Collins then told them how he and his deputy had found Dr. Roberts dead and Breanna missing. He described to them the indications at the doctor's office that Breanna had not left on her own accord. Given this evidence, plus her failure to contact anyone in town that she knew, a kidnapping seemed the only answer.

"I assume you found no evidence that would indicate who might have taken her," said the Wells-Fargo agent.

"If I did, I'd be on their trail this minute," Collins said flatly.

"What are you going to do?"

"Willie and I are going to see if we can pick up anything that looks like a trail. We'll circle the town and see what we can spot."

Washburn started to turn away, then stopped, faced Collins again, and said, "Oh, I almost forgot. I took Miss Baylor's things into the office last night so's they'd be safe. Barry's got 'em locked up in a cabinet. If you...*when* you find her, you'll know where to tell her the stuff is."

"I'll see that she gets it."

Deputy Yarrow snapped his fingers. "Wait a minute, Marshal! What about Miss Baylor's medical bag. She had it at the doctor's office last night. It sure wasn't there this morning."

"Hey, you're right. That means her disappearance likely has something to do with her being a nurse. The bag went with her." He pondered it a moment, then said, "It still has to be a kidnapping, though. I can't believe she would leave Doc for any cause if he was still alive. And if he was dead, why didn't she cover his face? It's the accepted thing to do. She'd also leave a note so we would know where she'd gone."

"Especially since she said she'd let us know whether she was goin' with us on the stage or not," Washburn said.

Collins rubbed the back of his neck. "I'm trying to think who would need her services so bad that they'd force her to go with them."

"Outlaws of some kind?"

"Could be," said Yarrow. "What about that Pflug dude? He and his pals weren't exactly the kind you'd want as next door neighbors. Miss Baylor did patch him up. What if he developed some complications, and his pals came back to take her to him?"

"Makes sense, Willie," nodded Collins. "You just might be hitting the nail smack on the head. Let's you and me saddle up and make us a circle around the perimeter of town. Maybe we'll be able to spot something."

The lawmen bid the stage crew and passengers good-bye and headed for the stable. Moments later, they rode to the west edge of town to begin their search. When they passed the last row of houses, their eyes beheld the wide swath of chewed-up earth where the herd of cattle had passed at sunup.

"If there was any evidence, it's gone now," Collins said. "It'll be the same north, south, and east, too."

"What're we gonna do now, Marshal?" asked Yarrow.

"This wide-open country's too big for us to just start riding and hope we get lucky and bump into them. Best thing to do is start asking around and see if somebody happens to know where those hombres live. If that doesn't turn up something, all we can do is hope and pray that whoever has her won't hurt her...that when she's done her job for them, they'll turn her loose."

FIVE

Breanna Baylor was dreaming about the man she loved. In her dream, she had just asked his forgiveness for sending him away. He had forgiven her, and they were in each other's arms when she was rudely awakened by a harsh voice.

"Hey, lady, wake up!" boomed Turk Dunphy. "Your patient ain't lookin' so good, and we want a female-cooked breakfast."

Breanna's joints were stiff. Blinking against the sunlight filtering through the dirty, fly-specked windows, she sat up on the hard floor and looked at Mack Pflug. His face was a pasty white.

Towering over her, the outlaw leader growled, "Do whatever you have to for Mack, then get to work on breakfast. Everything you need is in the cupboard. Hec's buildin' a fire for you right now."

The weary nurse worked her way to a standing position. "Give me a few minutes, okay?"

"Yeah, but make it very few. We're hungry. It's almost seven o'clock."

Breanna glanced at Hec Speer, who had just struck a match at the cook stove, then watched Dunphy go out the door onto the porch where the rest of the gang had gathered.

Straightening her back, she brushed at some unruly strands of golden, honey-blond hair dangling over her eyes and turned to

Mack Pflug. The wounded gunfighter was still breathing, and his eyes were fluttering. Bending over him, Breanna said, "Mack, are you awake?"

He licked his lips with effort and nodded, trying to focus on her face.

"I'm going to get you some water," she said. "You've got to drink some water."

He nodded again.

Breanna hurried to the cupboard, a bit surprised to see her patient conscious. Dipping a tin cup in the water bucket, she hastened back to him, sat down on the chair beside the bed, and placed a hand under his head. Tilting his head upward, she placed the cup to his lips and said softly, "Come on, now. I want you to drink all of this."

It took Pflug several minutes to drain the cup. When it was done, Breanna said, "Good! We'll do this again a little later. We've got to get some liquid in your system."

Pflug lay still while Breanna lifted the cover and examined his bandage. "How's it doin'?" he asked with difficulty.

"Well, you've lost more blood, but considering the hole you tore in yourself, it's a wonder you're still alive."

His eyes were dull and his lips barely moved as he said, "Thank you for...coming out here."

"I didn't have any choice," she clipped. "Your friends forced me to come."

Pflug was about to reply when Dunphy's thunderous voice boomed from the door, "How's he doin'?"

"He's holding his own," Breanna said. She wasn't sure it was the truth, but it would do for the moment.

"Good! Then get to cookin'!"

It was after nine o'clock when Breanna finished cleaning up after breakfast. Each of the men had taken a look at Mack, then filed outside to mill about the corral and tend to the horses. Breanna pondered her situation, trying to figure out an escape. Her life was worthless once Mack was dead or improved beyond his need of her care. She told herself it would be a miracle if he lived. His blood supply had to be dangerously low. As she dried her hands at the cupboard, she decided her only chance would be to slip out to the barn at night, bridle a horse, and lead it out of earshot from the house. Once she had gotten that far, she would mount and ride.

She could hear the outlaws calling back and forth to each other as she crossed the room to check on her patient. If he was conscious, she would make him drink some more water. She drew up to the side of the bed and sensed the presence of death. Bending over the wounded man, she saw he wasn't breathing. Checking for a pulse, she found none. Mack Pflug was dead.

Then the horror of it hit her. *Mack Pflug's death signed the warrant for her own!* She heard Dunphy's deep voice, and it was growing louder as he talked. He was coming toward the shack! Her heart pounded and the flesh on her scalp crawled, loosed, and crawled again.

Breanna's mind was racing and the palms of her shaking hands were wet. Looking through the front windows, she saw Dunphy step up on the porch and pause to talk to Jade Whetstone. At first her feet refused to move, but she forced them to carry her to the cupboard. She picked up a tin cup and dipped it into the water bucket. She must make Turk and the others think Mack was alive until she could make good her escape.

Just as she turned from the cupboard, both Dunphy and Whetstone came through the door. They looked at her, then at Mack, and started toward the bed. Breanna felt herself crushed in a vise of panic.

Dunphy paused, eyeing the cup of water in Breanna's hand. "He awake?"

"Yes."

"Good, we want to talk to him."

Breanna dashed around both men, blocking Dunphy's way. "Not right now! He...he must have more water immediately. He's lost a tremendous amount of blood. If I don't replenish the liquid in his body, he won't make it."

Turk loomed over her like some huge, unearthly ogre. He looked past Breanna to the form on the bed and said, "Mack, Jade'n I'll be back in a little while. Got some things we need to discuss. Okay?"

Terrified, Breanna prayed, *Oh, dear God! Help me!*

"Okay, Mack?" gusted Dunphy, glaring impatiently at his prize gang member.

"Oh, dear," gasped Breanna, looking toward the dead man. "He's lapsed into unconsciousness again. It's going to be a couple of days before you can talk to him, Mr. Dunphy. Right now, he needs total rest."

"All we need is about two minutes, ma'am. You let me know when he comes around again. Understand?"

Breanna stood before the bed, blocking the outlaws' view of the body. "Yes, I understand. As his nurse I advise against it, but you're the boss, sir."

Dunphy lifted a hand and stabbed his forefinger straight at her, looking down at it like he would the barrel of a pistol. "And don't you forget it, honey," he rasped.

Dunphy and Whetstone left the shack and joined the others outside. Breanna's knees turned to water. Her head went light, and she dropped onto the chair beside the dead man's bed. She felt as though the floor had tilted under her and instinctively grabbed the edges of the chair. Her breath was coming in short gasps. *I can't wait till tonight. Turk will come back before then. He'll kill me when he learns that Mack is dead!*

She thought of her trip to the privy earlier that morning. Aaron Smith had stood on the back porch of the shack and kept a guarded eye on her as she made the thirty-yard journey there and back. She had noted that if she could slip behind the small structure, she could move through the thicket that lay between the privy and the corral. Part of the corral ran on the back side of the barn and was not visible from the shack. If she could get that far and hop on a horse, she could go through the gate on that end of the corral and escape without being seen.

Hoarse laughter from outside brought Breanna's head up. The outlaws were coming back into the shack. Her escape attempt would have to wait. As the sound of heavy boots thumped on the porch, she could feel her pulse pounding in her temples. If one of the gang members came too close, he might be able to tell that Mack wasn't breathing.

"You get the cards out, Jade," came Dunphy's big voice. "I want to look in on our fastdraw artist over here."

Nerves screaming, Breanna lifted the cover off the lifeless body with one hand while probing the bandage with the other. With the cover off Mack's chest, Turk wouldn't be able to tell he wasn't breathing. She struggled to bring her shaking hands under control.

"So how's he doin'?"

"Okay," she replied, keeping her head tilted down. "He's had a pretty rough time of it, Mr. Dunphy. It's best if no one bothers him. He hasn't come around since you were in a little while ago."

"He looks awful pale. You sure he's gonna be okay?"

"Yes. He's…just lost a lot of blood. It's going to take time and plenty of rest." Breanna was sure Dunphy could hear the hammering of her heart.

"Yeah, well, you see that he makes it, y'hear?"

Breanna still did not look at him. "I'll do my best," she replied softly.

Turk moved to the table and said, "Okay, boys, five-card stud. I'll deal. Get your money out."

Breanna dropped the blanket in place and placed a hand on her throbbing chest. It felt like her heart would hammer itself to death.

As the morning passed, the outlaws laughed, smoked, joked, and enjoyed their poker game. Turk Dunphy would never let them drink while playing cards. Sometimes a man would lose enough money to make his temper short. If they had whiskey in them, someone would end up getting shot.

As Breanna sat beside the corpse, she decided it was time to make a run for it. Sooner or later the outlaws were going to find out their partner was dead. It could very well be sooner. She couldn't conceal it much longer. She would like to wait till dark, but that was some six or seven hours away. The plan had to be put into effect now.

She loosened the cover on Pflug's body to disguise that he was not breathing, then rose to her feet. *Here goes, Lord. Please help me.* Moving up to the table, she said, "Pardon me, Mr. Dunphy."

Turk glanced up at her. "Yes, ma'am?"

"I...ah...I need to go out to the...ah—"

"Okay," mumbled Dunphy. "Aaron, you go on watch till she gets back."

"Aw, boss," argued Smith, "she ain't goin' nowhere. Let her—"

"Do it! You can stand by the door and read your cards. Go on."

Smith knew better than to say more. Scraping his chair back, he folded his cards together and glared at Breanna. "Okay, lady...git!"

Breanna hated to leave her medical bag, but she had no choice. She would replace it when she got to Denver. All that mattered now was to get away from these men and ride for Pueblo.

She went out the back door, crossed the porch, and headed up the path. She didn't look back, but she knew Smith was standing in the doorway, watching her. She was gambling that Smith would turn his attention toward the game periodically. All she needed was a few seconds to dash from the privy to the thicket behind it. From there she could easily make her way to the corral.

She went inside the aging privy and closed the rickety door. She peered back toward the house through a half-inch split between two warped boards. Smith was leaning against the door frame, his cards fanned out in his hands, and talking to the men at the table while looking her direction.

Patiently Breanna waited. Waited and prayed.

She had been in the privy about three minutes when there was joyful laughter from inside the shack. Someone had just won a big pot. Aaron Smith swore and disappeared from the door. Breanna took a deep breath and moved out quickly, making sure to close the privy door. Within a few seconds, she was in the brush, ducking down and looking toward the open door of the house. There was more laughter, followed by Turk's big voice chiding someone. Aaron said something she could not distinguish and appeared again at the door.

Breanna held her breath as Smith looked toward the privy, then leaned once again on the door frame. It worked! He thought she was still inside.

Spring had not yet come to Colorado, and the brush had no leaves. It grew thick enough that if she bent low, Smith would not see her movement. She ran as fast as she could until she was out of view from the house.

A bay gelding and a red roan mare stood closest to the rear gate of the corral. Breanna decided the gelding would be faster. Sliding the wooden bolt that held the gate in place, she swung it open and moved toward the big bay. The roan nickered and shied away. Breanna figured the animal may have never been ridden by a woman.

The bay was watching her warily, but stood facing her. Lifting an open hand toward its muzzle, she said softly, "C'mon, boy. You and I are going for a little ride."

Suddenly Smith's voice cut the air. "Hey, lady! You all right up there?"

Turk's voice boomed from inside the shack, but she couldn't make out what he said.

"Hey, lady!" Smith shouted again. "You all right?"

Breanna knew she had only seconds to get on the bay and ride. The animal bobbed its head, whinnied, and blew. It was nervous about her. These animals were accustomed to being approached by men. Her long hair and full-length dress were new and different.

Desperate, Breanna moved up beside the bay, patted its neck, and said, "Easy, now. Just let me get a good hold on your mane."

The bay nickered nervously, bobbed its head again, and backed away.

"Come on!" she whispered. "Let me get on you!" The other horses in the corral looked on. Some nickered in low tones.

Finally the bay stood still, and Breanna reached up, sinking her fingers into the long, thick mane. Getting a good grip, she hiked her skirt up to the knees with her free hand and sprang upward. Clinging to the mane, she found herself bellied down on the broad back of the bay. It was dancing about, making it difficult for her to balance herself and get into a sitting position.

Smith's voice pierced the air. "Hey! What're you doin', woman?"

As the bay made a complete circle, Breanna caught a glimpse of the outlaw standing at the privy, holding the door open. "Tur-r-rk!" he bellowed toward the shack. "That woman's tryin' to get away!"

Breanna heard a tiny mew of fear escape her mouth as she struggled to get control of the animal and right herself on its back. A hard pull on the mane brought her to a sitting position. Gripping the mane with both hands, she guided the horse toward the open gate, then gouged its sides with her heels and shouted, "Hyah-h-h!"

The bay plunged out of the corral into the surrounding trees and thicket, into a full gallop. Cruel, leafless branches whipped at her face and hands, snagging her dress and hair, but she kept the horse going at top speed as she bent low over its muscular neck. Soon horse and rider emerged from the woodland into a clearing.

Breanna aimed due west for Pueblo, hair flying in the wind. Topping a gentle rise, she looked back and saw men running around in the corral like harried ants. They would be mounted and on her trail within moments. She could only hope the animal beneath her was as fast as it looked, and that she had enough head start to beat her pursuers to town.

The land east of Pueblo was rolling, but the hills were low and the draws shallow. She had been riding west for about five minutes when she looked back to see three horsemen riding like the wind. Slapping the bay's rump, she shouted, "Hyah-h-h-h! Come on, boy! You've got to outrun them! Hyah-h-h-h!"

There had been enough warmth from the sun that Breanna had not donned her coat when she headed for the privy, but now she was wishing she had. The speed of the horse caused a cold wind and her body was chilling.

Looking back after another couple of minutes made her blood run colder yet. One rider was pulling ahead of the others. It was Turk Dunphy! The big animal beneath him seemed to have wings.

"No!" breathed Breanna. "Please, dear God, please! Don't let him catch me!"

Squinting against the cold wind, Breanna looked toward the towering, jagged-toothed Rockies ahead of her, taking their bite out of the clear, cobalt sky. Just below them was Pueblo. So near...yet so far. Turk was gaining ground fast.

Pueblo was no more than two miles away when the outlaw leader pulled up behind her. Another tiny mew of terror escaped her throat. Dunphy leaned from the saddle and wrapped his muscular arm around her waist. Breanna screamed as he yanked her from the bay's back. Holding her tight, Dunphy pulled rein and skidded his mount to a halt. The bay eventually stopped, looked back, then turned and trotted toward them. Breanna's body trembled as she looked through her disheveled hair at the outlaw's angry features.

Turk swore at her and snarled, "I didn't give you permission to leave, woman! You're lucky I don't beat you half to death! Only reason I don't is because I need you to take care of Mack."

Breanna said nothing. So he did not know yet that his gunfighter was dead. A sinking feeling settled in Breanna's stomach. He would know it soon. Turk placed her in the saddle in front of him and headed back toward the shack. The bay followed a few yards behind.

"You pull somethin' like that again and you'll be sorry. You hear me?"

Breanna did not answer.

Sinking strong fingers into her hair, he jerked her head around, making her look at him. "I said, you hear me?"

Her hair felt like it would tear loose at the roots. Gritting her teeth, she said, "Yes."

He let go and snapped, "Okay. When I ask you a question, you answer! Y'hear?"

"Yes," she said, looking straight ahead.

The rest of the ride was a silent one, but a time of terror for the young nurse. When they arrived at the shack, Dunphy would learn that Pflug was dead. Then *she* would die.

Breanna prayed, asking the Lord to spare her life. Her thoughts turned to John. How she needed him now! She lashed herself for sending him away. If she had let things develop between them, everything would have been different...and she would not be in this awful fix.

When they arrived at the hideout, Breanna saw the outlaws bunched up on the front porch of the shack. She knew by the look on their faces that they had discovered the truth about Mack Pflug. Hec Speer stood with his thumbs hooked in his belt and said solemnly, "Turk, Mack's dead. Has been for some time. He's cold and stiff."

Dunphy swore and grabbed Breanna by the hair again, twisting her head around to make her look at him. "Why didn't you tell me he was dead?" he roared.

Grimacing, she replied in a strangled voice, "I...I thought you would blame me." She was afraid to tell Dunphy that she had overheard him say he would kill her when Mack no longer needed her.

Turk swore again, let go of her hair, and slid to the ground. "Get off the horse!" he growled, then turned to Speer. "Take her inside and tie her up."

"What're you gonna do?" asked Speer.

"You boys are gonna dig a big grave."

"What do you mean 'a big grave,' boss?" asked Jade Whetstone.

"We're gonna bury Mack," said Dunphy. "And after we've had a little fun with the nurse here, we're gonna bury her. For now, she can just sit there inside the shack and think about it."

Panic rose in Breanna's throat, choking her.

"C'mon, lady," said Hec Speer, gripping her arm.

As Speer dragged her toward the door, Turk said, "Tie her up good, Hec. If she gets loose, I'll hold you responsible."

"She ain't gonna get loose, boss. You can scratch that off your worry list!"

"All right, boys," said the outlaw leader, "you know where the shovels are. Let's bury 'em over there on the south side of the barn."

As Whetstone and Smith headed for the dilapidated tool shed, Harold Eggert moved up to Dunphy and said, "Boss, I ain't one to argue with you about anythin'. You know that. But—"

"But what?"

Eggert cleared his throat nervously and said, "Well...I...I don't cotton to rapin' and killin' women."

Dunphy's cheeks went red as brick dust. "Is that so?"

Eggert nodded and took a deep breath. "My pa—"

"Come to think of it, I can't remember you ever gunnin' down a woman. It's always been me or one of the other boys who's done it when some woman had it comin'. You yella or what?"

"No! It ain't that. I just look at women as...well, as somethin' special. My pa always taught me—"

Turk Dunphy's meaty fist smashed Eggert on the mouth, knocking him down. He hit the ground hard and lay there shaking his head as Dunphy stood over him and bawled, "Get up!"

Eggert struggled to his feet, holding his hand over his mouth. His upper lip was split and bleeding.

"Don't you ever question anything I say or do again!" Dunphy hissed. "You hear me, Harold?"

Eggert nodded. "Yes. I hear you, boss."

"Good! Now, keep listenin'. I don't care what your pa taught you about women bein' special. They can be dangerous as rattlers! You got that?"

"Yes, sir."

"If that little blonde spitfire had made it to town, there'd be a U.S. marshal and probably a posse on our tails. We'd miss out on holdin' up the Pueblo bank, and prob'ly miss out on the big haul at the Denver bank, too. Can you understand that?"

"Yes," nodded Eggert, wiping blood from his lip. "I guess I hadn't thought about it like that."

"Well, you'd best do some thinkin', pal," grunted Dunphy. "Tell you what. Just to help you get over your squeamishness about doin' in women, I'm gonna let you be the one to kill her."

Eggert's face lost color. He swallowed hard. "Me?"

"Yeah, *you.*"

Harold Eggert had killed several men and never lost a moment's sleep over it. But now he felt sick to his stomach. If he didn't follow Turk's order to kill Breanna, Turk would kill him. He would have to kill the nurse. It was a matter of survival.

"I'll even let you choose your method," said Dunphy, walking toward the tool shed. "You can think about it while you're helpin' the other boys dig. C'mon."

Inside the shack, Hec Speer lashed Breanna to a straight-backed chair near the table. Her hands were tied behind her back and tethered to a wooden brace at the bottom. Her ankles were wrapped with cords to the front legs of the chair. She couldn't move at all, magnifying her feeling of helplessness.

Finishing the last knot, Speer stood and grinned. "Well, pretty lady, I guess you can just sit here and think about it for awhile. It'll probably take us a couple hours anyway to dig that grave. Ground's purty hard around here."

Hec moved out the door and closed it behind him. Breanna tugged at the ropes that held her wrists, just to test them. There was no hope of escape. Dreadful waves of horror washed over her. How would they kill her? And what would they do to her before? They wouldn't bury her alive...or would they? Men as vile as they seemed capable of anything.

"Dear Lord," Breanna prayed, "There isn't anything too hard for You. Please, don't let them kill me! You know I'm not afraid to die, but Lord, I want to live. I want to find John and tell him that I love him. Please. Don't let them kill me!"

Breanna had committed much Scripture to memory over the years. Suddenly she thought of Daniel in the den of lions and of his words to King Darius: *My God hath sent his angel, and hath shut the lions' mouths, that they have not hurt me.*

"Oh, great God of Daniel," she breathed with a shudder, "I need one of Your angels."

The outlaws had been digging steadily for over an hour when Turk Dunphy, who leaned against the south wall of the barn, said, "Okay, boys, take a break. Jade, go to the shack and bring some water." Jade Whetstone laid his shovel down and headed for the shack like an obedient son.

Dunphy measured the hole with his eye. They had it some five feet wide and a little over two feet deep. He wanted them to go down at least four feet, and decided the digging would be easier with a wide hole than it would be if he had them dig it deep enough to lay one body on top of the other.

Swinging his wicked gaze to Harold Eggert, the outlaw chief said, "Well, Harold, got it figured out yet?"

Speer and Smith looked at Eggert, waiting to hear his answer. Turk had announced to the others that Harold was going to be the one to kill the nurse.

Eggert still felt sick. Trying not to show it, he replied, "Yeah. A bullet to the head is quickest."

Dunphy pulled at his beard and nodded. "Can't argue with that."

Whetstone drew up with the water bucket in one hand and a dipper in the other.

"The lady secure?" asked Dunphy.

"Yeah, you might say that," chuckled Whetstone. "I think Hec figures to bury her the way she is. It'll take a half hour just to untie her."

Speer looked at his boss and said, "I told you I'd tie her good."

"She look scared?" Turk asked.

"You might say that."

Turk grinned. "That's what she gets for tryin' to escape. Let her sweat."

When the outlaws had taken their fill of water, Turk said, "Jade, you and Aaron go get Mack's body. Hec and Harold, dig."

Soon Mack Pflug's lifeless form lay on the ground near the grave. Noon had come and gone, but none of the gang members asked to stop and eat. Dunphy was intent on getting the bodies in the ground as soon as possible. Their stomachs would have to wait.

After another hour of digging, Dunphy eyed the hole and said, " 'Bout another six or eight inches, boys, and you'll have it."

Abruptly there was a loud bumping sound from inside the barn, and two or three horses whinnied. The barn door that led into the corral on the west side of the old structure had been left open so the animals could move in and out at their leisure. The feed trough was inside the barn.

Dunphy turned toward the barn. The others stopped digging and looked at their boss. After a few seconds, Turk shrugged his shoulders and said, "Guess one of the horses must've bumped into somethin'."

The gravediggers went back to work. Suddenly the sound was repeated and the horses whinnied again.

Dunphy said, "Aaron, go see what's happenin' in there."

"Probably that red roan," muttered Smith. "She's all the time bitin' at the geldings and givin' 'em trouble."

Smith stepped out of the hole, laid his shovel next to Pflug's body, and walked around the corner of the barn. He heard his friends digging in the stubborn ground as he moved through the east door. The big barn was spooky, even in broad daylight. Dark shadows lurked in the corners. The horses had left the barn and returned to the corral.

Smith gave the gloomy interior the once-over and decided the strange sound had been the horses playing around. No doubt the roan mare was being her cantankerous self. He was about to turn and head back out when he heard a shuffling sound in the far corner. The hayloft was nearby, running the width of the building. The shadows beneath it were deep.

The sound had come from a corner of the barn's large open area. The aging roof had many a hole in it, and at one spot near the peak of the roof, an entire section about a foot square was missing. The sun was still high in the sky, and its light was coming through the opening in brilliant, cone-shaped shafts.

Looking past the shafts of light, Smith saw movement. His hand lowered cautiously toward his revolver. Squinting to see the shadowed figure moving toward him, he tensed and said, "Who's there?"

A cold tingle slithered down his spine as a tall man clad in a black broadcloth coat with white shirt, black string tie, shiny black boots, and black flat-crowned hat stepped into the circle of sunlight. He wore a low-slung, tied down Colt .45 in a black-belted holster. The handle grips on the .45 were bone-white.

The peculiar man was slender, yet had wide shoulders. The formidable sight of him froze Aaron Smith on the spot. His heart drummed his rib cage as the man kept his gun hand close to the Colt and used the other one to thumb his hat to the back of his head, exposing his rugged features to the sunlight.

He was square-jawed and had a pair of identical white-ridged scars on his right cheekbone. His eyes were pools of gray that seemed to look through the outlaw, rather than at him.

Smith was sure he had never seen the man before, but by the cut of him, figured him for a gunfighter. He was beginning to find his senses, and his hand twitched above the butt of his gun.

The tall man spoke with a soft voice that carried a heavy weight of authority. "Don't be a fool and go for that gun. You'll share the grave out there with Mack Pflug if you do."

So he knew Mack, thought Smith. *He's a gunslick, all right.* He licked his lips nervously, running his eyes toward the south wall beyond which his friends were digging the grave.

"If you're thinking about calling out, don't," warned the man. "Right now, it's just you and me."

Smith bit down hard, his breath hissing through his nostrils. He wasn't about to just stand there and let this strange man shoot him. His gun hand snaked downward but froze before he even felt the coolness of the butt. The tall man's gun was in his hand, cocked, and aimed at Smith's chest in less than a heartbeat.

Smith's jaw slacked. The speed of the stranger's draw was uncanny. "Take the gun out of the holster with your fingertips, Aaron, and toss it away."

Aaron's scalp prickled. How did this man know his name? How had he found the hideout? What did he want? What was he going to do? Aaron was feeling the pressure of those eyes. This gunfighter was almost unearthly. The gang members' muffled voices and the sound of their shovels filtered through the cracks of the south wall as Smith obeyed in a slow, careful move. When the gun had been tossed across the barn floor, the stranger moved toward him.

Turk Dunphy pulled a cigar from his shirt pocket and bit the end off. Pulling a match from the same pocket, he flared it and lit the cigar. After puffing it into life, he cast a petulant glance toward the barn, wondering what was taking Smith so long.

"Hey, Aaron!" he shouted. "What're you doin' in there? Get out here! I want this grave done pronto!"

Speer, Eggert, and Whetstone were taking a breather. They exchanged glances when no answer came from inside the barn.

Dunphy swore and shouted, "Aaron! Answer me! What're

you doin' in there?"

Silence.

Turk's face reddened. Swearing again, he looked at Eggert and said, "Harold, go in there and see what that idiot is doin'. Tell him I want him out here *right now!*"

"Sure, boss," nodded Eggert. Dropping his shovel, he hastened around the corner of the barn. He reached the partly open door, jerked it open, and plunged into the dark interior, saying, "Aaron, the boss wants—"

Eggert's words were cut off by the sight that seized his eyes. In the shaft of sunlight that came through the hole in the roof, he saw a tall, broad-shouldered man holding a gun on him. When he looked like he was going to call for help, the man said quickly, "One word, Harold, and it'll be your last."

The look in the man's strange gray eyes told Eggert he meant business.

"Wh-who are you?" asked Eggert. "Where's Aaron?"

"My name doesn't matter," came the soft-spoken reply. "Take your gun out with your fingertips and toss it over there by the feed bin."

When it was done, Eggert asked again, "Where's Aaron?"

Pointing with his jaw toward a dark corner under the hayloft, the stranger said, "Back there. C'mon. I'll take you to him."

"Now, wait a minute!" gasped Eggert. "I ain't—"

"You *are,*" said the tall man. "One way or another. Believe me, you'll like the first way better than the other."

Eggert's knees felt weak as he moved toward the dark corner with the man-in-black flanking him. When they reached the corner, Eggert could make out Aaron Smith lying on the dirt floor with his own bandanna in his mouth as a gag. He was on his belly with both hands tied behind his back. A second rope had his ankles bound, then led to his neck. It was wrapped around his neck so as to choke him if he struggled to free himself. Eyes bulging, he ejected a piteous nasal whine.

Eggert swore under his breath, looked at the shadowed face of the stranger, and said, "What do you want? I've never seen you before. How do you know my name?"

"Too many questions. Turn around and put your hands behind your back."

Two minutes had passed when Turk Dunphy pulled the smoking cigar from his mouth, turned his face toward the wall, and bawled, "Harold! Aaron! What's goin' on in there? You two get out here now!"

Whetstone and Speer were digging once again and had the grave almost four feet deep. When there was no response from inside the barn, Whetstone paused and said, "Want me to go get 'em, boss?"

Dunphy swung his heavy body around. Anger burned in his eyes as the words jumped from his throat, "No! You keep diggin'. I'm goin' in there myself and crack some skulls!"

Jade and Hec looked at each other, glad they weren't the ones about to feel Turk's wrath.

Turk was cursing the names of Aaron Smith and Harold Eggert as he stomped around the corner, down the east face of the weather-beaten barn, and bowled through the door. Unable to find his two men immediately, he paused to let his eyes adjust to the dark interior.

Turk heard a slight scraping sound to his right. He turned in time to make out a dark figure moving toward him. Before he could react, something hard cracked violently against his skull. The barn's interior went into a spin, and a black curtain descended over Turk Dunphy's brain.

Turk had no idea how long he had been out when he came to and found himself sprawled on the floor of the barn. Shaking his head, he sat up and looked around. Pain stabbed his skull. He raised a hand to the point of the pain and felt a large lump. It was bleeding slightly. His hat lay within arm's reach.

His attention was drawn to the tall figure who stood in the slanting shaft of sunlight. On the edges of the light that struck the floor lay all four of his men. They were on their bellies, trussed up with ropes between bent-up ankles and necks, and their hands tied behind their backs. Each man was securely gagged.

Turk struggled to a standing position and squinted, studying the face of the mysterious man who stood before him. He let his hand brush his holster. His gun was gone. Knowing he was at a disadvantage, he scrubbed a hand across his mouth and asked, "Do I know you?"

"Nope."

"Well, what's all this? What do you want?"

"I'm going to punish you for the way you've treated the little lady, Turk. Then I'm going to put you and your cronies here in the grave you've so generously provided."

Turk's face blanched. "Y-you know about the nurse?"

"Yep."

"Who are you?"

"A man who cares about Breanna Baylor." As he spoke, the stranger moved closer to Dunphy, fixing him with those penetrating gray eyes.

Turk took a backward step, noted the tied-down gun on the man's hip, and said, "You're a gunfighter, ain't you?"

"Sometimes."

Quaking, the outlaw leader said, "Now, look, whoever you are...I didn't hurt the lady. Honest."

"No, but you were making plans, weren't you?"

"Plans?"

"Yeah. To rape and kill her."

Turk swallowed hard. "No! Of course not! What makes you think that?"

"That wide grave out there. I see only one dead person beside it. Were you going to kill one of these men and bury him with

Mack Pflug, Turk?"

Dunphy could not answer without incriminating himself. There was a stone-dead silence in the barn. The man who stood before him simply let his last words hang in the air.

"Are you some kind of lawman?" Dunphy finally asked.

"Sometimes."

"Is that why you know my name...and Mack's?"

"Could be."

Turk felt cold sweat running down his back. "Well, if you're a lawman, you sure ain't gonna kill me and my boys and put us in that grave, like you said."

Every one of the trussed-up outlaws on the dirt floor showed terror in his eyes.

The tall man's voice was barely above a whisper as he said levelly, "I don't recall mentioning anything about killing you and your cronies before I put you in that grave."

Dunphy's features went dead-white. "You...you don't mean you're gonna bury us alive!"

The stranger's piercing eyes narrowed slightly. "Precisely."

Jade Whetstone was so frightened, he forgot about the rope around his neck. Ejecting a tight muffled wail, he kicked both legs. The rope pressed hard against his windpipe, and he began to choke and gag.

The man-in-black looked at him and said calmly, "That won't happen, Jade, if you lie still."

Dunphy's face was a mixed mask of animosity and horror. "You can't do it, man!" he bellowed. "It ain't human!"

"Oh? You were going to put Breanna in there."

"Yeah, but I had it fixed so's Harold was gonna kill her fir—" His features went from white to purple when he realized what had just come from his mouth.

The tall man grinned tightly. "A wise man named Solomon wrote about you long ago, Turk. Proverbs 12:13: *The wicked is snared by the transgression of his lips.*"

The big outlaw's cheeks quivered. Eyes wide, he gulped, "You...you a preacher, too?"

"Sometimes."

"Well, no preacher's gonna bury human bein's alive!"

"Not till he teaches a killer and bank robber who was going to murder a helpless woman a lesson." As he spoke, the stranger slowly drew the Colt .45 from its holster, took a few steps to his left, and laid it on top of a grain bin.

When he turned around, big Turk Dunphy had a diabolical grin on his face. The outlaws on the floor looked at each other. They had seen their champion beat men to death with his fists. This black-clad man was a fool, after all. Their troubles were over.

The stranger spread his arms, showing the empty holster and said, "Okay, Turk. Now we're even. Time for your lesson. It involves something else Solomon wrote."

"Oh, yeah? Well, I don't believe none of that sissy Bible stuff, but what is it?"

"It'll be the last part of your lesson."

Dunphy laughed maliciously and spit in the dirt. "We'll see who gets a lesson, pal!"

The trussed-up outlaws looked on eagerly. This would be a circus. They knew Turk had the strength of a rock-crusher. There was an immense impression of power in his ropy shoulder muscles, in the girth of his muscular neck, and in his trunk-like upper arms. His fists were like clubs. There was a fire in his eyes whenever he was about to fight, and those eyes were now ablaze. He would tear the stranger apart, be he gunfighter, lawman, or preacher.

"I'm gonna put *you* in the grave, mister fancy-man," he growled.

"Talk's cheap," prodded the stranger.

Dunphy lowered his shoulders, clenched his fists, and charged. He was lithe and fast for a big man...but the tall man was faster. He sidestepped the charge and chopped Dunphy on the back of the neck with his hand. The big man went flat on his face and lay there stunned.

"C'mon, woman-killer. Get up. We haven't even started the lesson yet."

Dunphy swore and worked his way to his feet. His eyes were filled with wrath. He swore again and made a second charge.

The man-in-black dodged him again, but this time, seized Dunphy by the collar and slammed his head into the barn wall. The building groaned and shook from the impact. Turk's legs gave way. He started to fall, but his opponent held him upright by the collar. Snapping his head with a sharp jerk, the tall man said, "More lesson coming up."

With that, he dragged the outlaw back to the center of the open area and stood him straight up. Turk was having some trouble with his equilibrium. Blinking slowly, he staggered a few steps and unwittingly ran into a punch that lifted his feet off the floor. He fell hard on his back and lay there, moaning.

The gang members were no longer looking elated. Their champion hadn't even thrown a punch.

The strange man hoisted the outlaw leader to his feet and held him there by the front of his shirt. Turk's head bobbed like his neck was made of rubber; his eyelids drooped.

"Come on, now," chided the tall man. "Don't go to sleep on me. The lesson isn't over yet." He paused a moment, then said, "You know, they say a good, hard slap in the face will do wonders to revive a man."

The men on the floor looked on helplessly as their boss took a series of stinging, open-handed blows.

When Dunphy's eyes cleared from the sharp pain, the stranger grinned and said, "See there? It works."

Dunphy groaned, "Please, mister. I...I've had enough."

"Ready to go to the grave already?" taunted the stranger.

Eyes glazed and drooping, Dunphy slurred, "No! P-please! Don't bury me alive!"

"Oh, but I always keep my promises. But before we go, let me tell you the last part of your lesson. Are you listening?"

Blood was trickling down Dunphy's forehead. Nodding, he replied with thick tongue. "Yeah, I'm...I'm listenin'."

"Good. Proverbs 13:15. *The way of transgressors is hard.* You said you don't believe any of that sissy Bible stuff, Turk. You're a transgressor of the law, aren't you?"

Turk knew better than to deny it. Nodding slowly, he said, "Yeah."

"Well, then...was the lesson sufficient to make a believer of you, or do you need some more?"

"No!" he gasped. "I don't need no more!"

"So there *is* some of the sissy Bible stuff you believe, eh?"

"I guess so."

"And what is it?"

"That...uh...the way of transgressors is hard."

"Good boy! Now it's time to put you and these other transgressors in the grave." As he spoke, the stranger stepped to the feed bin, picked up his Colt .45, and dropped it in its holster.

Dunphy was staring at him with stricken eyes. A gasp escaped his bleeding mouth as he begged, "Please, mister! Don't bury us alive! I've—we've learned our lesson. Haven't we, fellas?"

"Sorry, gentlemen," said the stranger. "I'm not convinced. I want you to *really* believe the way of transgressors is hard. Down on your belly, Turk."

When the outlaw leader looked as if he might refuse, the stranger moved toward him and rasped, "We can go at this the hard way or the easy way. You can go to that grave out there with a little pain...or with plenty of it. Choice is yours."

Turk Dunphy dropped to his knees, sleeved blood from his mouth, and went to his belly. While he was being trussed up like his men, he wept, begging for his life.

"Why, I'm surprised at you, Turk. Do you think Miss Baylor would've acted like this before your boy, Harold, took her life?"

Turk did not answer. He only closed his eyes and whimpered.

The tall man finished tying him up, gagged him, then grabbed him by the bent-up ankles and said, "Better not stiffen your legs, Turk, or that rope around your neck might cut off your air. Be a pity to lose you ahead of schedule."

The stranger dragged Dunphy outside and to the grave on his belly. Turk was gagging and choking when the stranger rolled him into the wide hole.

Moments later, all five outlaws were crowded into the grave with room for some two feet of dirt to cover them. They knew even that much would suffocate them.

The man-in-black picked up a shovel and said, "Well, boys, the way of transgressors is hard. And this is a hard way to go...but it's the way you're going." With that, he began shoveling dirt on top of them.

Inside the shack, Breanna watched the sun's rays slant low through the dirty windows. She had been unable to move since Hec Speer tied her to the chair.

That had been at least five hours ago. Where were the outlaws? She had seen nothing of them since Jade and Aaron came in and took Mack Pflug's body outside. She figured that had been some three hours ago. The digging sounds had stopped not too long after that.

Were they adding to her horror by making her wait and think about her death? How much longer would they wait? Till sundown? Dusk? After dark?

Her heart spasmed at the sound of footsteps on the back porch. They were coming for her!

Breanna was positioned so she could see the back door without turning her head. Her scalp tingled as the door knob turned. When the door came open, she couldn't believe her eyes.

The face in the doorway was that of Pueblo's marshal, Jack Collins. A broad smile appeared under his droopy gray mustache.

"Howdy, Miss Baylor! We'll get you untied right quick, here."

Deputy Willie Yarrow came in behind Collins, and the two of them went to work on the knots.

The relief Breanna felt overwhelmed her. Tears spilled down her cheeks. "How...how did you find me? Where are the outlaws?"

The lawmen were hunkered on her right and left. While both worked on the ropes, Collins said, "Well, ma'am, I'll answer your second question first. Turk and his pals are buried out there by the barn in a big hole."

"Buried? You mean they're *dead?*

"Not exactly, ma'am. They're under about two inches of dirt. But they're all tied up with ropes so they can't move a muscle. Their faces aren't covered. They're gagged, too, so they can't holler. Only dead one's that gunfighter. We'll go ahead and bury him in the hole after we haul the others out, but we wanted to come in here and untie you first."

Breanna closed her eyes and her lips moved in a prayer of gratitude. Seconds later she was free. Both men helped her to her feet and steadied her as she rubbed circulation back into her arms, wrists, and hands.

"You gonna be okay?" queried Collins.

"I'll be fine," she smiled, taking a moment to wipe the tears from her cheeks. "I want to know how you found me, but first...first I have to ask about Dr. Roberts."

"Well, ma'am," replied the marshal, "he didn't make it. Willie and I found him dead yesterday morning at sunup."

"Oh, I'm so sorry."

"No fault of yours, ma'am," spoke up the deputy. "We knew you'd been taken away against your will. There was plenty evidence of that. Marshal Collins and I agreed that you never would've left Doc on your own."

"Of course not. I might have been able to save him if those filthy beasts out there hadn't forced me to come here with them. That makes them murderers, doesn't it?"

"Yes, ma'am," Willie replied. "But for Dunphy, Speer, and Eggert, at least, murder's nothin' new. Probably isn't for those other two, either."

"They'll face a judge and jury," put in Collins. "Justice will be done. I've got a wagon on its way from town right now to haul them back to town. Got some nice uncomfortable jail cells waiting for them."

Breanna looked at him quizzically. "Well, tell me, please. How did you find me?"

Collins lifted his hat, scratched his head, and dropped the hat back in place. "Sort of strange, ma'am. There's a farmer lives about two miles east of town. Duane Hillman. His fourteen-year-old boy, Billy, showed up at my office this afternoon about two o'clock. Willie and I were a couple of miles out of town, handling a family feud, but Hap Winkler, who owns the clothing store next door, saw him ride up and go to my door. Hap went out and told him Willie and I would be back soon. Well, 'soon' was another hour and a half. Billy waited, though, and when we got back, he tells me he has a message for me. Said a man gave him a twenty-dollar gold piece to bring it. It was written on this piece of paper."

The marshal pulled a slip of paper out of his vest pocket, unfolded it, and handed it to Breanna. It was written neatly, giving the location of the hideout and explaining that the marshal should ride out there without delay and bring along a wagon. Collins would find the Turk Dunphy gang tied up and waiting. They would find Miss Baylor safe and unharmed inside the shack. The note was not signed.

"I want you to know that we did everything we could to find the tracks of your kidnappers, but we couldn't pick up a trail at all," Collins said.

Breanna raised her eyes to meet his. "I understand, Marshal."

"And, ma'am, I'm really sorry we weren't at the office when Billy got there. If we had been, we'd have been here sooner."

"No need to apologize, Marshal. Did the boy say what the

man looked like?"

"No, ma'am."

Breanna shook her head slowly with a faraway look in her eyes. *Could it be him?* she wondered. Placing fingertips to her temples, she said, "Wait a minute, Marshal. Didn't you say Billy Hillman arrived at your office at two o'clock?"

"Yes'm. Hap Winkler definitely said two o'clock, and he's a stickler about time. So I'm sure it couldn't have been more than a couple of minutes either side of two when Billy showed up. Why?"

Handing the paper back to him, she said, "This note had to have been written at least an hour before I heard the digging stop out there. Whoever this man was, he must've been awfully sure of himself."

"I told you it was strange," responded Collins. "Of course, I'm figuring he had a pretty good bunch of men with him to help him carry out his plan. Hard to understand why he didn't sign the note so we'd know who he and his men are. Or more sensible yet, I'd think since they had them all tied up, they'd just put them on their horses and bring them into town for me to lock up. It's a mystery to me."

The sound of a wagon rattling into the yard met their ears. "That'll be Jeb," Collins said to Willie. Then to Breanna, "Ready to go, ma'am?"

"Yes. Let me get my medical bag."

Breanna followed the two lawmen across the yard toward the barn. Jeb Welch, Pueblo's hostler, had the wagon pulled up beside the grave. The marshal left the white-faced outlaws bound and gagged while he, Willie, and Jeb lifted them from the hole and dumped them in the wagon bed. Even though they were in the hands of the law, they were glad to be alive.

Breanna stood some distance from the scene while the outlaws were being placed in the wagon. None of them would look at her.

When the last man had been loaded in the wagon, Marshal Collins told Willie and Jeb to bury the dead gunslinger. Leaving them to do the job, he walked to where Breanna stood and said, "We've got to take their horses into town, ma'am. Would you rather ride one of them than ride in the wagon seat?"

"Yes, please," she nodded. "There's a bay gelding in the corral. I'll ride it."

"Okay. I'll throw a saddle on him."

"Marshal!" called Willie Yarrow, who was standing over the corpse of Mack Pflug, which still lay on the ground next to the grave.

"What is it, Willie?"

"C'mere."

When Breanna and the marshal drew up, Willie pointed at Pflug's chest and said, "What do you make of that? At first, I thought it was a silver dollar, but it ain't. Thought I'd better not touch it till you saw how it's just layin' there on his chest."

When Breanna saw the silver medallion, she gasped.

Collins looked questioningly at her. Picking up the medallion, he laid it in his palm, face-up, and said, "You know what this is, ma'am?"

"Yes," she said, tears filming her eyes.

"Could I see it, Marshal?" asked Willie.

Collins placed it in the deputy's palm. Willie studied the five-point star on the medallion, then said, "It's got part of a Scripture verse on it, Marshal. See? Says, '*THE STRANGER THAT SHALL COME FROM A FAR LAND*—Deuteronomy 29:22.'"

Collins observed Breanna wiping tears. "You must know what this means, Miss Baylor. I'm sorry it's upset you. We can talk about it later."

"I'm not what you call upset, Marshal," she sniffed, "and we will talk about it later. It's just that, now I know who wrote the note. I can tell you he had no men with him. He works alone. He captured these outlaws all by himself."

Collins, Yarrow, and Welch looked at each other, wide-eyed.

"Well, Miss Baylor," Collins said, "this stranger from a far land must be some kind of man."

"He is, Marshal," she smiled, wiping more tears. "You've never met one like him."

The sun had disappeared over the western horizon and the sky was alive with purple hue as Breanna settled in the saddle and rode between the two lawmen ahead of the wagon. She thought of what John had said to her when last she saw him. *"Good-bye, lovely lady. I will be out of your life, but you will never be out of my heart. From time to time, I may be looking at you, but you'll not know I'm near. I'll respect your request."*

Breanna shuddered and tears flowed. "Thank you, John, for saving me once again. I'm so sorry for so foolishly turning you away. And thank You, Lord, for answering my prayer. I needed one of Your angels, and You sent him."

Breanna was unaware that a lone rider sat his big black gelding in a stand of trees on a distant hill and watched the procession pull away from the hideout. He focused on the lady who rode the bay and felt a mixture of warmth and pain in his heart.

SEVEN

—◆—

Lantern light twinkled in the windows of the houses on Pueblo's east side as the procession neared the outskirts. Little sound had come from the five outlaws who rode uncomfortably in the wagon bed, except for a grunt or a groan when the wheels struck rocks or ruts in the road. Hostler Jeb Welch would never admit to it, but he purposely ran over rocks and ruts that were avoidable. Whenever the jolt of the wagon made the outlaws complain, Jeb smiled to himself.

The night air was cold. Marshal Collins and Deputy Yarrow, flanking Breanna, had their collars upturned as they discussed what they would do when they arrived in town.

Breanna rode in silence, her coat buttoned all the way up and the collar pulled tight around her neck. Her left hand held the reins while she clutched the silver medallion in her right. John had left this medallion for her, as much as he had the first one. Though he would not appear to her, he wanted her to know he had saved her life.

"I love you, John," she said in a whisper only she could hear. "I love you more than I could ever say. But I'll sure try whenever the Lord answers my prayer and lets me see you again."

Breanna pictured John's manly features. Some of the women in Wichita had said that he would be almost handsome if it weren't for those twin scars on his right cheek. Smiling to herself, she remembered how she defended his looks, telling the women how blind they were. They laughed in turn, saying it was Breanna whose eyesight was faulty.

No, she thought, *not my eyesight. It was my good sense that was faulty. Just because Frank tore my heart out, I was too thick-headed to realize that John was different. I thought all men were like Frank. Oh, how foolish, Breanna! You sent away the only man who ever truly loved you! And now you pay for your foolishness with a lonely and broken heart.*

When they turned onto Main Street, they could hear the discordant sounds of three pianos coming from the town's three saloons, though the saloons had their doors closed against the cold of the night. Street lamps cast their yellow pools of light along the way as the procession moved toward the center of town.

When they approached the Pueblo Hotel, Collins and Yarrow hauled up to the hitch rail, with Breanna still between them, and Jeb Welch halted the wagon.

Dismounting, Collins said to Welch, "Drive on down to the jail. Willie and I will get Miss Baylor situated in the hotel, then we'll put these outlaws behind bars."

"Okay. She goin' out on the next stage?"

"Yes," spoke up Breanna, who was being helped from the saddle by Willie Yarrow. "Whenever that is."

"Be day after tomorrow," said Welch. "Ordinarily would be tomorrow, but Barry Wilkins told me this mornin' the stage broke a wheel somewhere along the line. He got a wire advising him of it. 'Course if it's full, you might have to wait till the next one."

"You need to get to Denver by a certain time, Miss Baylor?" Collins asked.

"No," she replied, taking her medical bag from Welch, who had carried it next to him on the wagon seat. "I'm to see a doctor there who is willing to let me work out of his office in my visiting nurse work, but he only knows that I'm coming. There is no date set for my arrival."

The marshal was about to suggest that Breanna stay in Pueblo until a new doctor could be found, when the sound of a ruckus came from the Wagon Wheel Saloon, almost directly across the street. The saloon door came open and two men appeared, helping a third man, who was bent over with his hands covering his face. Blood was seeping through his fingers.

Marshal Collins hurried across the street. "What happened?"

"Aw, Bruce got into a fight with Lloyd Perkins," replied one of the men. "Got pretty dirty and Perkins broke a whiskey bottle on the bar and shoved it into Bruce's face. Louis and I are takin' him home to his wife. Maybe she can stop the bleedin'."

Collins looked back at Breanna, then said, "Willie and I just brought Nurse Baylor in. Take him on down to Doc's office. I'll bring her along."

"You hear that, Bruce?" one of them said. "That nurse lady who was takin' care of Doc Roberts is back."

Bruce nodded, keeping his hands pressed to his lacerated face. His friends ushered him down the street toward the doctor's office. Marshal Collins turned, intending to hurry to Breanna. She was already more than halfway across the street.

"Ma'am," said Collins, "he looks pretty bad. I—"

"I see that. Is the doctor's office locked?"

"Don't think so. Not unless somebody locked it up after Doc's body was taken out...but I don't know who it'd be. Let's go and find out." Turning toward his deputy, he said, "Willie, go in and register Miss Baylor at the hotel. Tell them the town will cover her bill. I'll make sure she can get into Doc's office, and then I'll be back to throw those blokes in jail."

Yarrow headed into the hotel, and Collins and Breanna hurried down the street on the heels of the three men.

The office was unlocked. Lanterns were lighted quickly. Bruce Lynch was laid on the table, still pressing shaky fingers to his bleeding face. "I'll take my leave, now, ma'am," Marshal Collins said.

"Gotta lock up my prisoners, then go after the man who did this to Bruce. I'll be back later."

"Fine," Breanna nodded wearily. Turning to her patient, she said, "You hold on, Bruce. I'll do everything I can for you."

"We'll help any way we can, ma'am," one of the men said.

"All right," said Breanna, rubbing her hands together briskly. "How about building a fire in that pot-bellied stove? It's cold in here."

Pueblo's jail had four cells. Turk Dunphy and his four cohorts were carried inside and crowded into a single cell. While Deputy Yarrow looked on, Marshal Collins took the gag from Dunphy's mouth and began untying him. The others lay on their bellies, watching.

"Why don'tcha have your deputy start untyin' these other fellas?" Dunphy asked Collins.

"Because you're going to do it. I've got another man to arrest."

The outlaw leader scowled. "My joints are too stiff. I won't be able to untie 'em."

"Oh, you'll manage," chuckled the marshal.

When Collins had finished untying Dunphy, he noticed the slow trickle of blood on his forehead. As Dunphy groaned to a sitting position, Collins said, "Lift your hat, Turk. I want to see where that blood's coming from."

"Why should *you* care, lawman?"

"I don't really, but as marshal of this town, I have a responsibility to my prisoners...even when they're as rotten as you. Take your hat off."

With a grudging look, Dunphy removed his greasy hat. By the light of a lantern that burned on the wall just outside the cell, Collins could see that the scalp was split about two inches from Turk's low hairline. Apparently the cold air had slowed the bleeding during the ride into town, but the warmth of the jail was causing the bleeding to increase.

"So how'd this happen?" asked the marshal. "Pretty bad gash there."

Dunphy thought of the way he had been manhandled by the stranger. Bitterness darkened his features. There was gravel in his voice as he said, "That dude got lucky, that's all. Rammed my head into a wall. Next time I see him, things'll be different."

Collins stepped out of the cell and locked the door behind him. Looking at Dunphy through the bars, he said, "Doubt there'll be a next time, Turk. When the circuit judge gets my letter telling him I've got you and your gang in my jail awaiting trial, he'll have witnesses from at least four other states or territories here to testify...including some lawmen. Your neck's going in a noose. You won't be taking out any vengeance on the man who captured you and your hoodlums."

Dunphy half-whispered, "We'll see, Marshal." Then to the four men on the floor, he said, "Okay, boys. I'll get you outta them ropes."

Collins said, "Speaking of those ropes...just throw them out here in the corridor when everybody's freed." He started to turn away, then paused and grinned at Turk. "That is, unless you boys want to hang yourselves and save us the trouble."

Dunphy chose to ignore the marshal's words. Instead, he asked, "How long till the circuit judge comes through?"

"Oh, about six weeks."

"Six weeks! We gotta stay cramped up in this stinkin' cell for six weeks?"

The marshal chuckled, exchanged glances with his deputy, and said, "I won't be that mean to you, Turk. All five of you smell something fierce, but I won't make you stay huddled up that close. Like I said, I have another arrest to make. I'll put that man in one cell, then divide the other three up among you." Scratching lightly at his nose, he grinned and added, "However, I'm serving notice right now that you boys are going to have to bathe tomorrow...and twice a week after that."

Turk eyed Collins with disdain and mumbled, "Ain't nobody gonna make me take a bath."

"I bet that fellow who split your head could do it." Willie Yarrow laughed at his boss's quick wit.

Turk gave the deputy a spiteful look, then said to the marshal, "You're cute, lawman."

"I'm also able to make you bathe," Collins clipped.

Dunphy palmed a trickle of blood from his furrowed brow and turned away.

"You want me to see if Miss Baylor will take a look at that gash, Turk? Probably needs some stitches."

"She wouldn't patch me up. She'd rather see me dead."

"Don't judge everybody else by yourself, mister. Just because your kind has no compassion for other people doesn't mean decent people don't. If you decide to have her look at it, let me know."

When the lawmen were gone, Dunphy cursed them and went to work untying his men. As the outlaws rubbed numb limbs and stretched their legs in the close quarters, Dunphy said heatedly, "That stinkin' marshal is gonna be first on my list. We're gonna bust outta here long before that circuit judge can set us up for trial...and when we go, Collins gets it from me *personally*. I'm gonna kill that pious badge-toter with my bare hands. If that deputy gets in the way, he'll die too. Then...then, I'm gonna find that fancy-pants dude who snuck up on us and kill him an inch at a time."

Dunphy's men eyed each other furtively, remembering how their leader quailed before the stranger earlier in the day. They hoped they never met up with the mysterious man again.

Jade Whetstone worked on his stiff neck and asked, "How we gonna bust out, boss?"

"I don't know yet. But no podunk marshal and jail are gonna hold *me*. Just give me a little time. I'll find a way. We'll be outta here in no time. And when we go, we're gonna clean out that bank down the street and hightail it for Denver. That's when we'll really stuff our pockets!"

As he spoke, Dunphy wiped blood from his brow.

Hec Speer said, "Boss, maybe you oughtta let that nurse work on that gash in your scalp. You're bleedin' pretty bad."

Dunphy looked at the blood on his hand. "Well, it ain't too bad. Maybe it'll quit by mornin'. She'd have that marshal and deputy handy so's I couldn't make no escape attempt. She just might decide with them there to protect her, she could make the gash bigger!"

They heard the outer door open, then close. The sound of boots on wood followed, then the door that led to the office came open. Lloyd Perkins appeared first, a bit wobbly on his feet, followed by Collins and Yarrow. The new prisoner's eyes were bloodshot and watery; it was obvious he was drunk.

Collins stepped around Perkins, pulled the door of the farthest cell open, and said, "In here, Lloyd."

Perkins shook his head. "Aw, c'mon, Marshal. I didn't mean to hurt Bruce. He jush made me mad, an'...an' I punched 'im. He cussed me shomethin' awful. I...I...my mind went kinda black. Next thing I knew, he was on the floor an' I was standin' there with a broke whishkey bottle in my hand. You cain't put me in jail fer that. I didn't know what I was doin'."

"You think that's an excuse, Lloyd?" asked Collins. "You'd already been drinking, hadn't you?"

"Well, yeah."

"You know what liquor does to a man's mind, don't you?"

"Yeah."

"What's it do?"

"Muddlesh it up a mite."

"To put it mildly. So you knew what you were doing when you started drinking, didn't you? You knew it could muddle your mind."

"Well, yeah...if I drunk too much."

"You almost killed Bruce Lynch because you were drunk. No

excuses, pal. In you go."

When the drunk man was inside his cell, Marshal Collins pulled the key to the cell doors from a coat pocket and locked the door. Perkins dropped on a bunk, laid on his side, and began to weep.

Pulling his gun and cocking the hammer, Collins moved to the cell where the outlaws waited. "All right, boys, we'll do this one at a time. One false move from any of you, and you're a dead man."

Willie Yarrow stood back a few steps with his gun drawn and cocked while the outlaws were moved to other cells. Jade Whetstone and Aaron Smith shared one cell, Hec Speer and Harold Eggert another, leaving Turk Dunphy with his own. Dunphy's cell was next to the one occupied by Lloyd Perkins.

With all the doors locked, Collins dropped the key into his coat pocket. "I'm going back to the doctor's office. Deputy Yarrow, here, will go to the café down the street and bring you some vittles." With that, the lawmen left the jail together, parting when Collins turned toward the doctor's office.

The marshal passed through the waiting room and moved into the clinic to find Bruce Lynch sitting on a chair and his wife, Doris, standing beside him. His face was bandaged below both eyes and across his nose. Breanna was at the cupboard, cleaning the instruments she had used to patch him up.

Collins spoke to Doris, whose face was ashen, then to Bruce. "I've got Lloyd in jail. You want to press charges?"

Lynch slowly shook his head. "No, Marshal. This whole thing's as much my fault as it is Lloyd's. Neither one of us should've been at the saloon drinkin'. He should've been home with his family, and so should I."

Looking across the room at Breanna, Doris said, "If nurse Baylor was a man, Marshal, she'd have made a great preacher. She just preached my husband a temperance sermon like I've never heard before. God bless her."

Collins looked at Breanna, who was drying her hands on a

towel. "Good for you, Miss Baylor. I'm thinking we ought to keep you in Pueblo. Maybe you could accomplish something no preacher nor this town marshal has been able to do, and that's close down the saloons. For sure, those three saloons are where most of my trouble comes from."

Breanna gave him a faint smile. "It would be wonderful if such a thing could be done, Marshal, but I'm afraid people who think like you and I do are in the minority."

"Well, I just joined your minority, ma'am," said Bruce.

Tears welled up in Doris Lynch's eyes. "Thank God," she said. "Too bad you had to get your face about cut off to learn your lesson."

"How bad is it?" asked Collins, looking toward Breanna.

"The bottle laid his nose open and punctured both cheeks," she answered with a note of concern in her voice. "The cheeks may heal without scarring, but he'll have a prominent scar running the length of his nose."

Breanna's mind went to John and the two jagged scars on his right cheek. He never said how he got them, and she had never ventured to ask. John volunteered no information about his past. She had no idea where he was from. The strange medallion he had left behind the day he rode out of Wichita had her wondering if he was from some foreign country. He spoke perfect English, though, without the trace of an accent.

Breanna didn't even know John's last name. Though he had saved her life and they had become friends, she never called him any more than "John." Perhaps if she knew his last name, it would give her a clue as to where he had come from. She would have many questions answered by now if she hadn't sent him away.

"Well, Doris," said Bruce, slowly rising to his feet, "I think I'm feeling well enough to walk home now. We need to be going. Nurse Baylor looks awfully tired."

"I have had a rough day of it," smiled Breanna, running fingers through hair that needed a good wash and brushing.

When the Lynches were gone, Marshal Collins said, "Well,

ma'am, I'll walk you to the hotel, check on my prisoners, then head for home myself."

It was late when Breanna stopped at the desk to obtain her key, but she ordered hot water for a bath anyway. There were a few toilet articles in the towel closet, including a brand new hair brush. Breanna was pleased to know she would be able to brush her hair.

Midnight came before she had brushed her hair dry, blown out the light, and slipped into the feather bed. She thanked the Lord for delivering her from the death Turk Dunphy had planned for her, breathed an "I love you" to John—wherever he had gotten to by then—and fell asleep.

At first, Breanna thought the pounding was part of her dream. She was watching John ride away from the east bank of the Arkansas River in Wichita, as he had done the last time she saw him. The pounding in her ears seemed to synchronize with the trotting hooves of John's horse. Suddenly she sat bolt upright in bed, opened her eyes to brilliant sunlight filling the room, and realized she was in the Pueblo Hotel. She had neglected to pull the window shades before going to bed.

The knocking on the door stopped, followed by a male voice calling, "Miss Baylor! Miss Baylor! Are you awake?" Then it started again.

Breanna recognized the voice of Deputy Willie Yarrow. She had no robe, since her overnight bag was at the Wells-Fargo office. She would have to put her dress on before going to the door. Jumping from the bed, she called toward the door, "Just a minute! I'll be right there, Willie!"

It took her about a minute to make herself presentable. She disliked being seen in her bare feet, but hastened to the door, turned the key, and pulled it open.

"I'm sorry to bother you, ma'am," said Yarrow. "I know you must be awfully tired, but we need you desperately."

"It's all right. What's wrong?"

"Well, ma'am, there's a farmer's wife about nine miles south of town who's having a baby. A neighbor lady was to act as midwife, but Mrs. Simmons—that's the farmer's wife—is having lots of trouble. Mr. Simmons rode into town a few minutes ago, expecting to find Doc Roberts, and when he didn't find him, he showed up at the office half out of his mind. He's waiting down on the street in his wagon. I told him I was sure you would go with him."

Breanna's empty stomach reminded her she hadn't eaten for a long time. She couldn't remember when the last time had been. Ignoring her hunger pangs, she said, "Certainly, Willie. It'll take me about five minutes to get ready." Her hand went to her forehead. "Oh, dear. I was so tired when I left the clinic last night, I left my medical bag there. Would you run and get it for me while I get ready?"

"Sure will," he grinned. "See you shortly."

Breanna hurriedly finished dressing, laced up her shoes, ran the brush through her hair, and bounded out the door. She usually wore her hair pinned up when she did her nursing, but there was no time for that. Every minute counted for the farmer's wife and for the baby.

It was one o'clock in the afternoon when Simmons drove Breanna up in front of the hotel and drew rein. Smiling from ear to ear, he said, "Ma'am, I'd like to know what your fee is for what you just did. I can't put a price on my wife and new baby, but I want to treat you right for saving their lives."

"There's no set fee, Mr. Simmons. I accept whatever folks want to pay me. Some can't do anything at all, some can do a little...and others who can afford it pay me quite well. It all balances out. Really, you don't have to pay me anything."

"Oh, no, ma'am," said Simmons, pulling a wallet out of his coat pocket. "It's only right that I pay you. My wife and baby would be dead by now if it weren't for you. Will fifty dollars be fair enough?"

"*Fifty dollars?*" she exclaimed. "Mr. Simmons, that's about what I average for two weeks' work! No. That's entirely too much—"

"I insist," the farmer cut in, smiling. As he spoke, he took out five ten-dollar bills, folded them, and pressed them into her palm.

While the surprised nurse looked at the money, Simmons hopped out of the wagon, ran around to Breanna's side, and extended a hand. "May I help you down?"

"Thank you," she smiled.

Simmons thanked her one more time, then drove off as she entered the hotel. Famished, Breanna went to the hotel's restaurant and sat down to a meal. She was about finished when she saw Marshal Collins enter and head for her table.

"Hello," he said, standing over her. "I met Don Simmons a little while ago heading out of town. He told me you had saved his wife and baby. You're working your way into the hearts of the folks around here real fast, Miss Baylor. Word has spread all over town about what you did for the Lynches last night. And it won't be long before everybody knows about Mrs. Simmons and her baby."

Breanna smiled. "Just doing my job, Marshal. My work is very rewarding."

Collins chuckled. "It's also a mite harrowing at times, too. Like yesterday, for instance."

"Well, thank the Lord that kind of thing doesn't happen every day. My job has put my life in danger only a few times."

Breanna thought suddenly of the day John saved her life on the prairie north of Wichita. That was the closest she had ever come to death. She had felt the grim reaper's cold breath that day, and the memory of it made her shudder. "Well, Marshal, I've got to get over to the Wells-Fargo office and see when I catch a stage for Denver."

Collins noted the meal ticket on the table and said, "You're to sign this and apply it to your room bill, ma'am. The town will buy your meals while you're here."

Rising to her feet, she picked up the ticket and said, "Really, Marshal, that isn't necessary."

Collins took the ticket from her and said, "Oh, yes it is."

Collins signed the ticket and handed it to the desk clerk, then walked Breanna to the street. "Thank you, Marshal," she said. "That was kind of you."

"Oh...before you go to the Fargo office, ma'am, I...uh...I have a favor to ask of you."

"Consider it done," she smiled. "What is it?"

"Well...uh..." He cleared his throat and his face tinted slightly. "Well, fact is, ma'am, I sort of volunteered your services without...without asking you first."

Breanna arched her eyebrows and put a mock what-have-you-done-to-me-now look in her eyes. "Mm-hmm. And who's sick this time?"

The marshal cleared his throat again and said there were four of Doctor Roberts's elderly patients waiting at the office. They had learned of Nurse Baylor's work on Bruce Lynch and had gone to the doctor's office seeking her. When they found she was not there, they sent a young boy to ask the marshal if he knew where Miss Baylor might be. Deputy Yarrow, knowing that the nurse was at the Simmons farm, told them to wait at the doctor's office.

Ten minutes later, Breanna entered the office, medical bag in hand. The number of patients had grown from four to seven.

Breanna's care for the local residents consumed the rest of the day. When darkness fell and the last of the patients had gone home, Collins and Yarrow showed up and offered to take her to dinner, which she gladly accepted. She had not been able to get to the Wells-Fargo office and buy a ticket for Denver. She promised herself she would first thing in the morning.

Bone-tired, Breanna entered her room on the second floor of the Pueblo Hotel, hung her coat in the wardrobe, and moved to the window that overlooked the street. She was reaching up to lower the shade when she saw, standing under the closest street lamp, a tall, broad-shouldered man in black, wearing a black flat-crowned hat.

Her uplifted hand went immediately to her throat. "John!" she gasped.

The man's face was hidden beneath the wide brim of his hat, but Breanna was sure it was the man she loved. Calling his name repeatedly, she dashed to the wardrobe, grabbed her coat, and bolted through the door.

CHAPTER

EIGHT

❖

Breanna Baylor rushed through the hotel lobby, heading for the door. The clerk behind the desk looked up and smiled as she hurried past him. Just as she reached the door, it came open and three businessmen filled the opening, involved in a deep discussion. Breanna paused to let them enter, pushing up on her tiptoes to look past them into the street. When the door was clear, she rushed out into the cold air, looking toward the street lamp where she had seen John standing a moment before.

He was not there.

Breanna looked up and down the street. "Oh, no, John. Where did you go?"

Across the street was the Red Dog Saloon. A group of men stood on the boardwalk in front, laughing and talking. Breanna stepped into the dust of the broad thoroughfare and made her way to the jovial men.

One of them noticed her and said, "Good evening, ma'am. You're Nurse Baylor, aren't you?" She now had the attention of the entire group.

"Yes," she replied breathlessly. "Did you—"

"My name's Clarence Buffin, ma'am," said the man who had greeted her. "I'm chairman of the town council. I want to say that I very much appreciate what you've been doing for our citizens in place of our dear departed Dr. Roberts."

Breanna had not noticed until that moment that the group of men were well-dressed. They were not drifters or cowpokes but successful businessmen. She assumed the three she had met at the hotel door had been with the group. "Thank you, Mr. Buffin," she smiled. "I...I wonder if you noticed a man standing over there under that street lamp a moment ago. He was tall, dressed in black, and wore a black flat-crowned hat."

The council chairman glanced toward the spot in front of the hotel. "No, ma'am. I didn't notice him." Turning toward his friends, he asked, "Any of you gentlemen see a man standing under that street lamp over there by the hotel porch? Tall...wearing a flat-crowned hat?"

Heads shook as they mumbled that they had not.

"How long ago, ma'am?" asked one of the men.

"About two minutes. Three at the most."

"We've been out here about five minutes, ma'am. The only people I've seen over there were the three men from Denver who were with us this evening. They left us and went to the hotel about that long ago."

Clarence Buffin moved closer to her. "Is this man someone you know, ma'am?"

"Yes. I...he's an old friend. I'd heard he was in this area and was so happy to see him right there in front of the hotel. I hurried down to greet him, but he was gone by the time I could reach the street."

"Well, he couldn't have gotten far, ma'am," said Buffin. "He's not from around here, you said?"

"No. He's just in the area...on business, I guess."

"Well, he's probably staying in the hotel. I'll bet you'll find him registered there. Ask the desk clerk. He'll tell you."

Breanna thanked Buffin for his kindness and headed back across the street. She stared at the spot beneath the street lamp as she crossed the boardwalk and entered the hotel lobby.

Approaching the desk, she smiled at the young clerk.

He smiled back and said, "Is there something I can do for you, Miss Baylor?"

"Well, I'm not sure. You probably noticed me come down the stairs and hurry past you a few minutes ago."

The clerk adjusted his horn-rimmed glasses. "Pardon me if I'm a bit forward, ma'am, but if you passed a man and he didn't notice you, he'd have to be stone blind."

Breanna appreciated the compliment, but at the moment, it was of little importance. "There were three well-dressed men who came into the lobby just as I was going out."

"Yes, ma'am. Businessmen from Denver."

"You're an observant man," she smiled.

"I try."

"Well, was there a tall man—late thirties—dressed in black, wearing a black flat-crowned hat who came in just before you saw me cross the lobby?"

"No, ma'am. Should there have been?"

"I thought there might be. I saw him from my window upstairs. He was standing below the street lamp out there, but when I reached the street, he was gone. No one out there saw him. I thought possibly we missed each other by a few seconds. That is, if he came in here."

"This is someone you know, I assume."

"Yes. An old friend. I'd heard that he was in the area and thought he might be staying here in the hotel."

"Easy enough to find out, ma'am," said the clerk, opening the register. "What's his name?"

"John." The name came off her lips before she realized how foolish she was going to look now.

"John—"

"Ah...Smith. John Smith."

The clerk grinned. "Unusual name to say the least, Miss

Baylor. Sorry. No John Smith registered."

"Thank you," she said, smiling weakly. "Good night."

"Good night, ma'am," he replied. When she was about to reach the stairs, he called, "Miss Baylor..."

Breanna paused and looked over her shoulder. "Yes?"

"If your friend should register, I'll tell him you were looking for him."

"Thank you," she said, and mounted the stairs.

Breanna entered her room, locked the door, and removed her coat. Hanging it once again in the wardrobe, she went to the window that overlooked the street and reached up to pull down the shade. The yellow glow of the street lamp showed only boardwalk and dusty street. Her heart felt like it would burst as she brought the shade down, then went to the corner window and did the same.

Having caught sight of the man she loved, Breanna lay in the darkness, wide awake. Sleep would elude her, at least for a while.

An unwanted thought crowded into her mind. Maybe she was mistaken. Maybe the man was only built like John and dressed like he always dressed...even to the flat-crowned hat.

"No!" she said aloud. "It *was* John! I know it! He was at the outlaws' hideout yesterday, and he was there in front of the hotel tonight."

Breanna thought once again of John's last words to her: *"I will be out of your life, but you will never be out of my heart. From time to time, I may be looking at you, but you'll not know I'm near. I'll respect your request."*

Breanna knew that John had learned she was staying in the Pueblo Hotel and what room she occupied. Somehow he always found out things he wanted to know. She had no doubt that though he had told her she would not know he was near, he wanted her to know it tonight. Somehow he knew she had seen him from her window, and conveniently disappeared while she was dashing down the stairs.

"You sweet thing," she whispered, "you said I wouldn't know

when you were near. But after what happened to me yesterday, you bent your word just a little to let me know you're still close by."

She thought of the many times she had found herself in John's presence between that stormy day she met him last July and the bleak, cold day in November when she sent him out of her life. She had been fearful of letting herself fall in love with him because of what Frank had done to her. But Breanna also found herself off balance in John's presence. After Frank jilted her, Breanna had lost herself in her work. Then came that fateful day when John so suddenly entered her life. Shortly thereafter, he began showing up regularly, and his presence disturbed her. Every time they were together, strange, wild currents ran through her.

She became afraid—afraid of the utter helplessness he produced in her. She hated to be detached from the certainty she had built around herself. John's presence shook the foundations of the ordered little world she had created to protect herself from ever being hurt again.

The scene on the river bank rushed through Breanna's mind. She would never forget it. John trotted the big black gelding eastward into Wichita, and before he was out of sight, she knew she had made a dreadful mistake. John was gone—at her own request—and would never hold her in his arms again. She was doomed to a life of loving the man with all her being, but never being able to have him.

"Oh, God," she breathed, "can You find it in Your great, abundant heart to undo my foolish mistake?"

Pueblo's night traffic had dwindled to nothing. There were no voices coming from the street and no sounds within the hotel. The room was silent as a tomb. The darkness seemed to press in on her.

Throwing back the covers, she padded across the room to the front window and found the bottom edge of the window shade. She gave it a slight tug, and the springs within the spindle carried it upward, winding it tight. She did the same thing at the corner window. With the soft glow of light from the street lamps filling the room, she returned to the bed and its warmth.

Still not drowsy, Breanna thought of that stormy day in July. Having worked as a visiting nurse out of doctors' offices in western Missouri and northeastern Kansas for over six years, she had returned to Wichita last June to make Dr. Myron Hunter's office home base. She had her own horse and buggy, in which she carried medical supplies procured through Dr. Hunter. She had spent a full week with farmer Will Scott and his wife, Althea, whose place was some sixteen miles due north of Wichita, near the small town of Newton.

Will Scott had fallen while repairing the roof of his barn and had torn his abdomen open when he struck a piece of farm equipment. A Newton physician had performed surgery on Scott in the farmer's bedroom, saving his life. The damage was extensive enough, however, that he needed medical supervision for several days. The doctor knew of Breanna Baylor and contacted her by wire through Dr. Myron Hunter in Wichita. Breanna was just finishing a job near Wichita and was available to come. Seven days of her expert care had seen the farmer through the critical period.

Tears filled Breanna's eyes as she lay in the hotel bed and thought of that day when she almost lost her life. Time slid back...

The early morning sun was throwing its cheerful light through the kitchen windows as Althea Scott looked across the table at Breanna Baylor's empty plate and asked, "Would you like more pancakes, dear?"

"Oh, no thank you, ma'am. I've eaten all I can hold. Besides, I really need to be on my way. I'd like to be back in Wichita by ten o'clock if I can. A close friend of mine is having a birthday party for her little daughter at one, and I need to do some shopping. I've sort of adopted her as my niece."

"Well, I hate to see you go. Will and I have about adopted you as our daughter."

"That's sweet," Breanna said as she rose from the table. "I'll always remember my stay here with you. And I will never forget your generosity."

Althea rose and said, "Will and I wanted to show you our appreciation for giving us a week of your life, dear."

"I know, but two hundred dollars?"

"We talked about it for quite awhile before going to sleep last night. No doubt there are people you care for who can't pay you anything. So we decided to help make up for some of those times."

"Well, my prayer is that the Lord will give it back to you a hundred-fold, Mrs. Scott," said Breanna, embracing her.

The two women walked to the bedroom together, where Breanna told her patient good-bye, thanking him also for his generosity. Breanna bent over the bed, kissed Will Scott on the cheek, and left him with tears in his eyes as she vanished through the door.

Having harnessed her horse to the buggy while Althea was cooking breakfast, Breanna embraced the farmer's wife one more time and climbed into the seat. She was about to say good-bye when the rumble of distant thunder met her ears. Both women looked across the Kansas plains to the northwest, where dark thunderheads were gathering. The sun was still shining clearly in the east.

"Maybe you shouldn't go till the storm passes," suggested Althea, standing on the porch.

"I'll be all right," smiled Breanna. "If I put Nellie here to a trot, we should beat the storm to Wichita."

"Well, on your way then," said Althea. "If the storm catches you, pull into a farm house and wait it out."

"I will. Good-bye."

Breanna had been on the narrow, rutted road for an hour when she topped a gentle rise and spotted a huge herd of cattle about a mile ahead of her. The herd was headed south to the railhead at Wichita, and was being driven by a crew of shouting, whistling drovers who rode back and forth on long-legged ponies.

The angry storm was closing in behind her. The sun had vanished moments before behind dark, rolling clouds, and lightning was crackling in the north, followed by the rumble of thunder.

It had rained good the day before and there was not the usual cloud of dust behind the herd. Breanna had no way of estimating how many head there were, but they covered the road and spread out on each side of it, a span of at least seventy yards. She was looking for a ranch or farm where she could go for shelter, but there was nothing in sight. She remembered a small community maybe three or four miles ahead. If she could get the drovers to clear a path for her, she could probably beat the heavy part of the storm to shelter.

Thunder boomed, and the wind was picking up as it swept over the rolling plains. Snapping the reins, Breanna put Nellie to a gallop and shortly drew up to the rear of the noisy heard. A pair of young cowpokes saw the buggy and rode up. "Howdy, ma'am," one of them said. "Were you needin' to get through the herd?"

Breanna figured that was obvious. "Yes! That storm looks plenty mean. I need to get through as fast as possible."

"All right, follow us! We'll guide you through."

Nellie showed nervousness as she pulled the buggy amid the milling, bawling cattle. Breanna noted the long, sharp-pointed horns that clattered as the steers jostled each other. She couldn't get past them fast enough. It took some ten minutes to bring the buggy out in front of the herd, but it seemed more like ten hours to Breanna. She thanked the drovers and put Nellie into a steady trot.

The entire sky was a black, swirling mass, and the wind was getting stronger. Breanna had gone another mile or so when lightning split the air above her. Nellie whinnied at the fearsome sound and tossed her head, slowing down.

"No, Nellie!" shouted Breanna, snapping the reins. "Go, girl, go!"

Deafening thunder clapped like a thousand cannons all around, and the frightened horse bolted, heading straight south on the road. The buggy bounced and fishtailed dangerously. Terrified,

Breanna screamed at Nellie to slow down and pulled back on the reins with all her might.

Suddenly the crazed animal veered off the road and plunged down a grassy slope. There was a two-foot-deep ditch some eight feet wide at the bottom of the slope. Breanna saw the ditch yawning at her and braced herself for the impact. The buggy hit the ditch full-force and came to a sudden stop against the far bank, sending Breanna headlong into a patch of long, thick grass. When she stopped rolling, thunder was shaking the earth, and Nellie was bounding across the field dragging reins, harness, and single-tree behind. The buggy was dug into the bank, with both front wheels broken.

Breanna scrambled to her feet, her heart pounding and her breath coming in short gasps. She was a bit dizzy and bruised, but the soft bed of grass had saved her from serious injury.

Breanna made her way back to the road. Rain began to fall, driven by the fierce wind. All she could do was keep going south and hope to find shelter.

As Breanna stumbled along the road, the rain pelting her face, she heard something different than wind, lightning, and thunder. It took her a few seconds to place its source, but when she looked behind her, she found it. It was the sound of rushing hooves. The lightning had frightened the cattle, and they were stampeding straight toward her. There was nowhere to run. An overpowering helplessness took possession of her, a foreboding of death.

The herd was no more than two hundred yards away. Breanna thought of the ditch at the side of the road, but the solid wall of wild-eyed cattle told her they were in the ditch, too. It could offer no protection.

Frozen with terror, Breanna steeled herself for what was coming. Then something out of the corner of her eye caught her attention. It looked at first like some kind of apparition speeding toward her, but it quickly crystallized into a horse and rider. The horse was jet-black, and the man in the saddle was dressed in black. He was risking himself and his horse to rescue her.

The cattle and the rider were closing in fast. The front line of steers was so close, Breanna could see the whites of their bulging eyes. Horror and panic stabbed her heart. She could scarcely breathe.

The herd was no more than fifty yards away when the horse drew near. The rider leaned from the saddle and snatched her off the ground, holding her tight against him as they veered to the right and headed south.

The black gelding quickly put space between itself and the deathly horns and hooves. The space widened the more as the gallant horse carried its master and Breanna Baylor on a beeline south, outrunning the pending danger. When the horse settled into a smooth lope, the rider shouted above the sounds of storm and herd, "Get a good hold around my neck, ma'am! I'll swing you up behind me!"

Breanna had been clutching the arm that held her. Letting go one hand at a time, she reached up and wrapped her arms around the man's neck. Twisting in the saddle, he swung her up behind him. Clinging to him with one hand, she used the other to adjust her skirt, then wrapped both arms around his waist. Breanna looked behind to see the charging herd losing ground. The big black was pulling farther and farther ahead.

"You all right, ma'am?"

"Yes, thanks to you!"

Rain continued to pour down from the heavy sky. Horse, rider, and passenger were soaked. Breanna clung to his waist, looking past his shoulder to the south. Water from his hatbrim sprayed her in the face. She didn't care. The Lord had sent this man out of nowhere to save her. Silently she thanked Him.

"We're safe now," the rider told her over his shoulder.

"Yes, thank the Lord!"

"That's right. Thank the Lord!"

"And thank you!"

"No need to thank me. I was just doing my job. We'll be in Wichita shortly. Ebony can run like this for hours."

Blinking against the spray in her eyes, Breanna asked, "How do you know I want to go to Wichita?"

"That's where you live, isn't it?"

A strange feeling went over the nurse. How did he know that? Perhaps he had seen her in town. "So you're from Wichita, too."

"No, ma'am."

"Then how do you know I live there?"

The man-in-black did not reply.

They passed through the small community where Breanna had intended to seek shelter. No one was in sight. Everyone was inside, out of the storm. To relieve her uneasiness in the presence of this strange man, Breanna said, "So your horse's name is Ebony?"

"Yes. Fits him, don't you think?"

"Perfectly! He's as black as any ebony wood I've ever seen." She paused a moment, then asked, "Could he really run like this for hours with my extra weight on board?"

The stranger laughed. "You're light as a feather, ma'am. He doesn't even notice you!"

Some time later Wichita came into view beneath the dark canopy of clouds. Lightning bolts were still chasing each other across the sky, and the deep-throated thunder continued to rumble. When they reached the edge of town, the rider slowed his horse and trotted him onto Broadway. There was little traffic on Broadway or any of the side streets.

Freeing a hand to wipe rain from her eyes, Breanna said, "I live on Kellogg Street, west of Broadway a block and a half."

Breanna cast a glance at the Arkansas River off to her right. It was swollen and muddy. Yesterday's rain had affected the river, and the present downpour was affecting it more. Her mind went to Nellie. She loved the horse and hoped Nellie was all right. Her heart felt heavy at losing her. There was no way of knowing how far she had run, or which direction she might have gone after Breanna last saw her.

And then there was her medical bag. It might still be intact, unless the charging steers had slammed into the wagon. She was sure Dr. Hunter would understand and replenish her supplies without charge, but it would be up to her to purchase a new bag. She was thankful for the two hundred dollars safely rolled up in her dress pocket. The generosity of the Scotts meant even more now.

Breanna had not noticed when they turned onto Kellogg Street, but she did notice when the man who had saved her life hauled up in front of the boarding house where she lived and dismounted. "Well, here you are, ma'am. Safe and sound. Wet...but safe and sound."

Breanna had not realized how tall he was until he eased her down and stood her before him. Looking up at him, she noticed twin scars on his right cheek. His eyes were silver-gray and seemed to penetrate to the center of her soul. He had coal-black hair and brows and wore his sideburns to the middle of his ears. His dark temples showed a few flecks of gray. His craggy, angular features were handsome in their own way, and he was clean-shaven except for a well-trimmed mustache.

Breanna wanted to ask him how he knew where she lived. Instead, she smiled up at him and said, "I don't know how to thank you for saving my life."

"You don't have to, ma'am," he smiled in return. "Like I said, I was just doing my job."

Breanna wanted to ask him what he meant by that, but couldn't summon the courage. She was a bit off balance with this man. "Well," she sighed, extending her hand, "my name is Breanna Baylor. I'm a visiting nurse."

He took her hand in his, did a slight bow, and said, "Very happy to know you, Miss Baylor. It is *Miss* Baylor, isn't it?"

"Yes, I—"

"Breanna!" came a familiar voice from the front porch of the boarding house. "What has happened? Where's your horse and buggy?" Katherine O'Reilly was the sixty-five-year-old widow who owned the boarding house.

Looking up at the portly Irish woman, Breanna said, "It's a long story, Mrs. O'Reilly. I ran into a problem on my way home, and this kind gentleman saved my life. Nellie and the buggy are gone."

"Oh, dear, was it that bad? Well, you can tell me all about it later. Right now you need to come in out of the rain."

Breanna hunched her shoulders. "Doesn't make much difference now. I'm soaked through and through. But I do think we should invite Mr.—" Looking at the tall man, she said, "You haven't even told me your name."

A sheepish grin spread over his lips. "You can call me John."

"Just John?"

"Yes."

"All right," Breanna shrugged. "I think we should invite John in for lunch, Mrs. O'Reilly. It is lunch time, isn't it?"

"Not quite, honey. It's only ten-thirty."

"Oh, I guess with all that's happened, my timing has gotten off kilter."

"But we can invite him in for coffee," said Mrs. O'Reilly. "He can get dried off and stay for lunch."

"Sorry, ladies," John said, raising his palms. "I appreciate it, but I really have to be going."

"Could you come back another time and let me cook you up a good meal?" Breanna asked. "I'd really like to show my appreciation for what you did."

"There's no need to do that, ma'am. But since I don't get home-cooked meals very often, I'll take you up on it."

"When can you come?"

"Tomorrow evening?"

"Good! Can you be here by six?"

"I can arrange that."

Breanna loved his soft-spoken manner. During the ride, he had shouted above the hooves and storm. She had not heard his normal speech until now.

John swung into the black leather saddle and smiled down at

her. "Six o'clock tomorrow evening, then."

"Don't be late," she chided playfully.

"I'm never late for good cooking," he said, and trotted away.

CHAPTER

NINE

After bathing and brushing her hair dry, Breanna Baylor put on a clean dress, fixed her hair in its usual upsweep, and prepared to go downstairs for lunch. As she passed a large calendar that hung on the wall, she stopped and stared at the date. "July sixteenth," she said with a quiver in her voice. "Would have been the date of my death were it not for John."

Entering the hall and closing the door behind her, she said to herself, "I wonder what his last name is. Funny, he didn't seem to want to tell me." Grinning, she added, "Maybe he has some deep, dark secrets in his past and doesn't want anyone to know who he really is." She shook her head as she reached the top of the stairs. "No. Not dark secrets, at least. His is a good and honest face, and he looks you straight-on. In fact, he almost seems to look through you."

Entering the large eating area just off the kitchen, Breanna found the usual lunch crowd gathering around the table. There were three elderly widows, two elderly couples, and an old maid. The other ten occupants of the boarding house worked jobs in the business district and did not come home for lunch.

Katherine O'Reilly had told everyone at the table as much as she knew about Breanna's scrape with death, and about the man who had saved her life and brought her home. During the meal,

Breanna had to fill in all the details. Mrs. O'Reilly then explained that Breanna was taking a couple of days off before returning to her work and was cooking a meal for John the next evening. The group's excitement at this news ended when Mrs. O'Reilly said the meal would be enjoyed only by John and Breanna, who would eat in the dining room at six. The rest of the tenants would eat in the kitchen at seven.

That afternoon the sky cleared. Breanna walked to the doctor's office on Broadway and told Dr. Myron Hunter what had happened. Hunter told her of several requests that had come in for her services, but agreed that she should take a couple days off and rest. He would replenish her medicine supply without charge, and offered to buy her a new medical bag. Breanna explained that with the money she received from the Scotts, she could buy a new bag. She added that with the loss of Nellie and the wagon, she would have to rent a horse and rig from the local hostler until she could afford new ones.

The next evening, the Kansas sun was lowering in the clear sky as Breanna finished setting the dining room table. Mouthwatering aromas drifted in from the kitchen. She was humming a nameless tune when the old grandfather clock in the corner began to chime. It was six o'clock. Mrs. O'Reilly appeared at the dining room door and said, "Honey, he's here. Just pulled up."

"He would be right on time," she sighed. "I've got to dish up the food and carry it to the table. Would you meet him at the door and keep him occupied for about five minutes?"

"How about a little switcheroo on that, honey?"

"What do you mean?"

"I'll dish up the food and you go greet John."

"Mrs. O'Reilly," Breanna said, heading for the kitchen, "this meal is my responsibility. Just meet him at the door and tell him one of your leprechaun stories. Make it a short one, and I'll be ready in two shakes of a lamb's tail."

"Breanna..."

The tone of Katherine's voice stopped Breanna in her tracks. Turning at the door, she looked at her, waiting for the rest of it.

"Dearie, believe me...*you* should go to the door. Go on. I'll take care of dishing up the food."

Breanna cocked her head at her older friend, puzzled by her insistence, and began to untie her apron. "All right, Katherine. Whatever you say."

When Breanna reached the open door at the front porch, a gasp escaped her lips. She couldn't believe her eyes. John was untying Ebony's reins from the rear of a brand new buggy, and in the harness was the runaway horse.

"Nellie!" cried Breanna, dashing to her horse and hugging her neck. The mare bobbed her head and nickered, glad to see her mistress. John tied Ebony to a hitching post while the reunion was taking place, then moved toward Breanna, smiling.

"John! How—where did you find her?"

"Out on the prairie. She wasn't too far from where your wagon hit the ditch. The new buggy and harness are gifts from an anonymous donor."

Breanna gave Nellie one last hug, then turned and said, "Anonymous? I have a feeling his name is John...that he dresses in a black suit, white shirt, string tie, black boots, and black hat, and that he stands about six feet...ah...well, I don't know...somewhere well over six feet."

"If you're talking about yours truly, ma'am," he grinned, "I'm six-four before I put my boots on."

"Well, I *am* talking about you. John, I can't let you do this. Buggies like this cost at least three hundred dollars!"

"No problem for a rich man like me," he chuckled, leaning inside the buggy. When he turned around, he had her medical bag in his hand.

"Oh!" she squealed, clapping her hands. "You found my bag too!"

"The stampede went around your buggy, ma'am," John said

in his usual soft tone. "I figured you'd like to have the bag back."

"Oh, John," Breanna said tenderly, "you're a wonder. Why would you do all of this for me? We hardly know each other."

"We're friends, aren't we?" he asked, fixing her with those opaque gray eyes.

"After what you did for me yesterday? Friends forever."

"Good. Well, what are friends for if they can't help each other out when there's a need?"

"John, you overwhelm me," Breanna breathed, shaking her head. "I don't know what to say."

"Just say, 'Let's eat.' I'm starved."

Breanna laughed. "All right, let's eat!"

While they ate together, John was full of compliments. He bragged about every item of food on the table, saying he had never eaten such a wonderful meal. He complimented her on her hairstyle, saying it fit her perfectly. When he commented on the beautiful dress she was wearing, she shyly told him she had made it. John looked across the table and said, "I understand your medical talents surpass even your cooking and sewing talents, ma'am."

"Oh?" she said, arching her eyebrows. "And just who told you that?"

"Some of your most ardent admirers."

"Really? And who might they be?"

"I'll tell you some day, maybe."

"You are impossible, my dear sir," she laughed.

When they were down to coffee and apple pie, Breanna said, "Well, John, you know what I do for a living. What about you? Are you really the rich man you said you are?" She noticed how the scars on his face stood out in the light of the small lanterns that burned in the chandelier above the table. She was curious as to how he got them, but had not the courage to ask.

"Mm-hmm," he said, tilting his head down slightly and looking at her with admiration. "I have more than any man could want in this world. However, I just became richer. Miss Breanna Baylor,

CMN, came into my life yesterday."

The faint break of a smile softened her countenance. "Oh, so you've been talking to Dr. Hunter. You found out about my certification."

"Maybe I learned about it from someone else."

Lines etched themselves in Breanna's brow. "I do declare, John, you like to keep a lady guessing, don't you?"

John shrugged and stabbed a piece of pie with his fork.

"So if you've got all this money," Breanna asked, "do you occupy yourself accumulating more, like most wealthy men...or do you do something else?"

"I do something else."

"Yes?"

"Do you remember what I told you yesterday when you thanked me for saving your life?"

"You said it was your job."

"That's right. That's the sum and substance of it."

"I don't understand."

"It's my calling in life, ma'am. Like a preacher has a calling...or like a nurse has a calling. It's what I do."

Breanna shook her head. "I still don't understand. A preacher preaches to save souls. A nurse works to save lives, healing the sick and doing what she can to relieve suffering. What do you do?"

"The same thing. Sometimes I preach. More often I work at helping people who are in trouble. Like I did for you yesterday."

"Well, I don't know why you happened to be right there when I needed you, but I've thanked the Lord at least a hundred times that you were there."

"You've placed your gratitude exactly where it belongs, ma'am," John smiled. "The Lord God of heaven is the One who has given me my calling."

"Well, praise His name," she breathed sincerely. "I wish there were more men like you in this world."

"You could get some opposition to that statement in some

places," he chuckled.

"I can't imagine anyone not liking you, John."

"Thank you, ma'am," he smiled. "That's real kind of you."

"I mean it. I've only known you a little better than a day, but I know genuine character when I see it."

Breanna took a sip of her coffee, set the cup back in the saucer, and said, "John, you said we're friends, right?"

"Yes."

"And yesterday you told me to call you John."

"Yes, ma'am."

"Well, since we are friends, I would like you to call me Breanna."

"Really?"

"Really.

"Well, I'm honored, ma'am—I mean, Breanna."

"That's better. So back to your calling...does this mission of yours involve travel?"

"From the wide Missouri to the Pacific Coast, and border-to-border. I've even crossed into both Mexico and Canada."

"Sounds interesting but wearisome."

"More interesting than wearisome. *Rewarding* is the best word for it. Like the circuit-riding preacher. Sure he gets tired, but the rewards far outweigh the bone-weariness that goes with it. Or take your own work. A visiting nurse knows the fatigue that comes from traveling and sometimes working on little or no sleep."

"That's true," she nodded. "But like you say, the rewards far outweigh the weariness."

John finished his pie and downed the last of his coffee.

"Would you like more coffee, John?" Breanna asked, pushing her chair back.

"No, thank you," John said, palms lifted. "I'm full to the brim. Wonderful meal, but I've hit my limit."

Breanna scooted her chair back in place. She still had half a cup of coffee to finish.

John studied her as she sipped at it. "You're very dedicated to your work, aren't you?"

"I am," she agreed.

"So dedicated that there's no room for thoughts of marriage...children?"

Blood flushed Breanna's neck, working its way up the jawline to her ears. This man had saved her life at the risk of his own. She had no desire to show him her flinty side, but he had edged close to a sore spot. He would have to know the subject he had just broached was off limits.

Forcing calm into her voice, she looked him in the eye and said, "John, I owe you my very life, and I will always be grateful for what you did...but the subject of marriage and family is one that I would rather not discuss."

Breanna saw no change in John's expression. "I will honor that. But let me say that if you ever come to the place where you'd like to talk about it with a friend, I'd like to be that friend."

John's response disarmed her. She afforded him a smile and said softly, "I'll remember that, John. Thank you."

"Well," he said, rising from his chair, "I really need to be going. May I put your horse in the shed for you?"

"Of course. I'll walk out with you and show you where I park the buggy."

When Nellie was in the shed and the buggy was parked beside it, Breanna walked with John back to the front of the boarding house. Twilight had purpled the sky, leaving deep shadows all around. John towered over her as they stopped beside his horse.

"Breanna, please forgive me for bringing up that subject. I obviously scratched some old wounds, and I'm sorry."

"You're forgiven," she responded softly. "Thank you for bringing Nellie back to me. And my medical bag. And thank you for the buggy. You have no idea what this means to me."

"Oh, I have somewhat of an idea. You can't carry on your calling without those things." While he spoke, he loosened the reins from the hitching post.

"You're so right about that. I've got to get back to work within another day. Your thoughtfulness and generosity came at the right time."

John looped the reins over Ebony's head, stepped in the stirrup, swung his leg over the animal's broad back, and settled in the saddle. Looking down at her, he said, "There's an old saying among the cowboys, Breanna. *A man who offers to loan you a slicker when it ain't rainin' ain't doin' much for you.*"

Breanna chuckled. "Can't argue with that."

Touching his hat, he said, "It's been a real pleasure spending the evening with you, Breanna. Thank you for the best meal I've ever eaten."

"Flatterer," she giggled. "You're welcome. I'll cook you another one some time."

"I'd like that."

Breanna paused a few seconds, then asked, "Will you be leaving Wichita soon?"

"Tomorrow morning."

"When will you be back?"

"Can't say for sure, but with that dinner invitation, it'll be sooner than it would have been otherwise."

"Can't you be a little more specific? I want to be sure I'll be home when you return. Most of the time I'm not here."

"How about August 1?"

"I'll do my best to be here August 1," she responded warmly.

"If you're not, I'll find you."

Breanna had no doubt he was capable of doing just that.

The tall man was barely a shadow now against the dying light. Touching his hat, he said, "*Adios, amiga.*"

Breanna smiled, though it was too dark for John to see it. "God be with you too, my friend."

It took only seconds for the strange man and his mount to become less than shadows. When the sound of trotting hooves faded away, Breanna turned toward the boarding house and whispered, "Please do be with him, Lord. Other than You, a finer man never breathed air in this world."

When the first day of August came, Breanna Baylor found herself in El Dorado, some thirty miles east of Wichita. There had been a bank robbery there, and several townsmen had shot it out with the large band of robbers. Most of the robbers had been soldiers in the Civil War and were good with their guns. Only two of eleven robbers were cut down, but seventeen townsmen had become casualties. Four were dead and the other thirteen were severely shot up. Six were in critical condition.

The town's doctor had wired Wichita, asking for medical help, and Breanna answered the call. The robbery had taken place on July 28, and she was in El Dorado the next day. As she and the doctor worked on the wounded men, it was obvious to Breanna that she would not be in Wichita on August 1. Somehow she knew John would show up in El Dorado instead.

August 1 was a hot, sultry day in Kansas. An old abandoned warehouse had been converted into a hospital for the wounded townsmen. By then, three men had been released to their homes, but the others were kept under Breanna's watchful eye. The town's doctor only came by periodically, for he still had to care for his regular patients.

Breanna had cleaned wounds, changed bandages, and supervised baths for all ten of the men when the sun began to set. The wives of the wounded men brought in their meals and worked shifts to help the faithful nurse as needed.

The inside of the warehouse was like an oven. Every door and window was propped open. Breanna and the women on duty with her were moving about, fanning the patients.

Breanna was fanning an elderly man when her attention was drawn to one of the doors on the west side of the building. A tall, broad-shouldered man wearing a flat-crowned hat stood in the doorway, silhouetted against the light of the lowering sun. She recognized the man immediately and, excusing herself to the patient, hurried to meet him.

"John!" she said excitedly as he stepped inside and removed his hat. "You did find me!"

"Told you I would," he said, smiling from ear to ear. "I understand you've got your hands full."

"To put it mildly," she sighed, sleeving sweat from her brow. "It's been rough. At least we've got the most critical ones out of danger now, I think."

"When do you eat?" he asked.

"Whenever I get a chance. The wives of these men have been bringing in their meals. They always bring enough for me, so I'm not going hungry."

"Do you get any time off?"

"Time off?" she chuckled. "What's that? I'm just kidding. Once I have them all bedded down for the night, I take a walk and get some fresh air. There are at least three wives here all night to assist me in case I need them, so the men are never alone."

"What time do you usually take your walk?"

"About nine-thirty."

"Okay if I come by and walk with you?"

"That would be nice."

"Good. I'll see you at nine-thirty."

John was at the same door at nine-thirty and found Breanna waiting. The night air was barely cooler than it had been at sundown, but even a few degrees less felt good. There was a three-quarter moon shedding its silver light on the quiet town, throwing deep shadows beneath trees and buildings.

Their stroll took a turn that led them out of town onto the road to Wichita. Frogs croaked at a pond nearby and countless crickets performed their nightly concert. Fireflies winked at them.

John had Breanna telling him of different cases she had

worked on since they had last seen each other. He showed genuine interest in her work and asked questions about her internship under Doctors Jacob Wellman and Myron Hunter.

Soon they came upon a small brook that flowed alongside the road, then ran beneath it through a wooden culvert. Halting beside the brook, they studied the moonlight that danced on its surface.

Breanna knelt to touch the coolness of the water. Looking down at her, John said, "I've thought a lot about you since we met, Breanna. I'm sure glad our paths crossed."

The tone of his voice shook her. It sounded too tender, too much like a man falling in love. Without looking up, she said, "I've thought about you too, John. But then, friends should think about each other when they're apart."

John said nothing. Breanna could feel his eyes on her. Rising to her feet and shaking the water from her hands, she said, "I really ought to get back."

Still he did not speak.

Breanna brought her gaze up to his. He was standing with his hat in his hand and the light of the moon illuminating his face. When their eyes met, Breanna felt her knees turn to water. There was something about this towering, quiet man that unnerved her, and yet charmed her. Before she could make a move, she was in his arms and their lips were together in a soft, velvet kiss.

When their lips parted, Breanna stiffened, gently pushed back from him and said, "John...I...I'm sorry. I shouldn't have let that happen."

"Why not?" he asked, placing his hat back on his head.

Her hands were trembling. Breanna had promised herself she would never let herself become vulnerable to any man again. "Well, I—"

"Who was he?"

"What do you mean?"

"The man who cut your heart out."

Off balance, Breanna avoided John's steady gaze, put shaky

fingertips to her temples, and said, "I need to get back, John."

"I wish you would talk to me about it. I know I said I would honor your request to stay off the subject, but this thing is going to gnaw at your insides as long as you let it. I'm your *friend*, Breanna."

"All right," she replied, making a sudden decision. "Talking to you about it may make me feel better, but it won't change anything between you and me, John. I have to tell you that at the start."

"Fair enough," he nodded. "We can head back while you tell me about it."

Breanna told John the whole story, explaining how she had been in love with a man named Frank Miller. She thought him to be a wonderful man who loved her deeply and would make a fine husband. They became engaged, and Breanna built all her hopes and dreams on Frank. Three days before the wedding, he sat her down and told her he was in love with another woman. The wedding was off.

The shock of it devastated her, surfacing bitterness deep within that had lain dormant for years. Her father had run off with another woman when Breanna was six years old. She watched her mother fold up under the shock and pain of it, and though in time her mother recovered somewhat, she never really got over it. She carried the withering desolation of her husband's deed to her grave.

They were at the edge of town when Breanna finished the story. Stopping, John took her hands in his, looked at her tenderly, and said, "You've been through the fire, Breanna. I wouldn't minimize any of the pain you've suffered. But if you'll let down your guard and allow yourself to love the right man...the man who will love you more than you can ever dream, his love will tear out those bitter roots. You can know real happiness sharing your life with that man."

Breanna looked up at the man whose last name she didn't even know. His presence was comforting and disconcerting. There was a gentleness in him like she had never seen in a man and an expression in his eyes that drew her like a magnet. But she must resist. If she let herself, she would fall in love with him.

No! a voice screamed within her. *You must never let yourself be hurt again!*

She cleared her throat and looked up at him. "John, I do feel better for having talked to you about all of this...and I deeply appreciate your willingness to listen. But I told you it wouldn't change anything between you and me, and it hasn't. We're friends, John. Good friends, but that's where it stays. I wouldn't hurt you for anything in the world, but this is the way it has to be. Do you understand?"

Nodding slowly, John replied, "I understand, Breanna."

She could read the hurt in his eyes and hated that she had put it there, but she was helpless to do anything about it.

"We'll leave it on a friendship basis, as you say," John said in his soft-spoken manner. "Is it all right if I come to see you whenever I'm near?"

Breanna reached up and stroked his cheek close to the mysterious white-ridged scars. "Of course, you dear man. You not only saved my life, but you have brightened it as well. Please come and see me whenever you can."

Moments later, Breanna stood beside the warehouse-turned-hospital and watched John ride away in the moonlight. Sighing, she brushed tears from her cheeks and went inside.

During the next three months, John visited Breanna seven times. Their moments together were sweet and refreshing, but they remained strictly friends. The seventh time, which came in late October, was a difficult one for Breanna. She realized she was letting her guard down a little at a time. Each time they were together, she found it harder to see him go. When she watched him ride away on that seventh occasion, she made up her mind she must break it off completely.

On a cold, bleak day in mid-November, Breanna was home at the boarding house in Wichita when Mrs. O'Reilly tapped on her door. John was downstairs, wanting to see her.

Steeling herself for what she must do, Breanna carried her coat and scarf with her. She greeted John warmly and asked if they could take a walk. John agreed.

Before they left the house, Breanna explained that she would have to be at Dr. Hunter's office in about an hour. They could walk down by the river, but from there, she would have to head for the doctor's office. John understood. He would take Ebony along and ride to his next destination from the bank of the river.

When they reached the street, John untied Ebony from the hitching post and said, "Guess what, ol' boy. You get to take a walk with this fascinating lady and me. What do you think of that?"

Ebony bobbed his head and nickered.

"See there, Breanna," he said, leading the horse as they moved down the street westward, "he finds you fascinating, too."

Breanna's heart went ice cold and lead heavy.

While they strolled toward the lazy Arkansas River that bisected Wichita on its journey to the sea, John asked about her work. With her stomach in knots, Breanna told of many patients put on the road to healing and good health, and spoke of how much she loved her job.

When they reached the east bank of the river, Breanna tugged absently at her upturned collar, swallowed hard, and looked John in the eye. Clearing her throat nervously, she said, "John, I...I have to tell you something."

"All right."

"I...John, this is very difficult for me, but...I've come to a decision."

"About what?"

The tender look in his eyes made her task more difficult. Wanting to get it over with, she blurted it out. "John, you saved my life, and I'll always be grateful. You've been so kind and good to me, and I could never thank you enough. But...I'm asking you not to come and see me anymore."

"You mean...never?"

"Never, John. I...I find myself growing more attracted to you than I should. I can never trust my heart to another man. Please try to understand."

"I'm not sure I will ever understand, Breanna," John said with obvious hurt in his eyes.

Her own heart was bleeding. "Please try," she said in a half-whisper. "This is the way it has to be. Please don't make it any more difficult for me than it already is."

"All right, Breanna. If that's the way you want it, I'll move on. I'm sorry for what Frank did, but his jilting you for that other woman doesn't mean all men are like him." Turning to his horse, he swung into the saddle, then looked down at her through misty eyes. "Good-bye, lovely lady. I will be out of your life, but you will never be out of my heart. From time to time, I may be looking at you, but you'll not know I'm near. I'll respect your request."

With that, he wheeled Ebony about and trotted toward the center of town.

Tears welled up in Breanna's sky-blue eyes as she watched horse and rider diminish in size. They were not yet out of sight when she realized she had made a horrible mistake. She was not on the verge of falling in love with John...*she already had!* His name was on her lips over and over again as she reached toward him. Then he vanished from her sight.

Breanna wept as she walked toward town. "Oh, dear God," she sobbed, "what a fool I am. John loves me. I know he does. And I love him, with all my heart! And now I've sent him out of my life forever!"

She struggled to control her emotions as she proceeded slowly toward the doctor's office. She would not want Dr. Hunter or his staff to know she had been crying. Arriving at the office, Breanna approached the desk of receptionist Rachel Franklin.

"Hello, Breanna," Rachel said cheerfully. "You're just in time. I have the list made up for you."

"Johnny-on-the-spot, aren't you?" Breanna smiled as Rachel

placed an envelope in her hand.

"I try to be. From that list, it looks like you'll be plenty busy."

"Good. I need to keep busy."

Rachel cocked her head and squinted. "Breanna, are you all right?"

"Why, yes. Why do you ask?"

"Well, you just seem a bit melancholy or something."

"I'm fine," Breanna assured her. Turning away, she said, "Thanks for asking though."

"Oh! Wait a minute," Rachel exclaimed, pushing aside a stack of papers on her desk. "This is for you."

Rachel picked up a white handkerchief that was folded around something about the size of a silver dollar. Extending it to Breanna, she said, "A tall, dark-haired man came in her a few minutes ago and asked me to give you this."

"Oh. Thank you."

When she was back on the street, Breanna paused and unfolded the handkerchief. The object was exactly the size of a silver dollar and was made of pure silver. It was a medallion. Emblazoned in its center was a five-point star, and around the edge were the words: *THE STRANGER THAT SHALL COME FROM A FAR LAND—Deuteronomy 29:22.*

Breanna was crying again. "John, what does this mean? Where *are* you from? Oh, I've made such a horrible mistake! I love you, John! I love you!"

CHAPTER

TEN

B reanna Baylor rolled over in bed and blinked at the sharp rays of sunlight that filled the room. It seemed only moments before that she was lying awake in the darkness, reliving the few short weeks that John had been a part of her life. Sometime after the heart wrenching memory of watching him ride away from her in Wichita, she had fallen asleep.

Rising from the bed, she went to the front window and looked down at the spot below the street lamp where she had seen the man she loved the night before. There was a dull ache in the center of her breast. *So close, but still so far,* she thought. *Oh, John, I must find you. I am dying to tell you that I love you.*

Forty-five minutes later, Breanna stepped out of the room into the hall and started down the stairs. She would go to the Wells-Fargo office and make reservations for Denver, then return to the hotel and have breakfast in the restaurant.

When she reached the bottom of the stairs, she saw a young woman rise from an overstuffed sofa in the lobby and look directly at her. Next to her lay a small boy with pale features. He was holding his stomach. Breanna knew she had another patient.

"Excuse me, Miss Baylor," said the young mother. "You are Nurse Baylor, aren't you?"

"Yes, I am," smiled Breanna.

"I'm sorry to bother you, ma'am, but my son is very sick. Marshal Collins told me you were staying here at the hotel. I didn't want to knock on your door, so Lenny and I have been waiting for you to come down."

Moving toward the child, Breanna said, "I wouldn't have minded if you had knocked on my door, Mrs.—"

"Proffitt. Sylvia Proffitt."

Breanna knelt at the sofa and touched the boy's brow. "No fever. That's a good sign. You say his name is Lenny?"

"It's Leonard, but my husband and I call him Lenny."

The peaked boy looked at Breanna with dull eyes.

"Lenny, I'm Nurse Baylor. How old are you?"

Lenny took one hand from his stomach and held up four fingers.

"So you're four years old?"

Lenny nodded.

Looking up at the mother, Breanna asked, "Any diarrhea?"

"No, just vomiting."

"A lot?"

"Three times starting about midnight. Last time was about two hours ago."

"He seemed all right at supper last night?"

"Yes."

"Did he eat anything new? Something he had never had before?"

"No."

"And the last time he ate anything was at supper?"

"Well, no. We took him to a birthday party about eight o'clock. One of his little friends who lives down the street."

"What did he eat there?"

"Some chocolate cake. That's mainly what he was giving up all night."

"How much did he have?"

"Just one small piece."

"And it took him all night to get rid of it?"

Sylvia Proffitt's face crimsoned. Setting stern eyes on her son, she said, "Lenny, you and Howie told his mother that the dog knocked the cake on the floor and ate it. Did it really?"

Guilt was written all over the boy's face. He thought a moment, then said weakly, "Some of it."

"Lenny, that was a big cake. More than half of it was left after we all had a piece. If the dog ate some of it, who ate the rest?"

Lenny's lower lip quivered. "Howie 'n me."

Sylvia looked at Breanna and shook her head. "Well, now we know."

Rising to her feet, Breanna nodded. "Yes, now we know. Let's take him over to the clinic. There are some sodium bicarbonate powders in the cupboard. We'll have him feeling better soon."

Sylvia picked Lenny up in her arms and followed the nurse toward the door. When Breanna opened it to allow mother and son to pass through, another young mother was crossing the hotel porch with a small boy in her arms.

Breanna smiled at her and said, "I'll bet his name is Howie."

"Why, yes, but...how did you..?" Then she saw Sylvia holding Lenny, whose face was as pale as Howie's. "I see," she said, giving the boy in her arms a reproachful look. "You storied to me, Howie. It wasn't Freckles who ate the cake, it was you and Lenny, wasn't it?"

"No sense denying it, Howie," Sylvia said. "Your partner in crime, here, has already confessed."

Breanna chuckled and said, "Ladies...follow me."

Twenty minutes later, Breanna watched both mothers pass through the waiting room door onto the boardwalk with their sons in their arms. She was about to follow them when she saw a man heading for the door, holding his hand wrapped with a blood-soaked bandanna.

A half hour later she sent the man on his way after stitching up and bandaging a bad cut. She cleaned the cupboard and was about to leave for the Wells-Fargo office when heavy footsteps sounded in the waiting room. She looked up to see the beefy face of town council chairman Clarence Buffin. Four well-dressed men were behind him.

Grinning from ear to ear, Buffin said, "Good morning, Miss Baylor."

"Good morning, Mr. Buffin. Don't tell me you and those men with you are sick."

"Uh...no, ma'am. We just want to talk to you."

Buffin introduced his companions as his fellow-councilmen. When all had greeted her, Buffin said, "Miss Baylor, we would like to ask a favor of you."

"Yes, sir?"

"Marshal Collins tells us that you are heading for Denver on the next available stage."

"That's right."

"But, as we understand it, you have no set date that you have to report to the doctor who is to sponsor you there."

"That's correct, sir."

Looking around at the other council members, Buffin said, "Well, ma'am, as you know, Pueblo has no physician since Dr. Roberts died. It's going to take awhile to find one and get him moved here. There's talk all over town about what a wonderful nurse you are. So...ah...speaking for the whole town, we would like to ask you to stay and be our 'physician' until we can get one."

Breanna smiled. "Mr. Buffin, you flatter me. I'm just a nurse with a certificate. There could be things come up that I can't handle."

"You've already proven that you can handle more than the average nurse, Miss Baylor. We won't expect miracles from you, but without you Pueblo will have no medical help at all."

"Tell her about our financial offer, Buffin," said one of the councilmen.

"Oh, yes, thank you," nodded the chairman. "Miss Baylor, we

realize that people may not want to pay you for your services as generously as they would a doctor, even though you'll be doing the same as a doctor would in most cases. So the town will pay for your hotel room and meals. We will also foot the bill for all medicines you have to purchase. Pharmaceutical salesmen are through here every few days. We figure with these expenses covered, you should make more than enough money from your medical fees to take care of your other needs. How does it sound?"

"You are being more than generous, sir. Since I am needed here more than in Denver right now, I'll stay until you can find a physician."

"Wonderful!" exclaimed Buffin. "The people of Pueblo will be happy to hear this."

"But, please, gentlemen," Breanna said. "You must make everyone in town understand that there could be times—and very well will be—when what I'm asked to do is beyond my knowledge and experience."

"We'll make that clear, ma'am," Buffin assured her. "And you will have the same office hours Dr. Roberts did."

"Fine," smiled Breanna. "It's a deal."

"Well, gentlemen," said the chairman, "let's go spread the word."

"Ah...one thing, Mr. Buffin," said Breanna.

"Yes?"

"I've got a trunk and some luggage at the Wells-Fargo office. Could you see that it's delivered to my room at the hotel?"

"Consider it done. They'll be there when you return to the hotel."

"Thank you."

"Thank you!" he said, and the council filed out the door.

They had not been gone more than five minutes when more patients arrived. Breanna was in her element, enjoying every minute of it.

Pueblo's jail had a "bath shed" in the alley behind the cell block. One at a time, the prisoners were taken to the shed at gunpoint and supervised by Deputy Willie Yarrow while they bathed themselves. At first they had refused, but changed their minds when Marshall Collins announced there would be no meals unless his bathing rules were observed. Even Turk Dunphy folded under that threat, though he let all his gang members bathe first.

When it finally came his turn, Turk reluctantly went to the shed and climbed into the large galvanized tub. While the deputy sat in a chair, gun in hand, Turk grumbled and scrubbed.

"Don't forget to wash your head, Turk," Yarrow said.

"I can't. The gash in my scalp hurts."

"Well, wash it anyhow, then we'll take you to Nurse Baylor before she leaves town."

Turk scowled. "I ain't goin' to that nurse. The way she feels about me, she'd probably fix me good. My head'll be okay."

"Then wash it."

Swearing under his breath, Dunphy applied lye soap to his long, matted hair and made it appear he was scrubbing.

The door squeaked and Marshal Collins entered the shed. "Well, Willie," he said smiling, "it worked."

"What's that?"

"Nurse Baylor. Clarence Buffin was here a few minutes ago and said she's agreed to stay till we can get a new doctor."

"Great! I think I'll develop some incurable ailment so's I can hang around the clinic."

"There may be several men in town who come down with some dread disease," Collins chuckled.

"Maybe even our illustrious marshal?" grinned the deputy.

"Well, if I was twenty years younger, you could bet on it!"

Collins returned to his office, and shortly thereafter, Yarrow escorted Dunphy back to his cell. When the cell door was locked and the deputy was gone, Turk glanced at the empty cell next to him, glad that Lloyd Perkins had been released. Then turning toward the other cells, where his men lay on their cots, he said, "You fellas feel any better now that you're clean?"

"Not me," replied Harold Eggert. "I'm about to freeze to death."

"Yeah, me too," Aaron Smith said. "All that dirt was keepin' me warm."

"Worst thing about this bath stuff," said Eggert, "is that we gotta do it again day after tomorra."

"Don't think so," Dunphy said, sitting down on his cot.

Every man sat up and looked at their leader through the bars.

"What do you mean, boss?" asked Smith.

"I mean I figured out a way to get us outta here."

"Let's hear it!" said Speer.

"Well...while I was in the bath shed, the marshal came in and told that stupid deputy that Nurse Baylor is gonna stick around this town till they can get a new doctor."

"So what's that got to do with us breakin' out?" asked Whetstone.

"I got this gash on my head that's hurtin' a whole lot," Dunphy said. "I really didn't want her messin' with it, but I been thinkin'. If I have Yarrow take me over there to the doc's office, once I'm inside, maybe I can get the jump on him and get his gun. Then all I gotta do is shoot him, put a gun to little blondie's head, and march her to the jail. I'll make the stupid marshal open your cells, then lock him up. We'll get our guns, go to the stable, conk the hostler, saddle our horses, and take a little jaunt over to the bank. We'll clean it out and hightail it for Denver. And we'll take Nurse Baylor with us."

"What do you want to take her for, boss?" Whetstone asked.

"'Cause I got more plans, Jade. You guys remember when you were all trussed up in the barn and I asked that strange dude who he was? What'd he say?"

"Said he was a man who cares about Breanna Baylor," volunteered Hec Speer.

"Right, and that's how I'm gonna get my revenge on him. He knew where she was when we had her at the hideout. Maybe he'll follow the scent if we take her with us. We'll use her as bait. When he comes this time, we'll be ready for him. It's gonna be my pleasure to make him die a long, painful death."

At noon, Deputy Yarrow carried food trays into the cell block. As he began sliding them under the doors, he said, "Here's lunch, boys. Good thing you took your baths."

Dunphy was sitting on his cot, bent over, holding his head. When Yarrow knelt to place the tray under the barred door, he said, "What's the matter, Turk?"

Turk looked up, keeping his hands over the wound. "I'm hurtin' purty bad. Maybe I'd better let you take me over to the doc's office after all."

"Okay," nodded the young deputy, sliding the tray into the cell. "You eat, then I'll take you."

After Yarrow left, Turk laughed, "He bought it, men!"

Soon Yarrow returned to pick up the trays. While he was doing so, Turk asked, "You takin' me now?"

"Soon as I deliver these dirty dishes to the café. Be right back."

When the door shut behind the deputy, Turk winked at his men through the bars and said, "Get ready, boys. You'll be outta here in no time!"

Less than five minutes had passed when the door opened and both lawmen entered. Dunphy was shocked to see a pair of leg irons in the deputy's hands.

Scowling, he blared, "Hey! What're those?"

Pulling the cell key from his pocket, Collins gave the outlaw leader a bland look and replied, "Ankle bracelets, Turk. You'll have to walk like a short-legged woman with these on. I guarantee you won't be doing any running."

Turk frowned, his heavy brows knitting together. The leg irons did not fit into his plan. "Aw, come on now, Marshal. Them irons ain't necessary."

"Well, I beg to differ," said Collins, drawing his gun and turning the key. Swinging the door open and taking a step back, he motioned for Yarrow to attach the irons.

Willie clamped the irons around the ankles of Turk's boots and secured them with a small key. Then he reached into his hip pocket and pulled out a pair of handcuffs. The handcuffs were no surprise. Turk knew as long as his wrists were shackled in front of him, he could still carry out his plan. But the leg irons had him worried. He would just have to make his move at the right moment. Once he was in control with the deputy's gun in his hands, he would force him to unlock the irons.

Turk was not disappointed. Willie placed the cuffs on him in front of his body. The metallic sound of the ratchets filled the cell block as Willie squeezed them down tight on the big man's thick wrists.

"All right, Turk," said the marshal. "You can go see the nurse now."

Dunphy cursed the leg irons as Yarrow ushered him toward the door that led to the office. The chain between them was so short, he had to take tiny steps, shuffling his boots noisily as he went.

"See you this evening," the marshal called after his deputy.

"Okay, boss. Have any idea what time you'll be back?"

"All depends on whether the Jones's are home when I get there. If they are, I should be back by about seven. If I have to wait for them to show up, it'll be later. Either way, they've got to sign these papers."

It took deputy and prisoner a full twenty minutes to get to the doctor's office, ordinarily a walk of about five minutes. The bearded outlaw scowled menacingly at the townspeople who stared at him along the street.

When they arrived at their destination, they found Breanna in the waiting room, filing folders in a cabinet. Her eyes widened at the sight of Turk Dunphy. She noticed the leg irons and laughed within at his awkward stance. Willie Yarrow was slightly behind

Dunphy, covering him with his revolver.

"To what do I owe this pleasure?" Breanna asked with a cutting edge in her voice.

"Turk's got a gash in his scalp, ma'am," said Willie. "Says it's hurtin' him. I suggested we come and let you take a look at it."

Turk's senses were keen, alert for the first opportunity to get the upper hand on the deputy.

"Come over here and sit down," said Breanna, gesturing toward a straight-backed chair near the examining table. "Let me take a look at it."

Turk shuffled to the chair and sat down. He was glad when he saw Yarrow holster his gun and take a seat on another chair across the room. Breanna stood over Dunphy, removed his greasy hat, and dropped it on the floor. She reached up and parted Dunphy's thick hair and eyed the swollen, enflamed gash. "How did you get this?" she asked.

"It...it was that evil-eyed dude. The one that snuck up on us at the hideout."

"Evil-eyed?" Breanna snickered. "You mean because he subdued you and your hoodlums single-handedly?"

When Turk didn't answer, she pressed fingertips around the wound and asked, "What did he hit you with?"

"He didn't hit me with nothin'. He rammed my head into the barn wall."

Breanna smiled to herself. *Good for you, John*, she thought. Then aloud, she said, "Well, the reason it's hurting you is because it's full of infection. The reason it got infected is because of all the filth around it."

"What filth?" snapped Dunphy. "I just washed it this mornin'."

"The filth I saw when I was at your hideout," she retorted sharply. "You know...like the filth on your hat. You need to get rid of that awful thing."

"Well, I ain't goin' to, so you can just forget it!" Turk

mumbled something else indistinguishable.

Breanna looked at the outlaw and said, "I'm going to have to lance the wound, Turk."

"*Lance* it? Oh, no you don't! I don't trust you. You ain't cuttin' on me!"

"Fine," she responded, taking her hands away from his head. "Let it fester some more. It'll only get worse till the infection reaches your brain. Then they'll bury you."

Turk's dark features stiffened. Looking up at her, he said, "Aw, you're just tryin' to scare me. No little cut like that is gonna kill nobody."

"It won't? And exactly how much medical training have you had?"

Turk licked his lips. After a brief pause, he asked, "It's really that dangerous, huh?"

"Yes, it is."

"Let's say I don't let you lance it today. How long would it be till it really got bad?"

"Probably four or five days."

When Turk heard that, he decided to make his break and find a doctor elsewhere to lance the wound. His mind was working fast. In order to lance it, Breanna would have to use a sharp instrument. Probably a scalpel. If he could get his hands on it...

"Okay. Go ahead. Get it over with."

"That's better, " said Breanna, heading for the cupboard. "First, I'll have to sterilize the area, then shave the hair around the wound."

"Shave it!" gusted Turk. "Why?"

"Because once it's been lanced, I'll have to stitch it. It won't stitch right unless the area is shaved."

"Okay, okay. Get it done." A razor would work as good as a scalpel.

Turk sat still as Breanna washed the wound with wood alcohol, wincing only slightly when it felt like it was on fire. When she stepped to the cupboard and pulled a straight-edged razor from a drawer, he glanced at the deputy. Willie sat cross-legged, watching Breanna at work.

Breanna took a shaving mug and brush and worked up a head of lather. She dabbed the lather on the wound, then set the mug and brush on the cupboard and picked up the razor. Dousing it in alcohol to sterilize it, she stood over the outlaw and said, "Now, hold real still. If you move your head, I'll cut where I don't need to."

Turk's nerves tensed. Just as Breanna lowered the hand bearing the razor, he brought up his shackled hands, seized her wrist, and wrenched the instrument from her fingers. Jumping to his feet, he looped the shackles over her head and placed the razor at the base of her throat.

Willie Yarrow was taken completely off guard. By the time he uncrossed his legs, sprang to his feet, and drew his gun, Dunphy was holding Breanna in front of him and pressing the blade dangerously close to her skin.

"Freeze, deputy," Dunphy hollered, "or I'll slit her throat!"

Willie froze, looking at Breanna. Her face was chalk-white, the fear clear in her eyes. She drew in short, gulping breaths as Dunphy blared, "Bring me the gun, Yarrow!"

"All right, all right. Just don't hurt her."

Willie lowered the revolver and moved closer. Turk pulled Breanna next to the examining table and said to Yarrow, "Put the gun on the table."

When it was done, Turk said, "Now, take out the key to these cuffs and get 'em off me. Then I want these leg irons off."

Willie's face blanched. "I don't have the keys, Turk."

"Don't play games with me, boy! The keys...right now!"

Turk's hand shook and the razor brushed the base of Breanna's throat. She whimpered at the cold touch of it.

"Turk, both keys are back at the office," Yarrow said.

"You're lyin'! If you don't produce them keys in five seconds, I'm cuttin' her throat, then I'm gonna kill you!"

"Turk, you've got to believe me! Why would I have brought the keys? You're not to be freed from those cuffs or irons till you're back in the cell. The keys are in Marshal Collins's desk drawer."

Turk Dunphy realized the deputy was telling him the truth. He would have to adjust his plans. He would force Breanna to pick up the deputy's revolver and place it in his hand. He would then hold the gun to her head and drop the razor. But what would be his next move? He couldn't very well force the deputy and Breanna to go with him back to the jail. Someone would see them and try to intervene. If something like that happened, his escape plot would fail, even if he were to shoot the nurse.

No. Dunphy was too smart to make that mistake. He would hold Breanna hostage and threaten to kill her if Yarrow failed to follow his instructions to the letter. Once he and his men were free, they could get their horses, rob the bank, and ride for Denver. To ward off a posse, they would take the nurse and the deputy with them. Somewhere along the trail, they would kill both hostages and dump their bodies in some remote place.

There was poison in Dunphy's eyes as he broke the silence. "Okay, I won't hurt the little nurse here as long as my instructions are followed."

"I'm listening," the deputy said, nervously licking his lips.

"Are you listenin' Nurse Baylor?" Dunphy asked. Breanna nodded. "Okay then...reach over there on the table and pick up the gun by the barrel."

Breanna's hand trembled as she obeyed.

"Now place the butt of the gun in my left hand."

When that was done, Turk dropped the razor. It clattered to the floor and lay near Breanna's feet. Turk thumbed back the hammer of the gun. Its dry, clicking sound filled the room. Pressing the black muzzle to her head, he said, "Now, deputy, you listen real good. Little nursie and I are gonna stay right here while you go to the jail and get the keys. While you're there, let my men out and give 'em back their guns. Tell Jade Whetstone to send the other three to get the horses from the stable. Bring Jade back here with you. I want to see both of you when I crack the door. I want you back here with Jade within twenty minutes." Looking at the nearby wall clock, he added, "If you don't make it by that time, I'm gonna blow this gal's head off. And somethin' else, deputy..."

"Yes?"

"Don't get cute and try to bring some heroes with you to rescue her. If I see anybody other than you and Jade, I'll kill her quicker'n you can bat an eye. I mean it."

"It'll just be him and me," nodded the deputy.

"Your thinkin' good, boy. Keep it up."

Willie looked at Breanna and said, "Don't worry, ma'am. I'll do exactly what he says, and I'll be back in fifteen minutes."

A ruthless look settled in Turk Dunphy's eyes. "You better get goin', boy."

Willie hurried to the door and was gone.

When Turk heard the outer door slam, he said, "Okay, nursie. Let's you an' me go to the waitin' room. I want to lock the door so's nobody else'll come buttin' in wantin' your services."

Releasing Breanna, he waggled the gun at her and said, "I'll follow you."

Turk made Breanna lock the door while he held the gun on her, then took the key and dropped it in his shirt pocket. Taking her back into the clinic, he sat her on a chair and tied her hands in back, telling her it wouldn't be for long. When his boys got there, she and the deputy would be going with them. He just didn't want her getting any ideas about trying to run out the back door because he was in leg irons and wouldn't be able to catch her.

Breanna kept a wary eye on Turk as he paced the floor, taking the small, awkward steps the leg irons allowed. Both of them followed the movement of the hands on the old wall clock.

"Why are you taking Willie and me with you?" she asked.

"I think they call it insurance. I figure if we've got a coupla hostages, the law will go kinda easy comin' after us."

"We'll just slow you down," said Breanna, shuddering at the thought of being in the hands of the outlaws again.

"I'll be the judge of what's best, lady, not you."

Breanna said no more. While Turk continued to pace, she kept eyeing the clock. The rattle of the chain between his ankles played havoc with her nerves.

When Willie Yarrow had been gone sixteen minutes, Dunphy glared at Breanna and said, "You got four minutes to live, lady. You better pray that deputy gets here pronto."

Breanna had been praying. God had delivered her from Turk's clutches once before. He could do it again.

There was a heavy knock at the outside door. Dunphy grinned and shuffled toward the waiting room, gun in hand. "Maybe you'll get to live a while longer after all," he mumbled.

Leaving Breanna tied to the chair, Turk entered the waiting room and approached the door. It had no window, and there was no window on that side of the room.

Hindered by the handcuffs, Dunphy laid the revolver on the desk and fumbled for a few seconds getting the key out of his shirt pocket. "Who is it?" he called out.

The familiar voice of Jade Whetstone said, "It's me, boss. Jade."

Turk worked the key into the lock, opened the door an inch, and peered out. Jade Whetstone stood there, holding his gun on Deputy Yarrow. Turk could see no one else.

Laughing heartily, Dunphy swung the door wide. "Hah! We did it, Jade! We did it! Now we'll—"

Dunphy's words were cut off when a dark blur whipped around the edge of the door and rammed the barrel of a Colt .45 into his face, splitting his lip. Dunphy stumbled backward, his feet locking in the irons. He fell flat on his back.

Standing over him was the gray-eyed stranger...the man Turk wanted to kill more than any other man in the world.

CHAPTER
ELEVEN

urk Dunphy's heart pounded wildly in his chest. Blood ran from his lip onto his beard. His eyes were popping, but they bulged the more when the man-in-black eared back the hammer of his Colt and hissed, "So you put a razor to Miss Baylor's throat, eh? I'm tempted to splatter what little brains you have all over this floor."

Dunphy could only whine and shake his head with little jerky movements.

"Oh, you don't agree? Well, if I squeeze this trigger, you'll never put a razor to her throat again. Right?"

"Yes...that's right!"

"And if I don't drop this hammer, what then? Will you ever put Miss Baylor's life in danger again?"

"No, never!"

"But how do I know I can believe you? Maybe you'll break jail and decide to take Miss Baylor with you as a hostage. That would make me real angry. And Turk, you haven't seen me real angry yet. Believe me, you don't want to see me get real angry."

Dunphy blinked tears from his eyes and whined piteously.

"Okay, Turk," said the stranger. "I'll let the judge and jury have the pleasure of putting you away. Deputy Yarrow, look in on

Miss Baylor. I'll take Turk and Jade back to their pals in jail."

John jerked Dunphy to his feet. Willie turned to Jade Whetstone, who stood like a statue, and said, "Okay, Jade, you can give me the empty gun now."

Yarrow took the gun and tucked it into his belt. Then he took his own gun from the desk where Turk had laid it and dropped it in its holster.

Turk stumbled awkwardly as John shoved him through the door onto the boardwalk. When the outlaw leader's gaze locked with Whetstone's, Jade trembled and said, "I'm sorry, boss. I didn't want to do it. He made me. He'd have killed me if I hadn't done what he told me."

"Enough talk. Let's go," said John crisply.

People on the street watched with interest as John ushered the outlaws down the street.

Breanna sat in the chair, listening to the strange sounds coming from the waiting room. She could hear a male voice, but it was muffled. After several minutes, the door opened and Deputy Yarrow came in, smiling. "Everything's all right, Miss Baylor. Turk's on his way back to the jail."

"What happened?" she asked, as Willie began untying her wrists.

"It was your friend, ma'am. The stranger..."

"John!" she gasped. "Where is he?"

"He's taking big ugly back to the jail."

Breanna's wrists came free. Rubbing them, she rose to her feet and asked, "Are you sure it was him? What did he look like?"

"I could describe his looks, ma'am, but this should settle any doubt about who he is. He asked me to give it to you."

As he spoke, Willie pulled a silver medallion from his vest pocket and laid it in Breanna's palm. It was exactly the same as the other two John had left for her.

Breanna headed for the door. "I've got to see him, Willie!"

The deputy hurried after her, catching up as she bolted through the outer door. Lifting her skirt, she broke into a run. People along the street gawked as they watched nurse and deputy sprinting toward the marshal's office. They were within a block of their destination when Breanna suddenly stopped, breathing hard and looking wistfully up the street. She recognized Ebony just before the magnificent animal turned the corner two blocks away. The man on Ebony's back sat tall and erect in the black-leather saddle. She caught only a glimpse of him, and he was gone.

Fighting tears, she said, "I missed him, Willie."

"Maybe he'll be back before long, ma'am," said the deputy.

Breanna opened her palm and looked at the shiny medallion. "Maybe." Then turning to the deputy, she asked, "How did my friend manage to get in on this?"

"Well, when I left the doctor's office to do as Turk had told me, your friend was standing right outside the door. He must have been listening at a window, because he knew what was going on in the clinic. He told me he was the one who had captured the Dunphy gang at their hideout and tied them up. Said if I'd do as he was about to suggest, we could get you out of danger and put Turk back in jail."

"So what was it he suggested?"

"That he and I go to the jail and bring Jade back with us, which we did. Jade recognized him right away and was afraid of him. Your friend—John, you say his name is?"

"Yes."

"John told Jade if he would cooperate with him, he would refrain from breaking his neck. So, of course, Jade agreed to cooperate. We got his gun from the marshal's office and emptied it. When we got to the doctor's office, I let Jade stand there in front of the door with his empty gun pointed at me. When Turk opened the door a crack and saw us, he laughed, thinking his plan was on schedule."

"Yes, I heard him."

"Well, of course, Turk didn't see John, who was standing with his back flat against the wall. John spun into the doorway and jammed the barrel of his gun smack into Turk's face. You should have seen it, Miss Baylor. Turk's eyes were big as saucers. John lit into him for putting the razor to your throat. I mean, he really had ol' Turk scared out of his wits."

Breanna cast another glance up the street to the spot where she had last seen John. Willie saw the longing look in her eyes and said, "He's really somebody special to you, isn't he?"

She gave Willie a faint smile. "Yes, he is. Somebody very special."

The sun was setting behind the towering Rockies as the stranger rode into Denver on Wednesday, April 6. The town was on the grow. Wagon trains were crossing the plains of Kansas and Nebraska, using the wide Missouri River as a jumping-off place at both Kansas City and St. Joseph. Many travelers had no definite destination in mind. They were simply headed west to build a new life on the frontier, and would drive down their stakes when they found the right spot.

Denver proudly called itself the Mile High Town because its elevation was fifty-three hundred feet above sea level. It was also the "gateway to the Rockies," and many wagon train travelers were finding it to be the "right spot."

It had been nearly three weeks since John had frustrated Turk Dunphy's escape plan and put him back in jail. Breanna was foremost in his mind as he rode along Champa Street toward the Westerner Hotel. The broad, dusty street was busy with people on foot, dodging wagons, buggies, and riders on horseback to get from one side to the other.

Next door to the Westerner was the Rusty Gun Saloon. As John swung in to the hitch rail in front of the hotel, he noticed a large group of men gathered around a tall, skinny youth on the boardwalk in front of the saloon. From his perch atop Ebony, John could see that the center of attention wore his sidearm low-slung and tied down. He was obviously a gunfighter.

Dismounting, John drew closer to the knot of men and picked up from the youthful gunfighter that he was heading for the town of Black Hawk, which was in the mountains some thirty miles west of Denver.

One of the men in the group said, "My advice, Tony, is to forget Clay Austin. You're not in his league yet."

The gunslinger swore and spit on the boardwalk. "That's what you think, mister! Austin ain't all he's cracked up to be."

"Well, within the last month, two others just like yourself came through here on their way to Black Hawk. Both of 'em's buried up there in the Black Hawk graveyard."

Another voice asked, "What's Austin doin' up there in Black Hawk, anyhow?"

"He's bodyguard to that bigshot mine owner, Charlie Westmore," Tony said. "Sticks plenty close to him so it makes him easy to find. He don't roam around like most of our kind."

"He doesn't have to," piped up another. "Seems Clay's got 'em comin' to him."

"I heard that ol' Curly Bender was headin' this way from down in El Paso a couple months ago," said another. "He was gonna brace Austin."

"You heard right," Tony said. "Only Curly met up with Mack Pflug in Walsenburg. Curly's pushin' up daisies in Walsenburg's Boot Hill."

The man who had first warned Tony about going up against Austin said, "Maybe you'd better hunt up this Mack Pflug and see if you can outdraw him before you take Austin on, kid."

"Too late," Tony grinned. "Hear tell that about three or four weeks ago, Pflug chose Bobby Lawton. Lawton was no slouch, but Pflug wasn't either. They killed each other."

It had taken John a few minutes to place this young gun-fighter. *Sure,* he thought. *Tony Halloran. From somewhere in Oklahoma Territory.* Halloran had been working his way up the "gunnie" ladder since he was seventeen...four years ago.

"So," said Halloran, "since Bender, Pflug, and Lawton are out of the way, I figure to go ahead and put a bullet in Austin's heart."

"And then what, kid?" asked the same man.

"Oh, who knows? When word gets around that I took out Austin, there'll be plenty of challengers."

"Yeah," spoke up another, "like Jim Fielder, Luke Stanton, or Rex Hobbs...or even Tate Landry."

Halloran's features settled in a grim mask at the mention of Landry, the most feared gunfighter around. Tony Halloran knew he was not ready for Landry. If he could outdraw Austin, he would be on a level with Fielder and Stanton. Word was that Hobbs was somewhere in Texas or New Mexico, and Halloran hoped he stayed there. He wasn't ready for Hobbs either.

The group began to break up, with some of the men wishing Halloran good luck when he challenged Austin. Soon the young gunhawk found himself alone. Stepping into the dust of Champa Street, he went to his horse at the hitch rail and untied the reins. He turned to mount and found himself standing face to face with a man taller than himself, clad in black, with a flat-crowned hat to match. He wore a white shirt and black string tie. The man's frock coat covered his low-slung Colt .45.

"Pardon me," the man said. "Could I have a word with you?"

Looking him up and down, Halloran said, "Sure, Reverend. Only if you're gonna try to get me in church, I ain't the church-goin' kind."

Letting the gunfighter draw his own conclusions, John spoke in his soft manner. "I wanted to see if I could talk you into using the brains God gave you. You're no match for Clay Austin, Tony."

Halloran's eyebrows arched. "So you know me, eh?"

"Vaguely. But I know enough to warn you that if you go up

against Austin, he'll kill you."

The grin on Tony's face faded and petulance darkened his eyes. "So who are you to tell me I'm no match for Austin, preacher? What do men of the cloth know about such things? You better go practice your Bible thumpin'. You're out of your territory."

"Am I? How about going down by the creek where nobody else will see us, and you and me square off?"

Halloran laughed. "Are you kiddin'? Me draw against a preacher? Hey, Reverend, just because I ain't a church-goer doesn't mean I hate Bible thumpers. I don't want to kill a man of God."

"Well, I was going to suggest that we empty our guns. I just want to show you that a nobody like me can outdraw you."

Halloran looked at him askance. "You got a gun somewhere near?"

John smiled and pulled back his frock coat, revealing the low-slung black gunbelt and bone-white handles of his Colt .45. "Just happen to have it right here."

Halloran's face mirrored his surprise. "Why would a...a preacher carry a gun? Especially ridin' so low?"

"This is tough country," smiled John. "Man never knows what kind of trouble he might encounter. Better to be safe than sorry, I always say."

"And you really want to let me show you how wrong you are?"

"Please," nodded John, lowering his coat.

"Okay. I've got to be headin' west pretty soon, but I'll go along with your silly little game."

It was only a few blocks to Cherry Creek. The western sky was still bright above the Rockies, leaving plenty of light for the two men to square off. Both men dismounted on the creek bank, and Tony began punching the cartridges from the cylinder of his .44 Navy Colt.

John emptied his .45, dropped the cartridges in a coat pocket, then slid the shiny revolver back in its holster. Turning to his saddle-bags, he opened one, pulled out a big black Bible, and said, "I have something I want you to see, Tony."

Halloran's mouth turned down. "I don't want you preachin' at me, Reverend. Let's just get this done and over with."

"In a moment, but I want you to see something here in the Word of God." Moving shoulder-to-shoulder with the young gunfighter, he placed his finger on a verse and said, "Proverbs 15:32, Tony. Read it to me."

Halloran gave him a sour look. "You mean read it out loud?"

"Yeah. You can do that, can't you?"

"Sure."

"Then do it."

Halloran cleared his throat and put his face close to the page. "'He that refuseth instruction despiseth his own soul: but he that heareth reproof getteth understanding.' Okay, I read it...so what."

"You know what reproof is, Tony?"

"I guess so. It means to rebuke, doesn't it?"

"It can mean that. It also means to warn of an anticipated fault. And you know what instruction is, don't you?"

"Yeah. It means to teach."

"Good," said John, closing the Bible. "I'm going to teach you something, Tony. By this lesson, I'm warning you of an anticipated fault. If you refuse my instruction and do not heed the warning, God says you despise your own soul. Understand?"

"Yeah, I understand. But no preacher is about to teach me anything about gunfightin'."

"Let's see," said the man-in-black, walking away. When he was some thirty-five feet from Halloran, he pivoted, facing him, and flipped the tail of his frock coat behind his holster.

Tony had already gone into his stance, knees slightly bent, his right hand hovering above the oak-handled butt of his .44.

John folded his arms across his chest and said, "Remember, Tony, I'm not a gunfighter. I'm just a nobody."

Halloran cocked his head. "Aw, come on now, Reverend. Surely you ain't gonna start your draw with your arms folded."

"You have your way...I have mine. Draw."

Halloran's hand darted downward, but the stranger's .45 was in his hand and leveled on Halloran's belly before Tony's gunsight cleared leather.

Tony's shock-widened eyes locked on John's gun. He let his own gun slip back into the holster. Fiery devils of temper danced in his eyes. "You ain't no preacher! You're a gunfighter! Who are you?"

"Like I said, just a nobody. Point is, this nobody just showed you you're not as fast as you think. Do you understand the instruction I just gave you?"

"All I understand is, I'm wastin' my time here." With that, Halloran stomped to his horse, mounted, and trotted away.

John called after him, "He that refuseth instruction despiseth his own soul!"

Halloran did not look back. He reached the street and disappeared around the corner of a large building. John mounted and rode back to the hotel, wishing the hot-headed gunfighter had taken the lesson given.

At dawn the next morning John rode out of Denver, heading due west. By the time the sun came up, he was climbing through a rolling sea of foothills. Towering above him were the snow-capped Rockies thrust upward against the azure sky. John knew that some of the peaks on Colorado's range kept their snow year-round. Since it was only the first week of April, it would be another two months before the thaw really set in.

Soon he was in high country, skirting deep canyons and curving around the rocky shoulders as he pushed his horse up the rough, steep road that led from Idaho Springs to Black Hawk and on to Central City. The wind whistled and whined through the giant evergreens that lined the road and graced the steep mountain sides. At one point, he rounded a curve along the rim of a rocky canyon and saw a thin mist rising up from the canyon floor. A thundering roar met his ears. Guiding Ebony near the edge, he looked down and saw a giant waterfall some fifty feet below.

A L   L A C Y

The canyon was at least eight hundred feet deep. The waterfall rushed down the face of the cliff like galloping white horses in a mad race to see who could first reach the river bed far below. High above the yawning canyon, two hawks rode the air waves, screeching and playing tag as they dived and swooped with precision.

The tall rider rode on and soon topped out on level ground with meadows spread before him, amid patches of conifer and thickets of chaparral.

Soon Black Hawk came into view, with its wide main thoroughfare lined by false-fronted, unpainted clapboard buildings. John knew that just beyond the town a mile or so was the huge gold mine owned and operated by Charles J. Westmore and his two sons. Westmore was headstrong, greedy, and ruthless. It was no wonder the man needed a bodyguard. In his rise to the top, he had stepped on everybody he thought was in his way, even men who had worked hard for him and trusted him. Clay Austin's fast gun kept Westmore's enemies at bay.

It was nearing ten o'clock when John rode into Black Hawk. He wanted to be there in time to see the shootout. Gunfighters always wanted to do their gunplay when the most people were on the streets. In towns like Black Hawk, that time usually came between eleven o'clock in the morning and two o'clock in the afternoon.

Black Hawk's business section was only one block long. As of yet, there was no boardwalk. The dirt street ran right up to the doors of the bank, shops, saloons, and offices. There were three saloons, but John saw no sign of a church or school.

People milled about the business district as usual, telling John that no gunfight had yet taken place. When he neared the Black Hawk Hotel, he noted a large, two-story building across the street. Swinging in the breeze was a large sign that read:

CHARLES J. WESTMORE & SONS
MINING COMPANY
MAIN OFFICE

Suddenly the hotel door came open and the tall, slender figure of Tony Halloran emerged, followed by a half-dozen men. Halloran stopped in the middle of the street, facing the Westmore building. He apparently was satisfied with the number of people on the street. Halloran lifted his gun slightly within its holster and let it down easy. John wondered if the young fool was thinking at all about the lesson he had been given yesterday. Apparently not. It had meant nothing to him. Nothing at all.

"Clay Austin!" Tony bellowed, looking straight at the Westmore building. "It's Tony Halloran! I know you've heard of me! I'm callin' you! Come out and face me!"

There was movement at an upstairs window, but nothing moved on the bottom floor.

The crowd was growing. Halloran grinned as he looked around at the expectant faces, then faced the two-story building again and shouted louder, "Hey, Austin! What's the matter? My name scare ya? Come on out here! You're bein' challenged!"

John dismounted and wrapped the reins around the hitch rail in front of the assayer's office next to the hotel. On the other side of the hotel was the Black Hawk Gun Shop. While Halloran continued to call for Austin to show his face, John noticed a man in his midtwenties emerge from the gun shop, sided by a well-dressed man in his early sixties. He knew the older man was Charlie Westmore. The younger one had to be Clay Austin. There was a look of irritation on Austin's face as he left Westmore near the gun shop door and pushed his way through the crowd.

"Hey, Austin!" laughed Tony. "What's the matter? You yella? Afraid to face a real gunfighter? These people out here are gonna wonder what you're made of!"

"*You lookin' for me?*" Austin thundered from behind.

Halloran wheeled around to meet him. Austin was moving in an arc toward the center of the street. Halloran's eyes followed him as he turned his body to meet his movement.

"Yeah," replied Halloran, eyeing the man with open disdain.

"I hear you're supposed to be a hot-shot gunhawk."

"Guess you think you're more of a hot-shot, Mister—. What did you say your name is?"

"Don't give me that stuff, Austin. You know who I am!"

Austin gave him a crooked smile. "Better yet, Tony, I know who you're gonna be."

"Yeah? Who am I gonna be?"

"You're gonna be the next man buried in the Black Hawk cemetery! Go for your gun. Let's get this over with. I've got more important matters to attend to."

Halloran's hand dipped downward and brought his gun out of its holster. But before he could fire it, a slug from Austin's gun ripped through his heart, killing him instantly. The crowd looked on as Tony Halloran lay sprawled on the street, his sightless eyes staring toward the blue Colorado sky.

Austin acknowledged the applause of a few people in the crowd as he went to his employer. "Sorry for the interruption, Mr. Westmore," he said quietly, "but when a pesky fly gets a man's attention, there's no rest till he swats it."

Westmore chuckled as they crossed the street together and entered the mining company office.

The crowd dispersed, leaving Tony Halloran's body in the street. Someone said he would fetch the undertaker. The man-in-black moved slowly to where Tony lay and stood over him, shaking his head. "I told you, Tony," he said softly. "He that refuseth instruction despiseth his own soul."

John turned and walked to his horse. No one paid him any mind as he swung into the saddle and rode out of town the same direction he had come from.

CHAPTER

TWELVE

———◆———

O n Monday, April 4, Breanna Baylor was washing her medical instruments at the clinic when she heard the outer door open and close. Picking up a towel, she began drying her hands as she moved across the room. There was a tap on the door just before she reached it. Turning the knob, she pulled the door open and found Clarence Buffin holding his right forefinger with his left hand. The pain showed in his face.

"Come in, Mr. Buffin," Breanna said, glancing at his hands. "What happened?"

"You know my assistant over at the store, Earl Long."

"Yes. Come over here and sit down."

Buffin eased onto a chair. "Well, Earl and I were doing some rearranging in the office. We were moving the safe and had it almost down on the floor when it slipped out of Earl's hands. I was able to free my left hand in time, but the entire weight of the safe came down on this finger. I think it's broken."

Breanna examined his finger and found that it was indeed broken. While she was putting a splint on the finger, Buffin looked at her with admiring eyes and said, "You know, we're going to miss you around here."

"I hope so," she smiled, "but I'm sure you'll like Dr. Mullins.

As I told you when you informed me that he was coming, I've heard many good things about him."

"Well, if he wasn't bringing his own nurse with him, I'd have tried to persuade him to twist your arm and see if you wouldn't stay here."

Breanna smiled again. "Those kind words are music to a nurse's ears, Mr. Buffin."

"How much longer will you be here?"

"I'm booked on the Denver-bound stage on Friday. That will put me in Denver on Saturday, the ninth. That's the date I gave Dr. Goodwin in Denver. He's made arrangements for me to live in a small apartment owned by his father-in-law, who's a retired physician. There won't be any charge for the apartment because he and his wife want to have a part in my work as a visiting nurse."

"Wonderful. I think people like you should be treated like royalty. After all, what would we do without—"

Buffin's statement was cut off by the sound of gunfire. There was a rapid staccato of shots, then a scream, followed by more shots.

Breanna carefully knotted the bandage that held the splint in place and hurried toward the door, with Buffin following.

There was bedlam in front of the bank. Two men were stretched out on the boardwalk. Women were weeping and men were kneeling over the fallen pair. As the nurse and council chairman drew up, Buffin asked, "What happened?"

Several voices spoke at once, saying that Turk Dunphy and his gang broke out of jail, robbed the bank, and rode out of town. Breanna examined both men on the boardwalk and pronounced them dead.

"Where's the marshal and the deputy?" Buffin asked, looking around.

"They're inside the jail," replied a man, just approaching. "Both dead. Hanging by their necks from rafters in the cell block. No way to tell how Dunphy did it, but he and his cutthroats somehow got the upper hand on Collins and Yarrow."

Grief stabbed Breanna's heart when she heard of the deaths of Pueblo's lawmen.

Citizens who had seen the shooting told others that the two dead men on the boardwalk were passing by the bank when they heard shots from inside. When the robbers came running out, the two men had drawn their guns to stop them.

At that moment, the bank president appeared at the door, eyes wild, saying that he had a teller inside who had been shot. Breanna dashed into the bank and found the teller, a young man in his early twenties, on the floor behind his cage. He was conscious, and a quick examination revealed that he had been shot twice in a shoulder and once in the upper chest. Breanna asked the men nearby to carry him to the clinic. She would have to perform surgery immediately.

Four men picked up the wounded teller, and Breanna proceeded them out the door. A larger crowd was now assembled in front of the bank, and a battered Clara Welch, wife of hostler Jeb Welch, was wailing and telling the people how Turk Dunphy and his men had come to the stable for their horses. When Jeb resisted them, they began beating him. Clara had jumped in to aid her husband, and two of the outlaws had pounded her into unconsciousness with their fists. When she came to, she found Jeb dead with a pitchfork buried in his chest.

Clarence Buffin told Breanna he would stay and try to help calm Clara. Breanna said if he needed something to sedate her, Buffin could bring her to the office for some powders.

Leading the four men who carried the wounded teller down the street, Breanna thought of the hatred Turk Dunphy held for John Stranger. Now that Dunphy was on the loose, she feared for John. If the vile outlaw found him, he would probably shoot him in the back.

As the sun was setting behind the Rocky Mountains two days later, Turk Dunphy and his four men reached the southern outskirts of Denver. Drawing rein, Dunphy said, "Okay, here's my plan. Virgil Cullen, my ol' pal from Leavenworth, lives here in Denver now. Last time I saw him, he told me he was through robbin', but if I ever needed anything, to let him know. So we're gonna stay at Virgil's house tonight and right up till just before the bank closes tomorrow. Oughtta be plenty of money in the place by then."

"Boss, I don't mean to tell you what to do, but if you want to hunt down that wolf-eyed dude, we oughtta do that first, then come back and rob the bank," Jade Whetstone said.

Dunphy looked at Whetstone, ran his tongue over his swollen lips, and said, "We're takin' that bank tomorrow, Jade. With that kind of money in our pockets, we can afford to spend time huntin' him down."

"But since we were told he passed through Colorado Springs a week ago and Castle Rock three days ago, chances are good that he's here in Denver. I mean, he don't seem to be in any hurry. Let's get him first, then rob the bank."

"When you're boss, Jade, you can call the shots. Until then, we'll do it *my* way, got it?"

"Sure," Whetstone said, shrugging his shoulders. "I was just makin' a suggestion."

"Well, if suggestions are in order," spoke up Harold Eggert, "I suggest we forget all about tryin' to track that man down. He gives me the creeps. The man ain't human, I tell ya."

Turk laughed. "Harold, he puts his boots on same as the rest of us. And when I run onto him, he ain't gonna know I'm around. I'll chew up his broad back with six slugs. I'd like for him to see it comin', so's he'd know it was me, but I'll forego that pleasure for safety's sake."

"Sun's goin' down, boss," put in Aaron Smith. "Maybe we'd better be findin' your friend's place."

A few minutes later, Turk Dunphy knocked on Virgil Cullen's

door on Glenarm Street. A few blocks away, the man-in-black checked into Denver's Westerner Hotel on Champa Street.

Dunphy and his men received a warm welcome from Cullen, but were given the cold shoulder by his wife, Ethel. She reviled her husband for taking the outlaws in when he had promised her he was through with that kind of life and those kind of people. Virgil ignored her and showed the gang where each man would sleep. He promised them a good breakfast in the morning and told them they were welcome to stay until just before the bank's closing time the next day.

After the outlaws had bedded down, they could hear Ethel and Virgil arguing. The thin walls allowed them to hear every word. When Ethel refused to cook breakfast for a "bloody gang of bank robbers," a sharp slap was heard. Ethel wailed for some time before the house grew quiet enough for the gang to get some sleep.

It was almost noon on Thursday, April 7, as Harry and Bertha Sloan were headed west toward their home in the mountain town of Idaho Springs. The elderly couple's wagon was nearly as old as they. It creaked and groaned as the team pulled it up the steep, narrow road. They were in high country, and the wagon was heavily loaded with supplies they had purchased in Denver. The horses were puffing and straining against the harness.

Wrapped in a shawl, Bertha looked fearfully into the gaping maw of the five-hundred-foot-deep canyon at the edge of the road. The wagon wheels on her side were barely more than two feet from the rocky lip. Grasping her husband's slender arm, she said, "Harry, I wish you had listened to me and taken the long way home. I don't like this road. We just barely made it past that place by the creek this morning."

"We'll make it all right, sweetie," the old man said, patting her hand. "We did all right comin' over. We'll do all right goin' back."

"But with the spring thaw getting a good start, that creek was running hard. If it's eroded that spot any more, we won't get through. And even if it hasn't, we've got all this weight we didn't have coming over."

Harry chose not to say any more. Within five minutes, the wagon approached the troublesome spot. The creek came down off the side of a mountain that soared upward on their left, its ragged, snow-capped peak rising up to touch the sky. The swift-moving creek passed through a natural tunnel under the road before it cascaded down the canyon wall and into the river below.

Bertha's eyes widened as Harry drew the wagon to a halt. The rushing water had washed away more of the road since they came through that morning. "Harry, it isn't wide enough for us to cross now. Especially with all this extra weight."

The old man set the brake, then slowly crawled off the seat to the ground. Bertha watched as he went to the narrowest spot and examined it carefully, measuring the width with his eye, comparing it to the width of the wagon. Hurrying back to the wagon, he climbed in and said, "We can make it. There's enough road left to get us past."

"No!" she argued. "It's not wide enough!"

"But it is! I can tell. It'll be all right."

"Even if it's wide enough, the weight of the wagon could break off more of the road. It wouldn't take much to send us to the bottom of the cliff. Please don't try it, Harry."

"But, sweetie-pie, we'd have to back all the way down to the wide spot in the road. That's about two hundred yards. We can't do it."

"I tried to get you to take the long way home, but you wouldn't listen!"

"Honey," said the old man, attempting to stay calm, "I tell you what. Since you're so frightened, why don't you climb down and wait on the road while I drive the wagon across?"

"All right. But I'll have to get down on your side. There's not enough room over here."

The old man climbed down, helped his wife to the ground, then climbed back into the seat. Bertha held the shawl close around her and backed a ways down the road. Eyes filled with fear, she watched her husband take the reins and urge the team forward. The horses showed nervousness as they pulled the wagon toward the narrow place, which was only inches above the stream.

Harry Sloan licked his lips and watched the danger side as he guided the team over the place. The front wheels made it, and Harry was about to let out the breath he was holding when it happened. The edge of the road gave way under the right rear wheel, dropping the vehicle with a sudden jolt to its axle. More road gave way, and the wagon slid a few inches to the right.

The abrupt drop of the wagon was enough to spook the already nervous team. In a panic, they fought their bits, danced heavy rear hooves, and thrust forward with great power, tearing the doubletrees loose from the wagon with a loud crack. The frightened animals bolted up the narrow road, reached its crest, and disappeared.

The load in the wagon bed shifted with its downward drop, throwing the bulk of its weight to the right side. The wagon slipped a few inches further over the edge, swaying.

"Harry!" Bertha screamed. "Jump! The wagon's going to go over the cliff!"

The old man gripped the seat, a look of stark terror in his eyes. "I-I don't dare move. One more slip and it'll go!"

"But you've got to jump!"

"No! I can't!" he shouted, jerking his body. Even that movement sent the wagon an inch or two farther over the edge. Harry swallowed hard and Bertha bit down on her lower lip. The roar of the swift-moving stream seemed to mock them.

Just then a lone rider on a black horse topped the crest and galloped toward them. The rider thundered in, skidded the gelding to a halt, and quickly slid from the saddle. Giving the situation the once-over, he said to Harry. "I'm going to get a good hold right here at this corner, sir. When I say go, you climb down past me."

Harry nodded and said, "Okay."

The man planted his feet carefully, gripped the side of the wagon just behind the left front wheel, and shouted, "Go!"

Bertha stepped up to assist her husband as he climbed down as fast as he could move. Quickly they were in each other's arms.

The stranger let go of the wagon and leaped back. The aging vehicle groaned and slipped another few inches. Then the weakened canyon rim gave way, taking the wagon with it. Down and down it sailed before smashing on the rocks below.

Harry held Bertha and studied the man who had come out of nowhere to rescue him. To Harry, the black broadcloth frock coat, the white shirt and string tie, the black trousers, boots, and flat-crowned hat could mean only one thing. While the stranger stood looking over the cliff's edge, the old man whispered, "Honey, he's a preacher!"

The tall man walked to them and asked, "You two all right?"

"We're fine, thanks to you," Harry replied, looking at his wife. "Aren't we, sweetie-pie?"

"Yes," Bertha said, her lower lip trembling.

"My name's Harry Sloan," said the old man, letting go of his wife to offer his hand. "And this is my wife, Bertha."

"Happy to meet you, Mr. Sloan," said the stranger, shaking Harry's hand. Then he touched the tip of his hatbrim and smiled at Bertha. "You too, ma'am."

It struck Harry that the man had not given his name. He was about to ask when the man said, "I saw your team just over the top of the hill, there. I assume you were coming from Denver."

"Yes, Reverend," Harry nodded. "You are a preacher, aren't you?"

"Sometimes," came the reply with a crooked smile. "Tell you what, Mr. Sloan," he said, pointing to a rock ledge on the safe side of the road. "Why don't you take Mrs. Sloan over there and both of you sit down while I go after your horses?"

"I can help you," offered the old man.

"No need," smiled the stranger. "I have a feeling your knees may be a little weak."

"Well, you're right about that, stranger," chuckled Sloan, turning Bertha toward the rock ledge.

The man-in-black moved up on Bertha's other side and took her arm. When they reached the ledge, both men eased her down to a sitting position. As Harry sat beside her, Bertha looked up and said, "How can we ever thank you for what you did, Reverend?"

"No need. It's thanks enough just to know you're both all right. Now...I assume since you had your wagon loaded with groceries and household goods, you were headed home."

"That's right," nodded Harry. "We live in Idaho Springs. About three times a year we make this trip and stock up. Prices are lower in Denver."

"So you need to stock up again, don't you?" asked the stranger. "I mean after you buy a new wagon."

The old couple looked at each other painfully, then Harry looked at his rescuer and said, "We don't have the money to do either, young man. If you can bring our horses down here to us, we'll just ride them on home."

"Without the supplies you need? How'll you make it? You have to have food."

"We'll make it somehow," Harry said, forcing a smile.

"Tell you what," the man grinned, "let me take you back to Denver and see if we can't work something out."

"Well, if you have the means so you could make us a loan, we'd be able to pay you back come fall. I do odd jobs for people all over the Idaho Springs area. It's already lookin' like I'll have plenty of work this spring and summer."

"We'll talk about that later. Right now, I need to go get those horses so we can start back down the mountain."

Twenty minutes later, the stranger returned with the team. He had removed the damaged harness and had left only the bridles. To Bertha he said, "Tell you what, ma'am, you can ride my horse.

You'll be more comfortable riding in a saddle. Mr. Sloan and I will do the bareback riding."

"You're very thoughtful, young man. I appreciate that."

The tall man excused himself, walked to the big black, and patted him on the side of the neck. "Ebony, this is a nice lady. You have my permission to let her ride. Understand?" The animal nickered and bobbed his head.

Turning to Bertha, he said, "Okay, Mrs. Sloan. You can get on now."

"Pardon me, stranger," Harry said, "but that horse acted like he understood you."

"He did."

"Well, I'll be!" gasped the old man. "You've got him trained so nobody can ride him unless you give the word?"

"Precisely. And believe me, nobody can stay on his back if he wants them off."

"Well, I do declare," Harry cackled. "Don't that beat all!"

The man helped Bertha into the saddle, then the two men mounted the team, and they headed toward Denver.

It was almost two o'clock when they rode into town and headed for the Rocky Mountain Wagon Works. Harry and Bertha looked on while their new-found friend purchased them a brand new wagon and harness. The horses were hitched up, then the man went with them to the various stores and duplicated the load that had gone over the cliff.

When that was done, the stranger looked at his pocket watch and said, "Well, folks, it's just past two-thirty. Seems a little late for you to be taking the long way to Idaho Springs. I'll put you up in the Westerner Hotel and you can head for home in the morning."

Bertha looked at her husband, who shook his head and said, "Stranger—uh...Reverend, this is awful nice of you, but if I let you loan me any more money, I never will get it paid back."

A broad smile graced the man's rugged features. "Tell you what, my friend. I'm not in the loan business. I leave that to the banks."

"But...but I told you I couldn't pay you till fall."

"That you did. But you don't have to pay me back. Not for the wagon, the harness, the food and supplies, nor the hotel room and meals. It's all a gift."

"Now, just a minute young feller. That ain't right. The wind's only blowin' my way here. I can't let you do this."

"Yes, you can. It's what I've decided to do."

Harry exchanged glances with his wife, who was already fighting tears, and said, "Sweetie-pie, what am I gonna do? This feller is flat stubborn."

Bertha was biting her lip.

"Tell you what, Mr. Sloan," said the stranger, "you spoke of the wind blowing your way. There's an old saying among seamen about that—*When you can't change the direction of the wind, adjust your sails.*"

Tears moistened the old man's eyes. "Well, young feller, you leave me no choice but to adjust my sails, then."

"Good. Let's get you and Mrs. Sloan to the hotel. I'll take the team and wagon down to the stable. The bill will be covered, so all you have to do in the morning is walk in and drive the wagon out."

Later, the Sloans were in their hotel room with the tall man, who was about to leave. He opened the door and said, "I'm not sure we'll see each other in the morning, so I'll say good-bye now. It's been real nice meeting you."

"I know there are only so many words in the English language, young man, so pardon the overuse of 'Thank you.'" Bertha said.

"No need for pardon, ma'am. I appreciate your gratitude."

Harry stepped close and said, "My curiosity's killin' me. Man treats us in such a wonderful way is certainly a friend. Seems to me friends oughtta know each other's names. You know ours. What's your name, stranger?"

The man grinned. "That's good enough."

"Pardon me?"

"Just call me Stranger. That's good enough."

"You got a first name?"

"John."

Harry smiled warmly, shook the man's hand, and said, "Well, thank you for everything, John Stranger."

CHAPTER

THIRTEEN

———◆———

While John Stranger was getting the Sloans settled in their hotel room, Turk Dunphy and his gang made their way up Champa Street toward the Frontier Bank and Trust Company, which was directly across the street from the Denver Gun and Ammunition Shop. Next to the gun shop was the Rusty Gun Saloon, which was sided by the Westerner Hotel.

Pulling rein at the corner a half-block from the bank, Dunphy said to his men, "Let's go over this again. I want you boys movin' into that bank at exactly two minutes till three. According to that clock over there, that's fourteen minutes from now."

"You said you wanted us to leave the horses across the street so as not to draw attention to ourselves, boss," said Jade Whetstone. "Looks like there's space right in front of the saloon, there."

Aaron Smith chuckled, "Guess ain't much drinkin' goin' on this time of day."

"No," grinned Turk, "but there sure are lots of customers goin' in and outta the bank. Nice of 'em to make deposits for us, eh?"

The others laughed, then Turk said, "Remember...when we pull up to the hitch rail, don't wrap your reins around the rail. Leave 'em looped over your saddlehorns. The animals ain't gonna go nowhere with me right there with 'em, actin' like I'm adjustin' a cinch or somethin'." Running his gaze over their faces, Dunphy added, "I want every dollar in the place, boys. If anyone gives you trouble, blast 'em."

"You mean like we did that smart-aleck teller in Pueblo?" chuckled Whetstone.

"Yeah, exactly. Be a while before he pulls a gun on bank robbers again. Since we give 'em a warnin' the minute we tell 'em it's a robbery, it's their own fault if they don't heed it."

Turk glanced at the bank clock again. "Okay, fellas, let's put it in motion."

The gang rode slowly along the wide street. The boardwalks were busy with people going in and out of stores, shops, and Frontier Bank and Trust. Vehicles moved both directions, along with riders on horseback.

Hauling up in front of the Rusty Gun Saloon, the robbers dismounted, leaving their reins looped over the saddlehorns. Turk shifted his glance to the bank clock, then said, "Okay, boys, you got one minute before you pass through that door. Walk slow and casual. I'll be waitin' right here."

Dunphy kept himself obscured from view by staying amongst the horses. He could hear the angry voice of a man coming from inside the saloon, but could not make out his words. He watched his four partners in crime weave through the traffic and head for the bank's front door.

At the same moment, John Stranger emerged from the hotel lobby and paused on the elevated porch. He glanced down at the Sloan wagon, which was parked directly in front of the hotel. He would take the team and wagon to the stable, then ride Ebony to the other end of town to take care of a couple items of business.

He was casually scanning the street when his eye caught the four men walking toward the bank. He did not see Turk Dunphy amongst the horses, nor did Dunphy see him.

The man-in-black did, however, recognize Hec Speer, Harold Eggert, Aaron Smith, and Jade Whetstone. They were too close to the bank for him to block their entrance; there was no way he could keep them from going inside. There was only one thing he could do. He would have to stop them when they came out.

Dashing past the saloon, he plunged through the gun shop door and quickly looked about. Handguns were displayed in four glass cases that also served as a counter. The proprietor was behind them, showing a pistol to a customer. No one else was in the shop.

Behind the glass cases were shelves loaded with ammunition boxes, and on the opposite side were gun racks filled with rifles, carbines, buffalo guns, and shotguns.

Stranger grabbed two double-barreled twelve-gauge shotguns from the rack and rushed to the counter. "Pardon me, sir, but I need a box of twelves real fast." Even as he spoke, he laid one shotgun on the counter and broke the other one open.

The proprietor was angry. "Now just a minute, mister!" he snapped. "I'm dealing with a customer, as you can see. You'll have to wait your turn."

"There isn't time. The Frontier Bank is being robbed. Hurry! Hand me a box of twelves!"

Stranger's words didn't sink in for a few seconds, so he hopped the glass case, grabbed a box of twelve-gauge shells, and popped it open. He loaded both shotguns, snapped them shut, stuffed a handful of shells in the pocket of his frock coat, and said, "I'll settle up with you later. Right now there isn't time."

The customer stood, mouth agape, looking on.

As the man-in-black rushed past the stunned proprietor and headed for the door, he called after him, "I'll have Sheriff Thorne on your tail!" Then he looked at his customer and said, "Do you suppose the bank really is being robbed?"

Together they dashed to the door.

Outside, Turk Dunphy's eyes were riveted on the front door of the bank as he pretended to be adjusting a cinch on one of the horses. He figured it would take his men no more than three or four minutes to clean the place out. Suddenly his attention was drawn to a tall man in the street, dressed in black and carrying a double-barreled shotgun in each hand. He was shouting for vehicles to stop and for people to run for cover because the bank was being robbed.

Dunphy's nerves tightened when he recognized the man. Hatred flared up in him like the eruption of a volcano. Just as he had dreamed, the stranger was presenting his broad back as a target.

People were clearing the street, taking cover between buildings and in doorways and looking on with anxious eyes.

John Stranger took his stance in the middle of the street, unaware that his mortal enemy was behind him, drawing his revolver. He cocked the dual hammers of each shotgun, rested the butts against his hip bones, and lined them on the bank door.

Just as Turk was earing back the hammer of his weapon, he heard the same angry voice inside the saloon behind him that he had heard a few minutes earlier. But this time the voice was louder. Turk looked back to see Sheriff Jason Thorne emerging with an angry man in front of him. The man had his hands cuffed behind his back, and Thorne's deputy, Bob Cadwell, was beside him.

Dunphy swore under his breath. He was going to miss the perfect opportunity to enjoy the sweet taste of revenge. He eased the hammer into place and holstered his gun. He dare not shoot the hated man while the two lawmen were present.

Both Thorne and Cadwell stood looking at the man in the street, wondering what he was doing there. Just then the gun shop proprietor dashed up and said, "Sheriff, that man there just burst into my place, grabbed those two shotguns, and said the bank's being robbed!"

Thorne whipped out his gun and said to the deputy, "You stay with our prisoner. I'll—"

Shots sounded inside the bank and the door burst open.

On the street, John Stranger waited until all four robbers were out the door, then leveled the two shotguns on them as they hastily crossed the boardwalk and stepped into the street. "Stop right there!

Drop those guns and put your hands up!"

All four men were holding smoking guns and fully-packed canvas bags. Whetstone cursed when he saw Stranger and said, "It's that man from Pueblo!" As he spoke, he swung his gun on the man-in-black and fired.

The others also swore and brought their revolvers up.

What happened next takes too long in the telling, for it all seemed to happen at once. John Stranger's right-hand gun roared a split second after Whetstone fired. Whetstone's bullet hummed past his waistline and plowed into a water barrel in front of the gun shop. Whetstone took the full blast of Stranger's charge in the center of his chest. The impact knocked him off his feet. He was dead before he hit the street.

The second to die was Hec Speer. Stranger unleashed the second barrel of the shotgun in his right hand. The blast hit Speer in the same spot the first one had hit Whetstone, and killed him just as quickly.

The die was already cast for Aaron Smith. He flicked back the hammer of his revolver and took aim from the hip. Stranger's left-hand gun boomed. While Smith was going down, Harold Eggert, caught up in the swift current of the moment, leveled his gun on Stranger.

"Don't do it, Eggert!" Stranger shouted. But his words were of no effect.

There was only one thing on Eggert's mind: destroy the man who held the shotguns. He dropped the hammer but never heard the shot. Stranger ended his life the same as the others...with a full charge of buckshot to the heart. Eggert's bullet went wild, plowing dirt a few feet in front of him.

While the breeze carried away the blue-white puffs of smoke, two men came out of the bank, shouting for someone to get a doctor. The robbers had gunned down a teller and two customers. All three were seriously wounded.

Turk Dunphy decided it was time to leave. He would have to

shoot the gray-eyed man another time. He dare not be seen by the stranger, or he was done for. Even the sheriff and deputy no doubt would recognize him if they got a good look at him. Wanted posters with his face on them had been circulated to lawmen all over the West.

Keeping his back to Deputy Cadwell, who still stood on the boardwalk in front of the saloon, Dunphy led his horse away from the hitchrail and headed down Champa Street. When he was a half-block from the bloody scene, he mounted and put the horse to a trot. He would return to Virgil Cullen's house and hide there until he could decide what to do. His whole gang had been wiped out by the man who seemed to have entered his life only to ruin it.

Sheriff Thorne hurried to the stranger and praised his adept handling of the robbers. He had never seen such a display of marksmanship. After a few moments, he said, "I don't believe I know you, stranger. You from around here?"

"No," John replied, looking over the lifeless forms of the men he had just gunned down.

"You a gambler?"

"No."

"Only reason I asked was because of the way you're dressed. Seems gamblers like to dress that way."

"That right?" John said, absentmindedly. Though the robbers had given him no choice, it still did something to him inside when he was forced to snuff out a human life.

"Only other thing that passes through my mind when I see a man dressed like you is that he might be a preacher," Thorne went on. "I didn't even ask about that. Then again, no preacher could so coolly stand face to face with four armed robbers and take them out with the precision you did. So...I figured you might be a gambler."

"You're not alone. Plenty of people have figured the same thing."

"Well, are you a federal marshal, maybe? I don't see a badge, but—"

"No. I just happened to be down in Pueblo a couple of weeks ago and ran onto these fellas. They were in jail for murder and bank robbery. Must've escaped. Only there's one missing."

"Yeah?"

"Gang's leader—Turk Dunphy."

"Turk Dunphy! This is his gang?"

"Yep. He used to have five. One was killed in Pueblo."

"I've got wanted posters on Dunphy and a couple others," said Thorne, running his eyes over the four dead men. "Yeah. These two right here."

"Hec Speer and Harold Eggert," nodded Stranger. "Seems to me Dunphy ought to be around here somewhere. Unless something's happened to him."

"Must have," said Thorne. "Otherwise, he'd have been in on the robbery for sure."

Two of Denver's doctors showed up, made their way through the crowd, and hurried inside the bank. Then Stranger noticed the gun shop owner heading his way. As the man drew up, he spoke to the sheriff, then looked at Stranger and said, "You weren't kidding about that bank robbery, were you? How'd you know it was going to happen?"

"Like I was just telling the sheriff here—I ran onto this gang down in Pueblo a couple weeks ago. They were in jail for murder and bank robbery. I came out of the hotel and saw them heading for the bank. I knew they had one thing in mind."

"Well, I'm glad my shotguns came in handy," said the proprietor.

Hoisting the weapons to chest level, Stranger asked, "What do I owe you for them?"

"You mean you want to buy them?"

"Well, not exactly, but they're used weapons, now. So I figure—"

"No problem," said the little man. "They have to fire them at the factory back East to see if they work properly. I can clean them up and still sell them as new."

"All right," said Stranger, "but I owe you for that box of shells I broke open."

"Naw," said the proprietor, waving a hand. "I can still sell what's left."

Stranger handed him one gun, then pulled the handful of shells from his pocket and said, "Here's the rest of them. But I do owe you for the four I used."

"No you don't," smiled the proprietor, stuffing the shells into his pockets. "I'll gladly donate those four to the cause." The little man took his guns and left.

Stranger and Thorne noticed that two bank employees were picking up the canvas bags. There was movement at the bank door, and a tall, slender man with silver hair appeared. He eyed the sheriff and the man-in-black and walked to them. "Sheriff, I understand this man put these robbers down all by himself."

"That's right," said Thorne. Then to Stranger, "This is the bank's president...Wallace Bryan."

They shook hands, then Bryan looked around at the dead outlaws and said, "Some piece of work, Mister—I don't believe Sheriff Thorne told me your name."

Before John could reply, there was a rumble among the crowd as the three wounded men were carried through the door. Every eye turned in that direction. One of the doctors went along with the wounded, while the other headed for Sheriff Thorne.

As he drew up, medical bag in hand, he glanced at Stranger, then said to Thorne, "All three will be all right. Dr. Hedling and I will have to do some surgery, but no lives are at stake."

The physician, who appeared to be in his early forties, smiled at the man-in-black and said, "They were telling me inside that you saved the bank and depositors like me a lot of money, sir." Looking back at the dead outlaws, he said, "You must be plenty good with a shotgun."

"*Two* shotguns, Doc," interjected Thorne.

"Yes. Two. Are you some kind of gun expert?

"I don't know that you could say I'm an expert, Doctor. I've used them some."

"Were you in the Civil War?" the doctor asked.

"Well, yes and no. I—"

"Oh, excuse me," cut in the sheriff, "I didn't introduce you two. This is Dr. Lyle Goodwin. And...well, here I am again, stranger. I still don't know your name."

As Stranger met Dr. Goodwin's hand, he smiled and said, "You can just call me John."

"John? That's all?"

"That's all that matters."

Goodwin decided to press it no further. "Well, then, John it is. You've done many people in this town a great service. You put your life on the line to stop the robbery, and we owe you a debt of gratitude."

"We owe him more than that, Doc," Bryan said. "Speaking for my bank, we're going to give you a one-thousand-dollar reward, John."

Stranger's face flushed. "Oh, no, Mr. Bryan. That isn't necessary. Just accept it as my contribution to Denver's welfare. I like this town."

"Well, this town likes you, too. Especially those who do their banking with Frontier Bank and Trust. I would really like to give you the reward."

"You're very generous, sir," smiled Stranger, "but I can't accept it. Let me ask you...is there some community project under way right now? Or one that is planned?"

"Why, yes there is," replied the bank president. "Our three doctors are in a fund-raising campaign to build a hospital. It'll be the only hospital within four hundred miles when we get it done."

"Wonderful," smiled John. "Then put the thousand dollars in the hospital fund."

Dr. Goodwin smiled broadly, shook the tall man's hand again, and said with exuberance, "God bless you, John! God bless you!"

John Stranger grinned and with a twinkle in his eye, replied, "He does, Doctor. He does." Then to the three, he said, "If you gentlemen will excuse me, I have an errand to take care of."

They watched the stranger move down the street and climb into a brand new wagon loaded with food and supplies. As he drove it away, Dr. Goodwin said, "There goes a very special man, gentlemen."

"I was thinking the same thing," agreed Thorne.

Wallace Bryan sighed and shook his head in wonderment. "That man saved my bank from ruin. I'll always think of him as a heaven-sent angel."

Bertha Sloan stood wrapped in her shawl on the porch of the Westerner Hotel in the early morning sunlight. Her attention was on the wide, dusty street, where she expected her husband to appear, driving the heavily laden wagon. After the Sloans had eaten breakfast in the hotel restaurant, they had gone to the desk in the lobby to ask in what room they might find the man who called himself John Stranger. The clerk had informed them that the man had checked out before dawn and had paid their bill in full.

Bertha's mind was fixed on Stranger, wondering who he was and why he had shown up to save Harry's life and help them out of a desperate situation. It was almost as if he were sent from the hand of God. Her thoughts were interrupted when she saw the wagon coming down the street with Harry at the reins.

The old man drew up, parked the wagon, and helped his wife climb into the seat. When she was settled, he stabbed a hand down in his pocket and said, "Just like John said, honey. The bill was paid in full at the hostler's. But John left somethin' on the wagon seat. I found it layin' there when I climbed up and sat down. Here, take a look."

Bertha's eyes widened as she focused on the shiny silver medallion. She adjusted her spectacles and read the inscription aloud while her husband made his way around the rear of the wagon. "The stranger that shall come from a far land. Deuteronomy 29:22." Harry was making his way up to the seat as she looked at him and said, "I know John left it for us to find, but what does it mean?"

"I'm not sure, sweetie-pie," he replied, taking the reins and putting the team into motion. "Seems kinda strange. Guess we'll just have to chew on that one for a while."

Bertha clutched the medallion in her hand as the old man guided the team westward out of Denver.

It was midafternoon on Saturday, April 9, when the Wells-Fargo stage came to a halt at the boardwalk in front of the Denver office.

The trip from Pueblo had been a rather dull one for Breanna Baylor. She had boarded at Pueblo early the day before and spent the night at a way-station some fifteen miles north of Colorado Springs. There were two businessmen on that leg of the trip involved in a seemingly unending discussion of commerce and investments, which she found uninteresting. On Saturday morning, a third businessman climbed aboard, and the day's journey was another dose of dull male chatter, making the sight of Denver a welcome one.

The three men stepped out of the coach, still talking business, leaving Breanna to get herself down from the vehicle. She sighed and started to climb down when a distinguished-looking silver-haired man stepped up and said, "May I help you, young lady?"

Breanna flashed him a warm smile and gave him her hand. "Yes, thank you."

When her feet touched ground, she saw two women standing together on the boardwalk, smiling at her. The younger one moved toward her and said, "Miss Baylor, I presume?"

"Yes," nodded Breanna.

"I'm Martha Goodwin, Dr. Goodwin's wife. He wanted to be

here to meet you, but he's tied up at the office." Gesturing toward the elderly gentleman who had helped Breanna from the coach, she said, "This is my father, Dr. Micah Sommers."

"I'm so glad to meet you," Breanna said.

Sommers bowed slightly and touched the brim of his hat. "May I acquaint you, Miss Baylor, with my wife, Florence?"

Breanna greeted Florence Sommers, noting the strong resemblance between the two women. Running her gaze back and forth, she said, "There's no mistaking that you two are mother and daughter."

"Many people have said the same thing," said Martha. "And, of course, I'm flattered when someone says that I resemble my mother."

"We have your apartment all fixed up, dear," said Florence. "I hope you'll like it."

"I'm sure I will. I want to thank you and Dr. Sommers for making the apartment available to me. I still feel that I should pay you something for living there."

"Nonsense," Dr. Sommers said. "We are honored to have such a lovely young nurse occupying it." He paused a few seconds, then said, "I assume you have luggage."

"Yes. The driver and his partner are unloading it now."

Breanna was taken a few blocks to a large two-story house that had a small but comfortable apartment built on the back side, overlooking a beautiful yard. The Sommers explained that Florence's mother had occupied the apartment until her death a few months ago.

Breanna was unpacked and settled in her apartment by suppertime, and had refreshed herself by the time Martha knocked on her door, ready to usher her into the house for the meal she and her mother had prepared. Upon entering the dining room, Breanna was introduced to Dr. Lyle Goodwin.

While they enjoyed their meal, Dr. Goodwin expressed his pleasure in sponsoring Breanna as a visiting nurse. He expounded on the great need for her services all over that part of Colorado Territory. With the growing population, she no doubt would have all the work she could handle.

"I understand there are two other doctors in Denver," Breanna said.

"Yes. Dr. George Hedling and Dr. Ralph West. Fine men. We get along quite well and help each other out at times. In fact, the reason I was unable to meet you at the stage was because of some patients Dr. Hedling and I are working on together."

Martha turned to her husband and said, "Dear, you should probably explain to Miss Baylor about the bank robbery."

"Bank robbery?" echoed Breanna.

"Yes," nodded Goodwin, pouring himself a cup of tea. "Happened yesterday at Frontier Bank and Trust. That's where we do our banking."

"And you're treating three men who were wounded?"

"One is a bank teller, and the other two are customers. They tried to pull guns on the robbers just as they were leaving the bank and got themselves shot in the process."

"Are they badly hurt?"

"The two customers are in pretty good shape, and we thought the teller was too, but he developed some internal bleeding about noon today that we hadn't expected. I was working on him when you arrived on the stage this afternoon. I think he's going to be all right. Dr. Hedling is with him now and will be all night. Dr. Hedling's a widower, so he told me to go on home to my wife."

"I suppose the robbers got away," said Breanna. "How much money did they take?"

"They most certainly did not get away," Dr. Sommers said. "Every dollar they took is safely back in the bank's vault."

"Did a posse run them down?"

"A one-man posse," said Goodwin. "But he didn't run them down, he gunned them down."

"You said there were *four* robbers, Doctor?" asked Breanna.

"Yes. Sheriff Thorne said they were what was left of the Turk Dunphy gang. You may have heard of them."

Breanna's face lost color. "Heard of them? I had a serious run-in with them in Pueblo. They were in jail awaiting trial for murder and bank robbery up until last Monday. They killed Pueblo's marshal and deputy and escaped, then robbed the bank and rode away. I'm not surprised they came here." She paused a moment. "Doctor Goodwin, there were five in the gang when they left Pueblo. Do you know who the missing man is?"

"Dunphy himself, according to Sheriff Thorne. There hasn't been a trace of him. Thorne speculates that maybe the four who came in here had decided Dunphy wasn't boss any more and did away with him. Who knows?"

"I doubt that," Breanna said. "Those men idolized Turk...and feared him, too. I don't think they would have the courage to try killing him, even if they found reason to do it. I think Dunphy wasn't with them for some other reason. He's probably alive and well."

"At least he won't be much of a threat till he can put a new gang together," observed Dr. Sommers.

"Doctor, did I understand correctly that one man, alone, stopped the four robbers?" Breanna asked.

"Yes'm," grinned Goodwin. "I wish I'd been there to see it, but what I saw when it was over was awesome enough. The man used two double-barreled shotguns. From what I was told, he gave the robbers a chance to throw down their guns, but they tried to gun him down. He blasted a man with each barrel, hitting every one of them square in the chest."

Breanna's heart was racing and her mouth went dry. "Dr. Goodwin...this one man posse, as you put it...did you see him?"

"Yes. And more than that, I met him. Sheriff Thorne introduced us."

"Was he tall and slender with dark hair...and eyes the color of gunmetal?"

"Why, yes. Do you know him?"

"Yes, I do."

"His name is John something. He didn't seem to want to divulge his last name."

"He's that way. He's always helping people, but he never asks for anything in return, nor does he want any publicity. Apparently he feels if he divulges his name, he'll be more apt to catch the limelight."

"You say you know him, Miss Baylor," Martha said. "Do you know his last name?"

"No, I don't. Dr. Goodwin...do you know if he's still in Denver?"

"He left some time early this morning. The reason I know is—well, I haven't told you about his generosity. Wallace Bryan, the president of the bank, offered to give John a thousand-dollar reward. He wouldn't take it. He told Bryan to give the money to our hospital fund. Dr. Hedling, Dr. West, and I have a fund-raising campaign underway to build a hospital."

"It's just like John to do something like that."

"Well, anyway, as I started to tell you, I went over to the Westerner Hotel early this morning to thank him once again for what he had done, and he had checked out."

"Did the clerk say if he knew where John might be headed?" Breanna asked.

"He didn't. I asked, and I also asked what name he had registered under. The clerk showed me the register. The name he used was John Stranger. Can you beat that? Nobody's last name is Stranger."

"Sounds like it fits him," Florence said.

"Perfectly," smiled Breanna. "I've never met a man like him."

Later that night, Breanna lay in her new bed and cried herself to sleep. Once again she had brushed close to the man she loved, but once again he was gone. She fell asleep praying that the Lord would bring them back together.

CHAPTER
FOURTEEN

—◆—

The next morning, Sunday, April 10, church services were underway at the Lander Methodist Church in Lander, Wyoming, some three hundred miles northwest of Denver. It was the only church in the thriving, growing town, and it was packed to capacity.

Reverend Philip Landrum walked to the pulpit after the choir had finished a rousing gospel song and opened his Bible. "How about that choir?" he smiled. "Wasn't that a great song?"

"Amens" came from all over the congregation.

"Now, turn in your Bibles to Ephesians chapter one and follow along as I read, beginning at verse one: 'Paul, an apostle of Jesus Christ by the will of God, to the saints which are at Ephesus, and to the faithful in Christ Jesus: Grace be to you, and peace, from God our Father, and from the Lord Jesus Christ. Blessed be the God and Father of our Lord Jesus Christ, who hath blessed us with all spiritual blessings in heavenly—'"

Landrum's words were cut off by a loud thump at the back of the room. Heads twisted around and Landrum looked up to see two men shuffling in. The younger man had been shot in the shoulder and was bleeding profusely. The older man was holding him up and carrying a large canvas bag.

In the congregation was Hugo Vine, the Butterfield Stagelines agent. He recognized driver Joshua Bridges, who was supporting his young shotgunner, Glenn Sebring. Many of the congregation also knew them. The Butterfield line ran coaches from Douglas, in eastern Wyoming, through Lander, all the way west to Moran, at the foot of the Teton Mountains. Bridges and Sebring often spent the night in Lander when on their run.

Also in the congregation was Lander's physician, Dr. Patrick O'Donnell, a widower in his late forties, and his twenty-one-year-old daughter and nurse, Katy.

Hugo leaped to his feet at the first sight of his two friends and pushed his way past the others in his row to get to them. Dr. O'Donnell was sitting on the aisle and hastened to them with Katy on his heels.

"Here, let's get you off your feet," O'Donnell said, and asked the occupants of the nearest pew to make room for the wounded man to lie down. While the doctor and his daughter examined Sebring, others got up and moved so Bridges could sit down.

"What happened, Josh?" Landrum asked

Joshua Bridges explained that the stage was delivering a large payroll from the Douglas bank to a representative of the Diamond J Ranch, who was to meet them in Lander. The Diamond J was a massive spread and ran thousands of head of cattle. Their work force was huge, and the payroll, which came only once every two months, amounted to a large sum. It was the payroll that Bridges carried in the canvas bag.

"We were about ten miles east of here when six riders came out of a draw, brandishin' their guns and hollerin' for us to stop. I thought about givin' the team the whip and tryin' to outrun 'em, but I told myself in a hurry that it was no use. They'd catch us quick, and with six guns against our two, we wouldn't have a chance."

"They must have known you were carrying the Diamond J payroll," Hugo said.

"Absolutely no doubt," said the old man, glancing again at his wounded friend. "They flat asked us for it."

"Well, it's obvious they didn't get what they wanted," Reverend Landrum said. "So what happened?"

Bridges lifted his sweat-stained hat, sleeved the moisture from his wrinkled brow and bald head, and said, "I tried to fool 'em by tellin' 'em that we weren't carryin' no payroll. I had it stashed right at my feet in the box, where they couldn't see it. Glenn had his shotgun acrossed his lap. We had our hands up, but Glenn had eared back both hammers just before he raised his hands. When I told 'em we didn't have the payroll, the youngest—prob'ly not more'n eighteen—cussed me, callin' me a liar. He aimed his gun at my face like he was gonna blow my head off. Ever'body was lookin' at him, 'cause one of 'em told him to put the gun down. He sassed the guy, sayin' he didn't need to put up with no lyin' stage driver, and sure enough, started to drop his hammer.

"That's when Glenn snatched up his shotgun and let him have it. The kid's bullet warmed my ear as it buzzed past my head. He took the load in his throat and peeled outta the saddle, and some of the buckshot hit his horse in the eyes. Man and animal both went down.

"I snapped the reins and put the team into a gallop. One of 'em was screamin' that we'd killed his brother, and they all started shootin' at us. So Glenn unloaded the other barrel at one of 'em, but he hit the guy's horse instead. In fact, part of the charge hit another horse, too. Glenn was about to turn around and reload, and that's when the slug hit him in the shoulder.

"I looked back, expectin' to see them outlaws comin' after us, but they was bendin' over that kid. They were really upset about him gettin' blowed into eternity."

"You think they'll be coming after you?" asked the pastor.

"I don't doubt it atall. I pushed the team as fast as they could run to get to town. That's why we're so early. Them guy's will have to ride double, Reverend, but they'll be comin'. I know it. I left the stage in front of the office, figurin' it'd take 'em a little longer to find us, but you gotta hide us!"

Landrum turned toward Dr. O'Donnell and asked, "How is he, Doc?"

"He needs that bullet to come out. If they know they hit Glenn, the first place they'll look will be my office. So I say let's take both of them to one of the Sunday school rooms at the back and hide them. Then go on with the service, acting like everything's normal. I have my medical bag in my buggy. If someone will go out and get it, I'll work on him back there."

One of the men headed for the door to fetch Dr. O'Donnell's bag. The doctor explained to Glenn that he would have to hold off removing the slug until he could safely take him to the office. He would make him as comfortable as possible in the back room and at least stay the flow of blood.

Four men picked up the wounded shotgunner and headed toward the door at the side and rear of the platform. Another used his bandanna to wipe up the blood that had spilled on the pew.

Just then, the man who had gone after the medical bag bowled through the outside door. "There are five men coming this way, and they look plenty mean!"

"Everybody take a seat!" commanded Landrum. "Let's make it all look normal. If we're all singing, it'll be best."

One of the men sitting near the center aisle pointed to the floor and said, "What about these drops of blood on the floor, preacher?"

Landrum noted the trail of blood-drops that stained the floor. "Let's hope they don't notice them. It's too late to do anything about them."

"Shouldn't somebody get the marshal?" asked a middle-aged woman.

"He's out of town on an errand," Landrum said. "I saw him leaving early this morning. Said he'd be back about one o'clock this afternoon. We'll have to handle this ourselves."

"Too bad we didn't bring our guns to church," spoke up a man in his thirties.

"I appreciate your sentiments, Ralph," said the pastor, "but if we started gunplay in here, our wives and children would probably get hit. We'll just have to keep calm and trust the Lord."

Bag in hand, Dr. O'Donnell hurried toward the classroom. Katy hurried alongside him and said, "I'll go with you, Daddy."

"No, honey. It's best that you stay out here. If those outlaws decide to take a look in the back, you'll be safer out here."

"But—"

"Please, Katy," he said, with that fatherly look that told her not to argue. With that, he was through the door and out of sight.

Katy O'Donnell had her father's Irish eyes and her late mother's attractive features. She had long, wavy hair that seemed to catch fire whenever the sun touched it...and a fiery spirit to match. She was working to obtain her Certified Medical Nurse certificate. She was good at what she did and had earned the respect of the townspeople.

As Katy returned to her seat, Reverend Landrum hurried to the platform and said, "Please, everybody. Stay calm. Do your best to look as if everything is normal. Pick up your hymnals and turn to number forty-nine." Looking toward the woman who sat at the pump organ, he said, "All right, Mrs. Wagner...music."

Ten miles east of Lander on the road to Douglas, outlaw leader Hank Foster knelt beside the body of his dead brother, Billy, and wept.

Foster's men—Reggie Atkins, Chice Reed, Jim Wurth, and Stan Cole—watched the stagecoach they had tried to rob disappear in a cloud of dust, then turned their guns on the three wounded horses and put them out of their misery. While reloading, they gathered around their grieving leader, looking down at him in silence.

Foster was a short, muscular man in his late twenties, and his temper had a short fuse; he was vicious when riled. Timidly, Reggie Atkins placed a hand on Hank's shoulder.

Hank looked up at him with moist eyes. "He was my kid brother, Reggie. Those dirty devils killed him."

Atkins scrubbed a hand across his mouth. "Hank...if...if you'd like to stay here with Billy, the boys and I can ride double and still catch up to the stage before it gets to Lander. We'll take care of those two skunks right and proper."

Turning back to look into the face of his dead brother, Hank said, "No, Reggie. Just give me a few minutes, then we'll go after those killers."

Finally Foster rose to his feet, pushed his hair back with splayed fingers, and put on his hat. Without looking at his men, he bent down and picked up the lifeless form of Billy Foster and carried it to a low spot beside the road, where it would not be noticed by travelers, and gently laid it down.

As he returned to where the others stood, they saw the wrath that flushed his hard features. Hank Foster had known smallpox in his earlier years, and his face was badly pocked, which added to his fierce look. The urge to kill the men who had snuffed out the life of his brother was a monstrous, gnawing need inside him. "All right, let's go. But I want it understood—when we find 'em, I'm goin' to do the killin'."

"We'll double up on mine and Stan's horses, boss," said Jim Wurth. "The way that stage was flyin' when it left here, it might beat us to town, but those two won't be hard to find."

Hank spit in the dirt and rasped, "Ain't nowhere in the world those two can hide from me, even if they tried. Let's go."

Atkins rode double with Cole, and Reed rode with Wurth. Foster rode alone. Some thirty-five minutes later, they trotted into Lander.

It was almost midday, and the reflection of the lofty sun off the surface of the North Popo Agie River made it look like a ribbon of silver. The Wind River Mountains to the west were majestic

against the clear Wyoming sky. Directly overhead a V-shaped formation of ducks winged its way from the south. Spring was on its way.

Foster and his cohorts did not notice the beauty around them.
They were intent on one thing—find and kill the stagecoach driver
and shotgunner.

Lander's main thoroughfare was practically deserted.

Stan Cole looked toward his boss and said, "Hank, where is
everybody? Town looks almost deserted."

"It's Sunday. Ain't no stores or shops open. Of course, the real
pious ones are no doubt sittin' in church listenin' to some hypocrite
preacher tellin' 'em how to live."

Chice Reed looked down the sun-struck street and pointed,
saying, "There's the stage, boss. Right in front of the Butterfield
office."

Foster chuckled. "Guess those two won't be hard to find."

"We'll probably have to deal with the agent, too," Atkins said.

"Well, if he gets in the way, you guys blast him. Just remember, the other two are mine."

"We'll only butt in if it looks necessary, boss," Atkins said.

"Just you make sure it *is* necessary."

As they drew up to the stagecoach, Reed noted the sign in the
office door. "Take a look at the sign, Hank. Place is all locked up.
Suppose they're tryin' to fool us?"

Foster read the sign. "So the agent's in church, eh? I bet."
Swinging from his saddle, he stomped across the boardwalk and
pulled his revolver. He took a moment to peer through the glass, then
raised a foot and kicked in the door. It swung hard and banged
against the wall. Atkins, Reed, and Cole were on his heels, guns ready.
There was a desk behind the counter, but the place was unoccupied.

"You suppose they went to the town marshal's office for protection?" suggested Cole.

"Maybe," Foster said, holstering his gun. "It won't help 'em,
I'll tell you that right now. So we have to shoot a hicktown tin star
to get to 'em. So what."

"Hank, come out here!" called Jim Wurth, who had remained outside.

"What is it?" asked Foster, looking toward the open door.

"I think I know why they ain't here."

Foster rushed outside, with the others following. He found Wurth standing beside the stagecoach.

"Lookee here," said Wurth, pointing to dried rivulets of blood that had trickled down the side of the coach from the seat. "Had to be the shotgunner. It's on his side."

"I hope he's in a lot of pain," Foster said. "Just so he don't die yet. I want the privilege of killin' him."

"I'd say the driver probably took him to the doctor," Cole said.

Wurth nodded and said, "Looks like it. There's a trail of blood leadin' up the street. See it?"

All eyes focused on the tiny drops of blood that ran up the boardwalk.

"Okay," said Foster, "let's go find 'em."

While Reed, Wurth, and Cole led the horses along the street, Foster and Atkins followed the blood trail on the boardwalk, expecting it to lead to the doctor's office. As they moved past shops and stores, Wurth called from the middle of the street, "Hey, Hank...town this size wouldn't have more'n one doctor, would it?"

"Not hardly."

"Well, there's a Dr. Patrick O'Donnell's office right over there on the other side of the street. You still findin' blood?"

"Yep," said Foster, stopping to look across the street at the sign over the door of Dr. O'Donnell's office. "Well, for sure they didn't go over there. C'mon, we gotta find 'em."

A minute later they came to the town marshal's office, but it was locked up. The blood trail led past it, so they kept moving. They heard singing up ahead. From his place in the street, Reed pointed forward and said, "I'll bet they're hidin' in that church up there, Hank."

"Yep," said Foster, "you're dead right. That's exactly where the trail's leadin'."

They reached the church and tied the horses to hitching posts. Drawing and cocking their guns, the outlaws made their way to the front door. They could hear the pump organ above the unified voices that were singing a hymn with vigor.

Foster pointed to the blood on the porch. "See? Leads straight inside. They're here, all right."

The gang leader swung the door open and charged inside with his henchmen on his heels. The preacher was behind the pulpit, leading the singing. He stopped suddenly, eyeing the intruders. Heads in the congregation spun around. The organ went silent.

"Everybody sit still!" boomed Foster, waving his gun in a threatening manner. "First one that moves dies! Understand?"

Men, women, and children looked on the five outlaws with trepidation. Reverend Philip Landrum remained behind the pulpit. He glanced toward his wife and two children, who sat three rows from the front near the wall. Mrs. Landrum had an arm around both son and daughter, eyes fixed on Hank Foster, who was moving up the aisle toward her husband.

"All we want are the driver and shotgunner, preacher," Foster gruffed. "We'll take 'em and be on our way. Nobody here needs to get hurt."

Landrum replied levelly, "You are interrupting our service, mister. Take your friends and leave."

Raising his gun, Foster aimed it between the pastor's eyes and hissed, "Those dirty murderers killed my kid brother! I want 'em, and I want 'em now! You hear me?"

Children began to whimper and women gasped.

An elderly man on the aisle stood, leaning on his cane, and said, "We don't know what you're talking about! What driver? What shotgunner? This isn't the stage stop!"

Atkins brought his gun barrel down savagely on the old man's head. Children wailed and women screamed as the man collapsed in a heap, his cane clattering to the floor.

Foster turned his attention from the old man back to the

preacher and snapped, "There'll be more of that if anybody else lies to us! We followed a trail of blood all the way from the stage in front of the Butterfield office. That trail brought us here, and it leads right up this aisle to that door back there." The hard edge in his voice grew harder. "Now, we want those two, preacher. And we'll spill blood till we get 'em."

"Who do you think you are, barging into the house of God, waving guns and battering old men? You'll answer to God for this!"

Foster laughed. "Yeah? Well, I don't see God sittin' anywhere in here." Looking back at his men, he said, "Reggie, come with me. Rest of you boys keep this crowd covered. Anybody gets out of line—even the holy reverend here—shoot 'em!"

The two outlaws started for the door beside the platform, but Landrum leaped in front of them. "You have no right barging in here and interrupting our worship service, and you have no business searching our building! Get out of here!"

Irritated by the preacher's insolence, Foster aimed his gun at his stomach and dropped the hammer. The loud report clattered off the walls, blending with wild shouts and screams.

Landrum buckled, clutched his midsection, and fell to the floor.

Foster bellowed, "Anybody else acts stupid like the reverend, and they'll get the same thing! Watch 'em, boys! C'mon, Reggie."

As Foster and Atkins moved through the door beside the platform, Katy O'Donnell stood and ran toward Landrum.

Wurth stepped in front of her and said tartly, "Siddown, lady!"

Katy's temper flared and she glared at him. "I'm a nurse, mister! My pastor needs me, and I'm going to him. You'll have to kill me to keep me from him."

Katy started around Wurth, but he grabbed her by the arm and jerked her back in front of him. "I told you to sit down! Now do it!"

Katy pulled her arm free, shoved Wurth out of the way, and hurried to the fallen preacher.

A bit embarrassed by the way the small woman had outmaneuvered him, Wurth looked back at his cohorts, cursed, and started to crack her over the head from behind.

"Jim!" Reed shouted. "Leave her alone. She ain't hurtin' nothin'."

Wurth checked his move, looking at Reed.

Dorothy Landrum dashed from her seat, after telling her children to stay put, and headed for her fallen husband. When Wurth saw her coming, he pointed his gun at her and railed, "Go back to your seat, lady!"

Katy's courage had emboldened her. She gave the outlaw a cold look and said, "That's my husband on the floor. Get out of my way."

Wurth looked at her with hard eyes for a moment, then stepped aside. "Oh, well, I guess you can't hurt nothin' either."

While the frightened children wailed and the adults tried to calm them, Katy tore off a large section of her petticoat to use as a compress. She knew Landrum's chances were slim, and every minute that bullet stayed in his bleeding midsection took him closer to death's door. Landrum was conscious and in great pain. When he opened his eyes, Katy could tell they were getting glassy. He would pass out any second.

Biting down hard on her lips, Dorothy said, "Katy...what do you think?"

"If we can get the slug out real soon, he has a chance. We've got to get Daddy out of—"

Two rapid gunshots interrupted Katy. They were followed by two more. The children wailed the more, and two or three women began screaming. The three outlaws grinned at each other.

Katy and Dorothy exchanged fearful glances. The four men who had carried Glenn Sebring to the Sunday school room had returned to be with their families. That left only Katy's father with Bridges and Sebring.

Rapid footsteps were heard from the rear of the building, and the door beside the platform burst open. Hank Foster appeared first, carrying the canvas money bag, followed closely by Reggie Atkins.

Katy started to stand up, but Dorothy grabbed her, whispering, "No, honey! Let them get out of here first."

"All right, boys," bawled Foster as he side-stepped the fallen preacher and the two women, "let's get outta here!"

The gang hastened past the old man who still lay in the aisle. Foster let the others go through the door first, then waving his gun in a threatening manner, he gusted, "Anybody tries to follow us, they'll get the same thing that preacher and those men in the back room got!"

With that, Foster followed his men outside, where Atkins and Reed were stealing horses from the church's hitch rails. Quickly in the saddle, the gang galloped away.

Inside the church, Katy said shakily, "Dorothy, you stay with your husband. I've got to go see about Daddy."

The tension the congregation felt in the presence of the outlaws gave way to relief. Families embraced and wept; others headed for their fallen pastor. Two women stayed with the Landrum children, holding them in their arms. A couple of men helped the old man to his feet.

Katy's heart was in her throat as she ran for the door to the classroom. Just as she rounded the corner of the platform, the door came open. Dr. O'Donnell's face was ashen.

"Daddy!" Katy cried, dashing to him and throwing her arms around his neck. "I was afraid they'd killed you!"

Embracing her, O'Donnell said weakly, "I'm fine, sweetheart. But I'm afraid the other two are dead."

"They shot Pastor Landrum too."

"Yes. They told me. Is he—?"

"He's still alive, but you'll need to get the bullet out in a hurry. The one with the pock-marked face shot him in the stomach point blank."

Dr. O'Donnell hurried to the preacher, told the people to step back, and made a quick examination. Looking around, he said, "I need four of you men to carry him to my office right away. Every second counts."

Fifteen minutes later, Dorothy and her children were in the waiting room at the doctor's office, accompanied by a few of the church women. The rest of the congregation waited outside on the street. Chester Platte, the town barber and chairman of the deacon board, led them in prayer, asking the Lord to spare their pastor's life.

While they were praying, Marshal Jake Morgan rode in and dismounted quietly, waiting for the "amen." When it came, he moved in among the crowd and said, "I assume from Chester's prayer that Reverend Landrum is undergoing emergency surgery. What happened?"

Platte quickly told Morgan the story, and a posse was formed on the spot. Shortly thereafter, marshal and posse rode out in pursuit of the outlaws.

Soon word of what had happened at the church spread over Lander. Townspeople who were not church members gathered outside Dr. O'Donnell's clinic, joining in the vigil with the church members. It was ten minutes after three when the door opened and the somber-faced physician appeared with Katy at his side. Dorothy and her children could be heard weeping in the waiting room.

Dr. O'Donnell told the people that Reverend Landrum had died on the operating table. He had done all he could, but the bullet had done too much damage and the preacher had hemorrhaged to death. When the people began to weep, Platte told the crowd that the Lord had taken their pastor to Higher Service, and they must not become bitter nor wish him back.

As darkness fell, Marshal Morgan and the posse returned empty-handed. The killers had dodged them. Unless Morgan and his men got lucky in the next day or so, the outlaws were going to get away with the murders of the two Butterfield men and the pastor of Lander Methodist Church.

A town meeting was held at the church, and Morgan

explained that the gang had given them the slip. Outrage showed on the faces of the people, but none blamed Morgan and the posse. The killers had enjoyed a healthy head start; the posse was simply at too great a disadvantage.

Standing before the crowd in front of the pulpit, Morgan said, "I wish there was some way to get help to track them down, but as you know, lawmen and law enforcement agencies are few and far between here on the frontier. The closest help is the U.S. marshal's office in Denver. Even if I took the time to ride there, the marshals are so busy, it might be months before they could send any men."

One man who was a member of the church said, "Marshal, nobody in this town could ask any more of you than you've already done. Besides, if you rode to Denver to get help from the U.S. marshal's office, it would leave us without a lawman until you got back."

"That's right, Ben," spoke up another man. "I wish there was telegraph service between here and Denver, but since there isn't, we'll have to let this thing sit where it is. The rest of us have jobs and businesses to run. We certainly can't make the ride to Denver. And for sure, we can't afford to have the marshal gone that long. We've got too many troublemakers passing through this town. So, as much as I hate to say it...it looks like those dirty killers are gonna get away with it."

Ben Frye—who had spoken a moment before—shook his head. "Not really, Fred. Pastor Landrum preached a sermon about that a few months ago. I remember it clearly. He kept quoting from Romans 12: *Vengeance is mine; I will repay, saith the Lord.* Those killers will get what's coming to them. Even though we can't lay on them their just due, the Lord will."

"Amens" came from all over the crowd.

The bodies of the Butterfield stage crew were picked up by the company two days later to be taken to their families. On the same day, Reverend Philip Landrum was buried. Every resident of Lander attended the funeral, as well as people from outlying areas. Chester Platte conducted the funeral, since there was no ordained preacher within a hundred miles.

Platte finished the graveside service and offered his condolences to Dorothy Landrum and her children. Then he stepped aside so the long line of mourners could file by and speak their own words of comfort. While observing the slow-moving line, Platte noticed Dean Foster coming toward him.

In his early forties, Foster was owner of Lander's only bank. Of medium height and build, he wore a handlebar mustache and always chewed on an unlit cigar. Foster had purchased the Bank of Lander some three months previously. The former owner, Ted Hrdlicka, had mysteriously disappeared in early January and was found dead of a gunshot wound to the head a week later in the hills to the south.

Only days later, Foster had shown up in town, saying he had heard about the killing and was interested in purchasing the bank. He met with Hrdlicka's widow, offered her a reasonable price for the bank, and closed the deal.

"Hello, Chester," Foster said quietly. "Can I talk to you a minute?"

Platte nodded. "I suppose."

Foster cleared his throat. "Well, it's about the mortgage your church has with my bank."

"What about it?" Platte was irritated that Foster would approach him on business matters at his pastor's funeral.

"I'm just a bit concerned."

"About what?"

"Well, there's a payment due June 1, and I'm concerned that the church won't be able to make it."

"Why?"

"You're a flock without a shepherd, that's why. I've seen churches lose their pastors before. If he isn't replaced quickly, the flock starts to scatter and the offerings drop off."

Feeling his temperature rise, Platte looked the banker in the eye and said, "Mr. Foster, you're going to get ulcers over nothing if you're not careful. Right now, in our checking account at your bank, we have enough money to make the payment, though it's not due for several weeks."

"Well, I'm glad to hear that, but there'll be another payment due December first. What about that?"

"We'll make it," Platte said flatly.

"Well, I hope everything's as settled as you make it sound, Chester. Because if it isn't, I remind you that you and the other men of the church signed the note. If the church defaults, I'll look to you men personally to keep the payments current."

Platte's irritation grew. "Was it necessary, Mr. Foster, that you approach me with your worries at this time and place? Couldn't this conversation have waited until later?"

Dean Foster's mouth turned down and his eyes grew cold. "I'm a businessman, Platte. Man in my position has to stay on top of things."

"I won't argue with that, but there's a time and place for doing business. This isn't the time nor the place."

"Now, listen here. I have a genuine concern in this matter, and I—"

"You have nothing to worry about," cut in Platte. "The men who signed that note—including myself—are upstanding in this community. We've proven ourselves to be responsible citizens of good character. We won't let the payments get behind."

"Yeah, but if you go very long without a pastor, the church will dwindle, and maybe some of the signers will conveniently forget their responsibility to the bank."

Platte sighed with exasperation. "Mr. Foster, for your information, the deacons—of whom I am chairman—have already written to the denominational headquarters in Kansas City, asking for a replacement. We should be hearing back soon that a new preacher is on his way."

Foster pointed his finger in Platte's face. "Okay, but just you remember...I won't tolerate any late payments."

The deacon chairman grinned. "Tell you what, Mr. Foster. If you're so worried about the church staying financially stable, why don't you start attending and drop a healthy check in the offering plate from time to time?"

Foster had a stricken look on his face. Without another word, he turned and hurried away.

CHAPTER
FIFTEEN

Banker Dean Foster sat in his plush overstuffed chair, reading a week-old New York newspaper by lantern light. It had been dark for nearly two hours when he heard riders come into his yard. They rode past the house toward the barn at the back.

Foster had purchased the large, two-story house on the west edge of Lander from the widow of the late Ted Hrdlicka. Mrs. Hrdlicka had gone to live with family somewhere in California and sold the house to Foster for a low price.

Chewing on his customary unlit cigar, Foster laid the newspaper down, left his comfortable chair, and crossed the den. He went into the hall and walked to the kitchen at the rear of the house. Two lanterns burned in the kitchen, one on the cupboard and the other on the table in the center of the high-ceilinged room.

Soon Foster heard voices, followed by the sound of heavy boots on the back porch. He leaned against the cupboard, arms folded, and watched the five men file through the door. First came Stan Cole, then Reggie Atkins, Chice Reed, and Jim Wurth. Behind them appeared the stocky frame of Hank Foster.

Hank took one look at his older brother's angry, ice-blue eyes and said, "Well, I guess you got my message."

Dean shifted the cigar in his mouth and fixed Hank with a

surly glare. "Yeah, I got it. Haven't you got any better sense than to send a runny-nosed, ten-year-old kid to me with a written message? What if he'd decided to just throw it away? Or worse yet, what if he'd gotten curious, opened the thing, and read it? Sometimes, Hank, I don't know if you've got half a brain."

"Don't be so high and mighty," countered the younger brother. "It was the best thing I could think of at the moment. Besides, the kid delivered it, didn't he? *Without* openin' it. I figured you'd want to know about Billy gettin' killed."

Dean's voice was as shrill as the scrape of a file against metal. "Of course I'd want to know about Billy getting killed. He was my brother too, Hank! Maybe it didn't dawn on you that I might like to be there when he was buried."

"Well, I thought—"

"You thought what?"

"I thought you had your hands full here and wouldn't have time."

Dean was red from throat to forehead. "Where'd you bury him?"

"In a grove about ten miles south of here."

"Okay, so our little brother is dead and buried, Hank...but I've got a bone to pick with you."

"About what?" Hank's own ice-blue eyes narrowed. He stood two inches taller than his older brother and outweighed him by fifty pounds.

"Your stupidity! How dim-witted can you get? You followed that driver and shotgunner right into the church and killed them!"

"And what was I supposed to do? Them two killed our little brother, Dean! They had it comin'."

"Yeah? Well, what about that preacher? He didn't have anything to do with killing Billy. Why'd you have to gun him down? Especially right in front of his whole congregation?"

The other outlaws stood in silence, wondering if the Foster brothers were going to come to blows.

"He got in my way! Man gets in my way, it's his own fault if he gets a bullet in the gut."

"He wouldn't have gotten in your way if you hadn't pulled such a stupid stunt in the first place! You go plumb crazy when you lose your temper, and you don't use your head at all! Your hair-trigger temper is messing up my plan!"

Hank and his men knew how carefully Dean had planned to take over the entire town of Lander. Kidnapping and murdering Ted Hrdlicka and buying the bank from his widow was only the first step in his scheme. The Bank of Lander held mortgages on most of the businesses in town, giving Dean Foster control over them if they defaulted on the loans. The bank also held mortgages on most of the homes. Since Lander had become the main stopping place for travelers crossing Wyoming, there was money to be made, and plenty of it.

Dean's cunning plan had been to covertly bring Hank and his cohorts into Lander and use them to slowly drain the merchants' assets through burglaries, robberies, and ransoms for kidnappings. This activity would go on until the merchants were unable to make their mortgage payments. Dean would buy them out one by one. Those whose businesses were not mortgaged at the Bank of Lander would be frightened into selling out and leaving. Soon the town and its potential wealth would be Dean Foster's.

Hank fought off the anger pushing through him, sparked by his brother's accusing words, and said calmly, "I'm sorry for messin' up your plan, Dean. I...well, I loved Billy an awful lot, and some-thin' inside me just had to have revenge on those two for killin' him. I wasn't thinkin' about all those people seein' my face and the faces of my boys, here. Guess if you want to take a poke at me, I've got it comin'."

Dean sighed. "Good as it'd make me feel, Hank, it wouldn't solve anything. I'll just have to change my tactics now."

"What're you gonna do?"

"Take over the town by compulsion. You and your boys here

will become my enforcers." He paused, shifted the soggy cigar to the other side of his mouth, and said, "I can't put the operation into effect, though, without more enforcers. With enough men to control the people of this town by fear, we'll charge the merchants protection fees, like those gangs back in New York do. Pretty soon they'll get discouraged, sell out to me, and leave town."

"Where you gonna get more enforcers, Dean?" Reed asked.

"They're around. You boys are gonna split up and go on some recruiting missions for me. Hank will stay here. It'll take you boys a week or better to garner me six or eight more men. When they hear how much I'll pay them, you won't have any problem getting them to come with you."

"So when do we start, boss?" asked Reggie Atkins.

"Tomorrow. There are men who know me down south in Green River City and Rawlins...and over in Laramie City and Cheyenne City. Come with me to the den, and I'll make the assignments."

The men followed the Foster brothers to the den, where Dean wrote down the names of potential recruits. He distributed them to Reed, Wurth, and Cole. Then to Atkins, he said, "Reggie, I've got a special mission for you. I'm sending you to Denver."

"Denver? Who's in Denver?"

"A man who was my cellmate when I was in prison down in Brownsville, Texas. He's supposed to be walking straight, now...married and all that stuff. But I think for the right price, he'll dump the woman and come with you. His name's Virgil Cullen."

Dean wrote Cullen's name on a slip of paper. Handing it to Atkins, he looked around at the others and said, "If these men have some pals who want to pick up some generous wages, bring them along. I wouldn't care if we had another dozen men."

Hank rubbed the back of his neck and said, "Big brother, what're we gonna do about the marshal? Morgan ain't gonna go along with your protection plan. He can't be bought, either. You know that."

"I've already thought about him," nodded Dean. "Jake's got to go."

"You got somebody in mind to replace him?"

"Yes. Our cousin, the almost-famous gunfighter."

"Clay?"

"Yep."

"But I hear he's pretty happy workin' for Charlie Westmore."

"Not as happy as he'll be working for me. I'm gonna offer him *double* what he's making with Westmore."

The outlaws exchanged wide-eyed glances. Noting it, Dean said, "And you boys are going to get a healthy raise too." As smiles spread over their rugged faces, Dean asked Atkins, "You know where Black Hawk is?"

"Sure. In the mountains west of Denver about thirty miles."

"Good. After you've recruited Cullen, I want you to ride up to Black Hawk. I'll write a letter for you to put in my cousin's hand. If I know Clay like I think I do, he'll come."

"With Morgan outta the way and Clay wearin' his badge, we'll be in control of Lander for sure," Hank chuckled.

"Clay'll be perfect for what I need," Dean said. "Sensible outlaws will stay clear of Lander, and Clay can keep the law honestly in this town." He paused, laughed, then said, "That is...to a point. He'll, of course, make things run smooth for me and my enforcers, no matter what we do!"

There was a round of laughter, then Hank asked, "So when do we get rid of Jake?"

"Not for a few days. The town needs him right now."

"I guess we could wait till Clay gets here."

Dean scratched at an ear. "Well-l-l...I don't know, Hank. You know how Clay is. He really doesn't go for murder. I hope maybe we can get him over that. But since you'll be staying here, I want you to take care of Jake two or three days before we expect Reggie to come riding in here with Clay and Virgil. And I want you to make it look like an accident. Clay might get hot if he thinks we killed Jake. I'll tell him I offered Jake a couple thousand dollars to move on to some other town. He was going to stay on till Clay got here...and then accidentally got killed. So you've got to make sure it looks like an accident, Hank."

Hank grinned. "Don't worry, big brother. I can handle it."

Dean clapped his hands together and headed for the liquor cabinet. While pouring whiskey in glasses, he said, "This calls for a celebration, boys. We're going to put a stranglehold on the citizens of this town and rule them with fear." As he handed a glass to each man, he added, "Some of them no doubt will pack up and leave, but most of them will have no choice but to stay. Once I own all the businesses in Lander, things will settle down, and everyone can live happily ever after." *Especially me,* he told himself. *I'm going to be the richest man in Wyoming.*

At Kansas City, Missouri, thirty-nine-year-old David Thacker left the Methodist bishop's office with a spring in his step and a smile on his face. The sun was shining brightly, but it had never seemed so bright as it did on that day. He jumped in his buggy, gave the reins a gentle snap, and put the horse to a trot. He couldn't wait to get home and share the good news with Peggy.

Twenty minutes later, Thacker guided the buggy off the street onto the property of the Oak Avenue Methodist Church. He grinned as he passed the sign that contained his name as pastor of the church, and thought, *Not for long.*

He moved past the white frame church building with its high-pitched roof, stained-glass windows, and towering steeple, and approached the front of the parsonage. The white frame house, which blended with the church building, was situated at the rear of the property beneath a stand of tall oak trees. Spring's warm sunshine had transformed the buds on the branches into tiny green leaves. Thacker told himself he wouldn't be there long enough to see them grow into their fullness this year.

Bounding from the buggy, he quickly tied the horse to the hitching post and headed for the porch. The parlor door was standing open behind the screen door, and before he had even reached it, he started calling, "Peggy! Honey! Peggy!"

There was no response as he moved inside the house. Hurriedly, he walked through the dining room into the kitchen, calling his wife's name, and noticed the back door was standing open. At the same time, he heard Peggy say from the back yard, "I'm out here, darling!"

Thacker rushed outside and saw Peggy at the clothesline, hanging up the wash. Running to her, he said excitedly, "I was right, honey! The Lord answered my prayer!"

Peggy finished pinning one of their son's shirts to the line and turned to meet him, smiling. "Really? Oh, David, you're not kidding me?"

Peggy knew her husband had long wanted to go to the Wild West and help tame it by preaching the gospel. Though she had some reservations about taking their fifteen-year-old son and twin thirteen-year-old daughters to the far away frontier, she would not share them with her husband. She would follow him wherever he felt God was leading him in his ministry.

"No kidding, here, sweetheart. Bishop Ames and the Advisory Board have just assigned me to the Lander Methodist Church in Lander, Wyoming!"

"Wyoming," Peggy repeated in a half-whisper. "No wonder you're excited."

Wrapping her in his arms, he kissed her cheek, held her close, and said, "Oh, I know you and the kids will love it, honey. Just think of it! Wyoming! Wide-open spaces, a bigger sky than we've ever seen, and a chance to begin our lives anew where I'll really have a challenge. Frontiersmen! Pioneers! Mountain men!"

Yes, she thought, *and gamblers, gunfighters, and outlaws.* "It'll be quite a challenge, all right, darling. How soon do we leave?"

"Well, Bishop Ames wants me to leave tomorrow."

"Tomorrow?" she gasped, drawing back to look him in the eye. "There's no way we can be ready to leave by tomorrow."

"Not we, Peggy. Me."

"I don't understand."

"Well, the pastor in Lander died quite suddenly, and the people are without a leader. Bishop Ames wants me to go immediately. You and the kids can come in a few weeks, once you've tied up all the loose ends here."

"Oh—I see. But...what about our church here?"

"Bishop Ames said he would appoint an interim pastor until a permanent one can be assigned."

Peggy nodded. "The railroad doesn't go beyond Denver, does it?"

"No."

"Can you get to Lander by stagecoach?"

"You and the kids will. According to the bishop, there's a stage route from Denver to Cheyenne City. Another stage goes from there to Douglas, then another one yet goes from Douglas to Lander. I'll be needing a horse in Lander anyway, so I'll just buy one in Denver, then ride straight for Lander from there. It's about three hundred miles."

"Maybe you'd better take the stage and buy a horse in Lander."

"I would, honey, but I can get there much faster on a horse...and from what the bishop said, they need me there as soon as possible."

"I wish you didn't have to ride that wild country alone."

"I won't be alone," David said. "The Lord will be with me."

"How can I argue with that?" she smiled. Then, soberly, "Do you know what caused the pastor's sudden death?"

"I don't know, honey. Bishop Ames didn't say."

Reverend David Thacker arrived in Denver on Thursday, April 14. Asking at the depot for directions to the nearest stable, he carried his two pieces of luggage four blocks and entered the hostler's shack. The young hostler looked up as David came through the door. "Howdy, Reverend. What can I do for you?" The hostler had been carving on a piece of wood and shavings clung to the front of his shirt and pants.

"How do you know I'm a preacher?" asked Thacker, returning the hostler's grin.

"Well, only two kinds of fellers dress in black like you...especially with a flat-crowned hat, frock coat, and string tie. Gamblers or preachers. You just don't have the gambler look to you, so I told myself, here's a preacher."

"Excellent perception," nodded Thacker. "I need to buy a good horse. I have to ride it all the way to Lander, Wyoming."

"I don't carry anything *but* good horses, Reverend. C'mon. Let's go out back. You can leave your luggage here till you're ready to go. I assume you'll want a bridle and saddle, too."

"Oh, yes, of course. I did neglect to say that, didn't I?"

It took Thacker only minutes to pick out a long-legged sorrel mare. When she was saddled and the two pieces of luggage were tied on behind, the hostler opened the corral gate and Thacker led the horse through the gate and toward the street.

The hostler hurriedly closed the gate and drew up as the preacher was settling in the saddle. Looking up at him, he asked, "You say you're goin' to Lander?"

"That's right."

"That's a good three-four days' ride. I don't see a bedroll or any food."

"Won't need them. I've got my route marked out on a map in my small bag, here. I'll spend tonight in Loveland, then cut northwest and head toward Rawlins. I plan to skirt the southern tip of the Medicine Bow Mountains, so I should make pretty good time. If I see I can't make it to Rawlins by dark tomorrow night, I'll put in at Swan or Warm Springs."

"Smart thinkin'. A little plannin' can save a fella some money."

"Man in my profession has to do all the saving he can," Thacker laughed.

"So I figure you'll cut around the Sweetwater Mountains the next day, and stay at South Pass City for the night, then ride on up to Lander the next day."

"That's the way I've got it planned," nodded the preacher. "Well, I best be going."

"So long, Reverend," said the hostler, giving him a friendly wave.

Early the next afternoon, Thacker was making good time when he reached the southern tip of the Medicine Bow Mountains in Wyoming. Leaning forward in the saddle, he patted the mare's neck and said, "We're doing fine, girl. If we can keep up the pace after I let you take this breather, we'll make it to Rawlins by dark...or at least not long afterward."

It was then that Thacker noticed the dark clouds coming over the distant mountains from the west. Within a half hour, the clouds covered the sky. Another thirty minutes brought lightning, flashing blue-white and silent overhead, followed by deep-rumbling thunder.

When raindrops began to fall, he started looking around for shelter. The black, swirling clouds were coming lower, and so was the lightning. He spotted a rock formation with a large overhang some two hundred yards due north. It was high enough and deep enough to give both rider and horse shelter.

A jagged bolt split the air overhead, missing Thacker and his mount by not more than fifty feet. The mare fought her bit and danced in a circle. Thacker knew he must get his frightened horse to the rock overhang as quickly as possible. Gouging the sorrel's sides with his heels, he put her into a gallop straight for the rock formation through a grove of huge cottonwood trees.

Suddenly lightning struck a tree just ahead of him with a deafening crash. The mare reared and screamed in fright, falling backward. Thacker tried to get his feet out of the stirrups before the thirteen-hundred-pound animal fell on him. He was almost free when the sorrel came down hard on her back. His left foot was snagged in the stirrup, and his leg took the full impact of her weight as he hit the ground hard, landing on his left shoulder. A sharp splinter of pain shot upward from his ankle to his hip. His head began to spin.

Thacker heard the mare whinny and felt her weight leave his leg. He was barely aware of the sound of the horse galloping away amid the roar of thunder, then his body went numb and darkness closed in.

The sun was shining through a curtained window when David Thacker opened his eyes. He blinked and rolled his head against the pillow beneath him. The window was open slightly and the morning breeze toyed with the curtain.

Thacker pulled his right hand out from under the covers and brushed away the hair that dangled over his forehead. When he tried to bring his left arm out, he found he could not move it. Then he discovered that he could not move his left leg.

Panic set in. *Where am I? What hap—*

Then it came to him. The electrical storm, the sorrel mare rearing, the pain in his left leg.

Someone had picked him up and taken him to a cabin. Smooth, grooved logs made up the walls. He was aware of voices in another room. Listening closely, he could tell the voices belonged to a man and a woman. Who were they? How had they found him? What had they done to his arm and leg?

Thacker raised his head, pulled the cover away from his left arm, and saw that it was in a sling and bound tight against his chest. He could recall nothing about any pain in his arm. Lifting the covers back further and rising to a sitting position, he saw that his leg was splinted and wrapped tightly with what looked like a torn sheet.

A wave of dizziness washed over him. He knew he needed to lie down again before it got worse. As he put his head on the pillow, he heard light footsteps, and the door creaked open. His head was spinning, but he looked and saw a middle-aged woman with graying hair smile at him. Before coming further into the room, she called over her shoulder, "Will! He's awake!"

Her long skirt swished as she hurried to the bed. "Good morning, Reverend Thacker. I imagine you're feeling awfully weak, aren't you?"

Above the sound of the woman's voice, Thacker could hear other footsteps. Then a man appeared, standing beside her. He was a little older than she; Thacker guessed in his late fifties.

"Yes, ma'am," Thacker replied, finding his mouth dry as a sand pit. "I...I'm awfully weak, all right. I—" Then it struck him that she had called him by name. "How...how do you know my name?"

The man picked up an envelope off the bedstand and said, "We found this letter from a Bishop Emory Ames of Kansas City in one of your bags. It wasn't sealed, so we took the liberty of looking at it."

"Oh, of course, the letter," nodded Thacker.

"So we assume you're on your way from Kansas City to Lander."

"Yes."

"Well, I guess we should introduce ourselves. I'm Will Hawkins, and this is my wife, Edie."

"I'm pleased to meet you," said Thacker, his dizziness subsiding. "How did you find me? Did you see my horse? Where—"

"Whoa, slow down," said Hawkins. "I'll explain it all to you in a moment, but would you like something to eat first? It's been nearly twenty-four hours since we picked you up and brought you home."

Thacker suddenly realized he was hungry and said that he would like something to eat. Edie told her husband to go ahead and explain how they found him while she prepared him some food.

Will sat down and said, "It was like this, Reverend. Yesterday Edie and me went to Rawlins for supplies, and we got caught in that awful storm. We were dashing for shelter under a rock overhang when we saw lightning strike off to our right. That's when we saw you being thrown from your horse."

David vaguely remembered seeing a farm wagon heading for the rock formation shortly before his horse fell on him.

Hawkins explained that he had been a medical assistant in the Union army during the Civil War. He was experienced in recognizing and treating broken bones. While the storm was lashing at them, they rushed to Thacker and put him in their wagon. Under the rock shelter, Hawkins examined Thacker and found that his left shoulder was dislocated and his collarbone broken. His left knee was severely sprained, but as far as Hawkins could tell, no bone had been broken.

Edie returned with a bowl of hot chicken soup, and while she fed it to the patient, Will told him that their place was in the western foothills of the Medicine Bow Mountains, too great a distance from Rawlins to have chanced trying in the midst of the storm to get him to a doctor. So they had brought him home and splinted and wrapped his injuries.

Thacker expressed his appreciation and said that as soon as possible, he would have to get another horse and be on his way to Lander. Hawkins smiled and told him it would be a while before he would be up to traveling. But when the time came, he and Edie would give him one of their horses so the members of Lander Methodist Church could have their new pastor.

C H A P T E R

SIXTEEN

On April 21, Chice Reed and Jim Wurth returned to Lander with seven hard-faced men they had recruited for Dean Foster. Foster was pleased to find that five of them were men he had hoped to include in his gang; the other two were strangers who had come along, enticed by the money. Stan Cole arrived the next day with three men, two of them friends of Foster's.

That same day, Marshal Jake Morgan was returning to Lander from high in the Wind River Mountains. He had pursued and arrested a rancher's son for getting drunk the night before and shooting up one of the town's saloons. The lawman and prisoner were riding along a narrow mountain road at the edge of a rocky precipice when they were caught in a sudden rockslide and swept over the cliff.

When the dust settled at the bottom of the canyon, Hank Foster stood high above the narrow road and smiled to himself. He had used a long iron bar to dislodge a boulder, and as the boulder tumbled down the mountainside, it had carried tons of rock with it. Hank returned to town unnoticed and waited for nature to take its course. When Marshal Morgan had not returned by the next morning, men who knew he had gone after the rancher's son rode out to look for them. Four hours later, they returned and reported that

Morgan and his prisoner had been killed in a rockslide.

The town council met immediately to discuss the need to find another marshal. Dean Foster knew it would take them a week or two at the least to locate and hire a new man. While the meeting was in session, he was behind his desk at the bank, laughing heartily with his brother. They had no doubt that Clay Austin would be arriving any day with Reggie Atkins. Once Clay was there, the Foster takeover would be put into action. Dean was hoping also that his old friend, Virgil Cullen, would be with Atkins.

On Sunday morning, April 24, Chester Platte announced to the congregation at the Lander Methodist Church that he had received a letter from Bishop Emory Ames on Friday. The letter stated that their new pastor was on his way. Platte gave them some background information about Reverend David Thacker and explained that he was coming alone so as to arrive as soon as possible. Bishop Ames estimated the new pastor would arrive sometime the week of April 17. His wife and children would follow a few weeks later.

Since it was now April 24, Platte assured the congregation that Thacker would surely be there to preach his first sermon the following Sunday. There was much excitement at the good news, and the people sang with great enthusiasm before Platte delivered the morning's sermon.

On Monday evening, Dean Foster was eating supper in a private room at the restaurant in the Wind River Hotel. With him were his brother Hank, Chice Reed, Jim Wurth, Stan Cole, and the ten unsavory characters Dean had added to his gang. When the meal was finished and the waitresses had cleared the table, the doors were closed so Foster and his men could have a private meeting. As the men smoked and drank expensive whiskey, Foster began to explain his scheme to take over the town. He was interrupted by a knock at the double doors.

Foster swore, looked toward the doors, and called loudly, "I told you people we didn't want to be disturbed!"

The door came open and the restaurant manager stuck his head in. "I'm sorry for this intrusion, Mr. Foster, but I have some men out here who insist on seeing you immediately. The one whose name is Reggie Atkins says you will want to see him and his friends."

Dean Foster rolled the cigar to the opposite side of his mouth and smiled. "By all means! Show them in!"

The manager swung the door open, ushered the four men in, and left. There was a hearty welcome from those who recognized the tall, slender form of gunfighter Clay Austin. Dean and Hank Foster left the table to shake hands with Clay, then Dean turned and greeted Virgil Cullen. A big, burly man stood with Cullen. Chewing on his soggy cigar, Dean asked, "And who's this husky fellow?"

"His name's Turk Dunphy, Dean. He's a friend of mine. Reggie said if anybody else wanted to join up, he was to bring 'em along."

Dean's brow was lined with thought as he shook hands with Dunphy. "Wait a minute. Dunphy...Dunphy...I know that name. Of course! You're a big-time bank robber. I'm plenty glad to have you, Turk." Dean laughed, then added, "That is...as long as you don't plan on robbing my bank!"

Everybody laughed, including Turk Dunphy.

When the laughter died down, Dean said, "I'm a little surprised that you'd want to be a part of this operation, Turk. Where's your gang?"

A deep scowl captured Dunphy's face. "They were wiped out durin' a robbery down in Denver."

"What happened? Townspeople arm themselves ahead of time?"

"Nope," grunted Dunphy. "One man did it."

"One man?"

"Yeah. Used two double-barreled shotguns. I'd lost a man down in Pueblo a few days before that, so I only had four left. This evil-eyed dude killed 'em all. One day I'll run onto him, and when I do, he's a dead man. In the meantime, the deal your man offered sounded purty good."

"Well, if you're a friend of Virgil's, you gotta be all right," Dean said. Then to Virgil, "I told Reggie if the money was right, you'd leave the old lady and come a-running. Sure glad you're here."

"Didn't have to leave her. She was puttin' up such a fuss over me hidin' Turk from the law, I had to send her packin'. She's been gone a couple weeks or better."

They chatted some more, then Dean made his way back to Clay Austin. Putting an arm around Clay's shoulder, he looked around and said, "I'm sure all you boys have heard of Clay Austin. He's some kind of gunfighter. Faster'n summer lightning, I'll tell you that much. Clay's going to be Lander's new marshal."

When introductions had been made all around, Dean Foster stood before his new gang and gave them the details of his plan to take over the town. The new gang members would be quartered in a large, two-story house he had just purchased from the heirs of an old man who had died last month. The house was located a block off the main street, near the center of the business section.

Under Dean's direction, the gang members would walk the streets of Lander and take care of anyone who rose up against the takeover. With Clay wearing the marshal's badge, none of the gang would be in trouble if they cracked some skulls or even had to kill a few men to convince the townsfolk they were under Foster rule.

The takeover would begin the next morning. Gang members would enter every place of business and offer "protection" for a weekly fee, the amount for each merchant to be set by Dean Foster. If anyone balked, the gang members were to smash up a few items in the store. Male proprietors who didn't fall in line were to be worked over. If any women showed resistance, the gang members were to break out windows, tear doors off their hinges, and in extreme cases, destroy all merchandise. They were to apply whatever pressure it took, within those limits, to bring the merchants into subjection. Hard cases were to be brought to Hank Foster. If Hank had any questions, he would take them to Dean.

Dean expected the takeover to arouse the wrath of the town council. He would demand a meeting with the council and there announce that they were no longer in control. He would have his gang members present in a show of strength. Once it was established that Foster and his men were in charge, he would announce that Clay Austin was Lander's new marshal. Austin would be there to protect the people of Lander from troublemakers. He would also be there to jail and prosecute all who defied the Foster regime.

By late afternoon the next day, the town of Lander, Wyoming, was in the iron grip of Dean Foster and his henchmen. Clay Austin wore the marshal's badge and was in command of the office and jail. A pall of gloom settled over the entire town. People milled about, filled with fear, not knowing what to do. There was talk that someone should ride to the U. S. Marshal's office in Denver. The idea was scrapped shortly after its birth, however, when Dr. Patrick O'Donnell warned that Dean Foster would probably track down and kill anyone who made the ride. In addition, there were not nearly enough deputy marshals to even begin to cover all the territory west of the Missouri River. It could be months or even years before Lander could get federal help. The good doctor's advice was to go along with Foster for the time being. Sooner or later, they would find a way to defeat him.

On Wednesday night, the Lander Methodist Church was packed to capacity. Foster wanted to show the people he was not all bad. He would allow them to have their church services. He wanted them to settle down and enjoy life...as long as their enjoyment didn't hurt his profits. Some of Foster's men stood around outside while the service was in progress, but they did not venture inside.

Chester Platte preached a brief message, encouraging everyone to trust the Lord to deliver them, even as He had delivered the

Israelites from their oppressors throughout the Old Testament. God would also give them a man to lead them in their time of oppression, even as He had given His people Moses and Joshua. When the people prayed, they thanked God for the man He was sending to be their new pastor...and they prayed earnestly that the Lord would deliver them from the hands of Dean Foster and his gang.

The next morning, Chice Reed and E.B. Snyder, one of Dean's new men, were on the street in front of the O'Donnell clinic. Katy O'Donnell was returning to the clinic from the general store. She greeted sad-faced people along the street with a smile and a cheery word, trying to lift their spirits. Suddenly Katy noticed Reed and Snyder in a confrontation with an elderly man named Jedediah Moore. The old man was yelling and waving his cane.

Katy, whose Irish ancestry kept her temper near the surface, was irritated. She knew they had done something to rile the usually docile old man. Stepping up, she asked, "What's the matter, Jedediah?"

The old man pounded the tip of his cane on the boardwalk and told her that Reed and Snyder had ordered him off the bench outside the clinic. Several benches stood along the boardwalks on both sides of Lander's main street. The elderly citizens of the town loved to sit and talk of old times. Most of them had their favorite bench and their favorite friends to sit and chat with.

The Irish lass's eyes flashed at the two outlaws. "So what's wrong with him sitting on this bench?" she demanded.

"New rule, ma'am," Reed replied. "No loitering allowed. If you'll check the other benches along the street, you'll see they're unoccupied."

Katy glanced up and down the street. "Just who came up with this stupid rule? The elderly folk in this town have been sitting on these benches as long as I can remember."

"That *stupid* rule, as you call it," came a voice from behind her, "has been established by Mr. Dean Foster."

Katy pivoted to locate the owner of the voice. He was a lanky, square-jawed man not more than three or four years older than she. He had dark-brown hair and eyes. His long sideburns fanned out at his jaw line, and he wore a well-trimmed mustache. A town marshal's badge was pinned to his vest, and he wore his gun low and tied down.

Looking him up and down, Katy said with disdain, "So you're the new marshal."

The man touched the brim of his hat and replied, "Marshal Clay Austin at your service, ma'am. And you are—?"

"My name is Katy O'Donnell. My father is Dr. Patrick O'Donnell. This is his clinic...and I'm his nurse. Now, what's this nonsensical rule that your Mr. Foster has come up with?"

"Mr. Foster believes that loitering leads to vagrancy, Miss O'Donnell. There are too many stumblebums passing through town. Mr. Foster wants them to do just that...pass on through. He feels if they see other people loitering, they'll stop and do the same. So...it's my job to enforce the rules Mr. Foster establishes."

People were passing by, observing Katy's petulant countenance and admiring her spunk.

"Well, let me tell you something, *Marshal* Austin. It so happens that this bench is the property of the O'Donnell Clinic. You have no jurisdiction over it." Turning to the old man, she said, "Jedediah, you can sit on this bench any time you wish."

Jedediah gave Austin and the two henchmen a nervous glance, said "Thank you, Miss Katy" to the fiery redhead, and sat down.

Katy sat with him and said, "Any of your friends who want to sit with you are welcome to do it."

Austin stepped close and said, "Ma'am, you're making my job difficult."

She met his gaze head-on and snapped, "Then quit your job! These two look like they're fog-brained enough to work for that skunk, but you strike me as a man with more sense than that. How did you get hooked up with him?"

The faces of Reed and Snyder turned beet-red at her insult.

Austin saw it, and said, "You boys go on with your patrol. I'll handle Miss O'Donnell."

"Well, what do we do with these benches?" Snyder asked. "What if others are privately owned?"

"I'll talk to Dean about it. Just make your rounds. Don't bother with the benches till I can talk to him."

The outlaws nodded, gave Katy surprised looks, and walked away. People standing near applauded and cheered her. For the moment, at least, she had won.

Austin looked back at Katy and said, "Let me warn you, little lady. It isn't smart to defy Mr. Foster."

"I'm not afraid of Dean Foster, *Marshal* Austin. He breathes like the rest of us, walks on his feet, sees with his eyes, hears with his ears, and feels with his hands. He's a mere human. He's built his throne real high for himself. Only problem is, when he falls, it's a long way down."

Austin would not show it, but he was captivated by Katy's spirit and striking beauty. He could only stand there and listen. When she wheeled without another word and entered the clinic, he glared at the people who applauded her as if she were an actress walking off stage after a stunning performance. Left off balance, he quietly walked away.

Katy entered the clinic and found her father at a front window in the waiting room. He had been watching the incident outside. She glanced at him, then moved through the door into the examining and treatment room and set the items she had purchased down on the cupboard.

O'Donnell moved up behind her and said, "I declare, daughter, the older you get, the more you're like your mother. I think she gave you plenty of her spunk."

"Really?" she said, turning to face him. "Well, since you were watching the whole thing, maybe you should have come out there and shown a little spunk of your own."

"I was about to come out at first," grinned the good doctor, "but you handled it so well, I figured whatever I could do would be anticlimactic." Taking her in his arms, he said, "I'm proud of you, honey. You left that cocksure so-called marshal with nothing to say."

Hugging her father's neck, Katy said, "Oh, Daddy, something's got to be done about these awful men. I saw Mrs. Benton at the general store. She told me they're leaving Lander tomorrow...and that Frank Wythe and his family are going with them."

"I'm sorry to hear that," sighed O'Donnell, releasing her. "I found out while you were gone that three other families are planning to leave."

"How can they do it, Daddy? I mean...just pack up and leave their land and homes?"

"Most people in this town won't be able to leave. The ones you just named and the ones I heard about—the Wilsons, the Hamms, and Tracys—are well off and can afford to move. But the rest of our good citizens are going to have to stay and ride this thing out."

"I wish the others would stay and ride it out, too," Katy said wistfully. "The Lord is going to take care of Dean Foster and his scum. He may not do it as quickly as we would like, but I know He'll do it."

O'Donnell smiled and playfully cuffed his daughter on the chin. "That's the spirit, sweetheart. I agree. It's going to be okay. We just need to trust the Lord and let Him handle it."

At the Lander Wood Shop and Funeral Parlor, carpenter and undertaker Coye Coffman was gluing struts in a chair at his workbench when the door came open and two men stepped in. A chill rippled over him when he saw who they were. Jim Wurth and Turk Dunphy had been there three days earlier to collect the week's "protection" money. Coffman was short on cash and told them he would not have the money until he received payment for some furniture he had built.

Coffman continued his work as the two men approached

him. Without looking up, he said, "I don't have the money."

Dunphy brushed against him and growled, "We told you to go collect it from your customers, little man. Why didn't you?"

"I...I tried, but they don't have the money right now to pay me."

"Three customers?" Dunphy said incredulously. "*Three* customers and none of 'em paid you?"

"Yes, that's right," nodded Coffman, dipping the tip of a strut in a can of glue on his bench. With shaky fingers he placed it in it's predrilled hole. "It's hard enough keeping food on the table for my wife and four children without having to pay you people too. You and your banker boss are being very unreasonable."

Dunphy looked at Coffman with undimmed hostility. "We don't want your opinion of what's reasonable or unreasonable, Coffman! We want our money! Now let's have it!"

Fear rose up and became a solid, palpable thing inside Coye Coffman. His lips quivered as he replied, "How can I give you money I don't have?"

Dunphy's big right hand flashed out and gripped Coffman by the throat. "Maybe you need some incentive to go out and collect what's owed you so you can pay us!" As he spoke, Dunphy slapped Coffman several times. When he let go of him, Coffman's nose was bleeding and blood was oozing form a wide split in his upper lip. Then Dunphy threw the little man on the floor, picked up the unfinished chair, and smashed it to pieces on the bench. He grabbed the can of glue, held it over Coffman's head, and poured glue in his hair.

"We'll be very reasonable, Mr. Coffman," Dunphy said. "You've got till Monday. Of course, you'll owe us two weeks' fees by then, so you better be ready to pay us in full...or else. Get my message?"

"Yes," nodded the little man, wiping blood from his nose and lip.

When the outlaws were gone, Coye Coffman groped his way

to his feet and headed for Dr. O'Donnell's office. His lip needed stitching. He didn't know what he would do about the glue in his hair.

Clay Austin was at his desk when the door burst open and Katy stomped in. Austin rose to his feet. Katy's eyes flashed as she moved up to the desk. "Are you wearing that badge for show, or do you mean to be lawman in this town?"

"What's happened now, Miss O'Donnell?"

Katy pointed in the direction of the O'Donnell clinic and said heatedly, "I just helped my father stitch up a horrible cut on Coye Coffman's lip. His nose was bleeding, and right now my father is trying to get glue out of Coye's hair! What kind of animals are you hooked up with, Marshal Austin? I hear you're some kind of hot-shot gunfighter. I don't have a lot of respect for gunfighters, but from what I know about them, they aren't brow-beating bullies who pick on helpless people."

"Well, I—"

"If you're not man enough to handle this situation, you ought to take that badge off."

"Well, I—"

"It's bad enough for the merchants of this town to have to pay that so-called protection fee, but even Dean Foster can't get blood out of a turnip! Coye Coffman is struggling just to keep food on the table for his family and a roof over their head."

"Miss O'Donnell, I—"

"He makes a decent living when people pay him, but his wife has consumption and he's had a lot of medical expenses. Daddy doesn't charge him anything for his services, but medicines do cost, and we have to charge for them."

"Look, I—"

"How can you be a part of this wickedness? Do you know that five families are packing up to leave, just because of Dean

Foster? How do you sleep at night? Is the money that crook pays you really *that* good? I see you shave—I'll bet you do it without a mirror. If you had any conscience at all, you wouldn't be able to look yourself in the face every morning knowing what kind of hellish scheme you're a part of!"

"If you'll just—"

Katy O'Donnell's words continued to come rapid-fire. It made Clay Austin think of a Gatling gun.

"If I were a man, *Marshal* Austin, and wore that badge, I'd arrest those two ruffians, lock them up in jail, and throw the key in the Popo Agie. On second thought, I'd put them in burlap sacks and throw *them* in the river! Or better yet, I'd make them pay for the damage they did to Coye's property, make them both drink a can of glue, *then* throw them in the Popo Agie. But you're the man here...and you're the marshal. Or maybe I'm wrong."

Clay Austin was overwhelmed by the fiery spirit of Katy O'Donnell, and taken by her beauty. He had not noticed Dean Foster start to enter the marshal's office, then slip back and stay out of sight while he listened through the open door to the one-sided conversation.

While Katy stood glaring at Austin, waiting for an answer, Foster stepped inside. Austin's features lost color. Katy saw it and noted that he was looking behind her. Making a half turn, she laid blazing eyes on Foster and without blinking, asked, "So how much of this conversation did you hear, Mr. Foster?"

"Enough to know that you've got a big mouth, girlie."

Undaunted, Katy shot back, "Well, I hope you heard enough to know that I think you're a swindler. You're worse than those two animals that beat up on Coye. You wouldn't dirty your hands, but you'd pay them to do it!"

"You're big mouth is going to get you into a heap of trouble, lass, so you'd better shut up! I'm running things in this town, and my men will do as I tell them. If that gets under your skin, it's just too bad."

Katy remained immobile, resisting Foster with every fiber of her being. Jerking her head toward Austin, she said to the banker, "Your badge toter, here, disappoints me. I've always been taught to respect the man behind a badge. Well, since he's one of your puppets and dances on your string, I don't have to respect what's behind that badge, because it isn't a man."

Katy's words pierced Clay Austin like burning arrows. He swallowed hard but did not speak.

Katy took two steps toward Foster and stopped. Looking him straight in the eye, she hissed, "And as for you, mister...have fun while you play your high and mighty game as king of Lander, because it's not going to last long."

Katy started past Foster. Face beet-red, he seized her by the arm and jerked her around. "How can you be so sure my being—as you put it—king of Lander won't last long? You know something I don't?"

"Let's just say I know *someone* you don't know."

Squeezing hard on her arm, he snapped, "What are you talking about? Is there somebody involved in this town I don't know about?"

"You weren't listening," Katy said, jerking her arm loose from his grasp. "I didn't say you didn't know *about* Him. I said you don't know Him."

"Who?" demanded Foster, grabbing her arm again.

Katy surprised him by breaking his hold a second time. "The God who said, *Though thou shalt exalt thyself as the eagle, and though thou set thy nest among the stars, thence will I bring thee down.* You haven't gotten quite that high, Foster, but when He does bring you down, it'll break your stiff neck."

Foster's right hand lashed out and stung her cheek with an open palm.

Austin rushed forward, saying, "Dean, stop it! There's no need for that. You told all of us we weren't—"

"I didn't know we'd have a wench with such a big mouth."

"Well, I don't want this kind of thing going on," said Austin. "Don't hit her again."

Katy wanted to rub her stinging cheek, but wouldn't give Foster the satisfaction. Looking up at Austin, she said, "Thank you, Marshal. Maybe there's a spark of manhood in you after all." With that, she wheeled and moved out the door.

When Katy was gone, Austin said, "Dean, there's got to be a better way to bring these people into line than what Jim and Turk did to that undertaker...or even what you did just now."

Foster settled his flat gaze on the taller man. "You're soft, Clay. You may be a cool-handed gunfighter, but if you're going to make it big in this life, you'd better learn to shoot sometimes when the other man's gun is still in its holster."

Hardly hearing his cousin's words, Austin looked toward the open door. "She's some kind of woman, Dean. You gotta admit that."

"Yeah...some kind of woman. Religious fanatic is what she is. So God's going to bring me down and break my stiff neck, eh? That'll be the day."

CHAPTER

SEVENTEEN

Sunday, May 1, came and the members of Lander Methodist Church were still without a pastor. Chester Platte preached from Isaiah 40:31—*"They that wait upon the LORD shall renew their strength: they shall mount up with wings as eagles; they shall run, and not be weary; and they shall walk, and not faint."* Platte encouraged the congregation to wait upon the Lord for their new pastor to arrive and for deliverance from the oppression of the Dean Foster gang. A special prayer meeting was held after the service to ask God for the courage to wait upon Him.

Before dismissing the people, Platte—having been urged by Katy O'Donnell to do so—brought up Coye Coffman's beating on Thursday and his need for financial help to pay Foster's protection fees. Platte said that since the Lord would soon answer their prayers and deliver the town of the Foster blight, it was best for every merchant to pay the fee, though the whole thing was wicked and unfair. A special offering was taken for Coffman and, through tears, he and his wife thanked the people for their generosity.

It was midmorning on Monday when Dr. Patrick O'Donnell and his daughter were laboring over a patient on the examining table. Footsteps were heard in the outer room, followed by a tap on the door.

"I hope it's not more of this," said the doctor, nodding toward his patient. "See who it is, Katy."

Katy crossed the room and opened the door. Marshal Clay Austin looked down at her, smiling, and touched the brim of his hat. "Mornin', Miss Katy."

Katy only stared at him blandly.

Austin cleared his throat. "I thought I'd drop by and let you know that after arguin' with Dean ever since that incident with Jedediah Moore, I finally convinced him to throw out that rule about people not sittin' on the benches. That problem is over with."

"Good." Then motioning behind her, she asked, "What about this problem?"

Austin looked past her to the man on the examining table. He recognized Lander's blacksmith, Vernon Roper. His face was a puffy mass of cuts and bruises. Austin stepped around Katy and crossed the room. Dr. O'Donnell had taken stitches in three places and was now smearing salve on the man's battered face.

"Who did this, Vernon?" Austin asked.

Speaking past swollen lips, Roper said, "Wurth and Dunphy. It's been festerin' in me for a week about havin' to pay that rotten protection fee. When they came into my shop an hour ago to collect, it was just more than I could stand. I told 'em I wasn't givin' 'em any more money. They started roughin' me up. I clobbered Wurth, but Dunphy hit me with a two-by-four. I went down, then both of 'em beat me till I passed out. When I came to, they were gone, and so was all my money. They broke into my cash box and cleaned it out."

"Was there more in the cash box than you owed for the week's fee?"

Roper's puffy eyes flashed. "My fee is twenty-five dollars. There was more'n eighty dollars in that box."

"Well, Marshal, are you going to get Vernon's money back?" Katy asked.

Austin nervously rubbed the back of his neck. "I'll talk to Dean."

"Why do you have to talk to Dean?" pressed Dr. O'Donnell. "Why don't you arrest those thieves? What's that badge for?"

"Well, Doctor, you don't quite understand. You see—"

"Oh, Daddy understands all right. And so do I. You don't own the badge; Dean Foster does. You're just his little puppet. You have to talk to Foster because he's the law in this town, not you. Vernon has been beaten and robbed, but you won't do anything about it but kiss Foster's boots. How do you sleep at night, *Marshal?*"

Austin's face was growing red. Suddenly there were rapid footsteps in the outer room, then an elderly citizen of the town appeared, face pale, and gasped, "Marshal, you gotta come! There's real trouble!"

"What is it?" asked Austin, heading toward him.

"Some drifters are out there on the street about to pound Chester Platte to a pulp!"

Austin dashed out the door. The old man and Katy followed.

Chester Platte was in front of his barber shop in a heated argument with three tough-looking drifters, who had obviously been drinking. People were looking on, wide-eyed and fearful. The window of Platte's shop had been smashed, and there was glass on the boardwalk and inside the shop. Katy and the old man joined the onlookers as Austin drew up and cut into the harsh words flying between Platte and the drifters.

"What's going on here?" boomed the marshal.

The drifters turned and regarded Austin with disdain. Before one of them could speak, Chester blurted, "These men broke my window, Austin. I was shaving Benjamin Hanks, and all of a sudden, here were these three saddlebums in front of the shop, each daring the other to kick in the window."

Hanks was standing in the open door of the shop with a chair cloth tied around his neck and lather on half of his face.

Eyeing the troublemakers, Austin asked, "Which one did it?"

"The one in the middle, Marshal," spoke up Hanks. "Once

he'd kicked the glass and got it started, the other two started kicking pieces out that were clinging to the frame."

"I ran out here and demanded they pay for the damages," Chester said, "and they started swearing at me, saying they would do no such thing. They told me I should go back inside and shut up, or they'd beat me to a pulp."

Austin considered the drifters in contemptuous silence, then he said, "You're going to pay Mr. Platte for the damage, then you're going to get on your cayuses and ride out of town."

The drifter in the middle laughed in a harsh, grating sound. "Now, Mr. Lawman, you shouldn't talk like that unless you're ready to back it up."

Clay Austin's voice was as cold as his eyes. "I can back up my words, mister. Don't make me prove it." Without taking his gaze from the trio, he said, "What's it cost for a new window, Chester? You'll need to figure in the clean-up, too."

"Be about thirty dollars for the window, Marshal. And...ah...let's say five for the cleanup."

The middle drifter, who seemed to be the leader, pulled himself upright, jutted his jaw, and rasped, "We ain't payin' it." As he spoke, he let his hand drop slowly and hover over his gun.

The crowd began to draw back.

Austin's voice was flat, emotionless. "Oh, yes you are."

The leader began backtracking into the street, fixing Austin with eyes like cold slate. As his cronies sided him, he said, "You'll have to take all three of us, lawman. Think you're that good?"

Looking around at the onlookers, Clay said, "You folks get out of here."

While people were scattering, Austin looked back at the drifters just in time to see them going for their guns. His own weapon seemed to leap from the holster into his hand and fire of its own will. The drifter in the middle took the slug directly through the heart. His gun never came into firing position. While he was falling, Austin fanned his hammer, unleashing rapid-fire shots on the other two. The two drifters' guns roared. There was the breath of a bullet on Austin's right cheek as it hummed by, and he felt a burning in his upper left arm.

The drifter to his right was flat on his back, and the one to his left was on his knees with a surprised look on his face. His gun was in the dust in front of him, and he was clutching his chest. The drifter worked his jaw in a soundless effort to speak, then fell heavily to the ground, his face buried in an inch of dust.

As the gun smoke slowly drifted away on the morning breeze, the crowd regathered. Austin holstered his gun, then bent over the dead drifters and began rifling through their pockets. Blood was soaking the left sleeve of his shirt.

Abruptly, Katy was at his side. Eyeing the bloody sleeve, she said, "Marshal, that was a fine thing you did there...but you're wounded."

"I'll be all right, ma'am," he replied, continuing his search for money.

Katy bent down, took hold of the sleeve, and said, "You're bleeding profusely. You need to let Daddy take care of it."

Austin found what he was looking for and said, "As soon as I give this money to Chester."

Katy followed while he went to Chester, handed him a wad of bills and some gold coins, and said, "There's over a hundred dollars here. Take out your thirty-five and give the rest to Coye Coffman as payment for buryin' the drifters."

Dean Foster suddenly appeared, shoving his way through the crowd with Hank by his side.

"Listen up, everybody!" shouted the banker. "What you just witnessed was the great Clay Austin in action. Now, what did I tell you? Clay'll protect the people of this town as a good marshal is supposed to do. Remember what happened here. It was a Dean Foster man who protected Mr. Platte. If you'll all cooperate, you'll be glad to be a part of the new Lander."

"How about Vernon Roper?" piped up a middle-aged man in

the crowd. "It was Dean Foster men who beat him to a bloody pulp! He's bein' patched up in Doc O'Donnell's office right now."

"I'm already patched up, Clem," came Roper's voice as he moved into the street from the clinic.

Foster shot him a piercing glance, then looked back at the man who had spoken out. "Mr. Roper didn't cooperate, sir. Like I said, if you'll all cooperate, you'll be glad to be a part of the new Lander."

Roper drew closer to Dean, his eyes flashing fire, and Hank moved in front of him, forcing him to stop.

"Outta my way, Hank! I want to talk to your brother."

"You'll have to go through me to do it."

Vernon Roper felt a hand on his shoulder. It was Dr. O'Donnell. "Let it lie, Vern. It'll only get worse if you push it."

Roper fixed Hank with a hard look, then slowly turned away.

"Daddy, Marshal Austin's been wounded," Katy said. "I think you should take a look at him."

Dr. O'Donnell and Katy escorted Austin to the clinic and had him lie down on the examining table to treat his wound. While they worked, the physician asked Austin what caused him to become a gunfighter. Katy listened intently as Clay told his story. Before he turned twenty, he twice had to pull his gun to protect helpless, innocent people from outlaws.

He quickly learned that he had a natural ability with his gun. In the second incident, he had unknowingly outdrawn and killed a well-known gunslick. Shortly thereafter, he was challenged by an up-and-coming gunfighter named Whip Farr. He killed Farr and his reputation grew. More challengers came his way, and before he knew it, he was caught up in the inescapable contest for top dog amongst the gunfighters of the West.

Clay said he had never gone looking for someone to kill. However, wherever he was, plenty of young hopefuls had shown up to challenge him. When Katy asked why he had hooked up with Dean Foster, she and her father were surprised to learn that Clay and the Fosters were first cousins. Clay told them he had been working as a bodyguard to Charlie Westmore in Black Hawk when Reggie Atkins showed up, saying Foster was offering twice the salary if Clay would come to Lander and become its marshal. "After all," Clay said, "what else is there but money? That's the big essential, isn't it? Your nobody if you don't have plenty of it."

Katy and her father exchanged glances, then Doc said, "I think one day you'll find out there's more to life than money, son."

"Yes," Katy said, "like knowing the Lord and having peace that everything will be all right when you die. And while you're on this earth, having those things money can't buy, like the love of a good wife, and children who'll put their arms around you and say 'I love you, Daddy.'"

Clay Austin was nonplused. His eyes met Katy's, but he could think of nothing to say.

When the wound was stitched and bandaged, Dr. O'Donnell said, "Come back on Wednesday, Clay, and I'll change the dressing."

Austin was a bit unsteady on his feet as he stood up. Reaching for his wallet, he asked, "What do I owe you, Doc?"

"No charge," the physician replied, lifting palms toward him. Austin's eyes showed surprise.

"Let's just say it's my way of expressing appreciation for what you did in going to Chester's aid. Katy's been telling me there's something decent inside you that makes you different than the rest of Foster's bunch. It could be I'm beginning to believe it."

Austin's face reddened and he cleared his throat. "I...ah...I'm much obliged, Doctor. Thank you." Turning to Katy, he smiled. "Thank you, too, Miss Katy."

As Clay headed for the door, Dr. O'Donnell called after him, "Don't forget. Come back Wednesday so I can change the dressing on that wound."

"Wednesday it is," the marshal said over his shoulder, and was gone.

"You know, Daddy," Katy said, "for a man who runs with

criminals, he could be a decent person if he wanted to."

The doctor rubbed his chin. "Maybe so, honey, but I think Dean's got a tight hold on him. It'll take a lot of doing to break it. Katy..."

"Yes, Daddy?"

"You aren't developing a liking for that criminal with a badge, are you?"

She forced a smile. "Of course not. But...he is handsome, don't you think?"

"I'm not sure what handsome is."

Katy wrapped her arms around him and kissed his cheek. "Well, really handsome is about half as good looking as you are."

It was Dr. Patrick Michael O'Donnell's turn to blush.

For the next day and a half, Clay Austin moved about town keeping order while allowing Dean Foster's men to have their way. When some of them got too rough with the townspeople, Austin clashed with Dean Foster over it. Wanting to keep Clay's fast gun close by, Dean reprimanded the offenders in Clay's presence.

Wednesday came and still the church's new pastor had not arrived. Chester Platte would give it a few more days, then he would send a letter to Bishop Ames, asking if Reverend Thacker's departure from Kansas City had been delayed.

It was almost noon when Marshal Austin left his office and headed down the street toward the O'Donnell Clinic. He found himself feeling excited about seeing Katy again. Even though she was not overly fond of him, she was frequently in his thoughts.

Austin entered the waiting room and saw Katy sitting behind the desk, pouring over a ledger book. When she looked up, she gave him a nod and said, "Good morning, Marshal."

"Howdy, ma'am," he replied, tipping his hat. "You do the bookkeeping around here, too?"

"Somebody has to do it, and since the good doctor is the boss and I'm the only nurse, I also get to keep the books." She paused a moment, closed the ledger, and said, "Daddy's seeing a patient right now, but he should be through in a minute or two."

"Fine," he said, easing down on one of the benches. "I'll just sit here and enjoy the scenery."

Katy glanced up, unsure of his meaning, and found his eyes fixed on her. To cover her uneasiness, she asked, "Has the wound been giving you any pain?"

"A little, but not too bad. That is, except when I roll onto this arm in my sleep."

Katy wanted to ask if he was sleeping better now that he had shown some compassion for the townspeople, but decided to leave it alone.

The examining room door came open and an elderly woman emerged, followed by Dr. O'Donnell. When she saw Austin, she sniffed in disdain and turned up her nose.

When she was out the door, Katy asked, "How does it feel to be on Lander's 'most popular' list?"

Austin did not reply.

"Come on in, Marshal," Doc said. "Let's take a look at that arm."

Katy followed and went to the medicine cabinet while Austin sat on the examining table and began rolling up his left sleeve. Her father was unwinding the bandage as she placed a bottle of alcohol and a fresh bandage roll on a small table next to him.

Doc examined the wound and found that it was healing well. He cleaned it, then said to Katy, "Honey, I'll let you put the new bandage on. Mrs. Spencer is due at twelve-fifteen, and I need to get ready for her."

"All right," Katy nodded, moving in as her father stepped to the cupboard.

Katy began wrapping Austin's arm, working slowly to get it just right. She let her eyes drift to his and found him gazing at her. Miffed at his boldness, she set her mouth and gave the bandage a quick jerk. Austin winced and stifled a yelp.

Doc turned around, "What's the matter?"

"My hand slipped," Katy said. Then looking at the marshal, she added, "Hope that doesn't happen again."

"Be careful, Katy," Doc said, and turned back to what he was doing.

"I'll do that," she replied, holding Austin's gaze with steady eyes.

Katy finished tying off the bandage, and said, "There you are, Marshal. All done. When do you want him back, Daddy?"

"Let's make it Saturday."

"That all right with you?" Katy asked Austin.

Before Clay could reply, a voice boomed from the street and carried clearly into the clinic. "Clay Austin, I know you're in there! It's Rex Hobbs. There's a nice crowd out here, and I'm sure they'd like to see you square off against me. I'm callin' you, Austin!"

Clay looked toward the street. His lips pulled into a thin line, and his face was devoid of color.

Katy saw the fear in Austin's eyes and asked, "Who's Rex Hobbs?"

"He's a famous gunfighter, honey," said her father. "One of the fastest men alive."

"Why's this famous gunfighter wanting to shoot it out with you, Clay?"

"It's the law of the West. Remember I told you about men looking me up to challenge me? Well, here's another one."

"I didn't know the big names did this," Doc said.

"Now you do," Austin replied. "It's had to come to this. I've been challenged by a couple of not-quite-so-famous names recently and killed them. Word spreads fast, and Hobbs considers me a threat to his fame. Only name higher than Hobbs is the big man himself, Tate Landry."

Hobbs's voice came from the street again, but this time it was louder. "Hey, Austin, what's the matter? Are you yella? Come on out!"

"Clay, you may be fast, but Rex Hobbs has been around a long time," Doc said. "You go out there, he'll kill you."

Austin pulled his gun and broke it open. Spinning the cylinder to check the loads, he snapped it shut and eased it into his holster. Setting his jaw in grim determination, he said, "There's no way around it. I have to."

He adjusted his gun belt and said, "Thanks for the free medical service, Doc. And thank you, too, Miss Katy."

Katy moved to a position partially blocking his path and laid a hand on his arm. "Why do you have to?"

"It's just the way it is, ma'am. I'd rather die as a man than live as a coward." Austin walked into the waiting area and moved out into the glaring sunlight.

There was a crowd. Austin figured the townspeople would love to see him die.

Rex Hobbs stood in the middle of the street, a starched figure already in his quick-draw stance. He was almost an albino. Against the sunlight's glare, the snowy hair that showed under his broad-brimmed hat and his mustache contrasted sharply with his ruddy skin. His eyes were nearly colorless. "Well, it's about time, Austin!" he spat. "I was beginnin' to think you was hidin' behind a nurse's skirts."

"Well, now you know better," came Austin's level reply as he stepped into the dusty street to square himself with his challenger. He was unaware that both Doc and Katy had followed him outside and were standing among the crowd.

Katy turned to her father and half-whispered, "Daddy, we can't let him die. We've got to stop this!"

"How?"

"Gunfighters live on ego, don't they?"

"That's for sure."

"Well, wouldn't it be a blight on Hobbs's reputation if he killed a wounded man?"

The physician's eyes lit up. "You're right, honey. Pray for me—I'm going to see what I can do," Doc said, heading into the street.

Every eye in the crowd followed Doc's movements, including that of Dean Foster, who stood on the balcony of his bank building with Hank. The rest of the gang was on the street.

As Doc drew up beside Austin, Hobbs blared, "Hey, what're you doin? Get outta the way!"

"I'm thinking of your reputation, Mr. Hobbs."

"What're you talkin' about?"

"You wouldn't want to square off with a wounded man, would you, Mr. Hobbs? Why, when word got out that you gunned down Clay Austin when he already had a fresh bullet wound in one arm, that'd put a cloud over your impeccable reputation as a gunfighter, wouldn't it?"

Hobbs left his stance and stood erect. "What fresh bullet wound?"

O'Donnell turned to Clay and said, "Roll up your sleeve."

"Now, look, Doc," he protested, "I don't want—"

"Shut up!" Doc hissed under his breath. "You want to live, don't you?"

"Yes, but not as a coward!" Clay whispered back.

"You're not backing down, Clay. Let him do the backing down."

Doc took hold of Clay's left arm, unbuttoned the cuff, and rolled up the sleeve. Exposing the bandage for Hobbs to see, he said, "This wound, Mr. Hobbs."

"Don't look so bad," snarled the gunfighter. "Besides, it ain't in his gun arm."

"No, but when your admiring public learns that Clay had a wound that could have slowed him down, they'll wonder if he might have beat you without it. You want to live with that?"

Hobbs stomped toward Austin and O'Donnell, growling, "I want to see that wound. Take the bandage off."

Quickly Doc undid Katy's work and removed the bandage, revealing the bright-red wound.

Clay said, "Look, Doc, I can't let this keep me from answerin'

Rex's challenge. "Now, get out of the—"

"Maybe you can't," Hobbs cut in, "but I can! Ain't nobody gonna say I killed you in an unfair fight. This'll have to wait."

Katy O'Donnell breathed a sigh of relief.

Hobbs adjusted his hat, looked Austin in the eye, and said, "There will be another day, Clay. I'll give you time to heal up, then I'm comin' back. A showdown between us is inevitable. You know that, don't you?"

"Yeah, I know."

Without another word, Hobbs wheeled, walked to his horse some thirty yards down the street, swung into the saddle, and rode away.

As the crowd was breaking up, Austin looked down at the shorter man and said, "I owe my life to you, Doc. He'd have killed me."

"Don't thank me, son," replied O'Donnell. "The idea was Katy's."

A look of gratitude claimed Clay's face as Katy came up and took the bandage from her father's hand. "Come on, Marshal," she said. "Let's go inside and get you wrapped up again."

That night, at Lander Methodist Church's midweek prayer service, the pew seats were wet with tears as the people knelt in prayer, weeping and praising God that their deacon chairman had been spared a beating. They also wept as they implored Almighty God to hasten the day of their deliverance from the Foster gang and to bring their new pastor to them safely.

CHAPTER

EIGHTEEN

I t was almost noon on Thursday when people on Lander's main street noticed a lone rider coming in from the south. He sat tall in the black saddle atop a long-legged solid-black gelding. Dressed in black except for his white shirt that was adorned with a black string tie, he gave off an air of alertness, of perpetual watchfulness.

Eyes followed him intently as he stopped at the hitch rail in front of the Wind River Hotel. When he dismounted, his long frock coat flared open, exposing the bone-handled Colt .45 that rode low on his right hip, snugged tight with a length of black rawhide. He tied the big gelding to the rail and unbuckled the flap of the left saddlebag. Eyes widened when he pulled out a large black Bible, and whispers ran like the wind along the street. The new preacher had arrived. When some questioned why he would be wearing a gun, others reasoned that between Kansas City and Lander there were robbers and hostile Indians. Even a preacher had to protect himself.

John Stranger was aware that people were staring at him as he rounded the end of the hitch rail and crossed the boardwalk. When he entered the hotel, someone called out, "Get Chester Platte! The new preacher's here!"

Inside the hotel lobby, Stranger found two husky men behind

the desk, holding a smaller and older man against the back wall. One of them had the clerk's collar twisted tight at his neck and was blaring, "You'll have to learn the hard way, Thompson. Nobody defies Dean Foster!"

Choking out his words, Darren Thompson said, "I told you before...I'm waiting for a letter from Mr. Pierce in Cheyenne City. I can't pay your protection fee unless he gives me permission. If I pay any expenses Mr. Pierce hasn't okayed, I'll lose my job!"

"Better your job than your life!"

John Stranger laid his Bible on the counter and cleared his throat. Luther Noles and Keith Oldham turned to look at him. They noted the Bible near Stranger's hand and the upper part of the frock coat, along with the flat-crowned hat and string tie.

"Well, lookee here, Luther," Oldham said to his partner. "Looks like the new holy reverend has done arrived."

"Yeah, it does at that. Whattya want, preacher?"

Stranger decided he had come upon an extortion in progress. Letting them think he was a preacher, he spoke in his soft, level tone, "I would like a room, and I can't get one until you release the clerk and let him do his job. *So do it.*"

Noles let a wicked grin curl his lip, looked at his partner, and said, "Did you hear that, Keith? The holy man thinks he owns the world. Sounds kinda bossy to me."

Keith Oldham was a brutal man whose strength always had won its way. "Yeah, sounded that way to me, too," he grunted, letting go of Thompson's collar and moving to the counter. "Maybe the reverend needs a lesson on who's in charge around here."

Stranger reached across the counter, sank his fingers into Oldham's vest, and yanked him over the counter top. Oldham's head cracked the floor hard, and he remained in a crumpled heap.

Thompson stood with his back to the wall and massaged his throat. He heard Luther Noles utter a string of profane words as he rounded the end of the counter, clawing for his sidearm. Stranger met him with a powerful punch to the jaw that landed the big man on his back.

While the man-in-black confiscated the weapons from the two unconscious men, Thompson peered over the counter and said, "I never saw a preacher like you before. You really gave those two what they had coming!"

Just then the front door opened and Chester Platte appeared. Platte took one look at Dean Foster's two cronies and said, "Darren, what happened?"

"You should've seen it, Chester! These two were trying to force me to pay the protection fees, and your new pastor laid them out. Look at them—they're still not moving a muscle! I've never been a church-going man, as you know, Chester, but with a preacher like this one...you just might see me there every Sunday from now on."

The barber smiled and extended his hand to the stranger. "Reverend David Thacker, right?"

Without saying he was, Stranger shook his hand. "And you are—?"

"Chester Platte, Brother Thacker. I'm the chairman of your deacon board and the best barber in town! I, ah, might add, the *only* barber in town."

Stranger smiled and said, "What's going on here, gentlemen? If I heard right, these two were trying to extort money from Darren."

"You heard right," Thompson said, rubbing his throat again. "We've got a bunch of crooks—"

"Ah...maybe we ought to tell Reverend Thacker about Dean Foster and his hoodlums a little later, Darren. He's had a long ride, and I'm sure he wants to rest."

"Since I heard right," said Stranger, "these two should be arrested. One of you needs to go bring your marshal."

Platte looked at Thompson, then at the man he thought was David Thacker. "I'll fill you in on what's happening in our town a little later, Reverend, but let me just say for now, it wouldn't do any good to call the marshal. He won't jail them or prosecute them."

"They broke the law," Stranger said. "Darren and I can both attest to it."

"Please bear with me," Platte said, "but you'll understand better when we've had a good talk."

Stranger's steel-gray eyes held the barber's gaze. "All right. I'll take your word for it." Breaking the confiscated guns open, he emptied them and handed the cartridges to Thompson, telling him to discard them. Then he stuffed the weapons back in their holsters.

Oldham was shaking his foggy head and Noles was starting to come to. Stranger seized both men by their collars and dragged them toward the door. Chester hurried ahead and pulled it open. A large crowd had gathered around the front of the hotel, looking on with keen interest. When the man-in-black had dumped Noles and Oldham in the street, Chester stood beside him and raised his hands to get everybody's attention.

"Ladies and gentlemen!" he shouted. "I want you all to meet the new pastor of Lander Methodist Church...Reverend David Thacker!"

There was a loud round of applause, whistles, and cheers. Platte saw the Foster brothers in front of the bank and some of the gang along the street, so he made no reference to what the preacher had just done to Noles and Oldham. They had seen "Thacker" drag them out of the hotel and would put two and two together.

The people came up and introduced themselves, the members of the church making sure the preacher knew they were part of his flock. Oldham and Noles pulled themselves together and stole away. Moments later, they moved up beside Dean Foster and told him what the preacher had done.

When the last of the townspeople on the street had welcomed the new preacher, Chester told Stranger that the parsonage was vacant and ready for him to move in. He was sure Mrs. Thacker and the children would love the house.

Platte and some of the other members took their new pastor

to the church and showed him the building, then took him to the nearby parsonage. There Platte told him the whole story—from the murder of their former pastor and the two Butterfield men up to that very moment.

When he had heard it all, Stranger decided to let them believe he was their new pastor. David Thacker would arrive some time soon, but he wanted to clean up the town first. He could do this easier if everyone—including the town's oppressors—thought he was Thacker.

All but three gang members were at Dean Foster's house that night. Clay Austin had learned that an old friend of his was living in a small mountain village in the Wind River Range and had obtained Dean's reluctant permission to make a quick trip to see him. Stan Cole and Turk Dunphy were on an errand to Douglas. They were to scout out the Douglas bank so Dunphy could go back and lead a robbery at the most profitable time.

Dean Foster paced the floor of his den, chewing angrily on his unlit cigar. The men were seated on chairs and on the floor. Luther Noles and Keith Oldham were still feeling the effects of their encounter with the man-in-black. "This guy ain't always been a preacher," growled Dean. "Most preachers are mild-mannered little men who wouldn't swat a fly. This David Thacker knows how to handle himself."

"I've been kicked by mules and horses, and I've been in fights with some mountain-sized men, but I ain't never been punched like that parson punched me," Noles said.

Oldham said nothing, but the memory of being yanked over the counter and slammed to the floor made his whole body tremble.

"So when are we gonna kill this troublemaker, boss?" asked Reggie Atkins.

Dean stopped his pacing. "I'll have to think on it. No question it'll have to be done, but if we move too fast, we could incite the townspeople. Right now, we've got them buffaloed, but this guy's already become their hero. If we don't handle it just right when we take him out, the people could unite against us. If they did that, we'd be finished."

"I see what you're sayin'," said Hank, "but this guy might just be the one who can become their leader and *cause* them to unite against us."

"I know that," nodded Dean, pacing again. "But we dare not get hasty, here. Let's bide our time and do it right. I'm going to keep a close eye on him. When the time's right, I'll know it, and I'll also have figured out how to take him out."

"Changing the subject, boss, but how many of us are you gonna use to rob the Douglas bank?" Chice Reed asked. "I'm thinkin' that we don't dare thin our ranks too much around here."

"You're right about that. I'll make that decision when Turk and Stan get back in the morning. Once I know the layout of the bank and what the lawman situation is, I'll decide how many it'll take to handle the job." Dean paused, then said, "Well, that's all for now. Get back out there on the streets and keep our own little town in order."

As he lay in bed that night, John Stranger stared into the darkness and thought about Breanna Baylor. He was glad she had been able to settle down in Denver. He often passed through that area and could look in on her. Yet his heart ached. All he would ever be able to do was look in on her. He could never hold her in his arms, kiss her, or whisper words of love to her.

His mind went to the situation at hand. Foster and his henchman needed to be behind bars. And what about Clay Austin? Dean must be paying him plenty to have enticed him to leave Black Hawk. Well, Austin would have to suffer the consequences for joining up with his crooked cousins.

The next morning, Stranger left Ebony in the small corral behind the parsonage and walked to the business section. He needed to purchase a few groceries and some other provisions. As he strolled along the street, people stopped him to chat, wanting to let him know how glad they were to have him as a citizen of Lander. Church members told him they could hardly wait to hear him preach. Those who were not members told him they were planning to be in church on Sunday.

Stranger entered the general store and was warmly welcomed by other customers and by the proprietor and his family. When he had finished his shopping and left, they all talked about Reverend Thacker still wearing his sidearm. The previous pastor had never worn one. They finally decided he was still wearing it because of his encounter the day before at the hotel. This new preacher was no man's fool. He knew what Dean Foster and his men were, and he was going to be ready for them if they gave him any more trouble.

Turk Dunphy and Stan Cole were trotting into town at the same time John Stranger was in the general store. They were coming abreast of it just as he came out the door. At first, Dunphy gave only a casual glance at the tall man, but when he saw his profile, he recognized him. Stranger was turning to head back to the parsonage and did not see Dunphy.

Dunphy jerked the reins, halting his mount. Cole was a few paces past him when he realized Dunphy had stopped. Pulling rein, he hipped around in the saddle. "What're you doin', Turk?"

"I...uh...I just thought of somethin' I need to get in the general store. You go on. I'll catch up to you shortly."

"What are you talkin' about? We're supposed to meet with Dean, and he ain't gonna want to talk to me without you. You're the expert bank robber. I'll just go to the store with you."

Dunphy had no idea why fate had so generously smiled on him. His nemesis was walking down the street right ahead of him.

This was his opportunity to follow him and shoot him in the back. At last he could avenge his four gang members and pay the stranger back for foiling his escape plans. He wasn't about to let the opportunity pass by.

"Tell you what," said Turk, wanting to take out Stranger all by himself. "Why don't you go over to the Bird Cage Saloon and get yourself a nice big drink? I'll see you there in a few minutes."

Cole knew there was more going on than met the eye. Turk was acting strange. He would play along, then watch and see what Turk was up to. "Sure, I could use a stiff one. Come get me when you're done."

Dunphy nodded, shifting his eyes to Stranger, who had stopped to talk to a couple of men on the street.

Dunphy hurriedly dismounted and led his horse to the hitch rail in front of the general store. He kept track of Cole, who was riding toward the saloon, and John Stranger as he conversed with the two men. Cole hauled up in front of the saloon and went inside. The instant he was through the door, he rushed to a window and peered past the dust and fly specks to keep an eye on Turk Dunphy.

On the street, John Stranger finished his conversation and continued on toward the church. Lander's streets were lined with tall cottonwoods and oaks. There were vacant lots filled with them, and every yard had trees and bushes. Dunphy was able to follow unseen at a distance of about sixty yards. He was puzzled why the man would be in Lander, and doubly puzzled that he was carrying sacks of groceries toward the edge of town. His puzzlement increased when he watched Stranger turn onto the property of the Lander Methodist Church.

Hastening his pace, Dunphy rushed up behind a tree only thirty yards from the front of the parsonage. Whipping out his gun, he eased the hammer back as quietly as possible and took aim at Stranger's broad back. He heard a rustling sound behind him and jerked his head around. It was Stan Cole.

"What're you doin' here?" Dunphy whispered angrily.

"I thought somethin' strange was goin' on, Turk. I wanted to see what you were up to."

"I spotted my worst enemy leavin' the general store. I don't know what he's doin' in Lander, but I made myself a vow to kill the dirty snake, and now's my chance."

"Has to be the new preacher. They've been expectin' him to show up any time. Guess he came in while we were gone. You're worst enemy is a preacher?"

Stranger was almost to the porch of the house.

"He ain't no preacher," Dunphy grunted brusquely, moving away from the tree and raising his left arm, laying the barrel on it to steady his aim. "He's a devil from hell."

John Stranger suddenly dropped the bags he was carrying, whirled while drawing and cocking his Colt .45, and dropped low.

Dunphy's shot rang out and the bullet whizzed over Stranger's head. Stranger's gun roared back. The slug bored into the outlaw's chest, knocking him on his back.

Stan Cole had been in many a shoot-out and did the instinctive thing. He whipped out his sidearm and leveled it on the man-in-black. Before he could drop the hammer, Stranger's .45 roared again. Cole took the bullet in the center of his forehead and was dead before he hit the ground.

Stranger dashed to where Dunphy lay sprawled on his back. His gun was still in his hand, but he couldn't lift it.

John Stranger was aware of neighbors emerging from their houses across the street as he stood over the dying man. The bullet had pierced Dunphy's heart. Only a spark of life remained in the outlaw's eyes as he looked with hatred at the man-in-black. He worked his jaw, but from his throat came only the chilling sound of a life terminating. Death's cold hand squeezed the last breath out of Turk Dunphy. His chest went still, and his vacant eyes stared skyward. Stranger thought the hateful look seemed frozen in his eyes.

Stranger turned to meet the neighbors—two young couples

and an elderly man. Shock showed on their faces as they looked at the man they believed was Reverend David Thacker, then at the two dead men.

The elderly man said, "Reverend, I'm Dobey Mills. I live across the street, next to Paul and Wilda, and I seen it all. Them killers was goin' to shoot you in the back."

Paul Owens said, "We all saw what happened, Reverend. You had no choice but to defend yourself, but I guess you know you killed two of Foster's thugs."

It did not surprise Stranger that Turk Dunphy had hooked up with the likes of Dean Foster. "Guess I did," nodded the tall man.

Lou Washburn scrubbed a hand over his mouth and said, "Looks like Dean Foster wants you dead, Pastor."

"We don't know that for sure," Stranger said. "Maybe these boys were just trying to make it big with their boss by taking me out of the picture. I did get pretty rough with a couple of their pals."

More neighbors were moving onto the church property, voices buzzing. As they closed in, staring at the corpses, the five eye-witnesses began talking at once, telling what they had seen. Soon Marshal Austin came on the run, having been alerted that gunshots had been fired at the church.

The chatter stopped when they all realized Austin was there. Because he had defended Chester Platte against the drifters, the marshal had gained a measure of respect from the townspeople. Austin surveyed the corpses and asked what happened. Everyone listened as Paul Owens told what he and the others had witnessed.

Austin looked at the man-in-black and said, "I was out of town yesterday, Reverend. I guess you've figured out that I'm the law here."

"Your badge should tell me that, but from what the people of Lander are telling me, you dance on Dean Foster's string. Seems to me if that's the case, Dean Foster is the law here."

"I won't deny that I'm here because of Mr. Foster's invitation...and that I look out for his interests. But the people you talked to should have also told you that when outsiders come into Lander and cause trouble, I protect her citizens."

"I know about that, too," nodded the man who towered over Austin by almost a head. "I commend you, at least for that."

"Reverend, you heard what Paul told me. Is that the way it happened?" Austin asked.

"Yes, it is," nodded Stranger.

Washburn faced Austin and said, "I want you to tell me something, Marshal. You work for Foster, so you ought to know. Did he order our pastor killed?"

"No, he did not," Austin replied flatly. "I just talked with Mr. Foster a few minutes ago, and he was wondering why these two weren't back from Douglas yet. Since neither Mr. Foster nor any of his men have seen Dunphy and Cole since early yesterday morning, there's no way they could have received orders from Mr. Foster to do such a thing. Their decision to shoot Reverend Thacker was something they came up with on their own."

John Stranger knew it was strictly Turk Dunphy's idea.

"But why would they do it?" asked Washburn.

"I guess since they're dead and can't talk, it'll remain a mystery forever," Paul Owens said.

Stranger was glad to leave it there. Looking around at the small crowd, he asked, "Any of you men have a wagon you wouldn't mind using to haul these bodies to the undertaker?"

Paul volunteered his wagon and Lou agreed to help him. The rest returned to their homes. Clay Austin headed for the bank to tell Dean Foster that Turk Dunphy and Stan Cole were dead.

"Dead?" bellowed Foster, who sat behind his desk with his brother standing beside him. "How? Who killed them?"

Austin explained to the Foster brothers how Dunphy and Cole had attempted to shoot Reverend Thacker in the back, and how Thacker had turned the tables on them, gunning them both down.

Rage reddened Foster's features. "That does it! Something's awry here. Thacker's more than a preacher. He's been a gunfighter, or something akin to it. He's got to go!"

"Now, wait a minute, Dean," Clay said. "The man was only defending himself. Granted, he did a pretty good job of it, considering the odds against him. But he hasn't done anything to you. Oh, sure, he bruised up Noles and Oldham, but I've talked to you about this protection fee business before. I tell you, roughing up Lander's citizens, especially it's business people, is going to cause you more trouble than it's worth. And as for killing Thacker...you know how I feel about murder. If that's your plan, I'm down the road in an hour. I'll have no part of it."

Dean Foster needed Clay's fast gun. He couldn't afford to lose him. He decided he would tell Clay what he wanted to hear, but one way or another, Thacker would die. He just needed to make Clay think it was someone else's doing.

Palms up, Dean said, "Okay, okay, kid. No murder. But what are we going to do about this preacher? He's one tough hombre."

"I don't think he'll be a problem as long as we handle things right, Dean. We can control this town by other means than violence, you know."

Dean would pacify his fast-handed cousin for the moment. "Sure, kid. I'll, uh...I'll work on it and see what I can come up with."

Austin smiled, trusting his cousin, and left. When he was gone, Dean chewed angrily on his cigar. "We'll let it ride for now, Hank, but when things are just right, that preacher is going to die!"

CHAPTER

NINETEEN

—◆—

On Sunday morning, Clay Austin stood outside the church, along with five of Foster's men. Dean wanted them close by, just to keep the church goers on edge.

"Reverend David Thacker" preached his first sermon to a packed house, and they were thrilled with his preaching. Everyone agreed they had never heard such powerful, poignant, dynamic preaching...and from a man who was so soft-spoken outside of the pulpit.

John Stranger stood at the open door of the church, shaking hands with the people as they filed past. Dr. Patrick O'Donnell came through the line and introduced himself and his daughter, making sure the preacher knew they were members of the church. As Doc and Katy headed for their buggy, Clay Austin angled toward them. Touching his hat brim, he smiled and said, "Good morning, Miss Katy...Dr. O'Donnell."

Both greeted him cordially, then Katy said, "You should have come inside, Marshal. You probably couldn't hear the sermon too clearly from out here."

"Well, Miss Katy," Clay said, scratching the bridge of his nose, "I'm...ah...I'm not a church-going man."

"Atheist, eh?" Doc snapped.

"Oh, no, sir! It's just that, well..."

"Well, what? You don't think you owe God anything?"

"Well, no, sir. It isn't that, but—"

"I'm not payin' it!" Coye Coffman's voice pierced the air.

All eyes swung to the spot where Jim Wurth and the other four Foster men had encircled the undertaker.

"You've made plenty of money lately buryin' those drifters and Turk and Stan," Wurth rasped. "We'll be by your shop tomorrow mornin'. Your fee's due, and you'd better be ready to pay up!"

Most of those who had attended the church service were still on the grounds. They saw the preacher heading toward the shouting scene and began to move that direction.

Katy looked at Clay, whose attention was on Wurth and Coffman, and said, "There's more extortion, Marshal. What are you going to do about it?"

"I'll handle it, ma'am," he said, and left her standing with her father.

Doc and Katy moved closer to the trouble spot.

Before Austin got there, John Stranger had pushed through the crowd and was standing between Coffman and Wurth, facing the latter. The other Foster men stood in a semicircle with their hands resting on their holstered guns.

Stranger's normally soft voice was raw and gruff as he blared at Wurth, "This protection fee business is going to end in this town, mister!"

"Not until Dean Foster *says* it ends, holy man!" Wurth shouted back.

"We'll see about that," Stranger countered levelly. "Now take your pals and get off this property."

Wurth pulled back, letting his gun hand hover over his revolver. "I think maybe it's time for you to go to heaven, holy man. I'll give you a sportin' chance. Go for your gun."

The crowd was wide-eyed as the man-in-black slowly spread his frock coat, showing that he was not armed. "I don't wear my gun into the pulpit," he said softly.

"Well go get it!"

Austin moved inside the circle of people and said, "Jim, take the boys and do as the reverend says. Get off the church's property."

Wurth turned hostile eyes on Austin. "What're you talkin' about? Whose side you on?"

"Dean and I have an understanding. The methods he's been using are going to change."

"Well, he ain't told me to change nothin'. Coffman's fee is due in the mornin' whether he or this...this stranger like it or not."

"Enough talk," Stranger interjected. "Like I said, take your pals and leave."

Jim Wurth was known for his volatile temper. He released a string of foul words and jutted his jaw. "Well, maybe you'd like to try to throw us off, holy man!"

Coolly, Stranger moved to within arm's reach of him and said, "Watch your mouth, mister, there are ladies present. After you apologize to them, you may take your cronies and leave."

"Apologize?" Wurth snorted. "I'll eat my hat first!" As he spoke, he threw a haymaker at Stranger.

Stranger dodged the fist and seized Wurth's arm, wrenching it savagely. The arm snapped, and Wurth howled as a sharp pain shot through his arm and shoulder.

Out of the corner of his eye, Stranger saw the other Foster men going for their guns. Quickly he had Wurth's gun out of its holster, cocked, and leveled on them before even one could clear leather. The people were scattering, expecting gunfire. Wurth was on his knees, unable to move his right arm.

Holding the gun on the four outlaws, Stranger said, "Okay, boys, very carefully take your guns out of their holsters with the tips of your fingers and drop them on the ground."

All four still had their fingers wrapped around the gun butts. E. B. Snyder grinned maliciously and said, "C'mon, now, Reverend...ain't nobody can shoot a gun fast enough to take out four gunmen. You might get two of us, but the other two'll get you."

Lining the muzzle of the revolver on Snyder's chest, the tall man replied in his low-voiced manner, "That might be, but you'll be one of the two I take with me." Then letting his pale gray eyes roam to the faces of the others, he said, "Which one of you wants to be number two?"

The three outlaws looked at each other. Then Hal Simms said, "E. B., this ain't so good. He seems to have the drop on us. Two of us gettin' killed ain't worth takin' him out."

Snyder wasn't ready to die either. Sullenly he grunted, "Do what he says."

When the four guns were on the ground, Stranger said, "Okay...off the property."

As the foursome started to move, Snyder said, "How about Jim?" Wurth was still on his knees, holding his arm and moaning through clenched teeth.

"Dr. O'Donnell will have to take care of him. I think he has a dislocated shoulder and a broken arm."

Giving Stranger a murderous glance, Snyder walked away with the other outlaws and said, "You ain't seen the last of us, holy man."

Stranger grinned at him. "I'm sure of it."

Dr. O'Donnell and Katy moved in as the crowd looked on in amazement at their new preacher.

Stranger approached Wurth and towered over him. "Now are you ready to apologize to the ladies for your language, or would you prefer to eat your hat?"

Still gripping his arm, Wurth could only shake his head in a stupefied gesture and gasp, "No...I'll apologize."

"Good. Do it."

Looking toward the crowd, he said, "I...I'm sorry for my bad language...ladies."

"Fine," said Stranger. "Let's not hear any more, either. Next time you might get your mouth washed out with soap."

Standing next to the kneeling, hurting outlaw, Doc looked at Stranger and said, "I'd appreciate your help getting him to my office."

Stranger told the people who remained that he would see them all at the evening service, then he turned to Doc and said, "Let's go."

Clay Austin said, "I think I better go along too, Reverend. Snyder and the others will run to Dean and tell him what happened. I'll need to know Jim's condition before I go and talk to Dean myself."

"Okay," nodded Stranger. "Why don't you help him off his knees and steady him as we walk to Doc's office?"

Stranger watched Katy as she walked alongside Clay Austin and noted the look in her eyes while they talked. One minute she scolded him for not helping the preacher subdue the outlaws, and the next minute she was complimenting him for telling them to obey the preacher and get off the property. She also showed interest in the "understanding" that had been worked out between Austin and Dean Foster. Katy was overjoyed when he told her the violence against the merchants who weren't paying their protection fees was going to stop.

With Katy's help, Dr. O'Donnell chloroformed Jim Wurth and put his shoulder socket back in place, then set and splinted the broken arm. When O'Donnell said that Wurth would be all right in a few weeks, Clay left to tell Dean Foster.

While the doctor was finishing up, Katy walked Stranger to the outer room as he was preparing to leave. Before he departed, he looked at her and said, "Katy, be careful with your heart."

Astonishment showed on her face. "Pardon me, Pastor? I don't understand what you mean."

"He's an outlaw, Katy. Unless there's a drastic change in his heart and soul, you mustn't fall in love with him."

A shaky hand went to her temple. "Are you referring to Cla— I mean, the marshal?"

"Mm-hmm. I've been around a while, little lady. I can read feelings and emotions in people's eyes. Are you going to tell me I'm wrong?"

Katy cleared her throat. Evading his gaze, she replied, "He...he's got some good qualities, Pastor. I've even seen a change in him since he first came. He's been showing some opposition to Dean Foster's brutal ways."

"That's good, but keep a guard on your heart. Unless he submits himself to the Lord and becomes a Christian, you mustn't set yourself up for a miserable life."

"I know what you're saying," she said softly, "and you're right. Thank you for caring enough to talk to me about it."

"What's a pastor for?" he chuckled. "See you this evening."

Katy watched the tall man walk down the street and thought, *Your discernment is uncanny, Pastor Thacker.*

Clay Austin walked into Dean Foster's den and found Hank sitting in his usual chair beside his brother's desk. The four men who had been disarmed by John Stranger were sitting together on a couch along one wall. The atmosphere was charged.

Dean looked up as Austin moved across the room toward him and said, "Well? How is he?"

"Broken arm...dislocated shoulder. Doc says he'll be all right in a few weeks."

"What is it with this gray-eyed man-of-the-cloth, Clay? Who ever heard of a reverend who can tear a man up like he did Jim and disarm four men? What's he made of, anyway?"

Austin raised his hat and scratched his head. "Looks like flesh and bone to me."

"Well, he isn't like the rest of us. Take Hank, here, for instance. He's tough as they come, but there's no way he could've done what that preacher did to Noles and Oldham, and to Cole and Dunphy...and now to these boys and Wurth."

"He's a bit strange, I'll admit to that, Dean. But I think when our tactics change, he'll be less of a problem. He just doesn't take to strong-arm stuff. The minute he heard Jim givin' Coye Coffman a hard time, he barged in and took over."

"Well, somethin's gotta be done. The man's a menace. I don't see any way to handle him but to kill him."

Austin's features hardened. "I told you, Dean, you start talkin' murder and I'm gone."

"Maybe we don't need to kill him," Greg Wolford said. "How about we all gang up on him and give him the beatin' of his life. That'd take the starch out of him."

"Yeah," nodded E. B. Snyder. "Maybe all we gotta do is break both of his arms and dislocate both shoulders. He's got a coupla scars on one cheek. Maybe we oughtta match 'em with some on the other side."

Austin shook his head. "Even if we jumped him, some of us would get hurt, I'll guarantee you. Besides, you talk about getting the people together against us! My advice is for us to simmer down on how we treat the merchants. If we do that, the reverend won't bother us."

"I'm not too sure it's going to work, though," said Dean. "Without proper pressure, they won't come across with the fee. And besides that, I'm planning on raising the fees in a couple weeks. I can't own the businesses in this town unless the merchants are so broke they're forced to sell out."

"While you two are discussin' that, boss," spoke up Hal Simms, "I think I should tell you that you probably shouldn't count on Virgil Cullen for any help for a while."

"And why's that?"

"Well, we've...uh...we've sorta been coverin' for him."

"What do you mean?"

"Ever since Turk got it, ol' Virgil's been hittin' the bottle. He ain't done any patrollin' since. He's over at the house in a stupor right now. Least he was when we left him."

"Well, I want him sobered up!" snapped Dean. "You guys go take care of it right now. When he's thinking clear, bring him to me. There's no room in this outfit for a drunken sot. He'll either straighten up or take a ride."

As the outlaws were filing out the door, Dean said, "Clay, I want you to be at the church for this evening's service."

"Just me?"

"Yeah. Inside."

"Inside?"

"You heard me. We've got to keep that crowd nervous. With you warming a pew, they'll wonder what's going on."

Austin's face was white as a sheet. "Aw, c'mon, cousin. Why not just let me and some of the boys stand outside like we've been doin'?"

"For one thing, most of them are busy. I've got the four who just left here with an assignment, and I need to talk to the others about collections tomorrow."

Clay Austin felt sick. He was going to have to sit and listen to a sermon. He hoped it wouldn't be a hellfire-and-damnation one.

Lander Methodist Church's evening service started at seven. As the marshal reluctantly headed for the service, he saw Katy O'Donnell standing in front of the church, talking to a small group of women. It was about ten minutes before starting time.

Katy's eyes strayed to the lanky man with the star on his vest, threading his way among a few clusters of men near the wagons and buggies. She excused herself to the women and headed toward Clay. As they drew together, Clay saw her hair catch the fire of the sunset, turning it the color of deep, burnished copper. Her exquisite features and feminine charms took his breath away. Never had a woman so captivated him. He found himself wishing his life had turned out differently. If things were not as they were, he would do his best to court her and marry her.

"Hello, Marshal," she smiled. "I assume the others will be coming along shortly?"

Austin was fighting the desire to reach out and take her hand. To touch her softness would be wonderful. "Ah...no," he replied. "It's just me this time."

"Is Foster mellowing?"

"No, that's not it. He just decided to do it a bit differently this time. I'm supposed to attend the service."

Katy's blue eyes enlarged. "Oh, really?"

"Yes'm. I...ah...do you suppose it'd be all right if I sat by you and your father?"

"Of course," she smiled. "I sing in the choir so it'll just be you and Daddy at first. I'll join you when it's time for the message."

Clay's stomach was more jittery as he entered the church than it had ever been before a gunfight. People in the congregation were astonished to see one of Foster's men in the service, but they gave him a warm welcome.

Dean Foster looked quizzically at E. B. Snyder. "What do you mean, you can't find Virgil?"

"I mean we can't find him, boss. When we got to the house, he was gone. We looked in the saloons, but they haven't seen hide nor hair of him."

"Well, he's got to be somewhere. I want him found."

"We'll do our best, but if we don't find him before dark, best we can do is search for him in the mornin'."

Dean gave him a petulant wave and said, "Okay, okay. But we've got to find him soon."

"I'm sure we will. He's probably stumblin' out there in the woods somewhere, blind drunk."

"Never knew he was a sot," grumbled Dean.

"Before I leave, boss, the boys and I were thinkin' that a couple of us oughtta break into the gun shop and get us some guns...you know, since we don't have ours anymore. Any problem with that?"

"Of course not. Just wait till the town's asleep."

"Gotcha," Snyder grinned, and headed out the door.

Reverend David Thacker had just finished a hellfire-and-damnation sermon, when he looked up and saw a man coming through the door. He was on the run and didn't stop until he was a few feet from the pulpit. He was holding a cocked revolver, and it was aimed at the preacher's chest.

Clay Austin, who was on the aisle on the second row, recognized Virgil Cullen. That Cullen had been drinking was obvious, by his stance, but he was not drunk.

Cullen fixed John Stranger with hard, bloodshot eyes and bawled, "You killed my friend Turk Dunphy, preacher! I been waitin' to get my revenge. I'm gonna gun you down like a rabid dog right in front of all your hypocrite church members!"

Without pulling his gun, Clay slowly rose to his feet among the shocked congregation. He wanted to talk Virgil out of his murderous intent, but was afraid if he pulled his gun, Virgil might start shooting. Keeping his voice level and soft, he said, "Don't do it, Virgil."

Cullen glanced over his shoulder long enough to see Austin, then he looked back at John Stranger, who remained behind the pulpit. "Clay, what're you doin' here?"

"Attending the service," Austin replied. "Now I want you to lower the gun, ease the hammer down, and back up to where I'm standing. Then put the gun in my hand. What you're doin' is all wrong."

Swearing, Cullen kept his gun and line of sight trained on the preacher. "No, Clay, we'll do this like I say. Take your gun out and bring it to me. And don't get any cute ideas about shootin' me, 'cause if you do, the preacher will still get it. C'mon! Now!"

From the platform, Stranger recognized the look in Austin's eyes. He wanted to draw and take Cullen down, but there was the chance that Cullen's reflexes might indeed pull the trigger. Clay had no choice but to obey.

The men in the congregation were eyeing each other, wanting to do something, but Virgil Cullen had the upper hand. Mothers clutched their children close to them, and everyone thought of that dreadful Sunday morning service not so long ago when Reverend Philip Landrum had been shot.

When Austin's gun was in Cullen's free hand, the outlaw said, "Now, go back and sit down, Clay. Hurry up!"

The marshal withdrew and took his seat next to Katy once more. He exchanged worried glances with Doc, who sat on Katy's other side.

Glaring hard at Stranger and holding the muzzle of his weapon dead-center on his chest, Cullen said, "Okay, Reverend, I'll give you a chance to pray before you die. That's more than you gave Turk. Make it short, though, 'cause I want to show all these people that you Bible thumpers don't really believe what you preach. Ten to one says you'll sweat good and tremble just like any ol' sinner before I send you into eternity."

Stranger was calm and cool as he said in his soft voice, "I wonder if you are ready to die, mister."

"Don't preach to me, holy man! Just get your prayer said!"

"You missed my meaning. I mean, since I have a cocked revolver trained on your heart, are you ready to die?"

Cullen blinked as he saw that the tall man's hands were out of sight behind the pulpit. "You're lyin'!" he snapped. "Ain't no preacher wears a gun into his pulpit!"

"Who says I wore it in here? It was already here as a precaution. Now lower the muzzle and ease the hammer down, like the marshal told you."

"No! You ain't got no gun! I came here to kill you, and that's what I'm gonna do! But I want to hear you pray, first. Now do it!"

The people looked on with fear. Some wanted to slip out of the building behind Cullen's back, but were afraid he would hear them and start shooting.

Holding Cullen's gaze steady with his own, Stranger said, "I'm not lying about the gun, Virgil. I can drop you where you stand."

Cullen forced a laugh. "Hah! Even if you had a gun, you wouldn't shoot me in front of all these sweet-faced hypocrites."

"I'll remind them of what you said when I conduct your funeral tomorrow."

Cullen's face started to twitch from the tension, and a sheen of sweat moistened his brow. "You're bluffin'!"

"Are you sure?"

"Yeah!"

"Then why are you sweating?"

"Shut up and start prayin', or I'll send you to your Maker just like you are!"

"I'm ready for that, but are you?"

Cullen swore and defiantly raised his revolver, lining it between Stranger's eyes.

A loud report racketed through the building. Women and children screamed. Virgil Cullen's gun discharged, but he was already dead. His shot went wild, the bullet chewing into the wall behind the choir loft, near the ceiling. The .45 caliber slug from John Stranger's weapon left a splintered path through the pulpit on its way to Cullen's heart. Blue-white smoke drifted from the back of the pulpit as the dead man fell to the floor.

Stranger carried the smoking gun with him as he rounded the pulpit and stood over the lifeless form of Virgil Cullen. Looking at the congregation, he lifted his voice above the frightened cries and said, "It's all right, now! The man is dead. He's no longer a threat."

Marshal Austin and Coye Coffman carried the body from the church. When they were gone, Stranger led the people in prayer, thanking God that no one in the congregation had been hurt.

When the people were leaving, several of them heard

Coffman say to Chester Platte, "Looks like the Lord may have dovetailed our prayers into one answer."

"What do you mean?" Platte asked.

"Well, we prayed for our pastor to get here safely, didn't we?"

"Yes."

"And we prayed for the Lord to rid us of the Foster gang, didn't we?"

"We sure did."

"Seems to me our safely arrived pastor is also ridding us of the Foster gang...one or two at a time."

The stagecoach rolled to a stop in a cloud of dust at Denver's Butterfield Stagelines office. As the afternoon breeze carried the dust away, the shotgunner slid to the ground and opened the door. A middle-aged man thanked him, stepped out, and offered his hand to Breanna Baylor. She smiled and took his hand. "Thank you, Mr. Warren."

"My pleasure," he smiled, then turned and helped an elderly woman down.

The stage driver handed down a small suitcase to Warren, who thanked him, then turned to the women and said, "I certainly enjoyed traveling with you, ladies."

Both women returned the same, then Breanna turned to the silver-haired woman and said, "I hope you like living in Denver, Mrs. Spaulding. I sure do, what little I'm able to be here."

The elderly woman noted a wagon rolling to a stop and said, "Ah, there's my son now, Miss Baylor. I do hope our paths cross again."

"I'm sure they will," smiled Breanna. "Denver isn't all that large."

Clara Spaulding hurried away, calling to her son. At the same time, Breanna spotted Dr. and Mrs. Sommers pulling up in their carriage. Soon her luggage was in the back of the vehicle, and the retired physician was driving toward home.

"Well, dear," Florence said, "how did it go in Cheyenne City?"

"It was a lot of work," Breanna sighed, "but well worth it. Their facility isn't near what our hospital here will be when it's finished, but for a medical clinic, it's the best thing they have in all of Wyoming, I understand."

"So did they find enough nurses to staff the clinic?"

"Yes, finally. They have six—two for each eight-hour shift. I stayed longer than planned when they originally asked me to come, but I just didn't have the heart to..."

Florence Sommers turned to look at Breanna, wondering why she had cut off in midsentence. She was staring up the street, lips pressed tight.

Before Florence could ask what she was looking at, Breanna said, "Dr. Sommers, did you see that man on the black horse ride through the intersection up there?"

"Yes, I did."

"Would you see if you can catch up to him?"

The rider had already passed from view on the cross-street. "I'll try," Sommers replied, snapping the reins and sending the horses into a fast trot.

"Someone you know, dear?" Florence asked as the carriage bounded toward the intersection.

"I...I think so," Breanna replied shakily.

Seconds later, the carriage rounded the corner at a good clip, forcing the women to grasp the metal rail in front of them. The rider on the black horse was just crossing the next intersection. Breanna wanted to tell Dr. Sommers to hurry, but checked herself.

They drew close to him, and Sommers slowed the horses. Breanna's heart was pounding. The man made a quick turn and hauled up in front of a blacksmith shop. They came abreast just as he swung a leg over the saddle. When Breanna saw his face, she realized it wasn't John Stranger. He was older and smaller, and the frock coat and flat-crowned hat he wore were dark-brown, not black.

Disappointment washed over Breanna like a wave of ice water. Since she did not call for him to stop, Dr. Sommers kept the carriage moving. Leaning past his wife, he glanced at Breanna and asked, "False alarm?"

"Yes. I...I thought he was an old friend. I'm sorry, I was mistaken."

As Dr. Sommers turned the next corner and aimed toward home, the heavy-hearted young woman cried inside, *Oh, John, I thought it was you. Where are you, my darling? I must find you.*

CHAPTER
TWENTY

Marshal Clay Austin lay awake, tossing and turning. The sermon he had heard was gnawing at him like a voracious rodent. The preacher had made hell so real, Austin could smell the smoke. He had also made Calvary so real that Austin had a vivid image of Jesus Christ on the cross, bleeding and dying *for him.*

The man who had walked away the victor from seventeen gunfights found his pillow and sheets damp with his perspiration. He was so caught up in his miserable lot as a guilty sinner that he did not hear E. B. Snyder and Carl Matthews as they left the big house just after midnight.

When Austin was finally able to steel himself against the sermon, he still could not sleep for thinking of Katy O'Donnell. He was in love with her. Beyond the fact that she was sweet and wholesome was something that made her different than any other woman he had ever known. He corrected himself. It was not some *thing* that made her different. It was a Person...Jesus Christ. He had not understood that until he heard Reverend Thacker's sermon.

Clay laced his fingers behind his head, stared into the darkness, and smiled to himself. Katy was exemplary of what he had always thought a Christian should be...except in one aspect. The few Christians he had ever been exposed to were outwardly pious and subdued. Katy had spunk. Beautiful as she was, he thought she was the most beautiful when her blue eyes were flashing fire, like they had flashed at him on a few occasions.

And then there was David Thacker. Clay had never known a preacher who could handle himself like this one. Thacker had a steel rod for a backbone and was not one to back down from a fight no matter what the odds against him. Clay liked Thacker. And he had learned something these past few days. Just because someone was a Christian did not mean they had to be somebody's rug, nor did it mean they had to sit back and watch evil in progress. They could stand up and fight it.

Snyder and Matthews crept through the dark alley and drew up to the back door of Benjamin Hanks's gun shop. Using a small crowbar, they soon had the door open and slipped inside. They felt their way in the darkness through the work room and into the front of the shop. Lander's main street was illumined with lanterns, and the nearest pole was some thirty feet from the front windows. It cast a measure of light into the shop, but left deep shadows in the corners.

As they moved up to the glass cases that held various handguns, Snyder whispered, "As long as we're here, why don't we just take 'em all? I mean, even the rifles and shotguns there in the rack? Maybe if we clean old Benjamin completely out, Dean can take the place over right away."

"Just one problem with that," Matthews said.

"What's that?"

"How we gonna carry it all? We should've brought a wagon."

"There's another problem, too," came a voice from the shadows near the front windows.

Two hearts froze, and two men went for their guns.

"Draw them and you'll die!" hissed the strange voice.

This time it was their hands that froze.

"Who is it?" asked Snyder, his voice quaking.

Ignoring the question, the man in the shadows said, "Pull your guns out nice and easy and lay them on the glass case."

Afraid to disobey, both men did as they were told.

"All right, now put your hands down inside your belts. I mean all the way to the wrists."

When it was done, the man moved in front of the nearest window, outlining himself against the dim light of the street lamp.

"The preacher!" gasped Snyder. "H-how did you know we were comin' in here?"

"That's for me to know and you to wonder about."

"So what're you gonna do with us?" Matthews asked.

"Put you in jail for burglary."

"Hah!" chuckled Snyder. "That won't last long. Clay'll let us out before you can bat an eye."

"I wouldn't be too sure of that," countered Stranger. "I think your marshal is starting to see the light."

"You'll never make it stick," Matthews growled. "Maybe we just happened by and saw movement in here. We came in to investigate, and you threw a gun on us from the shadows. Maybe it was you who did the burglarizin'. It'll be our word against yours."

"Wrong," Stranger said stiffly. "It'll be our word against yours."

"*Our* word? What're you talkin' about?"

"Come on out, gentlemen," said Stranger.

There was a shuffling of feet as men emerged from the other shadows of the room. "I think you gentlemen know Benjamin Hanks. And of course you know Dr. O'Donnell and Chester Platte. These fine, upstanding citizens of our fair town watched you break and enter and heard you talk about cleaning Mr. Hanks out so Foster could take the place over."

Benjamin Hanks picked up the outlaws' guns and said to them, "Things are changing around here, in case you boys hadn't noticed."

"Chester," said Stranger, "I'll stay here and keep my gun on these burglars if you'll go awaken Marshal Austin and bring him back with you. We need to get these criminals locked up."

"What do you mean, you can't let them out?" bellowed an angry Dean Foster. "I'm the law in this town, and I'm telling you to release them!"

The early morning sun was shining through the window of Foster's den as he paced back and forth, chewing on his cigar. Clay Austin stood with his back to the window. "There were four witnesses, Dean," he retorted evenly. "If I let them out, the very thing you fear the most will happen. The people will unite behind Thacker and your empire will crumble."

"Thacker! Thacker! Thacker!" screamed Dean. "Where'd he come from? Preachers aren't supposed to be like him. They're supposed to be mild-mannered and...and weak."

"This guy is neither," Hank Foster said from the corner. "He's got to be dealt with."

"I agree," nodded Dean, "but we're outnumbered here. As long as we can keep the people afraid of us, we can dominate them. But if we harm their hero, they're likely to get so mad they forget to be afraid."

"You're talkin' good sense, Dean," agreed Clay. "Like I've been tellin' you, ease up and things will get better for us."

Dean swore, jerked the cigar out of his mouth, and threw it across the room. "Cullen's dead! Dunphy's dead! Cole's dead! Wurth is laid up for weeks, and Snyder and Matthews are in jail! Our forces are dwindling, and it's all because of that stupid preacher!"

"Bad choice of words, Dean," said Clay. "*Stupid* the man is not."

"So what're we gonna do?" Hank asked.

"I don't know," Dean said. "I've got to have time to think on it."

"Well, I gotta go rustle up some breakfast for E. B. and Carl," Clay said as he made for the door.

"You explain to those two why I'm not getting them out right away, will you?" Dean called after him.

Clay waved an acknowledgment and was gone.

Hank rose to his feet and said, "Well, I've got some errands to run. When you figure out what to do with Thacker, let me know."

"Yeah, I'll let you know."

Coye Coffman was sweeping the floor of his shop when heavy boots sounded on the boardwalk and the door came open. He stopped sweeping and looked up to see Leon Shields and George McGurk, their faces hard-set.

"We're here for the money," McGurk said heavily.

Coffman nodded toward a freshly made coffin on the work bench. "I won't have the money till I get paid for burying the man in there."

Both outlaws glanced at the coffin, its lid loosely in place.

"So who's that?" asked Shields. "Virgil Cullen?"

"No. Someone else."

"Who?" demanded McGurk.

"Take a look for yourself."

The outlaws grinned at each other and moved to the coffin. As they stood shoulder-to-shoulder, McGurk took hold of the lid and swung it upward. A large mirror lay on its bottom, reflecting their own wide eyes and open mouths.

Suddenly a cool voice from behind them said, "Of course, the choice is yours. Instead of being buried, you can go to jail for extortion."

Both outlaws whirled and found themselves looking down the barrel of John Stranger's Colt .45.

"Real careful-like, I want you boys to unbuckle your gunbelts and drop them to the floor. If you cooperate, I'll assume you've chosen jail rather than burial."

The outlaws eyed each other and began to unbuckle their gunbelts. "Sure, Reverend," McGurk chuckled. "We won't be in there very long. Why should we argue with that gun in your hand?"

"How'd he manage that?" boomed Dean Foster, sitting behind the desk in his private office at the bank.

"Don't know the details, boss," replied Reggie Atkins, "but they're both in jail. Thacker made Clay put 'em in the same cell with E. B. and Carl."

"The same cell? Those cells are hardly big enough for two men. What's that preacher think he's doing?"

"Well, I may be wrong, but I think he's plannin' to put every one of us in jail...so he's gonna jam the first cell tight before he starts fillin' another one."

Dean slammed the desk with his fist and uttered a string of profanity. "Who does that preacher think he's dealing with, anyhow? I'm no amateur! As soon as I figure out how to get rid of him without bringing the house down on us, he's a dead man!"

Heading for the door, Atkins said, "I'm with you, boss. Let me know when you're ready."

When Atkins was gone, Foster crossed his plush office, which was on the bank's second floor, and stepped onto the balcony. Cursing under his breath, he tried to clear his mind while observing the traffic below.

Beneath the balcony, Hank Foster met Atkins as he emerged from the bank lobby, and said, "We need to talk. Come with me."

Dean did not see his brother and Atkins leave the boardwalk and move between the bank and the building next door. Hank led his friend to the alley, where Wolford, Noles, Oldham, and Simms were waiting.

"What's goin' on?" Atkins asked, running his gaze over the determined-looking faces of the four outlaws, then looking at Hank.

"I've had it up to here with that preacher!" Hank growled. "I killed me one before, and I'm in the mood to kill another one. Since Dean's so slow to figure out how to kill him, we're gonna do it for him."

"Okay," Atkins nodded, "I'm with you. So what's the plan?"

"No plan, exactly. We just walk the streets together till we see him and gun him down. He's always movin' about town. Ain't no reason we can't blow him to kingdom come and have this mess over with before noon."

All agreed. This was Reverend David Thacker's day to die.

Jock Canfield and Mason Crier stood stiff and mean inside the blacksmith shop while Vernon Roper worked the bellows of his fire pit and calmly said, "I don't rightly think I need to be payin' any more protection fees."

The big double doors that faced the street were propped open with short lengths of two-by-four, allowing the bright sunlight from the street to fill the shop.

Both outlaws gave Roper a hostile look. Canfield grunted, "Without protection, pal, you're in deep trouble."

The blacksmith glanced toward the street, which was to their backs, and countered, "It's not me who needs the protection."

Both outlaws turned to see the shadowy form of John Stranger against the stark brilliance of the street. He was leaning against the frame of the wide door, idly flipping a silver medallion in his left hand. "You two can take your guns out of their holsters and drop them on the floor. You're going to jail for extortion."

"You ain't no lawman!" blurted Crier. "And we ain't doin' no such thing!"

As Crier spoke, he clawed for his gun, as did his partner. Before they could clear leather, Stranger's gun was in hand, cocked and ready to fire. Both outlaws were like statues, gripping their weapons but knowing they were dead if they pulled them.

Hands high over their heads, Canfield and Crier mumbled curses while Stranger held his gun on them and the blacksmith emptied their holsters. Stranger dropped the medallion in his pocket and took the outlaws' revolvers from Roper one at a time, stuffing them under his belt. "Okay, boys," he said, moving behind them, "you know where the jail is. Lead out."

As Canfield and Crier moved into the sunlight, holding their hands high, the Butterfield stage rolled past the blacksmith shop and stopped in front of the stage office a few doors down the street. The stage's lone male passenger stepped out and asked the two-man crew up in the box, "What's going on?"

"Looks like a couple of bad dudes are goin' to jail, Mr. Whitehead," replied the driver.

People along the street caught sight of John Stranger and the two he was taking to jail. Recognizing them as Foster men, they began to shout their approval to the man-in-black, calling him "preacher."

The stage passenger hurried to the boardwalk and said to one of the men, "Pardon me, sir. Am I hearing correctly? This man's name is Preacher?"

"Nope," grinned the Lander citizen. "His name's not Preacher. He's pastor of the Methodist church here in town. Just so happens our preacher is cleanin' up a mess we've had here for a while."

Whitehead kept his eyes on the procession as it moved up the middle of the street. "That's really something to see a man of the cloth with a gun at someone's back."

"Oh, it's been better than what you're seein'," grinned the other man.

John Stranger and his prisoners were passing the Bank of Lander a half-block from the jail when suddenly six men rushed from between two buildings, guns drawn.

"Hold it right there, preacher!" Hank Foster blared as the others fanned out to surround the man-in-black.

Stranger halted, his gun still leveled on the backs of Canfield and Crier. "Don't interfere, Hank! These two are going to jail."

"That's what you think. Jock—Mason—get outta the way! It's the holy man's time to claim his reward!"

The jubilation of citizens on the street turned to fear and shock. Amid shouts and screams, they scattered for cover.

Canfield and Crier darted toward the boardwalk.

With the quickness of a cougar, Stranger hit the street rolling and drilled Hank Foster through the heart. While Hank was going down, the other five outlaws opened fire. Bullets were chewing dirt all around him while Stranger rolled back and forth, sending hot lead at Luther Noles and Hal Simms, who were coming at him from the left.

As both men were going down, Stranger rolled again and fired at Keith Oldham and Greg Wolford. One bullet took off Wolford's hat, making him stumble. The other slammed into Oldham's shoulder, knocking him down.

Wolford was gaining his balance and bringing his gun up when a shot rang out from the side of the street, and a slug tore through his wrist, sending his gun into the dust. At the same time, Reggie Atkins—who was about to unleash his gun on Stranger—saw that it was Clay Austin who had just shot the gun out of Wolford's hand. When he turned to fire at Austin, Clay shouted, "Don't do it, Reggie!"

Atkins ignored the command, swore, and leveled his gun on Austin. Clay's weapon roared, and Atkins went down with a bullet in the heart.

By this time, John Stranger was on his feet, covering the wounded men. Hal Simms had taken a bullet in the lower left side and lay in the street, gripping the wound. Wolford was on his knees, clutching his shattered wrist. Oldham lay flat on his back, holding his bleeding shoulder. Foster, Noles, and Atkins were dead.

Stranger smiled at Clay Austin, who was walking slowly toward him, a wisp of smoke trailing upward from the muzzle of his revolver.

Lander's citizens were coming out of their hiding places, gazing at the dead and wounded outlaws and talking of how the preacher and the marshal had handled them. There was special elation that Clay had sided with the preacher against Dean Foster's would-be assassins.

"Thanks, my friend," Stranger said to Austin as the younger man drew up. "You just saved my hide."

"My pleasure," grinned Austin, looking around at the three wounded men. "I couldn't just stand by and let 'em gun you down. We'll get Doc to patch these fellas up, then let 'em join the other prisoners in jail."

"Speaking of prisoners," said Stranger, "two of mine got away."

"No they didn't, preacher," came the lusty voice of Benjamin Hanks. "I got 'em right here!"

Stranger and Austin turned to see the gun shop owner holding a double-barreled shotgun on Canfield and Crier. Their faces were pale, and their hands were high.

Austin and Stranger moved toward Hanks while the crowd looked on. As they drew up, Stranger said, "Clay, I caught these two trying to collect a protection fee from Vernon Roper. Take them and lock them up."

"With pleasure," Austin grinned.

"I...ah...guess you know," added Stranger, "you changed sides by what you just did. Your cousin isn't going to want you any more."

"I should never have been on his side to begin with. I've played the fool long enough."

"That's music to my ears," smiled Stranger.

Katy O'Donnell was standing near, and Stranger saw a look of delight in her eyes. For once he didn't feel overly concerned. Then he turned to Hanks and said, "Benjamin, I'm sure glad you saw what was going on out here in time to throw a gun on these two."

"Would've been a shame if they'd gotten away, preacher."

"I have one question, though. Most gun shop owners don't allow their guns to stand in the racks loaded. You must've moved plenty fast to load that shotgun in time to keep these two from getting away."

"Well, Preacher," chuckled Hanks, "it wasn't quite like that. There wasn't time to load the thing, so I just grabbed it off the rack, eared back the hammers, and dashed out the door."

Crier and Canfield swore under their breath.

"What's the matter, boys?" Hanks laughed. "You didn't ask me if it was loaded!"

Austin leveled his revolver on the outlaws and said, "Okay, you two. Let's go."

"Be sure to make them comfortable, if you know what I mean," Stranger said.

"I know exactly what you mean," grinned Austin.

"And when you've got them locked up, go over to the big house and arrest Jim Wurth, will you? He belongs behind bars, too."

"Will do," agreed Austin. "And...what about my cousin?"

"We've got enough on him to put him in prison for a long time. And, of course, there's Chice Reed, yet."

"I'll go after them as soon as I've got these guys and Wurth in jail."

When Clay and his prisoners were out of earshot, Stranger turned to Katy, who had her eyes on Clay, and said, "Keep a watch on your heart, little lady. We're halfway there with him...but only halfway."

"I know," she smiled, "but I have faith that the other half isn't far behind."

Katy joined her father, who looked on as several men picked up the dead outlaws and carried them toward Coye Coffman's funeral parlor.

The people gathered around the man they believed to be Reverend David Thacker. He was their hero, the answer to their prayers. Stranger talked with them briefly, then said, "Please excuse me, folks. I've got a little more work to do."

John Stranger headed toward the Bank of Lander. He had

taken but a few steps when a man stepped in front of him and said, "Pardon me, Reverend, but I just want to say that I've never seen such efficient handling of weaponry in all my life. You were something to behold!"

"Thank you sir, but I—"

"Oh, forgive me!" exclaimed the man, extending his hand. "My name is Worley Whitehead. I'm a drummer from Denver. Been coming up here on business for several years."

"Glad to meet you, Mr. Whitehead. I don't mean to be rude, but I really am in a hurry."

"I understand," grinned the drummer as the tall man hurried on. "God speed!"

Dean Foster watched the entire shootout from the balcony outside his office. He could hardly believe his eyes. His own brother and two of his men were lying dead in the street. The preacher had killed Hank and Luther, and his traitor cousin had killed Reggie. Between the two of them, they had wounded Hal, Greg, and Keith, and those three would be jailed after Doc O'Donnell patched them up. Anger burned within him toward Clay Austin, but it was a seething, unholy hatred he felt for the Reverend David Thacker.

Thacker had stolen Dean's empire. His entire gang, except for Chice Reed and Jim Wurth, was either dead or in jail. Where was Chice? He needed Chice Reed.

A wave of nausea washed over him, bitter bile rising in his throat. Turning from the balcony rail, he shuffled inside the office and eased himself down on the overstuffed couch. Cold sweat beaded his brow, and there was a sharp pain in the center of his chest.

As he put a shaky hand to his temple, the face of Katy O'Donnell flashed on the screen of his mind. He could hear himself saying to her, "What are you talking about? Is there somebody involved in this town I don't know about?"

Katy's retort echoed in his mind. "You weren't listening. I

didn't say you didn't know *about* Him. I said you don't know Him—the God who said, *'Though thou exalt thyself as the eagle, and though thou set thy nest among the stars, thence will I bring thee down'!* You haven't gotten quite that high, Foster, but when He does bring you down, it'll break your stiff neck."

Foster loosened his necktie and gasped for air. The pain in his chest was getting worse.

There was a knock at the door. Foster's head jerked up, and he found the breath to call, "Who is it?"

"It's Chice, boss!"

"Chice—come in!"

Chice Reed opened the door, saw Foster's pallid features, and rushed to the couch. "Boss, you okay?"

"You've got to help me, Chice! You're all I've got left."

"Best thing for us to do is get outta town in a hurry, boss. We can go out the back way and down the alley. My horse is at the house, so I'll have to ride one of yours. We'll head for your house and—"

"No! I can't make it to my house. I...I'm too weak to walk that far. Go get my horse and buggy. We'll get out of town before they know we're gone."

"Okay...okay, boss. I'll be back in a few—"

The office door flew open with a bang, and John Stranger filled the doorway. His gun was in its holster.

"Seems you two are the only ones left. You can come peacefully or the hard way, but you're going to jail with the rest of your bunch...those that are still alive, that is."

"Not me!" yelled Reed, going for his gun.

Stranger's weapon was out, cocked, and leveled at the outlaw before he could draw. Reed stood there, his hand frozen on his gun. There was a wild look in his eyes.

"Don't do it, Reed," warned Stranger.

While the outlaw was trying to make up his mind whether to make a fight of it, Dean Foster struggled to his feet. Like a madman, he stumbled toward the balcony, babbling, "Not me! He's not going to get me!"

Foster was out the door and onto the balcony. Stranger moved up to Reed and snapped, "Give me your gun!"

Reed hesitated, then reluctantly handed over his weapon. Stranger ran toward the balcony just in time to see Dean Foster stumble hard against the railing. It gave way with a splintering sound, and the babbling man fell to the street below.

Stranger wheeled and ran through the office, noting that Chice Reed was gone. He darted down the stairs to the bank lobby and out onto the street. A crowd had already gathered around the crumpled form of Dean Foster as he lay between the boardwalk and the hitch rail.

Stranger looked both ways and across the street, but he could see no sign of Reed. He began asking bystanders if they had seen Reed come out of the bank, but no one had. The outlaw had given him the slip. John Stranger didn't feel Reed was worth hunting down. No doubt he was already hightailing it to parts unknown. As long as Lander was rid of him, Stranger was satisfied.

Doc O'Donnell came on the run with Katy right behind him, holding her skirt calf-high in order to keep up. Stranger pushed his way through the crowd and knelt beside Foster, and was soon joined by Doc and Katy. Foster had landed on his head and lay with his neck twisted in a grotesque manner.

Doc laid an experienced hand on Foster's neck, felt for a pulse, and said solemnly, "He's dead. I think his neck's broken."

Katy stood and whispered, "Thence will I bring thee down."

Doc looked up at her. "What's that, honey?"

"Nothing, Daddy," she replied softly. "Just a little something I told Foster once."

The following Sunday, Lander Methodist Church was forced to hold its morning service outside. The pews and pulpit were set up in the open area between the church building and the parsonage, and chairs were borrowed from private homes and the town hall. Still, a great number of men had to stand during the service.

Songs of praise were offered to the Lord God of heaven for the deliverance He had brought. There was also a testimony time before the sermon, and many members of the church expressed their thanks to the Lord for giving them such a pastor.

The service was over and John Stranger had been in the parsonage for about half an hour when there was a knock at the door. Opening it, he found Clay Austin standing on the porch with tears in his eyes.

"What can I do for you, Clay?"

"Well, sir, I want to...I want to talk to you about becoming a Christian and a responsible citizen. I've walked with the wrong crowd long enough, as you well know."

"Come in, Clay," smiled the tall man. Closing the door behind him, he said, "Each man has a choice in life, my friend. He can approach it as a builder or a destroyer, a lover or a hater, a giver or a taker. You are about to make the right move. When you receive the Lord Jesus Christ into your heart and life and give your all to Him, *He* will make you a responsible citizen. And *He* will make you a builder, a lover, and a giver. Sit down over there at the table. I'll get my Bible."

Twenty minutes later, Clay Austin rose from his knees and thanked the preacher for leading him to Christ. As Clay was about to leave, Stranger said, "This is going to make a certain young lady very happy, Clay."

"I know, preacher," he said with a smile. "She's a wonderful girl. I'm going to find a good job and prove to her that I'm a new man. When I feel the time is right, I'll tell her how much I love her."

Stranger smiled and said, "That's the way to do it, Clay. But as for a good job, what's the matter with the one you've got?"

"Pastor, I was given this badge by Dean Foster, not the people of Lander. I've been wearin' it the past few days because somebody needs to watch over this town and feed those men we've crowded into those two cells."

Stranger grinned. "I sent a letter to the U.S. marshal in Denver yesterday. It may take a few months to get some deputies up here to take them to Cheyenne City for trial, but just think how much they'll appreciate their nice big cells when they go to prison.

"And as for your job, you're aware that the town council was re-formed yesterday."

"Yes, sir."

"Well, the councilmen brought it up themselves. People all over town have been saying they want you to stay on as marshal. The council voted to ask you to stay on as Lander's permanent marshal, and they asked me to talk to you about it. I was going to approach you tomorrow, but what's wrong with hiring a lawman on Sunday?"

Clay Austin left the parsonage with joy in his heart. He had a new life in Christ, a permanent job as Lander's marshal, and an opportunity to prove himself to Katy. Maybe one day he would ask her to marry him.

CHAPTER

TWENTY-ONE

———◆———

Breanna Baylor was sitting in the Bluebird Café with Dr. and Mrs. Lyle Goodwin. They were enjoying a fine meal together and discussing the work Breanna had been doing in Bennett, a small town east of Denver. Somehow the water at Bennett had been polluted, and a typhoid epidemic had broken out. It was now under control, and Breanna had returned to Denver for a much-needed rest.

As the Goodwins and Breanna chatted, she happened to pick up on a conversation between two men at the next table. She didn't mean to eavesdrop, but as she heard one man tell his story to the other, she excused herself to Dr. and Mrs. Goodwin and leaned toward the neighboring table. "Pardon me, gentlemen, but I couldn't help overhearing your conversation."

Both men smiled and stood. The younger one said, "Since I was doing most of the talking, ma'am, I assume it must have been something I said that interested you."

"Yes," smiled Breanna. "But first, let me introduce myself and my friends."

When introductions had been made all around, Worley Whitehead said, "What was it that I said that interested you, Miss Baylor?"

"Well, I heard you say that while in Lander, Wyoming, a few days ago, you witnessed a shootout involving a preacher and the town marshal and six outlaws. You said that when it was over, three of the outlaws were dead and the other three were wounded, but the preacher and the marshal were unscathed."

"Yes, ma'am. I wasn't surprised at the way the marshal handled himself, but to see a preacher wield a gun like that—I never thought in all my days I'd see anything like it. I mean...how many preachers would even get into a gunfight, much less make it look like he'd done it a hundred times before?"

"Remarkable, I agree," nodded Breanna. "It was your description of the preacher that caught my ear. You said something about him being tall and dressed in black. Then when you made mention of his pale gray eyes, I thought he might be someone I know. I heard you say you talked to him. Did he tell you his name?"

"No, ma'am, he didn't. He was sort of in a hurry when we talked."

Breanna's heart went to her throat. "May I ask you, Mr. Whitehead...were there any distinguishing characteristics about his face that stood out to you?"

The drummer thought for a few seconds. "Yes, ma'am, there was. He had two jagged scars on his right cheek. They were quite noticeable."

A chill riffled through Breanna Baylor. "Are you assuming he's a preacher because of his clothing?"

"Oh, no, ma'am. I heard people talking on the street. He's pastor of a church there in town."

"Do you know which one?"

"Well, ma'am, I think there's only one. I've been going to Lander for several years, but I never go to that end of town. I don't even know what kind it is."

Breanna's heart was pounding. John was the pastor of Lander's church, which meant he would probably be there for a while. She thanked Whitehead for the information, then turned to the

Goodwins and said, "Since I'm between jobs, I'm going to take a few days and make a trip to Wyoming. I'll take the next stage that's going."

Martha Goodwin said, "This scar-faced preacher must be someone pretty important to you."

"Yes, he is," Breanna nodded. "Very important."

On Monday evening there was a meeting at the town hall in Lander, called by the town council to publicly welcome Clay Austin as the permanent marshal. When the meeting was over, people stood in line to offer their congratulations. Last in line were Dr. Patrick O'Donnell and his daughter. The doctor spoke to Clay, then smiled at his daughter and walked away to join in a conversation with a group of men.

Katy looked up at the handsome young marshal, smiled warmly, and said, "I'm so proud of you. I just knew there was something good in you, even when you were running with those criminals. I know you'll make us a great marshal."

"Thank you, Miss Katy," Clay grinned. "And thank you for believing in me. That means more to me than you'll ever know."

There was a magnetic pull between them, but neither let on. Clay wanted to tell her that he had become a Christian, but somehow the words wouldn't come. Maybe he would wait until next Sunday morning's service when he presented himself for membership in the church. Yes, Katy would get her surprise when he stood before the whole congregation and told them of his conversion. He would spend the rest of the week anticipating the look on her face when she found out.

Katy bid him goodnight, then rejoined her father. Soon they were walking away with Katy holding onto her father's arm. Clay saw it and prayed that someday she would be holding his arm.

He was about to leave when Chester Platte left the group of

men Dr. O'Donnell had been talking with and called, "Oh, Marshal!"

"Yes?"

"I didn't think to mention it to you before, but the other day when all that shooting took place, I talked to the stagecoach driver, who's an old friend of mine. He told me there was a big gunfight over at Douglas that same morning."

"Oh?"

"That white-haired gunslick who said he'd be back to make you draw against him...ah...Rex Hobbs?"

"Yes?"

"Well, you won't have to worry about him. He was killed in that gunfight. Seems the big daddy of 'em all had been trailin' him to force a showdown."

"Tate Landry?"

"Mm-hmm. Landry got him."

Austin felt his scalp prickle. "Thanks for telling me, Chester."

"Sure. Just thought you'd want to know. Figured it'd be a relief for you to know Hobbs won't be breathin' down your neck."

"Yeah, thanks. I appreciate it." As he walked toward home, Clay hoped Tate Landry hadn't heard that he was in Lander.

The next day, John Stranger found Clay Austin walking on the street and joined him. "So have you told Katy the good news yet?"

"No. I thought I'd let her hear it when I give my testimony on Sunday."

"How about a little advice from a friend?"

"Sure."

"That young lady has been very concerned about your spiritual condition, Clay. I happen to know she has prayed real hard for you conversion."

"She has?"

"Yes, and she deserves to hear it from you before you make it public."

"Well, in that case, I'll tell her right away. Maybe I ought to go into the clinic and ask if I could take her to supper tonight. If she'll take me up on it, I'll tell her tonight."

"I have no doubt she'll take you up on it," grinned the taller man. "Tonight would be a perfect time to tell her."

The attention of both men was drawn to the middle of the street when the sharp voice of a lone rider pierced the morning air. "Hey! You with the badge! You're Clay Austin, ain't you?"

Clay's blood ran cold. He had heard Tate Landry's description too many times to mistake what he looked like. His throat was tight as he left Stranger and moved toward the rider. "Yes, I'm Clay Austin."

Dismounting, the infamous gunfighter grinned and said, "I'm Tate Landry, and I came here to brace you. It's time we met and cleared the slate. I guess you heard about me killin' Hobbs."

"Yeah, I heard."

People on the street were gathering around. Everybody knew that Landry was the king of gunfighters. Young Clay Austin could never match his draw, much less beat it. Clay knew it too, but there was no way he could get out of facing off with Landry. He had earned the reputation that had brought Landry hunting him, and now he must pay the price. He couldn't live with himself if he backed down.

John Stranger knew what was going through young Austin's mind. He was every inch a man and would take Landry's challenge.

Katy O'Donnell heard the excited voices through an open window at the clinic and hurried to the street. Her father was delivering a baby for a rancher's wife several miles away.

Clay saw Katy as she edged to the front of the crowd. She was now aware that Tate Landry had come to town to challenge the man she loved. Fear etched itself on her features.

Clay met Landry's hard gaze and said, "I guess it's time to clear the slate, Landry. Tie your horse up. I want to talk to someone for a couple of minutes, then I'll be back."

"Sure, kid. Just don't be too long. Me and these folks might get the idea you're stallin' 'cause you're scared."

The crowd was growing larger as Landry led his horse across the street.

Austin could feel Katy's eyes on him as he turned and stepped close to the man he believed to be Reverend David Thacker. In a low voice, he said, "Thank you, Pastor, for leading me to Christ. At least I know where I'll be when this is over."

"You don't have to go through with it, Clay," Stranger said.

"I couldn't stand myself knowing I'd played the coward, Pastor."

"I understand, my friend, but it's sure death if you face him."

Clay stared at his feet, rubbing the back of his neck for a long moment.

"Thinking it over?" Stranger asked.

Lifting his gaze to meet Stranger's, Clay said, "I'm wondering how this situation looks to Jesus. I mean...He certainly was no coward when He faced the cross. I know that wasn't the same thing as this, but just because I'm a Christian now, does that mean I should back down to Landry? What I've done in the past is simply catching up to me. Pastor, I've got to do it. I've just got to face Landry, or live with being a coward for the rest of my days."

John Stranger usually had an answer for any occasion, but this one had him stumped. How could he tell the young man to play the coward? This was something only Clay Austin could decide, and it was plain that the decision had been made. Laying a hand on Clay's shoulder, he said, "Do what you have to do."

Clay nodded silently, somberly, then said, "It's what I have to do."

Clay left Stranger and moved along the edge of the crowd. When he came to Katy, he said, "Could we go inside the clinic and talk?"

Katy's face was white as she took Clay by the hand and led him through the clinic door. When the door was closed, she gripped his forearms with both hands and pled, "Don't do it, Clay, please! I don't want you to die!"

"Katy, listen. I couldn't live with myself if I didn't face him. Like I told you the day Rex Hobbs rode in here, I'd rather die as a man than live as a coward."

Tears filled Katy's eyes. "I don't understand you men. This is so foolish! So utterly foolish! You're young, Clay. You can live it down in time. At least you'll still be alive."

"It would be a living death, Katy. A man who's a man can't look in the mirror at a yellow-bellied coward. I have to do it. But first there's something I need to tell you. I, uh...I want you to know your prayers haven't been wasted."

"My prayers? How did you know I—"

"There isn't time to explain, except to say that last Sunday, I received Jesus into my heart, Katy. I'm a Christian."

Katy O'Donnell wrapped her arms around Clay Austin, hugged him tight, and sobbed, "Oh, thank You, Lord! Thank You!"

Taking hold of her shoulders, Clay said, "I have to go, Katy, but there's something else I must tell you." Clay started to speak twice before finally managing to say, "I'm in love with you, Katy. I wanted to tell you before, but I knew there was a wall between us. Well, that wall is gone now, and I couldn't go out there and...and face Landry without telling you."

Tears streaming, Katy sobbed, "Oh, Clay, I'm in love with you! Please don't go back out there and draw against that awful man. Please. I want to spend my life with you."

"It wouldn't be much of a life living with a man who hated himself." Clay started to go, then turned back toward Katy. "May I...may I kiss you before I go?"

"Yes, of course," she sobbed.

Cupping her tear-stained face in his hands, Clay drew his lips close and said in a half-whisper, "Let this kiss stay with you forever, Katy. I'll carry it to heaven with me."

On the street, John Stranger made his decision. After Tate Landry had tied his horse to the hitchrail and moved to the middle of the dusty thoroughfare to wait for his victim, Stranger stepped off the boardwalk and headed toward him. Every eye in the crowd was fastened on the tall man-in-black.

Landry set his stony eyes on the man who stood three inches taller than he and snarled, "What do *you* want?"

Before Stranger could reply, someone in the crowd shouted, "Watch him, Reverend Thacker!"

Landry's cold eyes matched his smile as he said, "Reverend, eh? Don't tell me you're gonna preach to me about the sin of gun-fightin'. I've already heard that sermon."

"I'm not here to preach to you, Landry. I'm here to tell you you're too slow. You couldn't stand up against a real gunfighter."

"I suppose you know one?"

"No—I *am* one."

Landry threw his head back and laughed. "Are you kiddin' me? You? A *preacher?*"

Stranger knew he didn't have much time. Clay would be returning any minute. Backing away, he flipped the tail of his black frock coat behind his holster and said, "You man enough to draw against a real gunfighter?"

Sudden wrath hardened Tate Landry's features. "Okay, preacher, you asked for it. Let's get this over with!" he gusted, back-ing up a few steps.

The throng on the street stood in horror. What had gotten into their preacher? Why was he doing this? He had shown himself good with a gun, but Landry was the undisputed king.

Landry was a natural-born killer. All the decency in him had been starved out long ago. Any man who wore a low-slung gun was his enemy and potential opponent.

"Go for your gun!" Landry hissed.

"Ladies first."

Landry went red with rage, and his hand made an almost

imperceptible move for his gun. He had just cleared leather when John Stranger's Colt .45 roared. Landry's body jerked as the slug ripped into his heart. The revolver slipped from his fingers and fell to the dust. Eyes bulging with disbelief, he clutched the wound with both hands. Staring as though he were seeing the fiery destination of his wretched soul, Landry swayed rigidly upright, staggered two steps, then fell on his face.

The people stood like statues, unable to believe what had just transpired before their eyes.

Having heard the shot, Clay came on the run with Katy following. Rushing up beside the man-in-black, who was holstering his Colt .45, he gazed at the lifeless form of Tate Landry and gasped, "What happened?"

"The man decided he would use me for practice while he was waiting for you. I told him he was too slow. And he just proved it."

The townspeople finally found their voice and a rousing cheer went up. For the rest of the day, the subject on lips all over Lander was the speed of Reverend Thacker's draw. Some were sure he used to be a gunfighter. Others said they didn't care if he had been, he was an answer to their prayers. God had used him to free the town of Dean Foster and his cutthroats.

At the Wednesday night service, Stranger asked Clay to tell the congregation of his conversion, instead of waiting until Sunday. While he spoke, Clay expressed the great debt he owed Reverend Thacker, both for leading him to the Lord and for saving his life.

At the close of the service, the preacher announced that Clay and Katy were planning to marry after a proper courtship. Dr. Patrick O'Donnell had given them his blessing. There was spontaneous applause, and when the service was dismissed, congratulations were offered by all.

Chester Platte had just opened his barbershop on Thursday morning and was waiting for his first customer, when the door opened, and a man in his late thirties stepped in. He was dressed in black, with white shirt and string tie. He wore a black frock coat and flat-crowned hat. Smiling, he said, "Deacon Platte, I presume? Bishop Ames told me you were the town's barber, so I just looked for the shop the minute I rode into town, hoping I would find you here." Extending his hand, he said, "I'm Reverend David Thacker."

When Chester had recovered a degree and had read the letter of introduction Thacker was carrying from Bishop Ames, he said, "Reverend Thacker, there's something I need to tell you."

Platte sat Thacker down and told him the story of Dean Foster's takeover of the town, and of how the tall man with the scarred face had been sent from God as an answer to prayer. When the entire story had been told, Thacker asked, "Who can this man be? And why would he pass himself off as me?"

"I guess the best way to find out is to go and ask him," said Platte. "He's probably at the parsonage right now."

Platte and Thacker hadn't walked far when people on the street met them and wanted to know who the stranger was. Chester saw no reason to cover it up, so he explained the situation, showing them the bishop's letter. Word spread fast, and before the two men could reach the church property, more than half the town was on their heels. Dr. O'Donnell, Katy, and Marshal Austin were among them.

When they reached the parsonage, Platte said to the curious crowd, "I'd like for Marshal Austin to be with us when we talk to him. The rest of you wait out here. We'll have some answers shortly."

Platte, Thacker, and Austin stepped up on the porch, and Platte knocked on the door. When there was no response, he knocked again, louder, calling, "Preacher, it's Chester Platte! I need to talk to you."

Still there was no response. The three men hurried to the church building, expecting to find him there. He was not. Clay then asked the crowd if anyone had seen the preacher that morning. No one had.

Two men ran to the barn in back of the parsonage and

quickly returned, announcing that the black horse was gone. Austin then suggested they look inside the parsonage. Platte, Thacker, and Austin entered while eager eyes waited for their return.

In a minute or two they filed out the door, and Austin said, "He's gone, folks, and he's taken all his possessions with him. But he did leave something behind." As he spoke, Clay lifted up a silver medallion the size of a silver dollar. "Has a five-point star in the center and words around the edge—*The stranger that shall come from a far land. Deuteronomy 29:22.*"

A silence fell over the crowd. They were stunned, wondering what twist of fate had sent the tall, scar-faced stranger to their rescue at the exact time they so desperately needed him.

"He left us something else, too," Clay said. "He left us a legacy. He taught us to stand up against evil, meet it head-on, and conquer it."

While they stood looking at each other, not knowing what to say, a young woman approached from the street, threaded her way through the throng, and drew up to the porch. "Pardon me, gentlemen. My name is Breanna Baylor. I'm from Denver, and I just came in on the stage. The Butterfield agent told me I could find a Reverend David Thacker here."

"I'm Reverend Thacker, ma'am," said the man from Kansas City.

"Oh," Breanna said, putting a hand to her mouth. "You're not...I mean...the man I'm looking for is dark-haired, very tall, and has a pair of matching scars on his face."

"Well, ma'am," spoke up Clay Austin, "it's a long story, but the man you describe has been masquerading as David Thacker for several days. He single-handedly delivered this town from a gang of hoodlums, and now we've just discovered that he's gone." Holding up the medallion, Clay added, "He left this behind. Does it mean anything to you?"

Breanna bit her lips as she eyed the medallion. "Yes, it does. The man who left this is known for helping people in need. I...heard he was here and wanted very much to see him, but I see that my trip has been in vain."

Late that afternoon, Breanna Baylor stood at the window in her room at the Wind River Hotel, clutching the silver medallion that the desk clerk had given her in a sealed envelope when she checked in. Her misty eyes gazed at the Wind River Range to the west as the sun slowly dropped behind the jagged peaks.

Leaving the window, she walked to the dresser and picked up the envelope to examine it one more time. She knew John Stranger's handwriting when she saw it. "Miss Breanna Baylor," it read. "Wind River Hotel."

Her lips quivered. "Oh, John, did you see me come into town? Or did you just know I was coming and that I would stay at this hotel? I have another medallion to treasure now...but I would rather have you. I love you, John. I love you."

She drew a shuddering breath and held the medallion tight in her hand. She returned to the window, and as she looked toward the mountains, there was a void in her heart and an ache in her throat.

The fiery rim of the blood-red sun dipped below the majestic peaks, staining the western sky a deep, glowing crimson. For a few moments the brilliant color hovered in a death-struggle, then slowly bled away into the pale embrace of dusk.

OTHER COMPELLING STORIES BY AL LACY

Books in the Battles of Destiny series: Dramatic, action-packed historical novels set during the War Between the States

☛ *A Promise Unbroken* (The Battle of Rich Mountain)

Experience the heartache and victory of two couples battling jealousy and racial hatred amidst a war that would cripple America. From a prosperous Virginia plantation to a grim jail cell outside Lynchburg, follow the dramatic story of a love that could not be destroyed.

☛ *A Heart Divided* (The Battle of Mobile Bay)

Ryan McGraw—leader of the Confederate Sharpshooters—is nursed back to health by beautiful army nurse Dixie Quade. Their romance would survive the perils of war, but can it withstand the reappearance of a past love?

☛ *Beloved Enemy* (The Battle of First Bull Run)

Faithful to her family and the land of her birth, young Jenny Jordan covers for her father's Confederate spy missions. But as she grows closer to Union soldier Buck Brownell, Jenny finds herself torn between devotion to the South and her feelings for the man she is forbidden to love.

Available at your local Christian bookstore